Jami
disco
drea

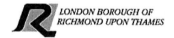

D0242959

NIGHT TIME COOL

NIGHT TIME COOL

PART I OF THE DREAMS OF SUN SERIES

JAMIE PARADISE

Unbound Digital

This edition first published in 2018

Unbound

6th Floor Mutual House, 70 Conduit Street, London W1S 2GF

www.unbound.com

ISBN (eBook): 978-1-912618-17-0

ISBN (Paperback): 978-1-912618-16-3

Design by Mecob

Printed in Great Britain by Clays Ltd, Elcograf S.p.A.

For my three angels, always: G, S and M XXX

Dear Reader,

The book you are holding came about in a rather different way to most others. It was funded directly by readers through a new website: Unbound.

Unbound is the creation of three writers. We started the company because we believed there had to be a better deal for both writers and readers. On the Unbound website, authors share the ideas for the books they want to write directly with readers. If enough of you support the book by pledging for it in advance, we produce a beautifully bound special subscribers' edition and distribute a regular edition and e-book wherever books are sold, in shops and online.

This new way of publishing is actually a very old idea (Samuel Johnson funded his dictionary this way). We're just using the internet to build each writer a network of patrons. Here, at the back of this book, you'll find the names of all the people who made it happen.

Publishing in this way means readers are no longer just passive consumers of the books they buy, and authors are free to write the books they really want. They get a much fairer return too – half the profits their books generate, rather than a tiny percentage of the cover price.

If you're not yet a subscriber, we hope that you'll want to join our publishing revolution and have your name listed in one of our books in the future. To get you started, here is a £5 discount on your first pledge. Just visit unbound.com, make your pledge and type ELVIS18 in the promo code box when you check out.

Thank you for your support,

Dan, Justin and John
Founders, Unbound

The 'Wade Long' Suite

Gary Abela
Huxley Acutt
Michelle Allen
Nick Ames
Alex Anderson
David Anderson
John Anderson
Steve Anglesey
Mike Anstead
Michael Armer
Joe Asbridge
Craig Ashmore
Steve Aughton
Michael Aylwin
Ryan Baldi
Nick Ball
David BDT Thomson
Damian Bell
Georgie Bingham
Martin Blackburn
Derek Brereton
Mandy Brereton
Ben Brigg
Dan Brook
Danny Bryan
Jamie Carragher
Gareth Carter
Marcus Christenson
Adrian Coombe
James Cooper
Jon Cotterill
Simon Crabtree

Iain Crabtree
Mark Critchley
Chris Croft
John Cross
Jonathan Cundall
Neil Custis
Seraino Dalgliesh
Dan Dalton
Uzi & Michelle Dar
Roger Dawes
Jack Dawson
Albert Depetrillo
Sara Dobson
James Ducker
Jonathan Easton
eCabs4U eCabs4U
Ben Edwards
Pete Ferguson
Dominic Fifield
Graham Fildes
Scott Fletcher
Ben Golding
Karl Greggan
Martin Haime
Andy Hampson
Cloud Hands
Simon Hardaker
PJ Harrison
Simon Hart
David Haskoll
Warren Haughton
Ric Hayes
Peter Hayter
Jon Henderson
Neil Hodgson
Lee Holden

Oliver Holt
Stephen Howson
Steve Hoyles
David Hytner
Al Ingram
Ben Irvine
Ian Irving
Blake Ivinson
Jake Jackson
Andreas Jackson
Mia Jackson
Patricia Jackson
Gaynor Jackson
Jamie Jackson
Rob Jempson
Richard Jordan
Michael Jump
Darren Kawonga
Oli Kay
Ian Keary
Suzy Kidd
Dan Kieran
Victoria Kloss
Matthew and Amy Lambert
Steve Lawrence
Alex Lowe
Darren Marchment
Jamie Marshall
Adam Marshall
Vicki Mathews
Emma Mayer
Emma Mayer
Noah Mayer-Hardaker
Ester Mayer-Hardaker
Dominic McGuinness
James McMath

Johny Mcpherson
Kevin Mitchell
John Mitchinson
Andy Mitten
Euclides Montes
David Mooney
Lee Moores
Jonny Morgan
John Niven
David Ornstein
Oliver Owen
Nii Ayikwei Parkes
Lee Phillips
Justin Pollard
Jim Powell
Harry Pratt
Simon Prosser
Tom Rey
Chrissy Rey
Dave Rey
William Rice
Ian Ridley
Adam Robertson
Alex Rowen
Lucy Sharman
Si:Fi
Ed Simons
Jonathan Smith
Jason Smith
Jonathan Smith
Rob Smyth
Zubran Solaiman
Ian Stanley Young
Becky Stevenson
Ben Stockdale
Andy Stoddon

Nicholas Sutcliffe
Nick Szczepanik
Daniel Taylor
Kristof Terreur
Danny Thompson
Richard Todd
Robert Tonge
Philip Townsend
Simon Trow
Gary Udall
lucy Warburton
Chris Wheeler
Arlo White
Kevin Whittaker
Cass Wild
Steve Wiley
Will Will Buckley
Matthew Wood
Ed Woodward
Stephen 'Lord Leopard' 'The Wooldozer' Wooldridge
Robert Woollard
Rachel Wulff

With grateful thanks to Jamie Carragher for helping to make this book happen.

Night time sounds

Night time sounds

Night time sounds

The sound of the night

Part One

High on Today

ONE

Elvis Street said, 'You going to do it – this time?'

Frederick shrugged and smiled. He said, 'What do you mean?'

The sound of the choir hit large. A hundred voices sang 'Silent Night' larger. The tone. *The tenor.* It floated from Shoreditch Church nave into the vestibule. It was groovy and Yuletide-rich. It was orchestral. It pumped senses and sent the world majestic. It had Santa Claus in town and the ages continuing. It was people rejoicing. It was possibility. *Possibilities.*

As the snow came down. As Xmas advanced. As Xmas *happened. The whirl of it all.*

Elvis said, 'What do you mean, "What do you mean?" *This time.* You actually going through with it – this time? Because what happened before was a joke. A complete hoot. It was hilarious. And I was the punchline.'

Frederick grinned. He buzzed and fritzed; grooved on control. *Saw the whole thing.* 'Of course I'm going through with it this time,' he said. 'I've told you that, haven't I?'

Elvis paused. The sound of the carol moved through him. Spirits rose – they soared when you let them. Let them *SOAR*. The snow outside; the traffic where Old Street/Shoreditch High Street/Hackney Road hit: it's the precise same thing.

Elvis said, 'Here's how this is all going to occur. Just listen, listen very carefully. Then there is no excuse. Just in case you try to back out again – like last time, saying you're not sure, thinking it won't work. This is simple. I set up the meeting, you have the cash.' Elvis winked. 'Ricky has the bugle. You're there, you're hidden, you wait for him to meet me, give me it – for me to move like I'm handing over the dough.'

3

Another stage-ham wink. Play this shit-head – enjoy it. 'At that point – you clout him, you have your collar. Your arrest. You've cleaned up your streets a little bit more. *We* get our score. Everyone's happy. Merreth Xmas, goodwill to all men. Except thicko dickhead Ricky Me.'

Frederick clocked the wall behind Elvis. A framed picture – it caught a smiling Prince of Wales. His features shone. He's a filthy rich/never worked royal. He's smug and the gang. He married the love of his life. He cracked it; didn't *think* he had.

Which was Elvis's problem. Thinking he's smarter than he is. He's smart but not *that* smart. If he was, he wouldn't think he was smarter than he is.

Correct?

Correctamundo.

Frederick smiled and killed a laugh. 'I'm arresting you too?'

In front of Prince Charles's grin, an Elvis grin. Unforced/easy, like the Prince's. It went to show – you smiled naturally, believed you were right, and you were not.

Elvis said, 'No. You are not arresting me.'

Like Frederick was denser than possible – duncey-bollocks from Duncey-Bollocks Central.

Elvis said, 'Fuck, I am glad we had this meeting. You are not arresting me. I'm with *you*. We're doing this together. You are arresting Ricky.'

Frederick smiled – again. He couldn't stop smiling; it's an affliction. His smile is Prince Chaz-esque: regal. 'I know I'm arresting Richard "Ricardo" "Ricky Me" Cliff. But if you're there, having just purchased a fat weight of chang, having paid him for it, what am I doing with you? What are my boys doing with you? Letting you go? Saying, "Thanks very much. Don't do it again. Pretty *pur-lease*"?'

Frederick could not believe Elvis. This was the problem with the other plan, the first one. It wasn't thought through. He scanned Elvis's face, scanned the Prince's. His eyes moved right, looked through the glass door.

He saw – thick flakes falling.

Streetlight-glistened snow.

East London was carpeted. The white stuff redecorated the world. Elvis said, 'That's simple. You're letting me go.'

Frederick chorted this time. 'If I'm not arresting you, then what is Ricky thinking? He knows straightaway something stinks if I'm arresting him and not you. You see that? I mean, you *can* see that? Come on, I have to arrest you. Or Ricky – whoever he's working for, whoever he owes a lump of chisel on tick to, whoever is down a sizeable weight, comes for *you*. After you.'

Elvis stopped, felt stupid. The plan was – *what?* He didn't consider it. He saw Ricky: being arrested. Frederick: ripping off the blow. He'd give Elvis a share. The split would be in Frederick's favour – this off-the-charts coke fiend. He slaved for nose candy like he slaved for eye candy and old-school house – that '88 second summer of love golden age shit he harped on about relentless.

Elvis smiled – the smile Frederick wanted to see. 'You're right, you got me.' He smiled different. 'But it has to look good, okay? *Authentic.* So this is how it will go. As soon as the deal happens and you appear, I'm running – that is, you go for Ricky so he can't get away and while you're doing that I am off, fast, your boys following me, a little after–'

A Frederick snort and a slow headshake. Play the role/play him. 'The part you forgot – forget to mention, maybe think of too, is I'm not arresting Ricky Me. Not exactly. I'm walking him and talking him. Telling him how it could be and how it's going to be. That he'll be processed and run by me. Become a good and faithful CI – a bigtime snitch of mine – if he possesses half a brain cell. You get this Elvino?'

Elvis nodded. 'I get it.'

The nave went quiet, the singing stopped. 'Silent Night' died: what else was there to say? A fresh ditty struck up – carol singers crooned 'The Holly and The Ivy'.

Elvis double thumbs-upped Frederick. He mind-whirred and jumped to *that*–

That subject – his name: NOW. Finally ask about why the fuck he was called Elvis; ask now with what he planned; what he planned to do *to Frederick*.

The choir and snow; the shakedown and scheme.

He caught a surge–

Now is the time.

Elvis said, 'While we're communicating so clearly – *so convivially* – like this, let me ask you a question about my nam–'

'If this is about *her* again, I thought we– I've apologised so many times, come on Elvino–'

Elvis smiled – store *that* up for the right time. Stick to the question of the name, being called Elvis.

Don't get into it now; don't recall what you saw.

How you found them.

'No, let's not mention Camilla, I am certainly not.' He winked. 'This is something far simpler, less involved for "Elvino".' He sighed, watched the snow fall outside. 'It's about this name you gave me, it's been bugging me for a long time. So, here I go – you're a house music nut, a second summer of love freak, never stop spouting about what a great time 1988–91 was, how it made you, the man you are, all that shit–'

Frederick, impatient: 'Yes?'

'So explain my name – Elvino, *Elvis?* Who calls their son Elvis unless they're stuck in the 1960s and a saddo Presley fanboy and *not* a near-fifty-year-old raver who still gobbles pills and thinks he's a cool cat?'

Frederick howls – relief this *wasn't* about Camilla fuelled them. 'Listen, I've never denied that you being a DJ – The Music Man, whatever you call yourself – is a boon. Keeps me in touch with the tunes now–'

'Answer the question – why am I called Elvis?'

Frederick shrugged. 'If I had my way it would've been Frank, as in Frankie, as in Frankie Knuckles, but your mum wouldn't–'

'She – *she* was into Elvis Presley?'

'Not really, in fact no. *Her* dad was and she liked the name. Throw in an element of wanting to spite me, and game over – that's the fairer sex for you, right?'

'I still find it hard to believe *you* allowed me to be called–'

Frederick, bored: 'You know *this* part of the story. I was never there – work had me before and after you were born.'

ONE

Work: boosting shit off goons you arrest/threaten to arrest, doing the shit in, partying with other women 'before and after' Mum died.

Frederick laughed. 'You're twenty-seven–'

'Twenty-eight.'

'Twenty-eight and you just ask me this. Your mother's dead, when, five years now? You never asked bef–'

Elvis fixed a smile on, hit a light tone: 'You and Mum divorced when I was six, remember, I never thought about it until – until now, recently.'

Frederick threw a beamer. 'Like I say, I wanted to call you Frank, even for your middle name. But your mum refused.'

A silence grew – Frederick's smile dropped, went to that vacant stare. Carol sound floated in muffled from the nave.

The powwow was over. Elvis said, 'Dad, see you soon. Keep safe, stay out of trouble. I'll be in touch. And listen, I like Elvis, as a name.'

Frederick cracked a grin. 'You should. See you soon.' He turned, exited, boosted onto snow-carpeted Shoreditch High Street.

Elvis opened the door behind him, made the nave. He walked down four rows, took a seat on the left.

He joined in the crooning. 'The rising of the sun/And the running of the deer.' That feeling again. The stuff inside, the stuff outside. Congregation voices. They rose upward; they rose to the church roof and beyond. Hit the skies; hit stars.

Like the whole thing was being left behind. Everyone, all of them, raised up.

Raised high for a moment that could not be forgotten if you felt it; wanted it to be this way.

His dad.

The powwow made it clearer. Confirmed this was the move: Frederick did his mother over. Frederick did Elvis over with Camilla, betrayed his own son with his girl. He did people every day of his life.

DI Frederick Street was out of control, needed bringing down.

Elvis was going to do it. For himself, for everyone else Frederick ruined.

His dad.

His fucking dad.

TWO

16 December, 1.17pm

Elvis at the apartment near Brick Lane. Thinking about Camilla. Wanting to avoid her, keep to his room, knowing he had to move out.

Seeing, *feeling,* finally it's over.

Wondering when she might be back. Not wanting her to be back. Not knowing when she would appear.

Who knew.

That was his ex-girlfriend. That had been her attraction.

Once.

The never knowing what she would do.

Not now.

Elvis crushed beans, let the coffee brew four minutes, watched time on his phone. He poured and sipped, watched snow; the white stuff kept falling, outside's a flake-fest.

He perched at his bedroom window and hit up the recording. The coffee was strong – java jolted.

He listened; Elvis to his dad:

'Fuck, I am glad we had this meeting. You are not arresting me. I'm with you. We're doing this together. You are arresting Ricky.'

The contempt now in his dad's tone before he buried it. The police training kicked in.

'I know I'm arresting Richard "Ricardo" "Ricky Me" Cliff. But if you're there, having just purchased a fat weight of chang, having paid him for it, what am I doing with you? What are my boys doing with you? Letting you go? Saying, "Thanks very much. Don't do it again. Pretty *pur-lease?*"'

Elvis chuckled. His dad was razor-sharp, his dad was a fat let-down. Elvis ran shades of Frederick; he knew that. He knew this, too: they were the same, they differed.

His own voice again: 'You're letting me go.'

He fast-forwarded the recording to near the end.

Frederick said: 'The part you forgot, forgot to mention, maybe think of too, is that I'm not arresting Ricky Me. Not exactly. I'm walking him and talking him. Telling him how it could be and how it's going to be. That he'll be processed and run by me. Become a good and faithful CI – a big-time snitch – if he possesses half a brain cell.'

Elvis smiled and drank coffee. He got what he wanted – Frederick, star Met Police DI, recorded spouting chapter and verse on turning over a dealer for a weight of coke.

No return from that. Frederick came off as bent as Ricky Me, the street joey they planned to rip off.

Next, ensure the plan went tickety-boo and record that as well. Allow Frederick no escape. Get it photographed, too. Filmed – shit yes. Elvis knew who could help him. Whose professional urge would match his moral/personal urge to document the fuck up that was Frederick.

The stunts he pulled and the people he ruined. It would all be over.

The shakedown of Frederick Street as he shook down Ricky Me would be slick and smooth. Elvis felt light-headed – he was going to pull this off. HE wouldn't know what hit him. Until it was over, too late. Until Detective Inspector Frederick Street was splashed all over newspapers, TV, websites, the MEDIA. Busted in plain view.

Next: convince Ricky to go through with his part. The right amount of dollar would do it. Ricky could not resist the spending stuff – who could?

This was a long time coming.

Elvis said the words out loud: 'A long time coming.'

The doorbell sounded; he made the entryphone. There's Dana, face on the monitor, he buzzed her in.

Dana Gabrielle – here she comes, smiling as always: enjoy that 365/ 24-7 beamer. She's Camilla's close friend. She's near polar opposite to Camilla. Dana has smarts, a lightness of self; a brain that makes her an ace reporter, ace to be around.

She said, 'Hi.'

She clocked the room for Camilla.

Elvis said, 'Camilla's not back yet. Surprise, surprise. She say she'd be here now?'

Dana Gabrielle in her smart business suit, blonde hair scraped back, those soft features showing.

Her smile went brighter. 'Not exactly. She called, said she needed to see me – she sounded upset. But *I'm* the one who's late. I got called on a job.'

'You want coffee?'

Dana nodded. 'Please. Black.'

'What was the job?'

Dana looked at snow out the window. 'This pills thing – the moody batch of Ecstasy putting our local respectable ravers in hospital. BuzzFeed are on it now so I'm stringing for them as well.'

'The moody pills offed anyone yet?'

'Can't be long. There's always someone who shouldn't be doing them in the first place who reacts badly. *Fatally.*'

'You speaking from personal experience?'

Dana laughed. 'Not me Elvis. I'm clean and serene, like you.'

'Of course you are.' There, again – that bolt of regret. Why go for Camilla? The headstrong girl with zero plans. Why not Dana, the cool one whose plans had plans?

He finished making the coffee, handed her a cup. 'What's the story?'

'A few busts, but only at street level. The police want to find the source, the big guy. Where it's coming from.'

'Where do they think it's coming from?'

He knew the answer. Frederick had to be involved. He braced pushers. Wholesaled the shit he ripped off back to street-level goons. Local bars and pubs got flooded; Frederick banana republic-ruled Shoreditch and Hackney.

Dana said, 'They're not sure where yet – the arrests have been on Old Street, Kingsland Road and the Cambridge Heath end of Hackney Road. That was the last one. Shoreditch Police Head of Media gave me the story, the bones of it anyway. That's what I've been doing.'

Elvis flicked through his iPhone, punched info into Google. He called Dana's yarn up on the *Shoreditch Today* website. 'Here it is – *Police Step Up Hunt for Dangerous Ecstasy*. By Dana Gabrielle. Exclusive.'

Elvis watched Dana loosen her hair; she said: 'It did read "Lethal" at first. As in, "Lethal Ecstasy", until I caught it, told the sub.'

'What happened to the journalistic license you bang on about?'

Dana shrugged. 'Until someone/something *dies* nothing is lethal.'

'You could have gone for "potentially lethal". That's correct? These bar snacks are potentially lethal. You said it yourself – always someone who shouldn't be taking them, does, and carps it.'

'Everything's potentially something.'

'You take the point.'

She smiled.

He said, 'What next?'

Dana sipped coffee and shrugged. 'Not a big enough noise yet for a press conference, so I'm hoping there'll be a proper briefing. The police want to try and hit some of the places where the pills are being sold and taken – get the dealers there. Try and lean on them. Your dad might be involved, right?'

She mentioned *him* – keep it vague; say: 'Who knows?' It's on his turf – so yes, maybe. As you say, may depend on how big time it gets. 'You said, lean on them?'

Dana nodded.

'Get them to grass?'

Dana nodded.

'Last thing they want to be known as, surely? Snitches.'

Dana smiled – he felt a soft wobble. The way her smile made you smile back.

Dana said, 'The idea is it's not known. No one goes around broadcasting it. Come on – you must know suspects, criminals talk. To get deals. It's like my trade – the whole thing falls down if no one blabs. On the quiet. A dealer is caught with fifty pills, a few wraps of coke, and he's going down – what do you think he's going to do?'

'I know.'

'Problem the police have on this one, from what the Head of Media says, is the scene constantly moving around. Brick Lane, Broadway Market, Mare Street, Kingsland Road, Hoxton, etcetera. Difficult to hit everywhere all the time, though the police would never say that.'

Elvis nodded, moved the conversation on. 'Fancy Ziggy's tomorrow night?'

'You DJing?'

'Was going to but not sure now.'

'If you do, I'm in.'

'Great.'

'Is Camilla coming?'

'Doubt it – why don't you ask her?'

Here she came, through the door, features screwed up. She went to Dana, they hugged, broke apart – Camilla eyed Elvis.

Dana to Camilla: 'Frederick?'

She burst into tears.

Elvis said nothing.

Frederick: he went with Camilla, behind his back. Then left her; left them *both* heartsick.

What could he say?

What was there to say?

It had all been said.

For months and months. It was old news. It still cut like it was fresh news.

It's another *reason.*

For what was going to happen.

One more *why* the turnover merchant was going to be turned over.

It might be THE BIG WHY.

Time moved on; days moved.

THE day would come.

He tingled.

THREE

1.17pm

Frederick watched the feed. He couldn't stop chorting. The show was hours in. It looked like it would run and run. Frederick nudged Wade Long. Wade lost interest. Wade kept falling the shit asleep. Wade garbed regulation Wade: Bermuda shorts, loud shirt, boaters. No coat. Despite the freezing fucking cold.

Frederick nudged him harder.

Wade opened an eye, primped his handlebar tache. He opened both eyes. 'It's still snowing.'

'Fuck that,' said Frederick. 'Watch these goons. Watch 'em.'

They sat in Frederick's unmarked Audi. He parked on Ezra, on the corner of Columbia, across from the place. Wade rigged the feed up. Frederick got him access, Wade did the rest: three pinhole cameras that beamed images live to the iPad propped on the Audi's dash.

They watched.

They saw:

Richard 'Ricardo' 'Ricky Me' Cliff.

He looked at the coke. Three knuckle-sized lumps plus a pile on his walnut-blanched coffee table. He looked at a rolled twenty note, a glass of vodka–7 Up. At a pack of Marlboro Lights. At Vanessa, his squeeze.

Ricky watched as she poured herself into a pink bikini.

He said, 'I don't see my phone.' His voice cut-glass clear on the feed. 'My mobile phone. I need it – you know that, it's essential to business. Where is it Vanessa? That student or whatever he is, Elvis, has been trying to call me. I've had three missed calls off the cunt – now I'm ready to speak, where's the phone?'

Ricky watched Vanessa. She smiled – read it as vacant. She fobbed the goon off. Smile and hope – hope he shuts up quick.

Was she vacant?

15

Ricky stood, Wade's second camera came into play. The iPad screen split three ways, one for each camera.

Ricky said, 'Fuck it. It'll turn up. Everything always turns up.' He looked on the table. 'Where are my keys? Time for another bump.'

Camera 3 caught Vanessa. She donned the bikini; burst out at all angles. She donned black heels, strutted her stuff.

Eyed the blow. 'Morning buster.'

Ricky said, 'Sweet'; and looked at his watch. 'Actually babe, it's afternoon. One-fifteen pm. More ice. He held his glass up. 'More in there will you – more vodka; 7 Up too.'

Camera 2 showed Ricky fixed on Vanessa's tits: who could blame him? Frederick near salivated – the zero wobble factor, how they held firm in the two pink triangles.

Ricky palmed her his glass and she disappeared. He said, 'I still don't see my phone but I do see my keys so things are looking up.'

He grabbed them, flicked one open, sat back down – the key showed a BMW emblem: classic street-dealer goon status sled. He poked the key in the chisel pile, gently brought it to a nostril. The bugle went down in one; his hand trembled from the hours-old session.

Ricky said, 'Why does anyone bother with a note? Why does anyone cunting bother?'

Vanessa moved back into shot, holding two glasses. 'Freshened up.' She palmed Ricky one, sat next to him on the sofa; she took the key and dipped it in powder and bumped one up her nose.

Frederick chorted, elbowed Wade. 'Here we go.'

Vanessa put a hand on Ricky's thigh. The street goon grimaced. 'You seen my phone or not?'

'I told you, I haven't.'

Ricky drank his vodka-7 Up, watched ice cubes wobble. 'I've got to find it.'

He stood up. 'Whooah!' He wobbled, nearly fell back on the sofa. Frederick and Wade howled – Ricky steadied himself, scoped the table again. 'You looked all over the flat like I told you?'

'Twice.'

'Try again.'

A Vanessa glare. 'Try not to fall over.' She looked for the phone, moving in and out of shot.

Ricky grimaced at her, bloated another bump. He killed half the vodka-7, scoped the table/room a millionth time.

He walked out of shot.

Frederick pointed out the Audi windscreen.

There – Ricky Me in shot in *real life,* at the first-floor window. They caught a clear view across Columbia.

Frederick and Wade ducked down; falling snow gave extra cover. They kept watching; Ricky lingered a few seconds, disappeared.

The audio still worked – they heard him say: 'Fuck it.'

He reappeared on camera 2, moved on to 1. He sat on the sofa: 'Vanessa – *Vanessa!*'

She jiggled on to camera 3.

'No luck?'

Vanessa shook her head.

Ricky said, 'What the fuck did I think you could–'

Vanessa, cutting him off: 'I think you should slow down on the partying – it doesn't agree with you.'

She followed with a smile – Frederick got this: she's a difficult read. She tied Ricky in knots. Her 'party' barb flew over Ricky's head.

The goon said, 'I have a plan – I've still got the landline, it's going to be our saviour. I'll call T-Mobile from it, see if they can send me a replacement.'

'A replacement?'

'Yeah, fuckwit. A new phone. That's where you come in. If they won't send it over straightaway you go get it for me, babe.'

'They're not going to give you a new mobile phone for nothing. Like they're not in business. Or only in business for you – to give you a new mobile phone for nothing.'

Ricky laughed, got a mean look. 'You're nineteen, you know it all because you go to college, right? Babe, I'm not expecting anything for free. Except for you to get with it. To catch the fuck up, sooner rather than later. You been doing sly bumps while you was looking for my phone? You more messed up than you should be, losing the plot already?'

He grabbed her chin. Forced Vanessa to look at him. Frederick laughed: 'You see this goon? He thinks he's an actual gangster. Can you believe this is actually happening? This is an underrated perk of the job – seeing how goons like this operate in private, in their own homes. He's watched *Scarface* too many times.'

Wade said: 'Ssssh.'

Onscreen, Vanessa said, 'No. But you have. You lost the plot a long time ago. *You* love a sly bump. You *love* a sly poke.' She giggled, grabbed at his dick. 'You love a sly anything.'

Ricky pulled her hand away. 'What are you talking about? I am paying for a mobile phone, babe. Understand *me*?'

Vanessa giggled. 'You don't get it do you? Why bother calling them? If you need it straightaway?' She pulled a face, made speech marks with her fingers. "For business." It won't come until later will it? Wait a minute.'

She did another bump and passed him the key. Ricky – addled; he put the coke-less key to a nostril, realised. Vanessa giggled, Frederick and Wade howled.

Vanessa: 'Oh dear.'

Ricky reloaded. He showed her the bird, did a bona fide bump this time.

Vanessa: 'I've got it – brainwave time – you're going to thank me for this. Use the landline phone, call your mobile, see if we can hear it ring.'

Ricky thought about it. He pulled the landline, dialled, put it on loudspeaker; they listened – nothing. He replaced the receiver.

'Try again,' Vanessa said.

He did – the same result, no mobile ring.

Ricky leered and laughed. 'Next bright idea.'

Vanessa said, 'Sure, and it will definitely help you. You've got insurance, for the mobile? You must as you are one tight bastard.'

Ricky grinned. 'Certainly.'

'Here's what you're going to do. *We're* going to do. You listening?'

Ricky nodded.

'If you're not going to listen forget it.'

Ricky grinned, his eyes half closed.

THREE

Vanessa said, 'Fuck this.' She pulled the landline, rang directory enquires, got the number for T-Mobile. Dialled and eyed Ricky. He bumped another bump, snorted loudly.

Vanessa covered the phone with a hand. '*Ssssh.*'

Into the handset: 'Hello. I'm calling about a stolen mobile phone.' She spoke for a few minutes, rang off.

A smile: 'You're going to like this.'

'Yeah?'

'All you have to do to get a new one for free is report it stolen. The insurance covers it.'

'But I haven't had it stolen.'

'You have now.'

Ricky threw a large grin. It lit up Wade's feed. 'Now we are cooking.'

'You report it stolen and the insurance pays for the new one. That's what the man said.'

Ricky beamed. 'A free phone. Off these insurance rip-off merchants. Who am I reporting it stolen to? The insurance company?'

'Not straightaway. First, report it to the police. Then it's official. Next, the insurance company.'

Frederick howled loud. He told Wade: 'Can you believe this? Ricky goes through with this, you know who's going to be the friendly community police detective who goes round to hear his tale of woe?'

Wade grinned. The shit-head liked *that*. 'I hear you my man. I hear you.' They watched the screen. Ricky – alarmed. Even his thicko brain sensed danger. 'Report it to the police? *Report it to the fucking police?* Why would I want to speak to them? Take a look around, do I look like someone who wants to be speaking to the police? How stupid are you?'

'You look like someone who likes to get something for free and who would like to fool the police, yes.'

Ricky shrugged, reached for another bump. Up it went. The powder worked instantly. Frederick knew the look he got, *felt* it: powder hit capillaries, Ricky's features changed. A soft breeze blew across them – *through him.*

Ricky grinned. He grew a *biiiig* pair of nuts, said: 'I report it to the police. Go on – then what?'

Vanessa, smiling: 'They give you a crime number, you give that to the insurance company and you get a mint new phone. Free. As simple as that.'

'That's my bitch. Here.'

Frederick/Wade guffaws; Frederick: '"That's my bitch"? Who is this goon?'

Camera 1 showed Ricky. He held a loaded key and Vanessa bumped it. He reloaded, wolfed it. 'Get me the number of Shoreditch pig shop.'

Vanessa opened the laptop – camera 2 showed the screen. It still played porn they had banged to earlier. Frederick and Wade caught the live stag flick in full.

Vanessa punched up Google, found the number, told Ricky: 'Pick up the landline and I'll read it to you.'

Ricky listened to her and dialled. He got put through, grinned at Vanessa, pointed at the handset, mouthed: 'Dickhead.' Into the phone: 'This Shoreditch nick?'

He put the loudspeaker function on. A voice came into the room, over the feed, Frederick and Wade heard it crystal.

The voice: 'Police station, yes. I'm Dan Holden, police staff at Shoreditch station. You wish to report a crime?'

'That's why I'm calling – I've had my phone stolen.'

'Yes sir. Name please.'

Ricky's face tightened – camera 1 showed it. Wade hit the iPad and went tight on Ricky's visage. It looked ridiculous. It *was* ridiculous. *He* was ridiculous.

Now – like he suddenly realised what he did. His tone ran reluctant. 'My name – Richard Cliff.'

'Address?'

'27a Columbia Road, Shoreditch.'

'Postcode?

'Postcode?'

'You do have one don't you sir?'

Frederick/Wade guffaws. 'This is good,' said Frederick. 'This is very fucking good. I know Dan Holden. He'll know exactly what kind of idiot he has here.'

'Sure,' said Ricky. 'Postcode – erm, E27RG.'

'What happened, sir?'

'What happened?'

'You said you had your phone stolen.'

Ricky's face said: get from my coke-addle and come up with a story; *fast.*

Here it came. 'I was at the top of the street earlier, Columbia Road, and these nig-nogs – black lads – pulled a blade and mugged me, took what I had in my pockets. My wallet, car keys and my phone. I was holding it. It wasn't in my pocket. Yeah. The bastards. That's what happened.'

A pause. Dan Holden: 'When was this?'

'I told you – today.' Ricky winked at Vanessa – it blared: this pig is a numb-nut, he hasn't got a clue. *Hahahaha.*

Frederick had read Ricky's record. It showed several arrests and prison time. *Ricky* was a numb-nut. *That* was funny.

Holden said, 'What time was this?'

'Don't know. I mean, not exactly. Say 10am.'

'"Say 10am"?'

'Yes mate. What I said.'

'And you've waited until now sir, 1.45pm, to report it?'

'Yes mate.'

A pause.

'You at home now?'

'Yes mate.'

Another pause. Holden played him; he knew how to squeeze goons. He said, 'Two detectives will be round soon to take a statement.'

Ricky looked at Vanessa. *She* looked at the blow, grabbed the key, stuck more up her nose. Rocked back on the sofa, closed her eyes.

'A statement? What for?' Ricky said. He whirled a finger next to his head: *how dim is this pig?*

Holden: 'That's what we do sir. Police procedure. Make a record of the crime committed against you and you get a crime number, for your insurance, if you are insured. I can't say we will catch who did it. In fact the chances are slim. That's the sad reality sir, I'm afraid.'

Ricky said, 'No problem.' He said it again: 'You're coming *round*?'

'That what I said sir – two of my colleagues from Shoreditch Police Station. Detectives. They'll take it from here.'

Ricky wasn't listening. He put the phone down, eyed Vanessa – she lay on a cushion.

Frederick nudged Wade. He pointed and near collapsed from laughter; managed to say: 'Look – *unbelievable*.'

Under the cushion was Ricky's mobile phone. Ricky saw it – he found his phone.

'For cunt's sake, Vanessa – look, my blower.' He pointed, Vanessa didn't move, her eyes stayed shut. 'What the fuck? Vanessa you daft cunt, *look*. My shitting phone – I've got the pigs coming round and they're going to see I found it and know I was lying about it being mugged off me. They'll probably search the whole place. They'll find my stash – I scored an ounce last night. I've got bags of pills that shouldn't be here as well. Shoreditch pig shop's around the corner – they'll be here soon.'

Vanessa kept her eyes closed. 'What *are* you talking about Ricky? How gone must you be.'

Frederick and Wade in pieces – they couldn't stop chorting, couldn't *believe* what they saw.

Ricky, raging: 'I asked you to look for it, didn't I? Twice. Fucking twice. What is the point of you if you can't do even that?'

She opened her eyes, reached for the key. Ricky intercepted. Ricky said, 'Allow me, dearest.' He took the key. Delved deep in the gak mound. It's a bumper edition, a Yuletide–scale portion. He cradled Vanessa's head, held the key to a nostril. He made sure she snorted it all the way down.

Vanessa's eyes gleamed. Frederick caught the look. The *expression*. Like earlier. She got the horn; was ready to blow Ricky. He's a goon but who cares: I'm *hornnnny*!

Ricky took his turn, did a bulging bump.

He looked at her a moment.

'Get me the hammer.'

Frederick nudged Wade. Wade nudged Frederick. They were in pieces – Frederick is decades time-served on the Met. Has seen a lot of shit. This is up there. Wade is ex-Met. Wade pulls stunts – he's seen a lot of shit. This is up there.

Vanessa, giggling: 'That's what you're calling it now is it – "The Hammer"?' She reached for his jeans and giggled again. Ricky gripped her hand.

He said, 'The hammer. The one I use to smash things up.'

'Fuck, Ricky, okay, okay. You're hurting, get off me.'

'The hammer. Can you find that? Do you think?' Ricky's voice squeaked on 'that'. He let go of Vanessa. The squeak made her laugh – she shouldn't be doing so – laughing in his face.

Who IS the bird?

Ricky pointed off-camera. '*Get the hammer now.*' Vanessa caught his tone, got up in quick time; moved off-camera, returned.

'No problem,' she said. 'It was hung where it should be, on the back of the bedroom door.'

Ricky ignored her – his eyes *wild*.

He snatched the hammer. She stepped away from him, flopped down back on the sofa. Back on the cushion. *On* his mobile.

He said, 'Now I'm going the fix the mess you made.'

Frederick said, 'I knew I should have brought popcorn. This is better than ripping the goon off.'

Ricky raised the hammer. He came towards Vanessa. He swung the hammer – at her, he aimed for her head. He *was* going for her head.

'What the fuck! RICKY!'

He missed. He hit the mobile phone under the cushion. The bit that stuck out.

Ricky's eyes bulged – he got madder.

Frederick and Wade re-corpsed. *What a show*. The sofa's softness neutered any hammer purchase. Ricky couldn't smash the phone. Like the hammer and phone were rubber. He picked it up – picked up the phone, threw it on the floor.

Now: he got the hammer and obliterated it.

See there – it *is* smashed to pieces *now*.

'That's what the fuck I'm talking about. Now pick up the pieces. All of them. And hide them. Hide them good.'

Vanessa, stunned: 'You what?'

'You deaf as well as dumb?' Ricky said. He dropped from a shout to a low voice. 'I told you to look everywhere for my phone. Except you didn't. Now the pigs are coming round to take a statement from me about my stolen phone and my phone's here. Except now it is smashed up and you're going to hide the pieces. Get it?'

Vanessa thought on it a moment. Like he was mad or smarter than she pegged him.

She nodded. 'Okay.'

She started picking up pieces of phone.

Ricky liked that – he smiled. Frederick watched Ricky's eyes. Frederick watched what Ricky watched: *that* pink bikini, *those* heels, *those tits.* Xmas has come nice and early.

OH, YEAH.

Ricky found the key, and reloaded. He did the bugle. He bugle-buzzed, caught a bugle-inspired eureka! moment.

He said, 'When you've finished that get me a piece of paper and a pen.'

Vanessa stopped picking up phone pieces. 'What for?'

'I need to write down my story for the pigs, make sure I don't forget anything.'

Vanessa: 'Jesus Christ.'

'And after that, hide the pieces of my phone if you're up to that. Then then we are done – these pigs are going to be mugged off. Season's greetings.'

'What about the stuff you've got here?'

'What about it? Have more if you like, just make sure you leave some for me.'

'No Ricky. We need to hide it. From the police. The pigs.'

Ricky looked at Vanessa. *Considered* it. He said, 'It's an ounce from the Albanians. You're right. You clean up here. Get rid of the pieces of my phone, hide them and clear up this table – it is filthy. I'll hide the stash. Hurry up, they'll be here any time.'

THREE

In the Audi, Frederick and Wade re-*RE*-howled. Frederick pulled his phone, speed-dialled the station.

Wade said, 'Who you calling?'

'Holden. Then Jefferson – this is one for him.'

Fuck his regular partner. Fuck Lee. Get the young detective on this. It might play good later. With what Elvis planned. The goon.

FOUR

16 December, 3.30pm

Frederick sat on the sofa at Ricky Me's place and admired the walnut coffee table. Thinking, it looked clean. Thinking, it had *just* been cleaned. *Knowing* it had.

Thinking: drugs, powder, coke. Towering, magnificent, shimmering senses popping blow.

This is a Blow Alert: hands on your head and don't nobody shitting move.

His eyes gleamed. They gleamed coke. They *pre-coked*. That's how they rolled.

This was playing sweeter than he imagined. Ricky's phone insurance play was a bonus. What a goon. It's a BIG bonus. An earned one. The beauty of surveillance. Of doing your homework. Of being a pro.

He left Wade behind. He met Jefferson outside the Royal Oak. Across from Ricky's. He worded the young detective up. Not completely. *Enough.*

Now: Frederick read what Richard Cliff of 27a Columbia Road said. About being mugged. Getting his phone ripped off. Frederick reading this *before* Ricky said anything. Richard 'Ricardo' 'Ricky Me' Cliff was yet to give his 'story'. Who cared? It's pretty clear what the story is. What he's going to say. It's written down on a piece of paper. On the table. Where it can be read – now, right now.

Hilarious.

As in – *fucking hilarious.*

Frederick looked at his colleague, DC Larry Jefferson. He caught his eye. He winked. He gave a this-will-be-fruity grin. He looked at Richard Cliff. The goon twitched, the goon was low-level dealer stock.

Frederick stood by the window. Frederick drank tea Vanessa made.

She packed calm eyes. She packed something else. Call it a *brain*. She sat on an armchair, sipped her tea, watched the whole thing unfold.

Frederick said, 'Before we get started, where's your khazi?'

'Khazi?'

'Yes, Mr Cliff, may I use it? The toilet.'

'Oh, right.' Ricky pointed towards the hallway.

'Thanks.'

He made it, took a leak. Scoped the mirror over the sink. Saw *under* the sink. He chuckled – these goons. Take it now? No, later – from Vanessa.

He went back.

They waited for him. He opened his pad, pulled a pen: showtime.

'What happened then, Mr Cliff?' Frederick eyed the note Ricky penned to himself.

Ricky said, 'It was awful, broad daylight, happened this morning at the bottom of Columbia Road, I was near the Stingray, that pizza place, and these fucking nig-nogs, black lads – whatever you call 'em – took out a blade and told me to empty my pockets. What was I supposed to do? There's two of them, one of me. If it's a fair go then it's different. I'll kick the fucking shit out of them.'

A watery grin. Confession time. A heartfelt mea culpa from Ricky Me: 'I did it. I'm not ashamed to say – I gave them my wallet, with all my cards in, cash. And I gave over my phone.'

Ricky looked at Frederick for the first time. Like he showed a sense of drama, occasion. 'And off they went. They robbed me in broad daylight. Left me fuming. I'm still fucking fuming, to be honest.'

'Your phone was in your pocket?'

'That's what I said.'

'Only it says here it was "in your hand". At the time I mean.'

Frederick held the piece of paper up. Jefferson took a look, read the note, laughed. Frederick threw him a look – he shut up quick. Vanessa read it. 'Jesus, Ricky.'

She laughed, too.

'It also says–' Frederick read slowly. '"The top of Columbia Road, near the shops". Not the bottom, near the pizza place, as you said.'

Ricky gave a smile and forced a laugh. 'And? So?? What's the Sherlock Holmes act for???'

Frederick – near impressed. The goon took a stab at cool. He packed a brains-deficit but had some street smarts. 'Which is it? Stingray or the shops? Top or bottom.'

Ricky laughed again. 'Whatever it says on there of course. Fucking hell.' Another laugh.

Frederick blanked. It *was* funny, but: he shouldn't show it.

Jefferson: 'Why have you written that down, sir?'

Ricky's watery smile. 'You're piping up now too are you? Why do you think? To make sure I wouldn't forget what had happened. Pretty important don't you think? Come on Mr Nice Policemen: why else would I?'

'You worried you'd forget being mugged? Pretty memorable experience, wouldn't you think, sir?' Jefferson spoke lightly – like he laid a trap.

Ricky blinked, looked at Vanessa. He scoped Frederick, went back to Jefferson.

Told him: 'An experience to shake you up, for sure. To put you in shock. Make you sure to try and nail the scum who did it. Do your best to get the facts straight so there's no escape for them. I mean, that's what you want too, right? Both of you?'

'We want what's right, that's for sure,' Frederick said.

'Of course you do,' Ricky said. 'And I'm here to help you do that. Course I am.'

A full-beam smile. He pointed at the piece of paper. 'Now we're clear, you might as well just copy down what I've written as hear me go through it again. You're all about statements, correct? Taking down statements. There you go then. I've helped you out – no need to thank me. I wouldn't expect it.'

Ricky's eyes narrowed – his grin went triumphant.

Frederick shrugged. 'Okay. Here we go.' He began writing, it didn't take long.

'You have your crime report. Here you go, you can make the claim. Can I have your full names and telephone numbers – best numbers to contact each of you on, please?'

'No point having my mobile number – it's been stolen after all.' Ricky laughed. He threw Vanessa a wink.

Frederick: 'Your landline number will do.'

Ricky read it Frederick, Vanessa gave her mobile number. He wrote them down and smiled. He stood up, looked out the window. 'Nice day. Can't remember so much snow at Christmas time. But I'm not complaining. Am I Jefferson?'

'No boss.'

Frederick's turn to grin. He looked at Ricky. 'You have something in your eye?'

Ricky considered it. 'Have I?'

'It's twitching. A bit out of control.' Everyone looked at Ricky. Frederick said, 'Maybe it's the shock. Still? You think so? Of your ordeal.'

Ricky said, 'Thanks for the concern. And for the report. If that's all, I've got stuff to do.'

'Could also be chemically induced, of course. Plus a lack of sleep. Going at it for a bit.' Frederick grinned. 'If you know what I mean?'

Ricky's answer came quick. 'Sounds like you're talking about an experience that's happened to *you*. That you know *all* about.'

'No,' said Frederick. 'You're the one who does cocaine and God knows what else. Don't bother pretending to protest. You've been done a few times, possession, possession with intent, you like to pilfer too, if I recall correctly. From your sheet. Did a few months in Brixton, right?'

Ricky grinned/grimaced. 'Old news,' he said. 'I'm the one who's been mugged, remember?'

Frederick to Vanessa: 'He's holding? In the flat? I don't mean a gram, an eighth for you to do, have a session, continue the good times you were probably enjoying before we came – that table looks rather polished, gives it away – I mean a weight. To serve up.'

Ricky shook his head, Vanessa shrugged. As if she gave a flying about Ricky.

'You mind if I take a look around?'

'Yes I do.'

'Thought so.'

'Why ask then?'

'Why not?'

Ricky said, 'Have you heard this policeman, Vanessa? He's supposed to be helping us.'

Frederick smiled, opened the laptop. Coke residue on the keyboard. Porn playing on the screen: young-hunk-on-grandma stuff.

He winked, said: 'You like old bid porn, Vanessa?' Jefferson laughed. Frederick watched the girl. She shrugged – she had heard it all before. This fucking pig.

Frederick said, 'You like granny porn Ricky? The geriatrics do it for you do they?' Jefferson laughed more, Vanessa too now.

Frederick closed the laptop. His voice went low. 'Don't worry Richard, Vanessa obviously gets off on your individual predilection. You know what I mean?'

He nodded to Jefferson. The junior detective killed more laughs.

'Come on. Let's go.' He winked at Ricky and Vanessa. 'See you soon, no doubt.'

At the door he paused. There – on the floor. A piece of Ricky's smashed-up phone. He picked it up, lobbed it Vanessa, addressed Ricky. 'Looks like she forgot a bit.'

He flashed them a look. He winked. Made a play of fighting back chorts.

They saw what it was, clocked what the detective found.

Ricky looked at Vanessa. Vanessa looked at Ricky.

DI Frederick Street looked at them.

It's that Fredster stuff. Groove on it.

The street, Columbia Road. Frederick and Jefferson turned towards the unmarked Audi on Ezra. Wade was long gone; Frederick stopped. 'Take the motor – go ahead. I've got a witness I need to see in the Oak.'

He pointed at the pub.

'I can walk back to Shepherdess – be nice in the snow. I'll feel all Christmassy. I'll like that.'

'Sure,' said Jefferson. The detective made the Audi, fired it up, boosted off down Columbia.

Frederick crossed the street. He entered the Oak, made around the bar, exited the other entrance. He crossed back over Columbia, pulled his phone. He took out his notebook, dialled the number and waited.

Vanessa answered.

He said, 'I'm outside. Yeah, the street. By your front door. No, stay there. Listen carefully. You need to meet me. For your own good. Do it. This is not over yet. There's a Thai place on Hoxton Square. Yelo. You know it? Good. Say 5.45 – yes, tonight. And when you come, make sure you bring Ricky's stash. No excuses – give *him* some excuse – and bring it with you. I know it's there and where it is, I've just seen it. If you don't you're both busted. I know you don't give a fuck about him. So, think of yourself. Don't let him know. He asks where it's gone, say that pig probably ripped it off when he went for a piss. Which is basically the truth. What's he going to do? Call the police?'

Frederick laughed the laugh – *that* laugh, which was deep yet high-pitched, like a baby who packed baritone vocal chords.

'So, bring the nose candy. Don't let him see you. Be there and your Xmas will still be merry.'

He rang off, laughed the laugh again. Baby-baritoned at this shit. What occurred. The sound hit cold air, passers-by. It sounded *off*.

Of course it did.

FOUR A

4.02pm

Elvis noshed a chicken kebab at Istanbul Sizzle on Brick Lane. His blower buzzed – an unknown number. He hesitated.

He took the call.

'Elvis?'

It took a moment. 'Ricky?' He was difficult to pin down. He *never* called, *never* answered.

'It's me, you student. Listen, this is–'

'What's this number?'

'Eh? It's – my bird's, so what? My phone died. It's a long story. But fuck that. This is serious, why I called.'

Elvis caught a sense: the joey's going to pull out, scupper everything. He said, 'Go on then – what?'

'It's weird, some kind of deep shit. Your dad's a pig? A detective. Is he called er – what the, I've–'

Elvis froze and popped a sweat. 'Frederick. Frederick Street. Yeah, he's a detective, can you just get on with this–'

'I'm trying if you don't interrupt me all the time – you know that's rude, when I–'

'Ricky!'

Jesus, how goosed is he?

'What? Right, yeah, sorry. Your dad has just been round to my place, if he is who we both think and say and seem to know he is–'

'*What?*'

Ricky snorted. 'You don't understand plain English? You a yid or something? Your dad has just been around to my pad. Which is why I'm calling – it was weird.'

'Why?'

Ricky went silent. Finally: '"Why?"'

Jesus – the goon runs an all-time record brains deficit. Makes him a liability *and* a workable joey.

'Ricky?'

'Right, yeah – the *reason* he came round was about my phone–'

'You said *that* was a long story–'

'It is – but it's why he came round – look, just shut up a moment.'

'Okay.'

'He came round because I reported my phone stolen and to get it replaced on my insurance I needed a police report, you know, to prove I'm not lying. I mean, I am lying, it wasn't mugged from me by some nig-nogs, but obviously I didn't tell the phone company that or the pigs, your dad, when–'

Elvis popped a fresh sweat and smelt a stink. 'Ricky, what did he do at your place?'

A pause. Revise earlier: this joey ran a *mere* quarter of a brain cell. And he ran it on a timeshare basis with *all* local joeys.

Ricky said, 'Nothing really. I mean, he wrote the report for me, that I needed for the new blower. But it was just the fact he was there. You know, with what we've got planned.'

Joey-features sensed right on *that*. Joey-features may have an iota of sixth sense. 'That was it?'

'He – he seemed suspicious of something. He saw my story written down – that set him off.'

Elvis paused, didn't compute. *Ricky* didn't compute. 'What story?'

'That I told the pigs, your dad. I wrote it down because I made it up. I didn't want to forget it, you see what I'm saying? He saw the piece of paper and thought I was lying.'

Elvis's Spidey sense ratcheted. Frederick – the old man knew/vibed something. His presence at Ricky's blared it. 'Anything else?'

Elvis brain-whirred. Frederick – he *couldn't* know anything. How could he?

Dismiss it.

Then, yes, it must be *this*: he checked Ricky out post the church meeting. Why he was at Ricky's pad. The old man wanted to see who they dealt with, who they planned to rip the gak off.

Ricky deep-breathed down the blower. His share on the quarter-cell ticked.

He said, 'Anything else? Dunno. Don't think so.'

Elvis made a decision. Fuck it, let's see how this plays. To Ricky: 'Good work calling me. You're earning your payola. I wouldn't worry about it. It's probably just a coincidence.'

Ricky wanted to believe it. 'You think so?'

'What else could it be?'

Ricky took a breath. 'We're still going through with it – the plan?'

Elvis laughed. The sound bounced around Istanbul Sizzle. Punters rubbernecked. 'Of course. Fuck him – my old man. He doesn't *know* what I'm up to. So as long as you keep your mouth shut about *our* plan it will stay that way. Get it?'

Ricky took a moment.

Ricky said 'Sure.'

Elvis hung up.

FOUR B

4.12pm

James Maroon sat on the terrace sipping bourbon. He was a suave-o sophisticate and a spiv. He knew what he was; prided himself on knowing.

Grooved on the knowledge: WHO THE FUCK WOULDN'T???

He possessed hinterland, too. He retained an interest in art. Had a small gallery off Hoxton Square. He was a reformed crackhead – the rock near ruined him. He got out. He retained his looks *and* his smarts.

His ambition.

He drew a fat well of strength from the experience. Strength money could never buy – only staring at the abyss could.

James was the coming man of Shoreditch. Frederick knew it. James was after Frederick: what the bent crook cop did and had; what he blocked James doing and having: CONTROL.

James knew about Elvis. He knew *all* about Elvis and Camilla. About Elvis and Camilla *and* Frederick. What a fine mess that was. Though he had to admit respect for Frederick doing *that* to his son. Banging Camilla because he could, and the fancy took him.

And: he knew this: about Frederick and Elvis: the feud; the shakedown Elvis planned of his dad – the exposé.

And James knew this, too: he was smarter than either. He would watch and monitor, spy and wait.

Wait for the right moment to take down Frederick.

Every move was about that.

His blower rung; he took the call on the first buzz. It was an unrecognised number.

He usually ignored any/all calls.

Not now – bring it the fuck on.

He said, 'Maroon.'

'It's Ricky.'

This muppet cousin of his. 'What?'

'Things are getting weird. The student's old man has just been at my place.'

James perked, sipped more bourbon. 'Spill.'

Ricky spun the yarn a second time in minutes. Ricky finished by relating his call to Elvis before he belled James.

James liked it – for three reasons. Because it confirmed how stupid Ricky was – check out the written-down story for the fuzz. It made him the ideal dupe in *James's* takedown of Frederick. He liked it second because he now *knew* Frederick was onto *Elvis's* plan to take his dad down. Maybe not all of it, but enough to get Frederick snooping. Even if Elvis didn't see it. There could be zero other reason for the 'coincidence' of the Ricky visit. James liked it third because Ricky came up *trumps* with the snitch info. It showed Ricky took seriously what would happen if he did not. Cousin or not. His supposed cut of the shakedown or not.

Ricky said, 'What do we do?'

James, toning surprise/befuddlement: 'What can you mean Richard, old boy?'

'Now, I mean now?'

James toned normal. 'Nothing. We carry on.'

'That's what Elvis just said when I told him about his old fella's visit.'

'Good,' said James. 'That's very good. Remember to focus, old boy. We do this right and we come up with a nice double score: the gak they're plotting to boost from you and the wedge. Ten K is not to be sniffed at, if you'll pardon the pedestrian punnery. That weight of showbiz will go for six times that. Best of all, I'll have enough dirt to do Frederick over so he's never coming back. Ever.'

He hung up, poured more bourbon. Didn't mention this was *all* about the dirt on shithouse Frederick Street. Forget the gak and the ten-large.

Didn't mention he left the whole thing open – this caper, how he planned it. Flexibility was key: who knew if the long game ran better by boosting the Streets' dipshit plan or letting it play out?

Because: it might be wiser to take on the victor of the Frederick-Elvis toe to toe. Let one consume the other – save James a job.

James knew Frederick worried Ricky. He knew Frederick worried Elvis. Frederick didn't worry James. He grooved on feeling the precise opposite emotion.

He could hardly wait.

FIVE

5.30pm

Frederick at Yelo on Hoxton Square. He wolfed stir-fry beef with holy basil. He sat outside under a heater. He watched snow fall. More fucking snow. It clumped everywhere.

He drank pale ale and ruminated.

People walked around in the white stuff like they were kids again. It made them smile. It made them HAPPY. It was odd, thicko tackle. Regular citizens showed no imagination. Regulation workforce were goosed from nine-to-five-ing. They lacked imagination, ergo they vibed this: zero snow meant zero jollity.

WHAAAAT???

Work it out. He couldn't.

The gig was grafting. The gig was grifting. The big G. Always be grifting. Always be GIGGING.

Find a caper; keep doing it. Keep on, and on. That way it wasn't work. He found the ideal patsy, for the latest gig.

Here she came; walking towards Frederick in the snow.

'Vanessa Compton. On time.'

Frederick got to his feet, offered a hand. He motioned her to sit down.

'Why here?'

'The food, you can sit outside, great view of Hoxton Square, the world passing. The poetry of the Smoke. That kind of thing.'

'That kind of thing.'

She scanned the menu, waved a waiter over. 'Pad Thai please, with extra peanuts and ask the chef to forget the spring onions. To drink, a mineral water and a Bloody Mary – double.'

The waiter ambled off. 'It's not often I get taken out. Especially by the police.'

'Ricky not treat you?'

'Not to anything outside the flat. All kinds of things inside.'

'I can imagine.'

'You don't need to.'

'True.'

He *didn't* have to – Wade's feed ensured that. He wondered if she'd reference the phone fragment he found. 'If Ricky's not the kind of guy to wine and dine you, why are you his girlfriend?'

Zero interest in the answer or question. Shoot shit to warm her up. There's no real need: once she got him access to Ricky's place she was his. In the gig, impossible to escape. The access was for Wade's cameras – he didn't tell her that – no need.

'Who says I'm with him?'

Frederick waited.

'I nearly never came.'

'Of course. *Good one.*'

He hooted. That was hoot-fest tackle. She ignored him: 'But I thought, why not?'

'You mean you thought: I have absolutely no fucking choice.'

Vanessa said nothing. Frederick got that sense again: she's smart.

Now, she spoke: 'Yeah, okay, you got me *detective*, I did, indeed, think that. You squeezed me, what else could I do?'

Frederick smiled. He could work with the girl – in the long term.

He said, 'I found his stash straightaway. As soon as we go round there, I see Richard Cliff – sorry Ricardo – Ricky Me – and know he's a dealer. I've read his record, his sheet before Jefferson and I roll up. Know him from around – whatever.'

She didn't tick – no question about *why* he got access from her to Ricky's pad. About what he did when she got him in the place the day before and got told to scarper. No sign/tell that she and Ricky got curious about the phone fragment he threw them as he and Jefferson exited. About his payoff line – 'Looks like she missed a bit'.

Maybe she hid it – that smart brain worked angles 24-7, for sure.

He riffed on Ricky: 'I can see he's wired – see you're more in control. He *knows* he's fucked up calling the police on this one. Before I took his statement from him, sorry before I took it from the fairy tale he'd written down, I thought: let's see if his stash is somewhere real obvious but where he *thought* it wouldn't be found. Unless his place is searched, which it wasn't going to be, as we're there to assist him after he's been "mugged".'

Pause, watch snow hit the square.

'If I've been inside one dealer's place I've been in most – understand? I excuse myself for a piss and find it. Behind the sink. Precisely where I'm thinking it will be. Unoriginal, yes? Lacks exactly the kind of imagination that keeps me in a job.'

Get to it: 'You brought the showbiz?'

'Sure.'

'Hand it over then, good girl.'

She palmed him the coke from Ricky's bathroom.

Frederick's features lit. It's a score/the grift – mucho amor.

He said, 'Merry Xmas.'

Vanessa shrugged.

The oz of chizz bulged in his hand. He palmed it in a jacket pocket and winked. 'Good girl.'

Vanessa's pad Thai arrived. She unwrapped chopsticks, started munching.

Vanessa said, 'Look – spring onions – what did I say to the waiter?'

'You're pretty full of it for a teenager.'

She laughed. Frederick waved the waiter over, ordered another pale ale. 'You haven't touched your drinks.'

Vanessa sipped mineral water, glugged Bloody Mary. 'I have now.'

'Why the confidence? Like you're forty-fucking-nine?'

'Interesting childhood.' She killed her Bloody Mary, ordered another when the waiter brought Frederick's ale.

She said, 'What do you want?'

'To keep you out of trouble.'

'*Hahaha.*'

She looked at Hoxton Square. Snow fell ceaseless. 'Come on – what do you want?'

'To keep you out of trouble, as I say. And – you can help me.'

The waiter returned with Vanessa's new Bloody Mary. She chinked Frederick's glass. 'How?'

'Someone I know is planning to turn me over and you're going to help me make sure he's the one turned over.'

'Who?'

Frederick chess-moved: mix truth/withhold some. He said, 'My son. Elvis.'

He eyed her: no sign she's familiar with him. That she/Elvis/Ricky schemed against him. Factor in her being a difficult read: impossible to rule out completely.

She said, 'Interesting. Why me?'

Frederick leaned back in his chair and drank pale ale. Snow swirled in Hoxton Square lamplight.

'He's going to use Ricky to try and do me. Set up a deal with him, for a few ounces of shit. The plan is to tax Ricky for the coke, split it between father and son. But he's secretly planning to record the deal and use it to bust me. Do me completely over. Something like that. Who the shit knows? As I say, *he's* the one who's getting turned over.'

Vanessa nodded her head. 'How do you know about it?'

'Not your business.'

'What's behind it? You could just walk away.'

Frederick laughed and glugged ale. 'Not your business either. But here you go. I quite like his style as it reminds me of my style, you know what I mean? Except I'm going to show him. By the time this is finished, the stupid thoughts in his head about what I might or might not be are over. It's why I didn't do Ricky – *arrest* him or you, when I found his stash. I have other plans. Well-thought-out plans. Trust me.'

'Sounds like bad father–son blood.'

'That's one way of looking at it.'

'You must have done something pretty bad.'

'I've done loads of stuff. I'm his fucking dad. What he would say is different. He would say it's about an ex of his. Mostly.'

'And?'

'We got involved. Her and me.' Frederick grinned. 'I don't usually get into this–'

'But you tell a low-rent teenager who's with a low-rent coke dealer.'

Frederick grinned.

'You went with her behind your son's back, when they were together? With this girl–'

'Camilla. But, no.' Frederick mock shocked. 'No. Afterwards, *later*. They weren't *together*. They were still friends, yes, but they'd broken up.'

'They'd broken up?'

'Yes.'

She watched him.

He said, 'Okay – they kept on getting back together, but that routine was a broken record I–'

'*Phewee*. That is a relief. For a moment it sounded like you might turn out to actually have a line you don't cross.'

They both laughed.

Frederick finished his drink, called for the bill. 'He thinks I'm a bad egg. A threat to society. He's beside himself with moral outrage. Elvis can't seem to handle that I'm where I want to be. That I have been for a while. And intend to be for a long long while. Understand?'

Vanessa nodded. Frederick said, 'Give me Ricky's landline number again – I seem to have mislaid it.'

She said, 'Why?'

'Because his mobile phone was stolen off him in a street mugging by some nig-nogs – remember?'

FIVE A

8.04pm

Frederick scooted the unmarked through snow to Columbia Road. He parked the Audi opposite the Oak. He pulled his phone, dialled the number, watched Ricky's place.

Ricky came on. He sounded weary. Like he had powdered on since Frederick and Jefferson departed.

He said, 'Yes.'

'Ricky – Detective Inspector Frederick Street here. Don't say a fucking word. Don't waste your breath, you'll need that to carry on snorting after we've spoken. I'm outside your place right now. The black Audi. I suggest you get yourself out of your hovel and into my motor, tout suite.'

'Eh?'

'*Now.*'

Frederick hung up, watched snowflakes fall. He gave him a minute – tops.

Here he came.

Ricky slid in the front passenger seat. He had to clear copious crap from it: Dunkin' Donuts boxes, reefer roaches, coke-snorting paraphernalia.

Ricky laughed. 'What a shithole, you call my place a hovel–'

Frederick went to grab him. Ricky shit three bricks and Frederick chorted.

He said, 'Listen, now. You're running about a thousandth of the average man's grey matter, and the average man is a prime thicko. So you won't have worked out my visit earlier wasn't purely on police business.'

Frederick paused, reconsidered. He eyed Ricky. 'You know what – I'm reserving the right. I'm making no definitive judgement on your precise intellectual abilities just yet. I'm holding back on that and will observe as we go forward with what you are about to be ordered to do. You cannot be too careful, and you cannot guard too much against the Big H. And that's not Horse/Hallucinogenics/Homeopathic fucking meds. I mean Hubris. Okay, so, you want a piece of advice from me, for free? Course you do. Here goes: don't resist what I'm about to propose. Instead, just ride on the warm glow of being co-opted by the fucking Fredster.'

Ricky started laughing. 'What are you–'

'Shut it Einstein, okay?' Frederick watched him. Saw he obeyed the order. 'I have a son called Elvis.' He fixed on Ricky – the goon showed no flicker, revealed zero tell. 'Said son is trying to turn me over and, guess what, he'll be using you as his patsy. If he hasn't already he's going to arrange a coke deal with you to buy so he can sell, as he's in a large amount of debt. So he is telling me. Cut a long yarn short, he's cut me in. On the deal. *Pretended* to. So that I can help. Use my PO-LICE credentials, general status in these parts as the gent to respect. Idea being he and me will rip thee off and split the shit. Except this is where the pretence comes in. He's having me on – *fooling me* – so that he can turn me over. Expose me. As he's got some ridiculous idea I'm a bent piece of filth. Cut an even longer story shorter: you are now working for me. Or else. Now, you talk. Answer a simple question for me.'

Ricky nodded.

'Good. Here it is: *do you understand?*'

Ricky nodded. 'Sure I do. Whatever he tells me I tell you. Correct?'

'Correctamundo.'

'And if I do, I walk away from this. Free.'

Frederick threw a crafty grin – look at this goon. 'As free as you're ever going to be.'

Frederick winked.

'I get it.'

'And?'

'And?'

'*Ricardo.*'

Ricky laughed. 'Okay, *okay*. You're bang on – Elvis has told me about his plan to turn you over. He's got something against you, like bad, you're bang on about that, too–'

'What's he promised you?'

'Come again?'

'Fuck off Ricky – spit. If he's told you all about it why would *you* go through with it? Agreeing to help rip off a so-called bent Met pig detective doesn't sound like an attractive proposition to a low-life street slave like you.'

Ricky stifled a laugh. Frederick made him as the thicko first thought. He wouldn't close the book, though: who knew with these shit-heads? 'Go on then Ricky Me: spit.'

'O*kay* – he offered me a grand–'

'A grand! To take me on, you must be particularly dense. There must be more. I *know* there is.'

'Okay, *okay* – you're right, I would be stupid to go through with it. And I'm not *that* stupid. I was – I wasn't going to go through with it. *I* was going to rip Elvis off–'

Frederick hooted. He double thumbs-upped Ricky. 'How?'

'How what?'

'How were you going to rip him off?'

'Dunno, hadn't worked that out. Maybe ask him for half of the money up front and do a runner.'

Frederick laughed more.

Ricky said, 'You *were* right. I wasn't going to go through with it.'

Frederick stopped howling. 'Well,' he said. 'You are now.'

FIVE B

8.31pm

James dined at the Skewered Lamb on Shoreditch main drag. He enjoyed a glass of Merlot. He noshed fillet mignon. Biz was good, biz was lucrative. He had just fixed two girls for high rollers who wanted to sex tour the Ditch.

Who didn't???

A call – that same number. He better store it.

'Ricky, twice in one day. What a pleasure. This better be good, cuz.'

Ricky sounded goosed. 'It is – I just saw that Frederick pig cunt–'

'I know this,' said James. 'You called me like a good boy before.'

'No, I saw him again. Now listen, this is good. You're going to want to hear this.'

James sipped Merlot and started listening.

He was *all* ears. It *did* sound good.

SIX

17 December, 11.17am

Frederick was in Rondon's Chicken Breast, the deli he favoured at Curtain Road/Great Eastern. He liked the chicken–salad cream sandwich here. He considered a second coffee, saw James walk in.

Maroon didn't see him at first. Frederick laughed: he sat at the window booth every time. Watched Great Eastern Street action every time. The cars, hipsters, working people, the dickheads.

The place wasn't big: how did James still miss him?

BINGO.

Here he came.

Mucho faux bashfulness.

James: handsome grin and wise eyes. Plaid suit and waistcoat. No tie, open-shirted. Somehow untouched by stuff. Somehow making Frederick feel good.

James sat, Frederick ordered java. 'You packing your phone?'

'Sure.'

'Put Curtain Road into Google, see if it has a Wiki page.'

'Why?'

'Why not?'

James shrugged, pulled his blower, hit up Google. He said, 'It's mentioned on the Shoreditch Wiki page. That's all.'

Their coffees landed. Frederick black, James a latte. Frederick: 'What the hell is that?' Then: 'What's it like to have your own Wiki page?'

James shrugged. 'Funny – especially when someone doctors it. Know what I'm saying?'

'Let me see if I remember: "James Maroon, nightclub promoter and entrepreneur. Is considered influential in the scene that flowered in Hoxton and Hackney from around 2003." Or some such shit.'

'Who else but moi?'

Frederick watched a cream Bentley pause on double yellows outside Rondon's.

He said, "'A candidate for Hoxtonian of the Year.'"

'It says that on my Wiki?' James punched his name into Google, hit up his page.

'No. *Shoreditch Today*.' Frederick shoved the free sheet across the table at James. 'Page three, take a look. Apparently, you're a "prime example of why the area continues to be hip even for those who don't care for any of that". You've got my vote, for sure.'

James scanned the story. A picture of him and three other local figures. A blurb about each. A fat paragraph of bull. He whistled. 'Who knew they even had this award? But then who knew newspapers still existed?'

Frederick and James laughed. 'You think this is working tonight at Ziggy's?' the DI said. 'This shindig of yours?'

'I hope so.'

'It'd better.' Frederick chorted. 'Or you lose my vote.'

James lowered his voice. 'These boys are perfect – shit-heads. They know how to sell, for sure. I – we – load them up at Ziggy's tonight, they sell as many pills, as much sniff as you can supply, Frederick: its pay-dirt time.'

'The place is full of pill heads *and* coke fiends?'

James shrugged. 'Everywhere–' he waved a hand out the window '–is rammed with drug heads. Shoreditch, Hoxton, Hackney, across the river. The whole city is on one. Or several.'

'I know.' Frederick flashed the endless shit he did. His boys into it like the punters they turned over. Made customers by arresting, scaring. They took what they held. Taxed what they seized.

He said, 'You ever see a flick called *Five Easy Pieces*?'

James slurped latte, shook his head.

'A Jack Nicholson movie. The guy he plays, his *character*, is this eccentric piano player, a near wacko. But he understands, he *gets* what's going on like no one else around him can. It makes him mad no one else does. He's the outcast of his family because he's the smart one. They all think he's angry. I mean, he *is* angry, but they're missing what else he is, that he can see, *gets* the shit they don't.'

James shrugged.

Frederick said, 'You should watch it sometime – see if you can understand it. Because it took me a while.'

James made an expression like he cared zilcho. 'Sure. And don't worry, they're mean bastards.'

'Who?'

'These goons I'm lining up. For business tonight at Ziggy's.'

Switcheroo: the shit-head thinks he's smart; trying to back-foot. 'I have every confidence in you, James. Now if you'll excuse me, my partner is here.'

'Okay, see you.'

'Sure.'

James took his time getting up. He passed a stocky blond man in a silver suit on the way out.

Lee Palm sat down. Frederick mind-flashed a highlight reel of their act: shaking down goons, snarfing boosted gear. Ten years of one-nighters and girls.

'You're late.'

'Gym.' Lee cradled a cup of herbal tea. 'How we doing this month?'

Frederick shrugged. 'If this goes well with Maroon – Merreth Christmas.' He laughed. 'Happy Diwali.'

'Diwali's been and gone and it's a Hindu thing.'

'Just being festive to all men.'

'I'm festive when the money rolls in.' Lee drained his tea. 'What's the new thing you mentioned?'

Frederick wolfed his sandwich. 'The usual thing. But a bigger score.' He lowered his voice. 'Half a kilo. This one we shake down completely. It is all ours.'

Lee's eyes gleamed. 'Happy Diwali.'

'There's a twist. You are going to like it. Oh yeah.'

Lee glanced around Rondon's. He took his time. 'I'm listening.'

'This one involves a young man named Elvis. Elvis Street.'

Lee took more time. 'You're going to pop Elvis? He's your son.'

Frederick smiled. 'I know that, Lee. Pop him?' He wasn't telling him it all. Not the way he saw this going down.

Frederick smiled at Xmas-lights voltage. 'Not exactly, no. I'll tell you all about it. But not now. Later.'

SEVEN

10pm

When James walked into Ziggy's the place bopped. The joint situated on the corner of Hoxton Square. The joint sub-gothic/hipped up. Stag heads wall-mounted. Baroque mirrors threw reflections. A cornucopia of ales and liquor bottles glittered bar-side. A pimped DJ booth showed the decks surrounded by Greek and Roman figurines in miniature.

It was going OFF.

Girls draped on boys. Boys draped on girls. They jigged near the bar. They grooved on the dancefloor, by sofas, everywhere. They did clothes/moves for a reason. It was mannered, early/endless weekend jive. Night time cool to forget daytime slog. It numbered drink and drugs and dancing. Punters desperate to part with the spending stuff. With copious amounts to part with.

The flyer was James M's design. It featured garish colours, a splash-paint font. It screamed: WISE AFTER THE EVENT – ZIGGY'S EVERY THURSDAY.

The night would last three weeks. The move: milk it while you can. James was, move-wise, chess Grandmaster genned-up. He knew how to milk the scene like a mo-fo.

Let the night flash and burn like the clientele flashed and burned and move on. Keep it fresh when it was stale as stale.

James stood at Ziggy's curved bar. He calculated money and profits until he opened up elsewhere. Put on the same night, call it *different*. Novelty was the IT factor punters went goofy for.

Frederick looked rough at the meet in the afternoon. Rough but in control. Knowing something about you you didn't. An expression Frederick didn't try to hide. As if he expected James to come at him. Wanted James to know it.

The threat. The power play. The action.

Bring it on. Here's the play, the action. Frederick was there to be done – taken out. And if he saw James aimed to do it: BRING IT THE FUCK ON.

Sinbad and Darren – in the corner. They punted tackle by the Ladies. Where James placed them.

He told them: 'Best for business is always quiff – they start buying and enjoying, their friends find out, the whole fucking joint is finding out – you know what I'm saying? That way they have to tell everyone everything about everything. Hey presto it's serving up shit like selling hot cakes time.'

Sinbad Williams and Darren 'Dazzler' De La Salle: a black boy–white boy duo; an interesting combo even in these enlightened times.

They were Hackney street flies. He knew them from the Dolphin, Mare Street's prime scumbag boozer. He slurped in there. A rare old-school juicer in an area that should have been razed years ago. Was finally being sucked into the city-wide gentrification craze.

He ordered a Jim Beam straight. He did so from Marie behind the bar. See that rotund derriere turn, *yeah*. Take a few pounds off it and she'd be in business. *He'd* be in business. She poured bourbon in the cut-glass tumbler he requested. She turned, spritzed water in a tumbler. A stripe of blow as fat as that posterior, a few more bourbons: *party time was on* – doing that from the rear. The way she positioned before turning.

James said, 'Thank you.' He felt a tug on his shoulder.

'We need more stuff.'

It was Sinbad, the black boy. He billed himself as a Detroit techno nut. *Contraire* to that. You're Numb-nut Central. His leather waistcoat with saggy dealer pockets froze him in a Staten Island b-boy time warp.

James took his time, sipped bourbon, looked up the bar, at Sinbad. 'Told you, you don't ever approach me, unless it's to say hi as you pass me by quickly, understand?'

Sinbad said, 'Sure.' Like the shit-head restrained himself.

James said, 'B.J. not holding?' He grinned, looked around for his house mule. Betsy-Jane, B.J. The dyke from central casting. She's crop-haired. Borderline obese. Pissed off about something she'll never compute.

There – a group of girls by the ladies parted and B.J. exited. She garbed that same Manchester United replica shirt. She's a United fan-girl, Cockney Red cliché. She looked goosed on the James/Frederick product – catch those pinned eyes, goofball grin.

James repeated himself: 'B.J. not holding? She fucking eat them all herself?'

He watched her say something to Darren. Dazzler head to toe in bleached white denim – jacket, knee-ripped jeans turned up. Too-small waistcoat. The outfit did nothing for his florid skin. Ziggy's disco lights strobed him ghoul-like.

'I told you,' Sinbad said – James caught the triumphant note. 'We need more stuff. No-one's holding nothing no more. We've been cleaned out. You were on the money about standing near the split-arses' shitter.'

'Out the back, by the bins, I told you. Go.'

Sinbad moved and James caught his elbow. 'Business spectacular, right?'

'Sure,' said Sinbad, cracking a smile. 'We're going to be cleaned out before midnight. The place is off its box already.'

James turned back to the bar, to his bourbon, to another look at Marie. Catch a sight of The Behind but she wasn't around. He put eyes back on the Ladies. B.J. disappeared, Dazzler waited for Sinbad. Here he came now with fresh supplies from out back, coming out the anteroom.

James moved, swerved Sinbad and Darren – ignore the shit-heads – and opened the anteroom door.

He closed it. Pumping bassline and crowd sound muffled. He pushed fire exit door bars and hit the yard.

There's the industrial-size containers in the corner. He felt behind the right-hand one.

The stash. Four fat rolls of notes, the best part of 15K. He felt behind the other bin. Five bank bags of gear – James pulled two pills, a wrap of coke. Marie would snap his hand off. Every piece did. He dry-necked a pill. This batch monikered clogs because they were made in

Amsterdam – land of the clumpy shoes: how very droll. Frederick said he ripped them off goons who bought them from a Dutch firm.

He opened the wrap, knuckled a bump of chang, headed back for the fire exit.

It burst open.

Darren rushed at him, breathless, *spooked*. 'We're in fucking trouble.' He grabbed James – his eyes little boy-fluttered, the punk cool came undone.

James said, 'Keep your voice down and grow a fucking pair quick. What is it, the pigs?'

'Pigs?' The thicko needed a few seconds. 'No – not yet anyway. But maybe soon. It's a split-arse, by the Ladies. She bought my last pill, took it straightaway – grabbed some of my pint to down it. Then I'm telling you man, can't have been no more than two minutes, she starts fitting, lying on the floor.'

'She still there?'

'She's been moved, thank fuck. Someone called an ambulance, I think.'

'Where is she?'

'In the office. Man I hope she's okay – I've had those clogs and they are hit and miss. She better not die, that'll be on my head, and I don't want or need that.' His face went redder, it heaved.

James gave zero fucks. If she keeled, Darren was right for once: he, Sinbad, B.J. were all prime for it.

They supplied the shit. With the help of Frederick Street, of course. Local filth – local *bent* filth.

James made sure Darren saw him smile. 'Come on, Dazzler.'

Dazzler said, 'Eh?' Dazzler followed.

Back inside the place bopped on. Music thudded, punters were goosed on James's supply.

Sinbad and B.J. vanished. They're not by the Ladies, can't be seen.

James told Dazzler: 'Find them, and get back to it. Fucking graft.'

Darren shrugged, like he remembered to be cool. James headed for the office.

It's Marie, the bargirl, The Backside. Her eyes rolled, mouth dryspittled. She's on the floor, a cushion propped under her head. B.J. doing the Mother-fucking-Theresa act.

At the table, Sinbad did lines with a rolled twenty. James liked his chutzpah.

He told him: 'Two things. First, don't offer me any of that shit with that note, I'll get hep B, some disease like that. Second, what the fuck you doing not out there grafting?' He eyed B.J. 'One of you is enough. Get there, go join pussy-dick Dazzler.'

Sinbad laughed – he couldn't care less about Marie.

James took a good look – like she fitted, eyes in the back of her head.

But, yes – no problem, it's cool. She won't keel – that shit-head Dazzler panicked.

Sinbad didn't move, he eyed Marie. 'You listening?' James said. 'What did I say? Go back out and carry on. The girl's okay – she *is* going to be okay.' He winked. 'You never know, she make a good recovery, maybe you can get her later.'

Sinbad shark-grinned. James: 'For a price, of course.'

It got B.J.'s attention. 'You a pimp now?'

James took his time. '*Now?*' He shook with laughter, got laughs from Sinbad.

He said, 'Sinbad, deal or not? Now clean the fuck up, there's an ambulance coming, I don't need you or your shit all over here.'

Sinbad did it easy, doing a slow stand, sloped out. Marie, now: coming round, her eyes stopped rolling.

James said, 'Don't worry'.

Then – *a buzz*. He felt his arms and legs freak, the pill started working. Tingles; his dick caught a warm sensation. He eyed B.J – she's an overweight dyke, a crackhead. They're technicalities, the way this E is working it's fucked-up magic.

Marie touched his arm, caught his eye. James flashed different. 'Fuck it,' he said. 'B.J. follow Sinbad, get there and graft.'

B.J. blinked. 'You sure?'

'Cool and the gang. You, Sinbad and Dazzler keep at it. We'll sell out before this plastic shit is over and the real music starts. Don't worry about her. There's an ambulance coming, I'll keep her company, all the rest of that shit.'

B.J. looked at Marie, at James. Like she saw what it was.

She left the office, headed for the Ladies.

Sinbad would have to wait for Marie. It could be a long wait.

James saw this – a play that worked on Frederick; would be another move against the has-been.

The wipers threw off fresh snow. James looked at Marie dozing on the backseat. He put the Merc in gear, spun it around the square, headed across Old Street, east to Whitechapel.

He made Boyd Street and kerb-parked. He was goosed, clog-fritzed. The pill was trippy, his head went gaga. A big horn gripped. The night had him. Senses shifted. This was mesmeric.

It was that feeling; *that feeling.*

He fire-lifted Marie. Snow fell hard, he punched the key code and entered the building. He made the lift to his apartment. His pad with panoramic views where he could scope the night-lit Smoke right now.

He got Marie inside, lay her on the sofa, poured a large one. He heavy-dosed Marie with Valium after the paramedics all-cleared her and left. When the barbiturates eased off a little it would be party time.

Play this like this: feed her more E. See what happened. If she got spangled, nothing else; give her the knight-and-steed act. She might be 'persuaded' to graft for him, working sad-sack needy men. Then bang her – another gratis piece of quiff. She should show *him* her stuff first. He poured *her* a bourbon, refilled *his.*

The alternative he liked too. He liked *more.* If the E turned her funny again – if it put her under and she didn't come back: watch out Frederick Street because *he* supplied the pills. He flooded Ziggy's with them. He was *responsible* for Marie Davies taking them.

He took the drinks over, whispered: 'Wake up.'

Her eyes slits, still *mucho* barbed-up: 'Your place?' Slurring badly.

'Uh-huh.' James surfed clog waves. He peaked – the crash would come soon. He pulled a bag from his pocket, palmed four Es.

He downed two, chased with bourbon.

He said, 'You feeling better?'

Marie Valium-smiled, tried to move, slumped.

James held out his closed hand. He said, 'You must have a splitter of a headache, all the booze and other shit you've done. You want a couple of pills? Paracetamol of course – nothing stronger.' He grinned, made it rakish. Double-bluff the piece.

She's barbiturate-juiced; he extrapolated how this would go.

Now, here she came. She held out a hand – he shook his head, gently opened her mouth, popped the two pills in – the two *Es*.

She smiled, grateful – eyes still slits – he threw bourbon in her, made sure she necked the clogs quick.

James rocked back, smiled back. He caught a massive surge from *his* double drop. His breath went short, like he needed air fast.

Marie, slit-eyed, slurring: 'I'm an epileptic – I – really – shouldn't – have done that pill – at – Ziggy's–'

She fell back on the sofa.

James – spangled, the ceiling like it caved in; the lights *BRIGHT*!!!

NOW: like it was half hour ago Marie noshed the pills, not thirty seconds. They hit instant, her eyes bulged and socket-jumped.

She started fitting.

Again.

A carbon copy of Ziggy's. She fell to the floor – there's zero to be done.

Dazzler *was* right: it requires zilcho time for pills to do her.

Here's the answer – she *can't* take them; can't take two.

Marie's face – purple; her eyes rolled. Her breath gasped. Like she *is* dying this time.

James got to his feet, wobbled, rode massive E surges, made it outside onto the terrace, his deckchair.

A star-spangled view.

Snow-topped buildings teetering, yellow lights across the city.

He rode the double drop.

Seconds, minutes passed.

Who knew how long???

Now, he came out of it, got some control.

Now, he thought.

Yes, the play with this thicko piece of quiff keeling.

How he chess-moved it.

He reached for his iPhone, dialled up Frederick to tell him a girl died at his place and he knew who sold her the fatal drugs.

It was him – DI Frederick Street.

He *supplied them.*

Not Sinbad, Dazzler or B.J.

It's leverage, juice. The result of putting this on him, what James planned for: Frederick would arrest *them*; keep the filth, media, everyone happy.

And, Street would know – *feel* – the play James made.

Here, now, Frederick picked up. 'Yeah?'

James started speaking. He said, 'Frederick, listen very fucking carefully.'

EIGHT

18 December, 11am

Elvis eyed the *Shoreditch Today* feed on his iPad. Dana hooked him up. Live-link hustle and bustle. A BBC crew showed. An ITV outside broadcast truck backgrounded. Sky News had two rigs. A reporter babbled to camera.

Dana stepped into shot. Dana looked fine, she counted to three, went live: 'You join us outside the apartment block on Boyd Street, Whitechapel, where Marie Davies, twenty-two, was found dead sometime in the early hours of this morning. An ambulance was called by James Maroon, the thirty-one-year-old owner of the rooftop apartment where Marie collapsed, but despite Mr Maroon's efforts to resuscitate her, and the paramedics' efforts on arrival, it was too late.

'Mr Maroon, a local businessman, is said to be distraught and police are treating Marie's death as suspicious. Just before *Shoreditch Today* began this webcast we learned that two men, Sinbad Williams, twenty-four, and Darren De La Salle, twenty-three, went to Shoreditch Police Station voluntarily, and are being interviewed. Last night, Marie had been working at Ziggy's bar on Hoxton Square and finished early apparently to enjoy the evening put on there – Wise After The Event.

'*Shoreditch Today* understands Williams and De La Salle may be asked about a dangerous batch of Ecstasy pills that have flooded this area of east London. Known as clogs, as they have a tiny image of a clog stamped on them, they have already hospitalised several young people and it is thought Marie Davies may have taken at least one prior to her death.

'Police have called a media conference for tomorrow at 2pm where the detectives leading the investigation, Detective Inspector Frederick Street and Detective Constable Lee Palm, are expected to offer more details and appeal for help from witnesses – anyone who was in

Ziggy's last night, who might have seen anything suspicious or saw Marie Davies. We will, of course, bring you live coverage of the conference.'

Dana paused.

'This is Dana Gabrielle, reporting for *Shoreditch Today*.'

She waited, went off air. Spoke quietly now: 'The body's found in the place – why have they not arrested James Maroon? Why has *he* not given himself up voluntarily? Why is *he* not being questioned, at least? That's what I will be asking tomorrow, at the press conference.'

Elvis killed the feed. Dana was right: this girl Marie Davies being found dead at James's place. It stunk.

Think now. *Think.*

He called up the movie file on the iPad, pressed play.

It's Ziggy's last night – Elvis turned down DJing for James and went along on other business: Frederick-involved business. See what he might find.

He hit – pay dirt.

Now, the video he filmed on his mobile had muffled crowd/music noise. Dim light that went brighter as the iPhone adjusted. He shot James through the fire exit window. It's hot fucking stuff. James is bang to rights: he went behind one bin, pulled something. He went by the other bin, pulled something.

'Nice,' said Elvis. The shot zoomed, went close in. He caught the roll of money James held. He caught the wrap – surely coke. The shot panned to catch James necking something – surely a pill – and he hit pause.

Paused it before the video finished anyway. He'd had to stop filming right then. Hide his phone, pocket it; get back inside the bar area quick in case James saw him.

He did so just in time. He made back by the bar, saw with his eyes the lumpy white boy serving pills up by the Ladies: how he headed towards the fire exit.

The white boy disappeared. Reappeared moments later with James. Whitey repositioned by the Ladies. His sidekick wasn't there – the black boy he served up with. James passed Elvis – he didn't see him – went behind the bar, disappeared.

Elvis refused James's offer to DJ to act on Wade's tip-off. His boss was 'good friends' with Frederick. His boss really *hated* Frederick. Wade Long fixed on wanting Frederick taken out.

On helping Elvis.

Wade told him Frederick supplied James. Wade said James would be punting at Ziggy's. Go and watch. It worked: Elvis got James on film with his stash. Now the girl died – Marie Davies – having been at Ziggy's too, at James's night.

What the–

Elvis *did* say yes to DJing for James tomorrow – at the Stars Bar.

His plan ran forward – a hit-and-miss strategy. Some shit stuck, some didn't. He built shit against Frederick. He built shit against James. Get James and Frederick talking, doing a deal: *even better.*

Marie Davies: Elvis was sure the two lads 'helping police with their enquiries' were Maroon's white and black boys. He was as sure Maroon was really behind Marie Davies's death.

Not as sure, but *close*: Frederick had to know James was in the frame for Marie Davies's death. So: Frederick protected James.

Otherwise?

Otherwise James would stop protecting Frederick.

He considered his dad again.

He's a Metropolitan Police Service-ranked detective who never burned: why?

The same answer: *Because* he's a Metropolitan Police Service-ranked detective.

Who's bent.

The blatant nature of it. Revile *and* admire. His job and status covered him. Surely *no one* would have the neck to do what DI Frederick Street did in *plain view.*

Tomorrow's press conference into Marie Davies's death was heart-breaking *and* high farce if you knew what really occurred.

Dana was covering it. He wondered how smart she was. How smart Frederick was. How smart James was. How smart anyone was.

He pulled his phone, called up Dana's number, phoned her.

She answered.

He said, 'Hi – I think we could do with talking.'

NINE

7.30pm

Frederick got to Moves Gym on Hoxton Square early. Earlier than Lee. He wanted to see the dark-haired number on reception. He was sure she was soft on him too. She had feed-me-coke-and-fuck-me eyes. She showed them to him – every time he met Lee here. It worked for Frederick – it was tremendous, *she was tremendous.*

She wasn't here. He howled. It was an older, blander number. A Sunday night piece, not a start-the-weekend balls-banger. The brunette was probably out, having Friday night fun in the Ditch. He might still see her, finish business with Lee and go out.

Though not hard, due to tomorrow's fucking media conference.

The Marie Davies thing needed tucking away neatly. James had to be dealt with. Handsome chops was starting to have fantastical ideas. The call last night – James trying to use Marie Davies dying on him as muscle.

Very interesting, *very stupid.*

Why he met Lee here. Make sure they were on-message. Frederick walked through double doors into the café. He could drink tea and watch gym joeys panting through surround-glass walls. It was large in here, spacious. Frederick relaxed, put his feet up. He felt why Lee liked the place. Except Lee was on the other side of the glass, pushing himself to a heart attack: the exercise, the steroids, the rest of the shit he did.

Frederick sipped tea and watched a stocky man in black cycling shorts and vest. He pressed a load on the weights machine. The glass sealed sound: shoulder muscles rippled as the load went up-down, up-down.

'You must really have the hots for that quiff, meeting here all the time. You hate it.'

Lee took the chair across from Frederick, his hair wet. He packed an isotonic drink, slurped from it, emoted smug.

Frederick said. 'You finished?'

'Good session. Cleansing. What I like before going out.'

'To business then,' said Frederick. He lowered his voice. 'The way I see it is this. The two from today, Williams and De La Salle, they're in the frame, it's out there, public knowledge. On the national and local news that they've been questioned.'

'They're out and about now.' Lee smiled. 'Released following questioning.'

'Which you and I know is perfect. It's a good play: are we going to arrest them soon? If not, when? If not at all, why not? If so, when, what's the charge and all that shit? It's a media wank-fest. And the media shit-heads love one of those.'

'They'll be happy.' Lee stopped smiling. '*Are* we going to arrest them?'

Frederick laughed. 'Who knows? If we need to. *When* we need to. The moral panic on this goes away soon, maybe not. If it doesn't – you know what it's like with fucking E snuffs – we bring them in and examine our options. They try and offer a deal, we hear it.'

Lee sipped isotonic drink. 'The only deal they could offer is Maroon. Say they'll give us the supplier, the big boy. That happens, how we play it? We can't be pulling Maroon in or he could try and do us. Say exactly where he's getting supplied from.'

Frederick smiled, remembering James's call about the tart dying at his place. He held it back from Lee. He said, 'Maroon tries that he is sunk and knows it. His word against that of Her Majesty's Met Police.'

'But that gets out, into the papers, the media – brass won't like it. It's a shitstorm. We can do without it.'

Frederick shrugged. '*If* he tries it. *If* it happens. *Maybe* he does try it. If he does – and it's a big if, if you think of the chain of events that has to happen to reach that stage – he's fucked anyway and knows it. When it comes to it we're clean, he's never ever got anything directly from us. Also, he tries, I mean really goes for it–' Frederick put two fingers, a cocked thumb to Lee's head. 'Pow.'

Lee said nothing.

'This is simple and hardly revelatory. If Sinbad Williams and Darren De La Salle offer us James, we use it to make sure James knows where he stands. We tell Williams and De La Salle we'll pull James. We see James, tell him what they're saying, that we're ignoring it, and that if anyone gets pulled in for this and goes down for it, it's them.'

'Seems to me that could be a waste.'

Frederick finished his tea. 'Waste?'

'Of Williams and De La Salle. We may need them later, for more serious shit. This is a girl who was a fucking epileptic. She knew she was at risk and still took Ecstasy. You know what I am saying here? Can't have been the first time, either. What kind of thicko does that?'

'It wasn't the first time for sure. She took one earlier – at Ziggy's. At that night James put on. She fitted there.'

'You what?'

'I told you to read the report. I left it on your desk.'

'I didn't have time – thought you'd fill me in. As you are doing.'

Frederick laughed. 'You're going to like this. She took a pill at Ziggy's, like I said. She had an epileptic fit there. An ambulance is called and she's treated by paramedics. They don't know she's taken a pill, of course. They think it's a fit, because of her epilepsy. It is, but it was trigged by taking a drug that basically makes people fucking have a fit. Marie Davies was bar staff at the place. James knows her, tells the paramedics about her being an epileptic. Tells them he knows her because she lives in the bottom apartment of his block. That's how she got the job – at Ziggy's. He tells the paramedics she can do this, have fits at work, have unfortunate incidents when working. He tells them he was unaware of this fit because he was elsewhere in the place and a new member of staff, who doesn't know Marie, doesn't know she's an epileptic, panicked and called an ambulance. Maroon tells them, the paramedics, *he'll* look after her when she comes out of it. Make sure she gets home safely, drive her back there himself. Which he does.'

Lee said, 'I like it. So, using my deductions as a detective with the world's oldest force, James plies her with drinks, maybe barbs, too, and feeds her the lethal pill. He probably wants to bang her and get her on his pimp payroll. I don't see the alternative, which is she had a private supply and she took another one herself, not after the fit she just had at Ziggy's.'

Frederick – a wide grin. 'I can see why you're high flying. But, not quite the full story. You're going to like this.'

'I like it already. Think I'm about to *adore* it.'

'You are – it isn't *one pill* but *two pills*. And the fucking lab report, the autopsy, says she did them both at the same time.'

Lee spluttered isotonic drink. 'She double-dropped. Two-for-joyed? With that condition? What a dickhead.'

'Come now, show some compassion. How many times have we done the same?'

'We're not fucking epileptics.' Frederick saw he got it, the play on this: some vintage Lee still remained.

Lee said, 'James fed her the two bar snacks. Has to be. He was going to have fun with her then get her working for him, if he could.'

'Correctamundo.'

Lee laughed. 'Can see why you're so Marvin Gaye about the whole thing. It's a mess and Maroon's in the middle of it. We'll get questions about him tomorrow. That's for sure.'

Frederick nodded. 'The mother should mention the epilepsy thing. You and I know these cases. She will want the dealers caught *and* to give a warning so no other young person will make the same tragic mistake. Try and make some good out of it. Try and make it fucking cathartic. All that bullshit.'

'Tragic' went in finger-shaped quote marks. He pulled a *what-a-tragedy* face, drew howls from Lee.

He said, 'Have you had one of those things yet?'

'The pills? The big bad clogs? Might have.' Frederick cracked a grin. 'What are you – a policeman? What I'm thinking is we coach the mum beforehand, you know the routine, go to town on her. This is your big chance to do the best you can for poor Marie, it's what she would have wanted – that kind of drill. If that doesn't work I'll be surprised. But if it doesn't, I'm sure you or I can introduce it during the press conference, as a nudge, a wink, a reminder she should be doing the right thing by Marie, in front of the media. Get the word out. While she has the chance. For the kids. Her beautiful daughter hasn't died in vain, all that shit.'

Lee shrugged. 'Or she says nothing but it gets out anyway. It "emerges". Casts an unfair shadow on Marie but there it is. Facts are facts. Et-fucking-cetera. This is the tragedy of an epileptic girl who couldn't say no. Not that she deserved the OD of course, but you know what I mean. Less is more for those media shit-heads. They'll love getting onto her epilepsy themselves, give them something else to go at. What *was* she doing? Taking another – two! – when she had just recovered from going under, fitting at Ziggy's after taking one there?!'

Frederick shrugged: the fucking youth of today. 'You want a tea?'

Lee shook his head. 'Just a Nutri-O, the apple one.'

'It won't do you any good. Fitness is all in here.' Frederick tapped his temple, got the bird from Lee. He grabbed his finger, tried to suck it. Lee said, 'Off you trot and get my magic bar.'

'Okay shit-face.'

Frederick came back with the Nutri-O and another tea.

Lee bit on the bar. 'I'm thinking we should bust some dealers, get the clogs off the streets. Two advantages I see: it would play well to our media friends *and* help us. A moody batch of gear is not good for business. Correct?'

Frederick liked it. 'Maybe those health bars do work.' He tapped his temples. 'We know *our* clogs are okay – they might have done Marie but she's an epileptic, what else is going to happen? Those pills are supposed to be strong – it's their USP. We've flooded the manor with them – and nothing. The ones that have done people over weren't ours.'

Frederick chorted, Lee chorted. They got up, boosted out the gym, made the pavement, across from Ziggy's.

Lights blinked – it's evening; *time*.

Frederick: 'I'm starving. Ravenous. And I know that funky health bar won't have sated you, my iron-pumping friend. Here.'

Frederick palmed a clog. Traffic chugged by, Lee stuck out his tongue. Snow fell, hit Lee's tongue. Frederick held the pill up – *Exhibit A* – and placed it in his partner's mouth.

Lee dry-wolfed it. 'These pills,' he said, 'Better fucking work.'

'Don't worry, they will. But if you want to double-drop just say the word. Marie Davies can highly recommend doing so.'

TEN

Late

Frederick leaned forward and barfed.

He yelled: 'Lee, get a number!'

He barfed again, puke hit pavement/studded frozen snow. Passers-by gawped – they laughed and cheered.

Frederick stood back up, wiped his mouth. He caught the blinking Starbucks sign. Fresh snow swirled in Old Street lamplight. He remembered Lee wasn't outside. He was back in the bar.

He shouted it again, for laughs: 'Lee, get a number!' The world tilted, wobbled – he wobbled. Christmas songs floated over from the 999 Club next to The Snooker Room and T–Bone where Lee better be lining more chasers up and getting the fucking number for girls. The horn needed addressing. Fuck a single-handed porn-watching session at the Ace Hotel. Lee's job was to get a number for girls. The useless shit-head.

He was near gone at the game. This was the latest proof.

Frederick made inside. Lee turned on his barstool. 'Drink.' He palmed a glass with tequila, lime, salt primed on a hand.

Frederick sat on his stool, slurped the slammer. He chomped lime, licked salt from Lee's palm.

He said, 'Nice palm Lee Palm,' and spluttered laughter. At the same joke. *Yet again.* Salt and lime juice hit Lee's face. Frederick's laugh that baby baritone. That mutant sound.

He took Lee's hand. 'How come your hand is brown, like you are, but your hair is blond Mr Palm? I may have to arrest you for false impersonation.'

Lee ignored him. He did the last time, the time before that. Frederick baby-baritoned more. It's a cartoon sound. It's off the fucking charts. He slapped Lee's back – felt the corded muscles through his suit jacket.

He said, 'That's what I like about you Lee – a sense of humour. No bypass for you. Not like some – all – the bitches I've been with.'

'Pray tell more.' Lee did his slammer and belched. Pulled his Red Stripe and sucked it.

'Angry,' said Frederick. 'They are all angry.'

'Anger is good or bad, like any elemental force. Depends how it is channelled. You know what Sarge was saying? He was talking about this the other day.'

Frederick wobbled in his chair. 'Don't give me the Sarge routine. Marge-the-Sarge is a heifer whose only use is to keep his fat trap shut.'

'He was saying nothing ever came out of anything apart from anger.' Lee smiled. 'He read that in a magazine, of course.'

'*Men's Health*? One of yours?'

'Ho ho.'

'Let me tell you about anger. And women. All the ones I've ever known – you're best off liking them without *being* with them.'

'Ho ho.'

'I'm serious. How attractive is a woman when she is not yours? I'm in love with copious tarts that way. A love that never extinguishes, either. *Can* never die.'

Lee said, 'If you say so.'

Frederick ordered more chasers. They did them. He pulled in two more Red Stripe. They sucked on them. 'Fairytale of New York' came on the bar system. It broke up the house music. The song was a thousand years old. It was stale Yuletide shit.

Frederick resumed the conversation. 'You're happily married Lee. That make you and Priti perfect?'

'No one's perfect. What Sarge was saying, before you rudely interrupted, was about psychos. The ones who are caught, or at least arrested for a crime–'

'Hurry the fuck up.'

Lee ignored him, took his time. He said, 'They are the sick fucks. We are all sick fucks but these sick fucks are the sickest of the sick. Some of the stuff they do, the crimes. They are angry fuckers. But why then don't they give themselves away? With their anger? You know what I mean? They're angry enough to murder, mutilate, be sex cases – interfere with children, all that shit. So why are they not angry enough, at some point, to lose control when we bring them in? You know, slip up.'

Frederick wasn't that drunk. 'They are cold-hearted calculating scum. When they kill they are the same. When they cover it up – guess what? The same.' He watched two blonde girls at the end of the bar. 'Which reminds me. A number for tarts. Give it the fuck up.'

Lee stared.

'You've always got a number.'

'Not this time. New phone.' Lee held up his Blackberry.

'What have you got one of those for?'

Lee raised a middle finger and cracked a grin.

Frederick said, 'Even that's last decade. And you do have a number for a girl. You have Maroon's number don't you? So you have one for girls in that phone. You hear me? Fucking hell Lee, I have to even think for you now.'

Lee blushed, recovered, gave Frederick both fingers. Frederick sucked more beer, scoped the blue lighting was supposed to supply the joint's ambience. The Pogues were over – Kirsty MacColl stopped wailing. Detroit house – old stuff – came on. The clog played mellow. Zilcho drama.

'Dial moron Maroon and arrange some girls. Tell them they're on the house as it's fucking Yuletide. Or else.' He paused. 'You in?'

Lee pulled his blower, started dialling. 'I ever out?'

Who shitting knew any more with his partner?

TEN A

Later

James was in position. He parked across from the Holiday Inn. Scanned the Merc's clock. The whores were due –

NOW. Here they were. He pulled his phone again. Hit the camera-zoom app up.

He went in close – there's Frederick and Lee at the bar, goosed. He caught them going in. They walked/vibed *off* – he worked it out instant: they snarfed pills. Catch those big eyes/goofball grins.

NOW. Frederick saw the whores, he careered from the bar to the door. He opened it – *wellllcommmmed* them in.

James shot Frederick on digital. *Snap, snap, snap.* He's cuddling one, he's gripping the other one's rear.

James's plan simple: keep tabs on Frederick, gather any dirt he could. Act/don't act: let's wait, let's *SEE*.

TEN B

Later

Frederick in a room at the Holiday Inn. A few doors down from the bar. Lee a floor up. James's girl for Frederick a Romanian/Albanian. She dressed again, held a cigarette up: could she light it in a non-smoking room?

He nodded. 'Go for it. Who they going to call to arrest you? The police? That's me. I *am* the pigs.'

Frederick laughed. The girl followed. She probably didn't understand. Frederick placed her money on the bed, made the window, watched fresh snow hit Old Street.

Think.

Marie Davies was about the same age as the whore.

Elvis, too.

Elvis.

What is he doing with this plan? Trying to fuck his own dad. He should know better. The right move now is keep it quiet. Away from the goons at the station.

'Bye.' The girl was at the door. Frederick watched snowflakes. He said, 'Bye.'

The room empty again. He pulled his phone, dialled Lee's number.

He answered.

'What room you in?'

'345.'

'You finished, Casanova?'

'I nearly fucking collapsed.'

'Spare me the details.'

'Don't be envious. I'm going to get my head down. Be bright-eyed for the press conference.'

'I want to talk. Come to the bar. We can have a couple, ease the rest of the pill off.'

'What you want to talk about? It's late.'

'I know what time it is.' This joker. 'You're going to need to know this.'

'Okay, sure'. Lee sounded spooked. Frederick boosted out the room and along the corridor. He wouldn't tell Lee everything, have to be careful – even with those you're supposed to trust.

The bar off-yellow lit – acceptable for a chain hotel. Soft seats and pot plants cast the place intimate. Music warbled to match the time of night.

They ordered Guinness and Bloody Marys.

Frederick faced Lee, his back to a window that showed Old Street. The 999 Club sign flashed. It was gone 1am.

Lee wearing that worried look. Frederick: 'Your girl the shits then?'

A Lee nod and watery grin. 'Maroon's usually are. The day he does us on whores *is* the day we do him.'

Frederick sipped Guinness. 'Only the strongest survive.' He eyed Lee. 'To Elvis. What I mentioned before at the gym. You've met him, of course.'

'You know I have. A few times. Good-looking boy.'

'True. But you don't know him. I mean, you've met him but you don't know what he's like.'

Lee blanked. 'If he's like you?'

Frederick shrugged. 'You hear what I'm about to tell you about him and you're going to think he is like his lovely pa, no doubt.' Frederick sighed. 'He is, he isn't – it's like that.'

'I'm intrigued.' Lee's worried look vamoosed. His features realigned – *this* is what this is about – back as Lee Palm, Met detective, shit-hot takedown man.

Frederick said, 'He's plotting to try and get me. *Me.*' He shook his head and chorted. 'Elvis hasn't got a clue. Trying this kind of shit.'

Lee – stunned. 'You sure?'

Frederick grinned.

'How?'

'How you think?'

Lee paused. 'He knows – knows everything then? *This* is what you meant at Rondon's?'

Frederick shrugged. 'He doesn't have to know *everything*.'

'True.'

'So what we're going to do is play along.'

'We?'

Frederick shrugged again – Lee played to type. 'You know it affects you. And once I'm telling you–'

Lee – worried again – spooked, something else on his features.

Frederick: 'I don't know what he's planning exactly and who else, if anyone else is involved.' It was correct/held stuff back. 'But he's set up a shakedown with me, a rip-off coke deal, and I think he's going to try and pull it then.'

Lee, again: 'How does he know enough to know?'

Frederick shrugged. 'Apart from being my son, you mean? Wade, I think. Good old Wade Long. I'll be seeing that porno sleazeball, for sure. Straighten him out. Then, we straighten Elvis out.'

Lee nodded, swigged Guinness. He drained it, picked up his Bloody Mary.

Frederick watched him. 'Here's how we're going to do it. You're going to like this. You're going to like this *a lot*–'

ELEVEN

19 December, 10.01am

Elvis asked Dana to meet him at Rainbow Studios on Meard Street, Soho.

He scored Wade's latest porno, *Cum Now, Cum Later*. It was the follow-up to *Always Welcome To Cum*. It was the final instalment in Wade's 'triptych'. The first flick was *Cum All Ye Faithful*. It targeted last year's Christmas market.

Elvis was bemused skin flicks worked like mainstream cinema – original/sequel/sequel. Bemused that skin flicks worked art house cinema language: 'triptych'. At Wade's grandiose notions – 'triptych'? In grunt-and-groan flicks?

Wade – tricky to pin down: what's tongue in cheek, what's goofiness?

The door buzzed, and here she was. Elvis let her in. To a Soho townhouse ground-floor space. It was surrounded by other townhouses. They accommodated other porno concerns, film companies, editing suites, IT start-ups. Soho: a jungle of bars, pubs, queer clubs, restaurants, fast-food joints and walk-ups. Two brothels operated above Rainbow Studios. The trade ran near 24-7 – sex procurement never stopped. The property would be Raymond family-owned. Or Liebling Pollack-owned. The two vied for Soho hegemony. The Raymonds were decades-established. They lorded sixty acres plus. Pollack's share ran minuscule. He's the coming property magnate/theatre impresario.

Dana – in the front room. *The* studio of Rainbow Studios. Wade's production company shot its shit here. Long Lotharios stretched to three high-res cameras, a sound rig and lights. The backroom was the editing suite.

Elvis walked Dana in there.

He pointed to the sofa by the window. 'Here.' He handed her a Starbucks. 'Caramel latte, how you like.'

She scoped the room. A faux Herman Miller chair, Mac screens, keyboards, laptops, two landline consoles.

'Your office.' Dana sipped latte.

'You've been here before.'

'At night – it was late. We did lines. We were at Bar One. I remember.'

Elvis thought about that night: what if?

What if?

Dana in another understated business suit. She knew how to dress, hold herself. She covered the press conference called by Frederick at Shoreditch Town Hall.

Later – after this.

Which was why they met.

'Come on,' Dana said. 'What's this about?'

Elvis sipped coffee. 'I can trust you?'

Dana shrugged. 'Of course.'

'I mean, really?'

'You mean the job – if you tell me something I might go and report it, broadcast it? No chance. Not if you tell me not to. Think of it like this: the police see a lot of things that are illegal each and every day, but do they act on all of them? Of course not. They use discretion and judgement to decide. And, anyway, you're a friend, so different rules apply.'

Elvis weighed it up. 'You're going to the press conference, right?'

Dana looked surprised. 'Marie Davies? Yeah, 2pm. You going to explain or not?'

Elvis made a decision. 'It's about her – Marie Davies. Actually, no. Not really, this is about my dad.'

Dana nodded.

'Your word, please.'

'Word?'

'You promise to keep what I tell you between only us.'

'I give you my word.'

'Okay.' He put his coffee down. 'Frederick, my dad, is leading the investigation into Marie Davies's death, as you know. Why I asked you to come here is because I'm sure my dad is bent, corrupt. I mean full-on bent. I thought he sailed close to the wind, but I was told stuff about him. Which I couldn't believe was true. Then I started digging, looking around, keeping my eyes and ears open. And realised it's true. It's difficult – fucking difficult – to accept the kind of person he is.'

Dana began to speak, stopped. Then: 'You mean, like him and Camilla? What he did with her?'

Elvis nodded. 'That's some of it – the kind of person he really is. Seeing her behind my back – all the time we're living together.'

Flash: finding them.

Frederick's defence: *who knew if you were on or off?*

His reaction: y*ou're my dad.*

He closed it down. 'Bottom line, he's a crook, bent filth. A rip-off merchant – into all sorts of capers. How does he get away with it? The answer's crystal clear. He's a corrupt policeman, corrupt detective running a corrupt operation.'

Dana looked sceptical.

Elvis ignored it: 'But I don't care about that.'

'What do you care about?'

'Nailing him.'

She paused. 'Because of him and Camilla? I'm not sure that is a good reason. I mean, I understand–'

'That's *a* reason. But it is not *the* reason. It's all wrong. What he does, as simple as that. Ripping off crooks, doing normal people – punters out for a good time and nothing else. He's out of control. You get it, right?'

'Of course, if you're sure about him–'

'I'm sure.'

Dana nodded. 'Believe it or not it's why I do *my* job – to try and get the bad guys. This Marie Davies thing, they look like they've got them, those two dealers who sold her the pills. But I'm not so sure. Why haven't they arrested the owner of the apartment where she was found? He's called James Maroon, the guy. Why haven't they taken him for questioning? Your dad – if he's in charge?'

Elvis nodded. 'I know James. And that's what I'm getting at. I don't know for sure, but Marie Davies dies, from a dodgy E. A pill she probably bought at Ziggy's, where she already collapsed. At a night put on by Maroon. James is an operator, a fucking specimen. Now, as a reminder, who is investigating Marie Davies's death?'

Dana nodded. Elvis: 'Exactly. Which might explain your question – why has Maroon not been arrested yet? It might explain where the drugs came from that killed Marie Davies.'

'Your dad? James? Both? Maybe they're in this together.'

Elvis nodded. 'The more I think about it the more I'm convinced of it.'

'How you going to prove any of this?'

'I don't want to. I'm setting him up on something else. I'm just giving you background, where I'm coming from.'

Dana sipped her latte. 'How's your relationship with him?'

'He thinks we get on – we do, enough for me to fool him into being set up.'

He held back the Ricky element; didn't tell her he was in on the plan.

Dana: 'Where do I come in?'

'I wanted to talk it through with you. See what you thought.'

Dana looked at the editing-suite walls. Stills and promo posters from previous Long Lothario flicks. A porno poster for *The Long Hello*. The legend: 'Starring Wade Long'.

She said, 'You compose music for these?'

'I wish. I source the music. Think of the *Pulp Fiction* soundtrack for cheap British porno that's trying to be American, and you can see where I am in life.'

'*Pulp Fiction*? Your boss blows his budget on music?'

'Not really. Wade wants below-radar stuff as it's cheap, often gives it that off-the-wall smut vibe. A dude called Patrick Cowley did a soundtrack for a couple of Yank porno films, one tune's called "Nightcrawler" – that's Wade's template. Helps his stateside porn aesthetic, as he calls it.'

'Peter Cowley? Never heard of him.'

'Patrick – you'll have heard his up-tempo stuff, disco. "Do You Wanna Funk", "I Feel Love" – he remixed those.'

Dana shrugged.

'You have to have heard "I Feel Love".'

'He sounds a sophisticate.'

'Patrick Cowley?'

'Wade.'

'Wade?'

'Yeah.'

'You've met Wade. That night we were at Bar One. You met him here.'

'I was so out of it I don't remember.'

'You must've been – you meet Wade, you remember him. You had a conversation with him, about porn, what everyone speaks to him about.'

'Yeah? What did I say?'

'You really don't remember, do you?' Elvis had total recall on it: the night they might have got together. 'You told Wade you had nothing against porn but couldn't it be more realistic, like seeing the girls really enjoying it, instead of faking it.'

'I'm surprised *you* remember it. The amount we drank and sniffed.'

Elvis laughed. 'It's why I gave up that shit. Dickhead dust makes us all dickheads. That's why I'm clean and serene.'

'What did Wade say?'

'Wade?'

'When I told him to make it more realistic, instead of girls looking like they faked it?'

'Wade said, "What do you mean? It's bang on the money. Isn't that what women do, anyway, in real life? Fake it?"'

Dana smiled. 'Nice answer. He's smart then, Wade?'

'Jury's out. Permanently.'

'How many of these films of his have you done?'

'Enough. They don't pay great, Wade's a tight fucker, but it is music – and I get to choose it, so it's not cheesy shit.'

'Example?'

Elvis opened a Mac. It showed the current scene he soundtracked on *Cum Now, Cum Later*. The vista was sun-bleached, numbered a pool, a lounger with a tanned blonde who donned a tiny light-blue bikini, big sunglasses. A muscled man with a buzz cut and bulging briefs entered to a booming bassline.

He pulled the blonde to her feet and they danced in the sun.

'Dancing? In porn?' Dana said.

'Wait.'

Here came a tall man with a handlebar tache. He wore a cowboy hat, white linen suit. The music faded, the man said, 'Don't let me stop you.'

Elvis hit pause.

'That's Wade?'

Elvis nodded. 'And that's Essex. Essex, Malibu.' Elvis laughed. '*Cum Now, Cum Later* was shot on location, at Wade's Chigwell pile. That's his pool, his porno-money mansion in the background.'

'The blonde girl helps the West Coast feel,' said Dana. 'Looks like he has done well for himself. Porn really pays.'

She took another look around the room. Scoped a poster for *CUM ALL YE FAITHFUL*. It featured a smiling Wade. He hung over the title words – clock that tache, those over-white teeth. Garish tinsel hung on a boner of length that went through the 'A' of 'ALL'.

Elvis: 'Where he gets his money is the zinger. From his alternative life.' He speech-marked 'life'. 'Wade does good from this business but no way it buys him a £1.5 million pad in Shangri-La footballer land.'

'Right,' Dana said.

'I'll give you a hint. Wade is who weighed me in about Dad.'

'He's mixed up with him?'

'Big time. He was – kind of still is, probably. With Frederick, once he's got a hold of you, it's difficult to get away. Wade's a coke dealer – *was*. A few ranks above street level, more of a trader. Dad "went into business" with him. Wade did very nicely from it, Frederick better.'

'Go on.'

'Simple, really. Dad threatened to bust Wade unless he cut him in so what choice he have?'

'Wade told you this?'

'Yeah.'

'Why?'

'Because Wade hates him. I don't know the exact details but they had a big fall out. Wade came in here one day, when we were in post-production for *Always Welcome To Cum*, the follow-up to that–' Elvis pointed at the *Cum All Ye Faithful* poster. 'I was doing the sound for the last few scenes. It was the angriest I've ever seen him. He did a couple of lines of gak, where you're sitting now. He offered me some, I turned him down. Wade said: "Not like your dad. Congratulations." In a funny voice. It was the first time he ever really mentioned Frederick. I kept my mouth shut and off he went, gave me chapter and verse about what a bastard Frederick was. Said he was into some heavy shit. I couldn't believe it at first. Didn't want to.'

'When was this?'

'That one came out–' Elvis scoped the poster behind Dana. The letters of *ALWAYS WELCOME TO CUM* dripped white effluence. This time Wade was done up as a man of the cloth. He stood in a church doorway, his flock two buff men, two pneumatic women in crosses, dog collars, nothing else. Below, it read: 'Released on Good Monday, of course!'

Elvis said, 'Yeah, out Easter this year, whenever that was. March or April.'

Dana: 'When did you find out about Camilla and your dad?'

'Around then.'

'So before any of this? You already knew about them when Wade told you about your dad?'

Elvis nodded. She thought he got into this because his dad cheated with Camilla. She probably ran a second thought: he goes up against the big bad crooked policeman, there's only one winner.

She might be right. Who knew?

He said: 'Wade's problem is – how does he get out of it? The hold my dad has over him. He doesn't deal any more, I'm pretty sure. But as I said, my dad's still got a grip on him.'

'Where you come in?'

'Maybe.'

'He knows what you're trying to do?'

'Not the whole thing.' Elvis paused – the front door sounded. 'Here he is now.'

Wade walked through the studio into the edit suite. He donned white chinos and a purple Hawaiian shirt. He had an iPhone to his ear. He winked at Elvis, double-winked Camilla.

He quick-fired into the phone. 'I guest star for you, you get the Wade Long name, the m-o-n-i-k-e-r on your product. Let me inform you now – that name stays above the title. No negotiation and I'll tell you why.

'I'm Wade Long. That means something in this shitty business.'

He put a hand over the phone. He over-loud whispered. 'This joker is certainly packing a short dick or he has no excuse.'

Back into the iPhone: 'I've got eleven inches. *No one* can match that this side of the pond or stateside, and what I'm telling you is – *what?* Listen, I met the dude and he and Wade are tight. I mean tight.'

To Elvis and Dana in over-loud whisper: 'This guy is fucking smaller than a light switch, I know it.'

To the iPhone: 'The budget was blown on me, so keep my name where it should be or I am out, trust me. And you *will* regret that.'

Wade rang off. 'It's all bullshit isn't it?' He addressed Dana. 'Great to meet you. I'm Wade. Wade Long.'

He pointed to the promos for *The Long Hello* and *Cum All Ye Faithful*. 'But you probably already know who I am. Who the *hell* are you?'

'Dana Gabrielle.' She coloured. 'We've met before.'

Wade stroked his chin. Like he considered it a matter of some importance. 'Are you sure? I'm sure I would have remembered *that* occasion.'

'It was a while ago, at night. Here.'

'At night?' Wade gave Elvis a hammy expression, put it on Dana. 'What was a lovely broad like you doing in here at night?' He seemed puzzled. 'I haven't done a night shoot in here for a long while–' Wade's eyes narrowed – he assessed Dana's chest, scrutinised her legs. 'I *really* am sure I would have remembered, I mean we get stand-ins all the time, a broad gets stage fright, it's her first time and–'

He looked to Elvis for help, waited for Dana to speak.

She said, 'I'll try and remind you. I was with Elvis in the pub around the corner and we came back here for something. You were leaving – you must have been working late. We said a quick hello and goodbye as you left.'

He winked at them again, slow finger-tapped his face. Like he agreed to keep something hush-hush. To never mention it again.

Elvis said, 'This is my friend, the girl I told you about, Wade. Dana's a reporter, for *Shoreditch Today*.'

Wade to Elvis: 'You didn't say she was a reporter.'

'I did, you must've forgotten. Listen, don't worry. She's with me. We can trust her. Her job can help us get my dad. I told you on the phone – Frederick's investigating that girl who died two nights ago in Hoxton Square. He's called a press conference about it this afternoon – Dana's going. I – we, think he's mixed up in it. It happened at a bar called Ziggy's. There was a night there put on by James Maroon. You *know* him.'

Wade nodded. 'Sure do.'

Elvis said, 'He bills himself as a local businessman. A night-club promoter but really he's all about the take from selling Es and coke, whatever else, at his events. I think – we both do – the girl who died from a dodgy pill was supplied by James. And she died at his pad. We think the chances are, especially with what you tell me about my dad, that James must've got his shit from Frederick.'

Wade shrugged. 'What you planning this afternoon?'

'Dana's going along – the idea is try and catch Frederick out. Ask a question that could trap him.'

The same Wade shrug. 'I don't want to bring a downer but this is Frederick-fucking-Street we're talking about here. No one catches him out. He must have done one thousand press conferences in his life. Everyone knows nothing is ever said in them by a pro like Frederick. Right, Dana?'

She shrugged. 'More or less.'

Elvis: 'Sure. But it's worth a go right? She's there anyway, it's her job, so why not? Maybe he says something, gives an answer we can use later. He's in front of the media, on live TV, he might let something slip.'

Wade primped his moustache. 'I don't see it. The dude's a major operator, clever with it. Most crooks I know, and I know a few, are not smart. Not your old man. Best not to fuck with him. That's why I don't want my prints anywhere near this.'

'They won't be,' said Elvis.

Dana: 'If he's as smart as you say, won't he guess that you might be part of this with Elvis?'

Wade – like he saw her for the first time.

'If you're smart enough to know he's smart you should be smart enough to consider this.'

Wade smiled. 'Very perceptive. You'll go far in your business, probably any business you choose. Ever think about writing scripts?'

'Haha.'

'You should.'

'I've gone from stand-in porn girl to porn writer.'

Wade eyes fizzed – booted on showbiz. 'I've one idea, needs fleshing out – a car-porn flick.'

Dana smiled, waited.

'This is not standard big-titted girl sucks off mechanic in garage and takes nine inches while spread on the bonnet.'

Elvis said, 'Can we keep to the point? My answer is, no he won't guess what's going on. He's not a mind-reader, God. He's never met Dana before – she's just one more annoying reporter looking for a headline.'

Wade's eyes glittered. 'This flick is more *atmospheric*. Moody. Cars in porn are like swimming pools. They're part of the language, they're shorthand for tits and dicks and cum shots. Know what I mean?'

Dana: 'I can imagine.'

'I want to go more fetish.' Like it was crystal what he meant, the greatest idea this millennium.

'And that's where I come in?' said Dana. 'You think this could be my field of expertise?'

Wade – lackadaisical. 'Who knows? It's my latest idea. Wade Long's ideas tend to become blockbusters in the trade.'

Dana pointed at the promo posters on the wall. 'Fetish doesn't really seem your style. It doesn't seem the Wade Long thing. It's not mainstream, commercial. In porn, or anything else. Elvis?'

He shrugged – this is old news.

Wade said, 'I agree. But you misunderstand me. It's all fetish. The tits, the dicks, the money shots, the pools, bikinis, *the cars*. Welcome to porno-land. The land of a fetish frenzy. Except no one says so. That is all.'

He was booted big time. 'Okay,' he said. 'If it makes you feel better, more at ease, I'll withdraw that word. No problem. Fuck fetish. Shall we say then – I want cars to be the stars as only second billing to the porno stars – the broads. I want to upgrade the metal. The Yanks use Porches, Hummers, limos. The Brits anything that's low-rent. You understand?'

'You said moody?'

'It's what I mean. Up the car, up the mood. Bang a Ferrari in the flick and we have a hit.'

'You're going to hire a Ferrari?' Elvis said.

A fat Wade grin – wide. 'Hire? Buy the motherfucker, brother.'

'Come again?'

He nodded. '*Have* bought actually. As of last week – an early Christmas present from Wade to Wade. I have to pay the thing off, of course. For tax reasons.'

He clocked Dana like he made a decision. 'Another reason why Frederick needs taking out. He's slicing me too thin. I'm an anorexic fucking salami. It's become worse and worse – he wants more and more. It's why I put Elvis onto Ricky to cook up his scheme.' He stopped talking. 'You told her. The whole thing, I mean?'

'Not yet. Just like I've more to tell you. Just like we've been telling you. That's why we're here. Why I want Dana's help, got her involved. You're probably right about Frederick being too clever to be tripped up this afternoon. But I can trust Dana – *we* can. Like I said, this all works she can help nail him, really put the shit-head under, by reporting the story how it should be.'

Wade shovelled out lines next to a MacBook, did a fast one up a twenty-pound note, offered Elvis, Dana. They knocked him back. He shrugged and did theirs, grew a broad smile.

He said, 'You might as well tell her the whole plot. Dana – it's like a Wade Long porno classic, the shakedown we have here, 'cept Elvis scribed this motherfucker.'

Dana, quick. 'Maybe you should get him on-board then – as your writer.'

'I've asked. I keep on asking. I'm close to begging. But he always turns me down. It's "music, music, music". He can't do other things. As if branching out wouldn't help Elvis's obsession. But Wade cannot be too harsh – if he manages to take the old man down that is a service Wade L, most street dipshits and dealers in east London plus bent filth waiting to take over from Frederick will be grateful for.'

Wade threw a lit-up grin. 'Drink?'

They left Rainbow Studios and ate pavement along Meard Street, Wardour, Peter and Berwick Street. Snow fell light, winter air braced them.

It was Xmas, Xmas. Everywhere.

The season was goosed.

Half merry crowds filled juicers. Smokers chuffed outside and swigged pints and mulled wine. They passed two Santas. A group of elves eyed a gang of girls draped in tinsel on Berwick. A homeless man was given alms by a fruit-and-veg stallholder – he grumbled at being palmed an apple, an orange. He wanted cash, now.

They snagged a table at the Blue Posts on Berwick, along from the market. Elvis and Dana ordered coffee, Wade a Jack and coke to wash down lines he hit the Gents to snort. Elvis filled Dana in on Richard 'Ricardo' 'Ricky Me' Cliff and the plan: the takedown of Frederick. He *still* kept Ricky being complicit out of it.

Wade listened, vibed tense. Dana said, 'You say you tried this with Frederick and Richard, Ricky Me, before, what happened?'

'I know Ricky from around – for years. He's a coke-head, he likes pills too. The Royal Oak on Columbia Road is gentrified now, a gas-tro joint. A few years ago, around 2002–4, it was *the* early morning after-party place. Open at that time because of the flower market – had a licence for the traders to have a drink early, something to eat. Ricky's pad is on Columbia, across from the Oak. Back then we'd have a laugh in there, on a Sunday morning. Then – I didn't see him for a while. Then – I did. When I'm out playing, DJing around the Ditch. He's out of his box, as always. *Then* I get to know he's deal-ing, coke, like serious weights, not street-level stuff, because he–' Elvis pointed at Wade, 'told me. Wade was Ricky's man, his supplier. Ricky was one of Wade's dealers. Used to be. Ricky gets it from elsewhere now Wade's out. The first time I told my dad about Ricky, that we could shake him down, rip him off, which my dad adores doing, he agrees to it. Then, he backed out, before it happened.'

'Why he back out?'

'Who knows.'

Dana looked at Wade – a Wade shrug. Elvis: 'Why does it matter?'

Dana kept looking at Wade.

Finally: 'You want my take? Okay – here you go. This is your dad. What does that mean? Simple – he doesn't do anything he doesn't think about from all angles. And I mean, all fucking angles. Ricky didn't know about it? The first plan?'

'No.'

'You were going to try to get him in on it too? Include him in the plan to do over Frederick?'

'I thought about it. Wasn't sure, like I told you. He backed out before it got that far down the line.'

'Uh-huh.' Wade to Dana: a fuck-it look. Elvis clocked it, let it fly.

Wade said, 'Why's he agreed to it a second time?'

Dana nodded. 'Yes, why?'

'He didn't,' Elvis said. 'That's not how it happened. Frederick came to me about it. I'd given up on getting him through Ricky, was thinking of something else, had cooked up a few ideas. That's how I moved onto James Maroon, who I'll get to. But Frederick calls me a couple of weeks ago, says, "I'm ready to do the Ricky Me thing. Let's go."'

Dana face-palmed, Wade grimaced. Elvis: 'I was surprised as you look. Trust me.'

'He's playing you,' said Dana. 'He *knows*.'

'What I said,' said Wade.

Elvis shrugged. 'What I said too – at first. Look, the possibility can't be discounted. But I don't think so. Not any more. If he is playing me, then tell me why?'

Dana and Wade – quiet.

Elvis: 'Think about it. He owns Shoreditch, Hoxton, that end of Hackney. He's bent and has been for years. Who knows what else he's into? He doesn't *need* to play me. Tell me the reason he does, because

I don't see one. This is not worth the risk. Just walk away from it if he knows. What I'm thinking is he's thinking he is doing it as a favour. He thinks I need the money we're supposed to get from ripping off Ricky Me. The money I'd make from punting the coke we're going to take from him.'

Dana, Wade: 'Why?'

'Because of Camilla – I told you both this. It's as simple as that. He feels bad, been trying to make it up to me ever since.'

Elvis mind-flashed the scene, *that day*. Finding them. NO, pull back. Don't *see it again*.

'You know he told me what he told me,' said Wade.

Elvis shrugged. Dana said, 'Which is?'

Wade looked at Elvis, said: 'That Elvis and Camilla were virtually split up – and Camilla gave Frederick no choice. She was messed up – you're her friend, you must know what she gets like. And that – *that was that*–'

Elvis, trembling: 'We were still together. But what's the difference?'

Wade – a hand on Elvis. 'I'm just saying what Frederick says. How he sees it. Sorry.'

Elvis, trying to be calm: 'However he sees it, he sees it *now* as something he regrets so he wants to sort it out. Good luck with that one. But I can use his deep and lingering regret to get him. He's a sad and sick fuck.'

Wade shrugged – his eyes coke-pinned. He kept quiet – like he still didn't buy why Frederick went to Elvis to revive the Ricky plan.

'I caught them at it Wade. My dad and my girl. You need a picture? You're the sleaze king, so think about it. At my place, *our* place. It wasn't the best day of my life.'

'I can imagine.'

'You can't. Trust me. But guess what, that wasn't *the* worst day.'

Dana as Camilla's friend throwing off a *tell-me-NO-more* vibe.

Wade: 'I've heard enough.'

Elvis ignored him: 'Try the day Camilla told me she was pregnant and it wasn't mine.'

Wade – wall-eyed. 'They have a kid? No wonder he feels bad. That kid is your–'

'No they don't – there is no kid.'

'She lost it?'

'She had an abortion. Which I was against.'

Wade – a leave-it-there look. Dana – misreading. She knew the story, tried to hurry him up. 'Then Elvis finds out it was his after all.'

Wade put eyes on the Gents. He wanted more blow, to escape. 'I don't follow.'

'I had a big fight with Frederick, during which he told me for the first time he couldn't have kids any more as he'd had the snip. I couldn't check it out – my mum's dead.'

Wade wanting out of this powwow now. Dana squirming too.

Elvis – near rage. They should see the *need* to have this crystal. The WHY. What the fuck this is about.

Wade said, 'How *did* you check then?'

'How do you think? Camilla.'

Wade didn't compute. 'Why you think it was your dad's in the first place? Why didn't you think it was yours?'

'I did. At least, *thought* it might be mine. It was a toss-up. Did I have a kid or a half-fucking brother/sister on the way? So we had a test, a paternity test. Or Camilla did. And guess what?'

Wade, like he couldn't guess – it was the last thing he wanted to do. Like he wished – not for the first time – he didn't know Frederick Street. 'I can't.'

'When the results came back she said Frederick was the father. My dad was the dad.'

Wade stood up. For a line, another drink. The Blue Posts rubber-necked – check that Hawaiian shirt/big hair combo: far out, even for Soho.

'She lied to you.' It wasn't a question, no need to ask any more. Wade saw the picture, the full picture.

'Yeah.'

Wade couldn't resist: 'Why?'

'Cut a long story short, Camilla's a bit odd, screwy. Know what I mean?'

'I have to agree,' Dana said. 'Elvis is underplaying it. She's got issues, almost like paranoia.'

'Okay,' said Wade.

A silence, Elvis killed his coffee. This was over, they got it. 'Moving swiftly the fuck on to James Maroon. I was at Ziggy's on Thursday, the night Marie Davies ended up dead at his pad. Wade – this is what we meant earlier, about him and Frederick. James has to be a suspect at least. But, no, doesn't look that way. It has to be because of Frederick. I filmed James on my phone at Ziggy's, going outside to the back where he stashed the coke and pills he was serving up through those two joeys he had grafting in the place, the ones who've been questioned by my dad about Marie Davies's death. They stood by the Ladies all night, far as I could see. Later, the girl dies from a bad E at his pad and Frederick makes no jump? That Maroon is at least worth investigating? No. But the dickheads serving up for him are. They did almost certainly sell the pill to Marie Davies. You see how it's clever? Because if they sold the pill that killed her, then it IS on them. That's why they're in the frame. But how did Frederick know to arrest them? He did it in double-quick time as far as I can see. Broke the world fucking record for nicking a pair of suspected murderers. It has to be Maroon, grassing them up. And that's why Maroon hasn't been arrested, is unlikely to, because you know what else? I'm sure he gets his gear from Frederick.'

An Elvis laugh. 'My dad is, ultimately, the supplier of the Ecstasy that killed Marie Davies – how fucking fucked up is that? Think about. My dad is effectively investigating himself and his own operation.'

Wade supressed a laugh. Dana said, 'It makes sense why James has not been arrested. Have been asking myself this. Say the fake deal between Ricky and your dad does go off as you plan – then what?'

'I'm going to record audio. And I thought you could help me film it, that was my idea.'

'Then?'

Elvis sat back. 'Then it's champagne time – we've got Maroon on film, my dad filmed, recorded. You publish it as a *Shoreditch Today* exclusive. You win a load of awards and Frederick is fucked forever.'

Dana said, '*If* it works–'

'It will.'

'More drinks?' said Wade.

'No thanks. We're off to the media conference. With Frederick Street, highly respected Met Police detective, lead investigator in the tragic death of Marie Davies. What a load of shit.'

They said goodbye to Wade, boosted outside and back to Rainbow Studios, where Elvis's Volks was parked up. They had half an hour to get over to Shoreditch Town Hall.

Elvis opened the passenger door for Dana. 'I'm DJing tonight. At the Stars, the place down from the town hall. I think you should come.'

She said, 'I'll still be working – after the press conference.'

'Work, then come. Will be worth it – Maroon has a night on there. His big Saturday Ditch production, Were Kids Once. A Croatia–Goa beach thing. Painfully hip. And as its cooler than Yule I'll be playing tunes.'

'He'll be there?'

'Of course. He will have all kinds of shit he has to make sure goes off.'

Elvis got in the driver's side and drove off, balled the Volkswagen over to Old Street.

TWELVE

2pm

They parked on Hoxton Square, walked the corner and made Shoreditch Town Hall.

TV crews, photographers, journalists throwing questions: a media scrum.

Shanique Mannan, Dana's *Shoreditch Today* cohort, on the steps. Two men in suits and four uniforms passed as she spoke to camera.

Shanique said, 'Detective Inspector Frederick Street, lead investigator, and Detective Constable Lee Palm just walked by on their way to this highly awaited media conference in which they will offer more information on the tragic death of Marie Davies and take questions. They are expected to offer information, too, about the men, Sinbad Williams, twenty-four, and twenty-three-year-old Darren De La Salle, they have been interviewing. *Shoreditch Today* understands Williams and De La Salle may have been spoken to under caution but have not yet been arrested or formally charged.'

Elvis and Dana stopped near the bottom of the steps. Elvis said, 'The Frederick show. He loves it. I mean A-D-O-R-E-S. The circus is what it's all about.'

Dana nodded. 'Come on.'

They followed the media scrum inside.

There's the main hall, where the press conference will go off. Elvis said, 'I'll watch from the back. Make sure Frederick doesn't see me.'

'Sure.' Dana walked past rows of seats and bagged one at the front.

Elvis caught a clear view of her from the back.

The top table was empty. On a velvet-covered dais: four microphones, name placards, glasses, two water jugs. It awaited the Fredster Show.

Here, now.

Frederick and Lee entered from a side door. A slickly made-up woman headed them. She was dark-haired and mid-late twenties. A weary-faced woman followed. She was grey-haired and pushed fifty. They all walked slowly, rounded TV cameras and photographers. The place went quiet. Elvis saw Dana 'hi' people she knew. Her oppo numbers from the circuit: TV and national press. She glanced at her notepad, her questions. She had told him what she was going to ask, rehearsed it on the way over.

In their seats: Frederick, Lee. The beat-up woman was Marie's mother – Elvis recognised her from the news. The girl in make-up must be Leesa, Dana's Shoreditch Police PR contact.

Frederick tapped his microphone, wolf-grinned as sound bounced off high ceilings and ornate walls. Dana had told Elvis the town hall was famous for an inquest into Jack the Ripper's last victim.

Frederick in a blue suit, crisp white shirt, black tie. Elvis had to laugh: the handsome fuck.

Leesa did the introductions.

Then:

Frederick kicked off. 'First of all may I thank you all for attending what is a very sad and grave matter. I am Detective Inspector Frederick Street, this is my colleague, Detective Lee Palm. This is Loretta Davies, Marie Davies's mother. This is Leesa Zapata, our media officer. We are from Shoreditch Police Station. We're here to offer more information and take your questions about the tragic death of Marie Davies, of which Detective Palm and I are the lead investigating officers.

'Marie was a twenty-two-year-old girl, who died in the early hours of Friday morning at 5 Boyd Street, Whitechapel, a four-floor apartment block, Marie passing away in the top-floor apartment of James Maroon, a local businessman. This much we already knew. What we can now say is that she was an epileptic, which had an unfortunate bearing on her death.' Elvis's hackles went haywire, Loretta flinched. The hall squawked and gasped.

Frederick continued: 'On Thursday night, Marie was working at Ziggy's, a bar on Hoxton Square, which is just around the corner from here. After she finished working, we know Marie decided to spend some time at the evening taking place at Ziggy's called Wise

After The Event. This is when the night began to take a tragic turn. At some point she took an Ecstasy tablet and reacted badly to it. As I said, Marie is – was – an epileptic.'

Loretta blanched. She stared at Frederick, who continued: 'And this fact, together with the tablet she took, a kind known as a clog, which is from a batch we believe to be particularly toxic, put Marie in difficulties. An ambulance was called to Ziggy's and by the time the paramedics arrived she had recovered. So she was checked over but did not require any further treatment and the paramedics left. As we understand it, they – the paramedics – were not told she had taken the Ecstasy tablet. They were told that a new member of staff had seen her collapsing and panicked. As it was known generally to staff and management at Ziggy's that Marie was an epileptic. And what they should do should she suffer an attack while working. They knew she could suffer fits occasionally and that, while this can be harrowing to see, knew how to react and deal with it. But this new staff member did not know any of this and, quite reasonably, called 999 for an ambulance.

'So, the paramedics having been assured it was just a fit, left as Marie checked out okay, appeared okay and had recovered. Mr Maroon, who was the promoter of the event at Ziggy's, further assured them that Marie would be looked after and personally taken home by him.'

Elvis's phone pinged – Dana WhatsApp-ed: 'Safe for paramedics to leave Marie at Ziggy's?! They left it to Maroon to get her home!'

Frederick continued. 'Marie Davies lived in the same apartment block as Mr Maroon, on the ground floor, three floors below Mr Maroon's place. His apartment is the top apartment of the 5 Boyd Street building.'

Dana gasped loud. Heads turned, Frederick, Lee, Loretta Davies and Leesa gawped. Elvis's phone pinged: 'Does this let Maroon off the hook? Give him a get out?'

He answered: '???'

Ping: 'Your dad just said Marie lived in the same block. It means it's a logical explanation for the chain of events. How she ended up in Maroon's place.'

Elvis watched the stage. Frederick and Leesa clocked Dana. Lee watched space. Loretta – stupefied.

Frederick continued. 'A little later, Mr Maroon drove Marie Davies back from Hoxton Square to Boyd Street in his car. Still concerned and wanting to make sure she was okay, he took her up to his apartment.'

Elvis's phone pinged again. Dana: 'Why not her place, it's the ground floor? Why not put her in her own bed??!'

Elvis replied: 'This fucking stinks and is glaringly obvious.'

Frederick covered the microphone and leaned into Lee and said something inaudible.

He came back to the mike. 'Unfortunately – and we understand the sensitivity of this to Marie's mother, the rest of her family and friends – unfortunately, when in Mr Maroon's apartment, Marie decided at some point to take more Ecstasy. Another of the so-called clogs, another of the tablets we think are toxic, dangerous.'

A whole room gasp/squawk. The girl took *another* after fitting at the bar. It's new information. The reports said she took one. *In total.* She took TWO.

Frederick eyed Loretta. Elvis clocked the move – Frederick's MO: dramatic pause time, play the moment.

'In fact, she unfortunately took two. At the same time it would seem – according to the autopsy, which–'

The hall went WHAT?? TWO?? AT THE SAME TIME???
WHAT THE FUCK???

Elvis waited for the phone ping. The message: 'Another *TWO*. This is easy for Frederick. It looks like Marie brought it on herself. That she had it coming.'

A second message pinged. 'AS IN WHAT ELSE DID SHE EXPECT??? You know what I mean?'

Elvis pinged back: 'Yeah, it's a fucking gift for him.'

Frederick performed. He knew how to stop the show. 'This was unknown to Mr Maroon, he says, and unfortunately this time, given, as I mentioned, Marie was an epileptic, together with the strength, the toxic nature of this batch of Ecstasy, meant her system failed, despite the paramedics, who Mr Maroon called to his apartment, trying to save her at the scene. Mr Maroon, too, had previously tried to resuscitate Marie.'

Frederick paused. Did he throw Dana a half grin? Sense bad juju from her? 'My colleague Lee Palm will now speak.'

'Thank you,' said Lee. 'As you can imagine, this is a very difficult time for the Davies family. And we thank and salute the bravery of Marie's mother, Loretta, in being here today. Marie has a brother and sister and, together with their father, all of the family considered being here today to appeal for help and any information that might catch whoever did this. But understandably they decided it would be too painful. We do, however, have a message from the family, which we will read out in a few moments, words they hope may persuade someone to come forward.

'Now, about the men we have been questioning. They are Sinbad Williams, twenty-four, who is of Afro-Caribbean heritage. And Darren De La Salle, twenty-three, who is Caucasian. Each of these men resides in Hackney. And we continue to question them. As Detective Inspector Street indicated, we continue to look for leads and want anyone who thinks they may know something to come forward.'

Lee paused and looked at Frederick. 'We want to know who sold Marie Davies the Ecstasy tablets she took. This means not only who she got the tablets from directly, on that night if it was that night, but who the main supplier is, who is flooding the streets with this Ecstasy. This batch is, as we have said, very dangerous.'

Lee looked at Leesa. She nodded. 'Thank you Detective Inspector Street and Detective Constable Palm. As I mentioned at the start, I am Leesa Zapata, a Met Police media officer. Now, before we take your questions, Loretta, Marie's mother, wishes to say a few words.'

Loretta nodded. Lee gave her a be-brave shoulder pat. She bowed her head. 'I first of all wish to say how beautiful a girl and daughter our Marie is – was.' Trembles: 'A lovely girl who touched everyone who met her. But I also want to say–' Her voice dragged. She looked far from wanting to say anything. Lee whispered in her ear, Loretta nodded.

'Yes, I also wanted to say, to be clear, that Marie was an epileptic and so, while she was young and we all make mistakes, she should not have been taking drugs.' Her voice, wavering: 'Any kind of drugs, as she was obviously more at risk. So I say to anyone out there, any youngsters – *anyone* – do not take this evil stuff, especially if you are more at risk of something terrible happening because of a medical condition–'

Another trail off. Frederick's face respectful.

Loretta said, 'I – this is very hard for me, sorry, and all of Marie's family and friends – but please, *please* if anyone out there knows anything, or thinks they do, please let us know. Let the police know. We have to catch whoever did this, whoever is selling this evil stuff–' She stopped and dry-sobbed. The sound held the room.

Lee placed an arm around her, the dry sobs faded.

Leesa allowed a respectful pause. 'Okay – now, questions from the media please.'

Someone behind Dana said, 'Have you arrested or charged Williams and De La Salle?'

Frederick and Lee looked at each other. Frederick: 'They are still being interviewed.'

The same person again: 'That is a no, then?'

'That is correct.'

Someone else: 'Do you think they sold the Ecstasy to Marie?'

'We're not able to say anything on that at the moment.' It's a non-denial from Frederick.

Dana, now: 'What about the Ecstasy, are you testing it to see how toxic it is?'

'Yes,' said Frederick, smiling. 'We are.'

'And James Maroon,' Dana said, 'Is he being questioned?'

Frederick – like he waited for the question. 'He has given us a full statement.'

Frederick waited – he expected more.

Dana said, 'So he's not a suspect then?'

'That's a bit of a sweeping question,' said Frederick. 'I'm sorry but, with respect, maybe you don't understand the process, at the moment we have no suspects.'

It was smooth. Dana said, 'But you're not interviewing Mr Maroon?' said Dana. 'Like you are with Sinbad Williams and Darren De La Salle. At length, I mean. As an ongoing thing.'

A pause and a Frederick shrug. 'What's the question?'

'The question is, why not?'

He stifled a laugh and threw the hall a grin. Elvis riffed on Frederick: he's transparent – surely everyone sees it? What he is.

Frederick said, 'Sorry, your name is?'

'Dana Gabrielle, of *Shoreditch Today*.'

'Ms Gabrielle, I am really not at liberty to offer a walk-through of this case or our procedure. For that, my apologies. However,' he indicated Leesa, 'we can offer you and anyone else interested as much background as we can, afterwards. We are always keen to help as much as is possible and any investigation allows. Be assured of that.'

Dana paused. 'Thanks. But my question stands. I'll rephrase it. Marie Davies was found dead at James Maroon's apartment. Does this not make him a person of interest? Of particular interest?'

'Of course, you are correct,' said Frederick. A smile flashed across over-white dentures. 'As in any investigation, anyone and everyone connected with a case is a person of interest. James Maroon is as much in this category as anyone.'

The tone grated – over-polite; *so so humble*. Dana's colleagues failed to follow up. They got sucked in by Frederick's charm: gravitas delivered via a sly embarrassment.

Someone asked how long it was before Sinbad Williams and Darren De La Salle had to be arrested – if there was a time frame?

Lee replied 'No issue.'

Dana stood up. Elvis got it: she wanted eye contact, give him something more to chew. Frederick avoided her, answered the next question.

Dana moved off – questions continued – she made Elvis, they went and stood outside.

Dana said, 'What a performance.'

Elvis nodded. 'You get it now? What he's like? What he is?'

She nodded. 'We're right. Knowing what we thought and what we knew before, then this display from him. I'm convinced.'

'Me too.'

Dana pointed at a clock on the wall. 'Deadline time, I have to file. I'm going to work in the café here. I'll catch you up.'

'You know where the Stars is, right?'

Dana nodded, walked off.

THIRTEEN

5.31pm

The Stars was a lager-and-guest-beer boozer. Its pumps gleamed chromed metal – James pimped the house lights to oranges/yellows, hung drapes to resemble a cocktail joint on a beach somewhere hot.

Elvis watched the barman pull his third drink. Mid-afternoon creeped to early night. TV news spewed reruns of the Frederick show.

The Marie Davies death was headline news. The sound was down, his dad muted. Body language rendered Frederick as play acting – if you knew his shtick.

Post-Dana, the questions ran redundant. Were easy for Frederick to answer.

The barman looked at the TV. 'The surprise is that girl is the first to carp it.' He placed a fresh Guinness on the bar. 'A pal of mine was at Ziggy's on Thursday. He had two of those clogs, said they were rocket fuel. Sent him loopy – I've heard other people getting freaked out on them. Like, *too* off it. They're funny-farm gear.'

Elvis laughed. His dad held a media conference: a TV star, the day's big news, leading the investigation. He asked for any information *please* about the supplier of the dangerous pills that killed Marie Davies. HE supplied the dangerous pills that killed Marie Davies.

Elvis chewed on the Ricky plan: Frederick had to be taken down. It would save more people from being broken. There's his real trade: breaking people.

Wade warned him. Like he didn't know what his dad was.

Elvis said, 'Why did she take two more of them? That's what doesn't make sense.'

The barman blanked. 'Sorry?'

Elvis said, 'Marie Davies – the girl who died, took one of those pills, nearly died, recovered. Then took two more for some reason, then

111

carped. That's stupid, right? She didn't deserve to die but she had a warning. *And*, she was a fucking epileptic.'

The barman shrugged, walked off.

Elvis slurped Guinness and clocked the joint. A banner splashed faux graffiti, hung over the Technics at the bar end.

It read: WERE KIDS ONCE.

The name of Maroon's night. DJ Elvis kicked it off, *The Music Man* spun his shizzle.

The place filled up, Saturday night came on. Mobs of revellers. The bar ran three deep. James coined it in. Elvis flashed on him as a younger version of Frederick – *as* his dad, wanting to be the man. He flashed on this, too: maybe James tried to screw his dad over.

Elvis made the decks, Dana came through the door, he waved her over. Dana – *needing* a vodka and orange, quick. Elvis got her a double, a fresh Guinness for him.

Elvis said, 'You finished?'

'Until Monday. Long day, all kinds of complications.' She scoped the boozer. 'It's busy – only just after seven.'

'How James likes it.'

'He's here?'

'There.'

Elvis pointed behind the bar. There he is sporting a plaid three-piece suit. Hair: slicked/styled/groomed.

Dana said, 'He's good-looking.'

'Yeah.'

'Not like your dad. He's handsome.'

Elvis didn't like it, kept his tone neutral. 'There's a difference – between good-looking and handsome?'

'Yes.' Dana sipped her drink, watched James as he laughed with a bargirl. 'He knows Frederick is your dad?'

Elvis laughed. 'How do you think I got this gig? And the last one? The one before that? Frederick. How do you think I got my job working for Wade?'

'That's what I thought. So, what's the deal exactly – why are we here?'

Elvis shrugged. 'I'm playing records, you get to meet James. I introduce you, you see what he says – get a feel for him. I play more tunes, the rest of the night's the night.'

'When do you start?'

'About now.'

'Alright then – go DJ.'

'I prefer Music Man.'

'What's wrong with DJ?'

'There's nothing *wrong* with it.'

'DJ sounds better. It scans.'

'Maybe.'

'DJ Elvis: does it get any better than that?'

He cracked a grin – did it get any better than *her*? He powered the Technics on, hit a first record up. It's early '80s Kraut, a track called 'I Wish'. A sweet melodic number: you closed your eyes, you imagined you saw the sun setting *faaaat*.

The place moved. Mobs of girls downed drinks and ordered more. Boys did lines in the Gents. Pills got popped, ketamine imbibed, booze thrown down.

Elvis brought in the next record. A Rheingold number. James bowled over, his eyes twinkled. He smiled. He shook hands with Elvis and Dana.

He said, 'Elvis, aren't you going to introduce us?'

'Dana, Dana Gabrielle – James Maroon.' Elvis left it there. He sang to the chugging rhythm: 'Auftakt/im takt/im viertakt/soll es klingen.'

James bowled off, bowled back with drinks.

The Stars wobbled. Punters loosened. The night came down. Elvis's next tune oozed a fat bassline. The joint bounced, the same lyric repeated. This was the night, right here, right now.

James said, 'Dance?' He held his hand out to Dana and gave her a look: she's only human, how can she resist?

Elvis didn't like it: Maroon's a crook charmer slimeball, in cahoots with Frederick.

Dana accepted Maroon's hand. They twirled, they danced like they had danced a thousand nights together.

Elvis still clocked it, mixed another record.

A theory: Dana might be playing James. Get him onside to extract info. They twirl in the orange light. James dizzied Dana. But did Dana dizzy James – *spill your guts, let something slip.*

Dana came over. 'Keep the music playing.'

'How's it going? You working on him?'

She nodded, went back to James, his smile/snake charm. He's see-through. And yet, Elvis didn't *want* to believe it. Maybe that's his thing, trick, how he pulls it off: it's no act, it's natural.

Elvis snagged another drink, downed half the pint, caught twenty-twenty vision. His dad was going to be caught. *He* was going to pull it off.

Boozy sense showed it all interlinked, logical. Frederick Street was going down by his son. Elvis would take Lee Palm, James Maroon and anyone else with him. Then, he would move on. Strut forward, slowly, coolly.

Zen-like.

The Strut.

Yeah – The Music Man. Yeah – *The Strut.*

A punter made the decks, leaned in. 'I've got the clogs – you know what I mean? As advertised on TV, on the news. These aren't fucking duds.' Elvis caught a whiff of bad breath. 'James says you want any, they're on the house.'

His eyes were zapped. He walked off, got lost in the crowd.

Confirmation: James *did* serve up clogs in here. Frederick and Lee Palm surely *did* supply them for James to peddle. Two days after Marie Davies died. She's dead from two moody pills and business continues on. They're open 24-7.

They're shameless.

FREDERICK is.

Elvis fought a grin off. He couldn't help it – you had to admire his dad's unbounded front.

James walked up. 'I've met Dana before?'

'Don't know. She's a friend of–'

'Camilla's. That's right, your old squeeze.'

Elvis said, 'My fucking ex.' He hit up the next record. A piano track that built and built, took them towards midnight and beyond.

James grinned. He made a packet at the bar, from his mules serving pills up.

Elvis dropped the next tune. Its hook was simple: 'It's like ecstasy/ When you say that to me.'

Repeat.

James the other side of the bar, exited the door. Like the move at Ziggy's when he went outside to the stash.

Dana came over. Elvis, rhetorical: 'Wonder what he's up to?'

Dana, giddy: 'He's got to run the place, it's his night after all.'

'It wasn't a question. I know what he's up to. This is the same as at Ziggy's, he keeps the stash outside, to supply the lads he has in here serving up for him.'

'You really think he's doing that after what happened with Marie Davies? Selling in here?'

Like she swooned under his charm.

'He, James, does not give a fuck about what you, I, anyone who's normal cares about. That's why he's perfect for Frederick cos he's the same. I guarantee you, the gear being done in here, most of it will come from James. And that means – from my dad. While you were dancing with him – sorry, virtually falling over the guy – a lad came up and offered me a clog. Told me James was offering them for free. Clogs *are* being bought and sold in here and he's behind it.'

'Falling over him? *Him?*' She laughed. 'Really? That's what you think?'

Elvis flushed. 'James will have at least two dickheads in here working for him. He makes the cut from the bar as well. And worse, Frederick sits back and coins it in, too. Rips stuff off from the day job and earns big time from the night job – except he has James and other mugs working for him.'

Dana nodding, believing now about James.

Elvis said, 'See if we can clock who's working for him. The lad who offered me the freebie pills has disappeared. I'm just about finished; I'll play one more tune then I'm over.'

He hit the twelve-inch lined up on the deck. It's a test pressing, *pre*-white label. Sound stew engulfed the Stars. A Dutch–Italo house number, electro-fizz on a pulsing beat. Elvis's sound.

An echoey voice and guitar rhythm took hold.
The vibe: like the place would never close.
James came over.
'My round,' said Elvis.
'Great set. But no more drinks, we're going. Come on.'
'Where?'
'The next party. Where else are we going to go?'

FOURTEEN

Moments later

They jumped in James's silver Merc. He parked it in the alley behind the Stars. The heaviest fall yet of snow recoated windows. James brushed it off the windscreen, took the driver's seat. Dana rode next to him, Elvis in the back.

Dana, a joshing tone: 'Should you even be driving?'

James said, 'Maybe not. But frankly my dear I don't give a damn.' A cheesy line. It drew near-hysterical laughter from Dana. She must be – *surely* – hustling him.

James placed the Merc in first, hooked his iPhone to the sound system, balled the accelerator. They made Great Eastern Street to make Old Street roundabout. They headed towards town, street lights blurring by.

James slowed the Merc, balled metal again, and hooted. Elvis said. 'Slow down, it's fucking icy.'

Dana hooted too. Elvis frowned – these two. James eased the Merc, did so for good this time, cruised at a nice pace. He tooled along City Road, past closed shops, tower blocks, maisonettes and townhouses. He hit left along Goswell Road, hit right past Smithfield Market and made Charterhouse Street.

James pulled to a stop, on yellows – no parking snitches at midnight on pre-Christmas Saturday. 'Here is where we're going next.'

He pointed at Fabric nightclub.

Elvis said, 'Nice. Has a boss sound system, speakers under the dancefloor. It's been a while.'

James said, 'A friend of mine met his wife in there. They're still together. *Very* romantic.'

Dana said, 'That's Fabric?'

'You've never been?'

'A long time ago.'

James said, 'Time to refresh the memory.' That act: dazzling smile, air of other.

That charm. 'Come on.'

FIFTEEN

20 December, 0.01am

They hit the queue. They walked up the queue. The doorman pulled aside the red cord. The two-lane VIP queue was longer on the street side. There was no queue on the club side. It's *VVIP*, that's why. James hit the club side. Elvis and Dana followed. The doorman slid a door open and they glided in.

James stopped on the stairs. 'It's fucking Saturday night, it's midnight, it's coming up to Christmas Day. I've had a girl nearly die at my Thursday night, then go and die at my place. Where I *live*. The police are sniffing around and are bound to start crawling all over me soon. What does this speech mean? That I intend to get royally boxed out of my head in here. And you're both welcome to join me.'

Dana giggled. Elvis looked at her. James hit speed dial on his phone. Carried on up stairs that went wide.

He dropped his voice, said into the phone: 'Do the place now. He's with me and about to get mashed up if I have anything to do with it. Hit it.'

'You don't have to tell me twice,' said Lee, and hung up.

Lee Palm, the big man gone small. Too long with Frederick's foot on his throat. Do this job right and Lee would be talked to. See if he really wanted to get out from under Frederick. That could be arranged.

James got him inside the place – now it was up to Lee.

They made the top of the stairs, headed for VIP, were waved through.

James soaked up high fives, handshakes. He kissed, hugged. He's The Man, Mr Saturday Night. The joint was a riot of red. Red carpets, red lights, red tinsel for red Yuletide. Christmas stunk, Christmas was faux faux. Christmas was money and drugs and fandango. And money. Money, money, money.

One end of VIP looked over Room One's dancefloor. The other had the bar. James positioned there, beaming at everyone who said 'Hi'.

He pointed across the room. 'Look, there's a fucking white dove in here.'

Elvis and Dana rubbernecked. James pulled a bag of chisel. He wet a finger and dabbed. He left/right-nostrilled chizz.

Dana and Elvis turned back. Elvis said, 'Dove?' They 'caught' him doing chisel. Dana giggled, James pulled a spoon, offered it. She looked around.

Elvis said, 'Careful!'

Dana told him: 'Sssssh!' She spooned the white stuff up both nostrils.

James grinned – Dana offered Elvis the spoon. He said, 'No thanks, let's have drinks.'

Dana felt an instant coke rush, her eyes gleamed. 'Come on Mr Clean and Serene.'

Elvis fobbed her off with a smile. James said, 'Drinks on me. What'll you have?' He saw Elvis cracking: they were all the same, booze was gateway tackle to the hard stuff.

Their drinks arrived. Doubles: vodka–tonic for Dana, gin–tonic for Elvis, Jim Beam for James.

James wanted more coke. And one of those pills that offed the girl. Doing that was a sign. He popped it, glugged bourbon. He was ready to fly until Monday night. The spoon came back out. He reloaded, fed his nose, Dana did the same. Elvis hesitated, waved it away.

James's phone buzzed. He pulled it, put the spoon away.

It was Lee – FaceTiming.

James hit answer – Lee's face on the phone. James hid the screen from Elvis and Dana, didn't try *too* hard: fuck them.

'Yes?' He tried not to laugh. This shit house. Frederick's lieutenant. Fuck's sake.

Lee's face big, ugly, trying to burst through the phone screen. He said, 'What was the key code again? To his place? I can't get through the door of the building.'

James laughed. It perked Elvis and Dana. She tried to see the screen – he shook his head, winked. 'Private business.'

To Lee: 'You're police. Filth. You can't get into an apartment building on fucking Princelet Street? On your turf? Your *hood* – whatever you idiots call it?'

Elvis staring – like he heard, the daft fuck. James smiled, switched his camera on so Lee could see him. Sotto voce: 'Just wait a minute thicko, I'll look this up on my phone.'

He told Lee the four-digit code – the one he and Ricky's camp act swindled from that dumb fuck Miss Nice outside the place earlier today.

Sotto voce again: 'When you get to the door of the actual pad it's the same code. Do not fucking call me again on this. You're getting paid. Earn it.'

He dropped the low voice, went *loud*. 'Thought *I* popped one of those clogs. You sure it's not you?'

He howled and hung up. Elvis and Dana must've heard – no reaction: a red light; they don't want him to see.

Interesting.

James held up his phone. 'This guy.' It's OTT, hammy. Their faces – moral fucking outrage. They *did* hear. They didn't *like* the clog joke. They *didn't* approve. Big deal.

James, more OTT: 'WHAT?' They didn't blink. Even the quiff, who was supposed to be cool, vibed thought police. Fuck it: dick with these two shit-heads.

'Okay, *okay*. Kidding about those Es is not your taste. But it's to mine. I'm sorry about the girl, of course I am, but fuck, you have the kind of few days I've had, then–'

They saw it: he didn't give a flying. 'Let's take a table.' He corralled a bar slave. 'Champagne and a bucket on the balcony, my account – James Maroon. Make sure there's a load of ice.'

VIP was off the leash. Punters noshed gear. Walls dripped E/coke/ket perspiration. Fabric's uber-cool unisex restroom rammed out with goosed punters. Room One packed underfloor bass drums. They ripped *up* through punters. Senses spasticked. Normal sense went south. Something took over.

James peered over the balcony. Look at the scene – it's craaaazy. He filled flutes with champagne. Punters screamed as the latest tune climaxed. The whole thing went *off*.

They clinked glasses, threw back champers. James's phone vibrated again.

If it's that prick–

He pulled his phone: Lee – FaceTiming.

James hit answer, picked up his Jim Beam and drank. He felt in his suit jacket for his bag of clogs, popped a second, chased it with bourbon/champagne.

He pointed at his phone, mouthed: 'Business.' Sotto voce: 'Lee, this is going to be funny. Shoot.'

Lee's face screen-bulged. It disappeared. Elvis and Dana watched James.

Lee: 'Which door is it, left or right?' The image blurred; Lee spun his phone left–right, left–right.

James full-throated laughed. 'Slow down, you lunatic. You're on the wrong floor if there's only two doors. I told you three, the middle one.'

Lee's face appeared onscreen. 'Why not say so?'

James dropped whispering. 'I did say so dickhead. A trillion fucking times.'

Lee – ecstatic. 'There *is* a third one, down the corridor.'

Elvis – on his feet, leaning towards James, refilling James's flute. James – 'Thanks.' He jerked the phone away from Elvis.

Lee was getting his head banged. James, *again*: 'Do what you're getting paid for.'

Lee had hung up.

'You're just busy tonight, or is it all nights, all day, every day?' said Dana. She gushed, James perked – *brainwave*: she and Elvis worked on him. Some plot, shakedown.

He eyed Dana: half-drunk grin *and* watchful eyes. Elvis: watching freaks walk by, studiously *not* looking at James.

James told Dana: 'Business never stops.' An E rush gripped – it was tremendous.

Elvis – *this:* he wanted to get on one of those sweet clogs. The way he gulped champers, aped blissful content. Had no self-control, the muppet.

So: get him ON ONE.

James drained the champers into their flutes, ordered two more bottles, a fresh ice bucket. He ordered a tray of shots, dark/light sambuca. Tequila, salt and lemon. The round ran four rounds deep.

James poured.

Arctic-chilled £69 Veuve Clicquot into their flutes.

Sambuca/tequila shots down his throat and chased these with Clicquot and watched Elvis and Dana follow.

He poured more Clicquot and finished the last shots and chased these with Clicquot and felt a sweet clog surge hit.

Like he floated and surfed and spun the same time.

It was magic. It was going to be FUCKING magic.

He started on the second bottle of Clicq.

He poured.

More waves hit. The room kaleidoscoped: colours, sensory shift. Mood uplift. Attitude and mean edge blunted. Stuff made sense, didn't matter. Was forgiven. Fabric's Yule time tinsel town red was *alriiiight*.

Vision blur. He saw – Elvis and Dana finish their shots. They blanched and wretched.

Now's the time.

James felt a goofy grin. The bar snacks like bucking broncos. Limbs pins and needled. Stars burst through his eyes. Stars burst back through his eyes. These Es – absolutely brillo.

Time to share the love. To Dana and Elvis: 'Fancy a pill, a little fella? Come on, time to celebrate, it's the weekend, Christmas.'

Yes, CELEBRATE.

Celebrate Frederick's impending demise. He couldn't keep up. Time moved, shifted eras. Mr Bent Filth was an abacus in a James Maroon digital age. Frederick's existence: dependent on the constant calibration of who he could keep quiet, who he had to end.

Friday – a *long* day. James watched news and stayed inside. He was watched. Today, the same: waiting for Frederick to call, make a move: nothing.

He sat tight since the quiff died. He gave a statement to Frederick's mob. He made *his* move – informed Lee what he had to do, break in to Elvis's pad.

Elvis glugged champers and looked at James – BINGO: the joey can't resist. 'What have you got?'

James kept a straight face. 'You know what I'm packing, Mr Music Man. Pills. Es. Little fellas. These ones are the God of all known bar snacks.'

Blurred vision hit – E waves juddered – *they are bar snacks beyond compare.*

Dana said, 'Yes, please.' She's a greedy piece of quiff – feast on a wide James smile.

He pulled a pill, leaned over the ice bucket. He stuck his tongue out, placed the E on there. She got it – out came her tongue and James flicked the clog onto it.

She swallowed. She glugged champers to chase it.

'Thank you.' It came out high-pitched, slurred. Dana giggled, James joined her.

Then: they looked at Elvis.

He said, 'I'd love to but you know – clean and serene, I–'

'Ditch the Betty Ford act,' Dana said. 'Come on. What kind of fucking DJ doesn't do pills on a Saturday night? At Fabric? Before Chrimbo in fucking VIP?'

James gave Elvis the smile. 'She has a point.'

Take the chance now – it's about timing – the same act – pill onto tongue, lean over.

Elvis reflex – Elvis in a nutshell – he didn't want to take/he totally did. Out came his tongue – Elvis trying to see the pill, it's impossible without taking it off his tongue. Impossible to see its yellow speckles, embossed clog symbol.

He gulped it down – his eyes darted, he *knew.* 'That was a *clog.*'

Dana said, 'Good.' She threw James a smile, Elvis got a scowl.

James reconsidered – maybe she wasn't plotting with him? The way she talked to him.

Maybe Elvis flew solo – a *flash*: maybe Elvis worked against him with Frederick.

Fuck it. He surfed clog waves, heard Elvis talking.

Saying: 'Where have you got these pills from? They're the ones that killed the girl at your place aren't they?'

'Good, aren't they? She must have carped it because she was epileptic because these are–'

Leave it there. The pills *were* strong: Frederick fronted a neat PR line: they *might* kill an epileptic.

Otherwise: no problem. Buckle up, enjoy the ride.

These – something else. Sensations dipped, fingertips fluttered. Moments passed. He couldn't get a handle on them: *they're over, they begin again.*

James E-ed how James was straight. His self was enhanced. He was made more right. More smart, slick, handsome, hip. He was *even more* the Night Time Cool no other shit-head knew existed. Es were euphoria and empathy and they surged. Empathy for James Maroon. The rest of the fuckers could go fuck themselves.

That was euphoria: it made him *euphoric.*

VIP – out of control. Fabric – off its rocker.

Elvis – opposite. Wait until that clog drops.

Elvis; *oh Elvis.*

His place was about to be turned over. Ransacked by Lee. His dad's partner. Lee's instructions: take his laptop, any other computer equipment. Wipe: the film of James going to the stash at Ziggy's on Thursday. Then: smash the pad up. Make it look good, scary.

And the pics – hang them.

Confuse/disturb.

James grooved on it. The info: finding out about the film. How: easy answer – he's James Maroon, everything needed to know is known.

Betsy-Jane: his eyes, snitch. Thursday night at Ziggy's she spied Elvis with his phone. B.J. left Sinbad and Darren by the Ladies, tried to find James when the girl collapsed. She found Elvis instead – the shit-head snooped on James through the fire exit doors; filmed him on his phone.

B.J. told him after Marie recovered in his office, when the ambulance and paramedics were gone.

Now, B.J. watched Lee. If he made a wrong move. She was a crack-head, she *watched* a crackhead. Crackheads were good for these jobs – they turkeyed for rocks, dare not fuck up the prospect of a bag.

James got E blurs, vision wobbled. He eyed Elvis: Lee smashes his pad up. Wipes the film/doesn't wipe it. Does what else he has to do. It doesn't matter: Elvis could have backups – he *should* have backups – stashed somewhere.

The *idea* remained: a message sent. Shake this shit-head up; shake *Frederick* up.

Elvis's place being turned over as he's being turned over in Fabric. What a hoot, a total howl-fest. He took one of the pills that killed a girl. She carped it in the pad of the dude he wants to take down. James pulled his phone, told Elvis, Dana to smile. He snapped pics. He did it fast, before they could think. He got into shot with them. He took group selfies. Snap, snap, snap. They're all spangled. It's dirt, *grift*.

Elvis – no turning back, zero way out. The muppet snarfed the same pill that killed Marie Davies. How that would mess up his head? His plan? Think of the blackmail possibilities doing that clog threw up. By the time James finished, Elvis was finished, his amateur plot finito. Au revoir Mr Fucking Clean and Fucking Serene.

He caught another flash. If Elvis tried to turn him over, did Elvis try to turn Frederick over? As part of the same plan? Was that *all* of his plan: double play James *and* Frederick, at the same time. That would be a laugh. A howl and a half. He heard stuff about them. A rumour. About that piece of quiff Elvis used to see – Camilla – that he *still* lived with her despite their break-up. Despite Frederick being mixed up in it. Despite Frederick banging her on the sly. *The not so sly.* Pulled a classic Frederick move on his own son.

James read Elvis with ease: he's a loyal, sentimental type. When that kind turned, they *turned*. Searing vengeance time.

James liked it: Elvis going against Frederick. Coolio – it could facil-itate this move, maybe: recruit Elvis, make him a sleeping partner.

It was an option, a play.

We have a common cause: Frederick.

Elvis, goofy-smiling, leaned over. His cheeks juddered, face dis-torted from the clog. The muppet's out of control.

James grinned wide – Elvis misread. 'I'm glad I did it. This pill is smooth.'

Looks like it mate – *notttt!*

James, full-on schmooze: 'They are smooth. Just like your tunes Mr Music Man. I may have given you a gig at first cos of your dad, but that was nepotism that was worth it. You're a total god with the sounds.'

No tell from Elvis. Not a flicker at Frederick's mention.

Elvis: 'I'll tell you a secret. I'm clean and serene for moments like this. Nights like this.'

What the –

What is he talking about?

Elvis – a good read of James. 'I'll explain, I'll tell you.' His speech E slurred. 'I am clean and serene so that when I do a pill, it's rocket fuel, it goes – *whoooosh!*'

Elvis's eyes half closed; James said: 'I'm feeling the fucker too, doing stuff to my cells and mind.'

James's phone buzzed – a laugh before he pulled it. Lee Palm was proving an absolute howl-fest. He's Frederick's partner in crime – that's a *hoot*.

FaceTime – it wasn't Lee, it was Betsy-Jane. Those worried eyes.

What did *she* want?

'B.J.'

'James.' The nervous tone, crack-induced wariness. 'It's Lee.'

James chorted: 'The suspense is killing me.'

B.J.'s eyes widened. She moved closer, face went larger. 'You're on those clogs, aren't you?'

'Two of the things. You must've done one.'

She shook her head – too hard.

'You've been punting them for me so you must've taxed one. A little test drive. James won't notice, so why not?'

'No way. I promise you.'

'Come on. Don't lie or it'll be worse for you.'

B.J. – zilcho backbone – a grin at the screen. 'Yes, and you're right. They *are* mad.'

James howled. Her ability to lie, zero – why he trusted her. 'Why did you call?'

'I told you – it's Lee. He's still in there.'

James looked at his watch. 'You sure?'

'There's only one way in you said.'

'Correct.'

'I'm in the bar across the street. On my fourth drink, at least. I can see the place easy. No one's come in or out of the building since he did.'

'How long's he been in there?'

'Has to be more than an hour.'

'Yeah.' He scanned his phone for the times Lee called. 'Just over an hour.'

'The light's still on in the apartment.'

James – past caring. He lowered his voice. 'Far as I know, the girl Elvis lives with – Camilla – she's out all night and Elvis is with me, out of his head. So fuck Lee. Whatever he's doing. I told him ten, fifteen minutes, in and out. He is one class-A muppet.'

'You could phone him.'

'I could. But you know what? Why? It could be funnier this way. The girl comes back, catches an intruder. She calls the pig shop – imagine if Frederick gets wind of it. Try explaining that one Detective Palm, Frederick's partner turning over his son's pad.'

James hooted.

B.J.'s face – confused. She wanted no complications. Do a job, get paid. Repeat.

James hung up, ditched any more thought of Lee, pulled the spoon, serviced both nostrils.

VIP jumped. VIP tripped.

Dana danced in front of the table. She shook her stuff, boogied cool. A punter buttonholed her. She pointed at James.

He waited – here she comes.

Indicating the punter: 'Can he buy one?'

His E mood became E edge. 'I'm not selling anything.'

It confused her. 'Okay – no problem.'

The punter sloped off.

Elvis watched James in action. He went to him, spoke E babble. 'Have to say tonight, taking us out, very good of you. And I always appreciate you booking me to DJ.'

E gush, full on. 'We going anywhere else, after here?'

James, smiling. 'Hold on cowboy.' He turned *his* E love on, maximum wattage. Feel the intimacy between us, sharing this *special moment*. 'This place not enough for you?'

'Sure. But it'll be seven in the morning like that.' Elvis clicked fingers. 'And we'll want to carry on.'

'Don't worry. There's a smorgasbord of places we can go to.'

A smorgasbord.

What the–

Forget/fuck it. Fuck everything thought, presumed, about James and Frederick.

See why it all made sense.

Forgive Frederick for betraying him with Camilla. Forgive the shithouses he surrounded himself with, the crime he did.

Forgive James for Marie Davies's death.

E vision: keeping the poor girl tragic and the whole thing an epic universe act.

Frederick and James and Lee – no choice. *They're in thrall to it.*

Elvis got his dad and Lee, who and what they were. Elvis got James – a crook because he knew nothing else, could control nothing else. It's grandeur and status, destiny and events.

It's HIM.

He got up from his seat, made James.

James's eyes moved.

They clicked off.

Shut down, quick.

Not fast enough: they flashed *something.* Elvis saw it; James built barriers. James was just the same as him.

Here goes:

He hugged him, kissed his cheek.

Elvis: 'You're a good lad, you really are. Trust me.'

James – no flicker, that smile.

Elvis – goosed from the clog: 'You know if you *know*. And *we know*.'

James – a thumbs up.

Elvis stood, came close to falling. It's ridiculous: the blitzed feeling, motor skills gone. He caught the table, knocked James's empty glass to the floor – stop the ice bucket following.

PHEW.

He repeated: '*We know*.'

Wait.

James – *whadda you know?* – brought a slow double thumbs up.

Elvis, emboldened, E STUPID:

Tell James it all. The whole scheme, full script. What's planned, *going down*. Taking Frederick and Lee out. Leave Wade out of it. And James. Say to him: this is what it's about. This is a warning. Understand?

OR.

The clog switched now. The vibe: subtle shift stuff. Difficult to discern. His mood told him – *you are mistaken. You know nada. You are goosed.*

KEEP YOUR MOUTH SHUT.

Thoughts, decisions, choices – *spinning.*

Say: 'I got it wrong. About you. Who you are.'

He saw now.

James – magnificent and seamless.

James – fast and loose.

Groove – on his easy rhythm.

James, smiling: 'Everyone does. Get it wrong about me. Who can blame them? I don't.'

Elvis looked over at Dana dancing. She panted like a marathon runner, sweated up a sweat like she coke-fucked for days.

Elvis joined her, started dancing.

James joined them.

They all started dancing, threw out beams – to each other; to punters.

James felt his phone buzz – B.J.

Clogs spritzed capillaries. His brain worked a thousand images a second. His brain got meat-sliced. His head lightly billowed in the breeze of the fucking tune the DJ brought in. Image stew, a million memories a second. Sun-bleached afternoons. Evening sunsets abroad. The gear and the birds. It all marched by. A lifetime in a moment.

He shouted to Elvis: 'THIS IS A FUCKING TRACK. NOT THAT KRAUT SHIT YOU LOVE.'

The phone kept buzzing. It's B.J. calling. He hit answer. He *knew* what it was. Lee – he fucked up.

'B.J.'

'James, it's Lee.'

'Meaning?'

'He's still in there.'

James bounced and bopped. High-fived Elvis and Dana.

'His funeral.'

'I wouldn't have called but it's worse than that. Frederick just turned up.'

James, narcotic-numbed: 'When?'

'About half an hour ago.'

Work angles, toss this fucking development around: what if Lee worked him against Frederick? If B.J. did?

The same answer: good, bring the cluster-fuck cabaret on.

To B.J.: 'Okay.'

He hung up, kept dancing. Elvis was in for a surprise when he got home.

His phone buzzed.

It was B.J.

A-*fucking*-gain.

'Yes?'

'They just left.'

'Lee and Frederick.'

'Yeah.'

He hit end call – what does it mean, have to know, park it for now. Certain: Lee's dead, done – by Frederick, or him.

He pulled another clog, popped it. Dana, fiend eyes, saw him: *one more please?* He palmed her the tablet and she wolfed it. He pointed at

Elvis, palmed Dana another and she tapped him, pulled the shit-head out of a deep E reverie.

She opened her palm: Elvis, opening his mouth, numero dos clogos went down – he dry-gulped it.

To James: 'Thank you.'

To Elvis: thumbs up.

The night floated and veered. Motion and flight. Stars in the ceiling, and toes. Deep understanding without going deep. There is *nothing* wrong or right.

They synched; they *got it*.

The DJ kept dropping those tunes: they hit 3.15am. They hit 4.54. They hit 4.55, 4.56, 4.57.

They recalled nada from 5am.

SIXTEEN

7am – surfacing. Still in VIP. Their balcony spot got retained.

Faces kept passing – morning – relentless – the DJ slid a sound in that brought the place down, *together*. It oozed adventure, set the joint free.

James couldn't help it – he lost that cool – couldn't care less. To Elvis: 'What *is* this tune, Mr Music Man?'

Elvis, smiling: '"E-dancer/Feel The Mood." Kevin Saunderson.'

James shook his head and howled: *really*? He told Dana: more howls. Elvis: he made it a group howl-fest.

James, smiling: 'Of course it is. What the fuck else would it be called?'

NOW:

The lights went up/the night finished. WELCOME TO SUN-DAY. Brightness glared, Fabric's mob got walloped.

James donned his shades: L.A. motor cop-cool; James M Fucking Cool. That X-factor shit.

To Elvis, Dana, a hand: 'What a night.'

Dana: 'Brilliant.' Her eyes glittered. Elvis nodded – catch that goofy smile. He pointed at James's sunglasses. '*Nice*. Wish I had a pair.' James smiled – a full beam. 'Close your eyes.'

Elvis did. James pulled a second pair of shades from his suit jacket. Ray-Bans – wayfarer chic for Elvis to glide out the joint.

Elvis – delighted. 'Thanks.'

'Come on.' They took the stairs from VIP, exited into a dark sky.

SEVENTEEN

8am

Fabric punters hailing taxis – jumping into parked-up sleds – on the club side – by Smithfields Market. They stood around in the snow. They talked and smoked, grinned and gurned.

James, still goofed: 'Now?'

'Anywhere.' Elvis grooved on the Ray-Bans. The view they gave.

Dana shrugged. James said, 'Let's go then.'

'Your car?'

'Not in this state.' He pointed to a row of taxis.

They made a hackney carriage. James told the driver head east. He'd give him an address when he got it. James pulled his phone and fired a message. They pulled into the City. They boosted through Barbican, St Paul's, Bank, Houndsditch, Liverpool Street. They hit Shoreditch High Street. They made north of Hoxton Square. They made Kingsland Road.

Streets, flying by. They were gone. They were morning ghouls. Snow melted on pavements. Street lights burned yellow. The driver asked for an address.

James showed his iPhone, the cab did a 180 at half speed, went back towards town. After a half mile: they hit Great Eastern, stopped at the top of Leonard.

James paid the driver. It's cold, snow fell relentless.

Elvis scoped up and down Leonard. 'We going Home Bar?'

James pointed. 'Next door.'

They made the adjacent house – Victorian, two steps up off street level. James hit the buzzer and the door swung open.

EIGHTEEN

8.22am

The place – cavernous. Done up like Honolulu. If Honolulu was situated in the Alps. Fake palm trees 'planted' in fake snow. Girls in grass skirts and coconut shells for brassieres, Hawaiian print dresses. The boys in Hawaiian shirts and rolled-up cut-offs.

The place rocked. Beamed onto walls: images of surf and sand and alpine fantasia. The music: smart-alec house and disco for musos and cool cats. For Hoxton hip. Boys and girls who knew what they liked.

Elvis – 'Wow.'

Dana – 'Wow.'

James grinned. 'Fuck this.' He led them to a lift – teak-walled, teak-doored. It ran five floors. They stepped in and stepped out at the top, entered a penthouse where the real hoedown occurred.

Wade positioned on a chaise longue doing blow from a platter. The joint swam in plastic-boosted women dressed in near nothing. Bikinis, swimsuits, high-end underwear. The quiff numbered porn stars, wannabees and connected pieces. They circulated. They were smashed out of their brains. The men – wised-up, smashed. Ceiling-to-floor glass walls showed the Smoke in panorama. A DJ spun deep house on a mezzanine. He sported bleached surfer-dude locks.

Wade pulled a face – corny *and* knowing.

He waved them over, said: 'James – what took you? Line? Of course you do. Have two. Elvis? Clean and serene? Doesn't look like it. Dana, hello again. You're *more* than welcome.'

Elvis said, 'Wade – what the?'

'You *know* I have a townhouse Elvino.'

'I didn't realise it was like – this.' He scoped the place again. He couldn't stop – Dana, the same.

NINETEEN

9.15am

They walked to a window. It's a glass wall. The vista showed the Thames, Tower Bridge, cars, buses and trains. Traffic chugged roads, hit arteries. It's a capital city Sunday morning moment, here *now*, gone *now*. White-*white*. Coked-up Dickensian Smoke. Time never moved. The scene hadn't shifted.

It's Victorian – *the big V.*

Elvis did chisel. Elvis did *Wade's* chisel. The rush came instant. It mixed with the clog blur. Wade's chizz is high-grade. Rocket fuel. It centrifuges with all the MDMA. Legs, head: clean, *laundered*. A mind shower. A brain wash. His eyes popped, flashes roved in.

ZOOM!!!

The whole thing brilliant through James's Ray-Bans.

London, a paperweight scene. Sensory fine-tune – *feeling soft-powdered through cells.* The brain houses an angel – celestial-imbue.

Tingles. Rushes.

NO.

The mood bent. *Backwards.* A *baaad* volte face.

Fear roved in; fear gripped. The E blanket got torn away. The coke took over.

Thoughts got poisoned: he took a pill with James Maroon. A clog – the same kind that killed Marie Davies.

Clean and serene?

A fraud.

This crusade of doing this to Frederick for the right reasons OVER.

He was the same as all the rest. He spilled info to James. He took an E that killed a girl Thursday. He just snorted gak in front of James.

He couldn't work it out, get a grip:

Did he blow it?

Did he reveal it all?

Everything he and Dana planned.

He looked at the London skyline, saw dawn lighten, caught his reflection in the glass and his blood froze.

The DJ dialled the volume down.

The place stopped.

Now: the DJ dialled the volume UP on the next record.

A voice sang: '*Higher.*'

Sang: '*A lack of love.*'

Over an acid house squelch.

The place went nuts.

James did coke from Wade's platter, Dana danced. Wade went up on the mezzanine by the DJ. He got a blow job from a silicone piece, caught Elvis's stare, saluted. Elvis forced a grin and turned back to the cityscape.

He fretted on Wade: Wade knew what Elvis and Dana planned. Wade plotted with them at the studio yesterday. Now, they were here. Work it out. James brought them here: a move between Wade and James? Engineered by Frederick?

He couldn't think straight.

He stared at London.

This was *it*. The reason *why* he went clean and serene. He felt in his pocket – there's a trump card: temazepam/blueys. He walked to the bar. This window showed east London going out to Essex. He took a Budweiser from an ice bucket, popped it and chased two blueys down. Amber waves would be incoming.

The sense that nothing mattered would be fucking incoming.

Here, now – all light. Heaviness floaty, senses blissful.

Elvis joined James on the chaise longue: a bluey dream, everything retreated/blurred.

He patted James on the knee and pointed to the platter. It's piled with chisel. Fresh powder, virgin snow, a coke stairway to heaven. The blueys' soft power was tremendous. What a bar snack. Mind and body blown. It neutered coke paranoia. Remade it as something wondrous.

James said, 'Go ahead.'

'Cheers,' Elvis said. He did a fat stripe, passed the platter, James followed. The platter came back to Elvis. He repeated. The platter came back to James. He repeated.

James's cheeks gleamed, his eyes glittered. 'You done eggs?'

Elvis nodded – James sounded distant, close. 'Want a couple?'

'What are they?'

'Tens.'

'I'll have one.'

Elvis pulled a bluey and James palmed it, chased with beer. He pointed at Dana. 'She gets better the longer we are out.'

'The more fucked up we get.'

'You been anywhere near her?'

'I wish.'

'Your ex is a big pal of hers.'

'Yeah.'

'That wouldn't go down too well.'

'Fuck that. Some of the stuff that happened between us – we're over any of that shit counting.'

'Your dad went with her, right?'

Elvis grinned. It didn't matter, in this moment. 'A few times.'

'He has a way of operating, your dad. What did you do about it?'

Elvis shrugged – tried to fight off the memory again. The narcotic haze made it hard – he started to get an image – hear a sound – yes, that was the first thing – on getting outside the flat – *that sound.*

He closed it down, snapped back to here.

He told James: 'What could I do about it? That's him, that's my dad.'

James got that look. 'Apart from doing it first – to your ex. Getting your retaliation in first.'

Elvis laughed: James knew *that,* did he? All about *THAT.*

'Did she catch you playing away, then? Like you caught her with your dad? In the act?'

'I was grassed up. By a grass.'

'Which dickhead did that?'

'If you find out be sure to tell me.'

James, grinning. 'I shouldn't say this, maybe, but my money is on your dad. I say that with no actual info, of course.'

'Don't worry, I've thought it myself.'

James a candidate too. The way he operated, vibed junior Frederick.

Lay it on him, see. 'I've also, at times, thought it might be you who snitched me.'

James, no blink. 'Why wouldn't you and shouldn't you? It was some dickhead around here for sure.'

Elvis believed him – instinct confirmed. 'I don't see the percentage in it for you. The *why*. You do everything for a reason.'

'True. Apart from the stuff I don't.'

James laughed – Elvis too. Elvis saw this: the way James let him know he knew about Elvis going behind Camilla's back before Camilla did the same with Frederick.

It's a play.

What's behind it needs considering.

Dana came over. Her eyes flickered: she wasn't that far gone. She took it all in.

To James: 'How do you know Wade?'

James's eyes coke-pinned: 'How does anyone know anyone? My line of business, you get to know people. London's a village, right?'

Wade made an act of coming down the mezzanine steps. Did the zipper of his Bermudas up slow. Pretended to catch his dick in the fly, got group howls. He flopped on the chaise longue, grabbed James and Elvis, pointed by the DJ, where the girl who just blew him danced.

Sighing: 'I'm all out of love, fellas, you know what I mean.'

He winked, James emptied an eighth of Chas and Dave out. He built little piles. *PARTEEEE* time. He did a line, passed Wade the snorter – up went a long line.

'Fuck and *fucketty-fuck.*'

Elvis grabbed the snorter, did the same. Dana next. Wade again. The stuff took hold. The joint spun, senses hyperspaced. Elvis got to his feet.

He needed a girl, *had* to have one.

The chisel was magic. The bluey effect brillo.

James's phone buzzed. He ignored it, felt in his pocket for another clog. He chased it with beer, went to the bar, pulled a bottle of Prosecco, poured a large glass.

The DJ started playing dropped Balearic sounds. Elvis to Dana and Wade: 'You ever been Ibiza? If not, you have to go.'

Wade shrugged. Dana to James: 'You got more clogs?'

James grinned, lobbed the pill over. She caught it, did the tablet. James lobbed one to Wade, he did it. James looked around for Elvis. Dana clocked him – she pointed at the mezzanine.

TWENTY

Moments later

James in coke/MDMA/egg heaven. Paradise flutters hit, eyes golf-balled.

It felt fucking ridiculous.

His phone went again.

He pulled it, hit answer.

'Good morning James.'

The voice – familiar – it took a moment to register – he got it – 'Frederick.'

'James.'

Here it is. This, right now.

'You're up early Frederick, if you have been to sleep at all.' He followed with a laugh – nervous – blitzed.

The laugh boomeranged back. 'I've been to sleep. A murder detective needs his shut-eye. Demands it.' Frederick talked slow, a near drawl. 'Even this one. Especially this one. We need to meet – there's been a problem overnight.'

Take a punt. Front it: 'This involve Lee, by any chance?'

'Correctamundo.' Frederick didn't pause. Cold sweats, they cut through the gear, the drug buzz flatlined.

Frederick knew he sent Lee to Elvis's.

Did Lee play him?

Major misjudgement if so.

Fatal.

Dana and Elvis watched. Let them.

'Go on.'

'It pains me, of course it does. But there you go. The fucking fuck-up was at Elvis's.'

'Doing?'

'That's the thing. He says doing me a favour. Didn't want to tell me because Elvis is my son, etcetera. Giving it that routine.'

'Okay.'

James waited.

'Lee says the favour he was doing me was to send Elvis a warning. He didn't want me to know because he's my son. You understand me?'

'The warning is? What?'

'That the little motherfucker is trying to turn me over. Elvis. My own son. I know this. I *knew* this. Lee *knew* I knew this. He thought rather than me have to deal with it he'd get involved. Do it for me. Intercede. Tell Elvis not to do it. Send a warning. Like I said.'

James paused. Compute: difficult. The drugs/Frederick on the fucking other end of the phone.

Play him for time. 'That's good of him.'

'You could say that. Or you could also say that Lee Palm is full of shit. Let me outline precisely why. Say, for instance, he's not doing it for me. Say, for instance, he's no longer doing it for me. Say, for even more instance, he is no longer working for me and is *fucking* with me.'

James played for more time. 'Two questions. Why is he doing it, then? And who is he doing it for?'

'That's good. You're out and messed up and still seeing the point. This is what I am going to find out. And you're going to help me. If, of course, that's okay?'

Sweats popped more. The shit-head played him – what is there? *Answer.*

'Sure.' Don't pause – show you know what's coming next. 'I'm at Wade's. His town place. Why are you not here? The Fredster's natural habitat. Porno quiff and enough blow to fuel a hurricane.'

Frederick chuckled. 'I'm entertaining as we speak. *Entertained.* I'll come get you. With Lee of course, once he finishes getting his cock sucked. The fucker was doing crack when I got there. I told him, "Keep some for me."' The chuckle. 'Now *we're* piping some peace. Finishing off.' Frederick didn't wait. 'I'm there in half an hour or I'm square.' That Frederick chort. 'Squarer than that son of mine.'

He hung up.

TWENTY

James looked at his Rolex – a fake – *très cool*. It showed 9.45.

He scanned the place – still going off. He made Dana. 'Where the fuck is Elvis?'

She pointed at the mezzanine again. 'Up there somewhere.'

'Fancy a drink?'

'Sure.'

'In a pub. In proper surroundings. This fucking place.'

'Shall I get Elvis?'

'Do what the fuck you like. The Griffin's open – let's go.'

Dana scoped the mezzanine, didn't see Elvis. The DJ dropped a disco number. 'I'll send him a text, the sleazeball.'

They walked to the elevator as the sounds kicked in an orchestra break.

They walked back through mock Waikiki. It still went off – they departed.

TWENTY-ONE

Moments later

They hung left down Leonard Street. Through snow to the corner. They made the pub – Dana pulled her phone and papped the Griffin sign. It was half covered in snow. She WhatsApped the image to Elvis, with a message: 'In here.'

They hit the bar. Dana said, 'Bloody Mary? I'm paying.'

James nodded.

Dana ordered doubles with celery, tabasco, salt and pepper. They took a table by the window. The snow still fell. The Griffin's windows were near whited out. James slurped his drink and his phone buzzed.

He *knew* who it was.

He answered.

That voice: 'Where are you?'

'In the Griffin, further down from Wade's.'

'See you in a moment.'

'I better come to you.' He closed a hand over the phone. 'I'm with a girl, a reporter.'

'The one from the press conference?'

James didn't ask how Frederick knew, why Frederick didn't ask if Elvis was there.

'That's the one. She's – she's with Elvis, if you know what I mean.'

Frederick hung up.

James put his phone back in his pocket. 'Got to go.'

'What?'

Here came Elvis.

'Tag team. You have company.'

'You coming back?'

James shrugged. He put his gloves on, high fived Elvis. 'Who knows.'

'You're going already?' Elvis said.

James nodded.

Elvis said, 'Okay.' To Dana: 'What's that – Bloody Mary? Let's have another.' He made the bar as James left.

TWENTY-TWO

Moments later

Leonard Street – the snow thick-flaked the vista. Like it would be deep drifts soon.

James rode drug tremors. He walked through the white in half wonder – substance-brave – ready to face Frederick.

He walked *past* the Range Rover. It was parked between Wade's and Home Bar. Snow near deluged windscreen, windows.

The driver and back passenger doors opened.

'JAMES!'

He heard his name, turned. Two men in black, hoods/mufflers covering their faces.

They motioned to him.

If this was a trap it was from a corny gangster film. He got in the back, one of the men sat next to him. The other hit the driver's seat.

'James.'

It's Frederick – sat behind James in the back row. James clocked another man – the passenger on the driver's side: it was Dazzler. The driver pulled his hood and muffler down – Sinbad. The man next to James pulled *his* hood, muffler down – Lee.

Frederick said, 'Take his mobile off him, pat him down. We don't need any clever moves.'

Dazzler held a hand out and James gave up his iPhone. He raised his arms and Dazzler reached and patted him down.

'Turn.'

James twisted, faced Frederick. He threw that matinee idol smile, got one back plus a Frederick wink. Dazzler finished patting him. 'He's okay.'

Frederick said, 'Turn back around.'

James did – the smile held.

Frederick said, 'Drive. Go by the pub – the Griffin.'

Sinbad put the Range Rover in first and inched through snow. Lee turned to James and winked. Frederick must have seen it – a double bluff, triple.

How many bluffs before any was the same as no bluff?

Showtime.

Sinbad in second gear – two minutes to reach the Griffin. He was careful not to slide the vehicle; to avoid getting stuck in snow.

He parked across from the boozer.

Its windows were snow-covered. A patch at the top clear – a view inside of Elvis and Dana at a table over Bloody Marys, pints of Guinness.

Elvis stood, walked out of view.

He reappeared by the jukebox.

Frederick chuckled. 'That's my boy.'

James and Lee laughed. Sinbad and Dazzler joined them.

Lee spoke for the first time. 'How you doing?'

James said, 'Never better.'

Frederick chorted. 'You seem more friendly than I remember. You two, I mean. Touching, very touching.'

No one spoke.

Then–

James: 'And?'

'You know what I'm saying. What my point is. *Here's* the point.'

Frederick pulled a Glock, pressed it to James's neck.

'You're going to hear this only once. Listen/don't listen. Your choice. Lee, my partner here, is in my son's pad in the early hours of this morning. The question is, what the fuck he's doing in there? The answer is, turning Elvis's place over. You hear me? My partner is doing all kinds of shit in there. He's on the pipe of peace but that's not the main thing. He's *in* the place is the main thing. The next question is, why: why is he in there, doing this stuff? That's my son's place.'

Sinbad and Dazzler watched space. Lee giggled – how blitzed was he? James shrugged. 'I take it you asked Lee. And didn't like his answer.'

'Sure.'

'Which is where I come in. I get it, don't worry.' James threw the grin. 'Well, what do you want me to say?'

Frederick brushed the gun across James's shoulders. He shivered. 'You're giving me E tingles.' It got laughs from Sinbad, Dazzler, Lee *and* Frederick.

Frederick – the Glock across his shoulders again.

James – 'Those clogs are the best garys you've had in a while. They Wade's?'

Frederick withdrew the gun. He pushed the piece against Lee's ear. 'More via Wade, but who's quibbling?'

'I can see how they fucked that girl up, her being an epileptic, the dipshit thicko piece of quiff.' James laughed, Frederick didn't.

He said, 'Lee's given me his version. About his being at Elvis's. What's yours?'

James laughed. It became a shrug. 'Mine? The truth? Before I get to that – what did he tell you? Lee, what did you say?'

Lee started to talk, James stopped him. '*Ssssh*. Don't worry. I *know* what you're going to say you said. I know what you are like. Just as I know what Frederick is like. And, not to leave these muppets out, I know precisely what Sinbad and Dazzler are like.'

Sinbad and Dazzler lunged at James. Frederick stopped them. James said, 'Calm down. Just calm the fuck down muppet boys.'

They calmed. They didn't look happy about doing it.

Frederick – the Glock on James. 'Cut the shit or you're over. Finito.'

'Okay,' said James. 'My version? The truth? The truth is I cooked it up with Lee. I have to be honest and say that I am just not sure about Elvis. You know what I mean. But he's your son, obviously. So what can I do? How can I come to you about it? Why did I go to Lee is the real question. Why the fuck not is the answer – my answer. Who else can I trust? Last night Elvis is playing at the Stars – my night there – then he's out getting fucking blitzed with me. It means he's out of action and I know exactly where he is. It means I know Lee can get into Elvis's pad and see if he's up to anything, you know what I mean.'

Frederick shook his head.

James shrugged. 'Look – I know he filmed me on Thursday night.

At Ziggy's. Going to the stash. So, I want to try and get hold of that. Destroy the file, the evidence. But I know I might not get it. You know what I mean? You know, be able to wipe it out completely even if Lee can find it at Elvis's, because if Elvis backed it up – clouded it, emailed it, memory-sticked it, whatever, then–

'But I really want to do is send a message. The message might be from me. Or from you. You know what I mean? How will he know exactly? I don't care. It plays better this way, for sure. I'm sure *you* can appreciate that, Frederick. A play of leaving shit open, make it a bit uncertain, confuse him. That's how you'd do it, right?'

Nailed it. What a show. The Fredster had to go for it. It was a performance he should admire.

It's a quasi-homage.

Frederick said, 'Lee, get out.'

He began to move. Frederick laughed. 'Hold it. You know what Lee, my soon-to-be-ex and deaded-up partner, told me? He didn't mention you once, James. Your name never came up when he told me what he was doing in Elvis's place.'

James nodded. He knew Lee would lie – lacked the smarts to hide behind the truth.

Lee said nothing. Sweat spotted his forehead. Finally: he *saw* what was about to occur.

Frederick said, 'Now you can get out.'

Lee fumbled with the door, stepped onto Leonard Street, hit thick snow.

Frederick fixed the Glock on him.

Frederick told Sinbad, 'Give James yours.' He reached under his seat. 'Lee said what he said. Made his statement – your turn.'

Sinbad held the gun. James took it. It wore a silencer – primed, ready. He stepped out of the Rover, the car drove off slowly.

It stopped after a few yards.

Snow fell. It whirled down.

Lee didn't try to run. He stumbled towards the Griffin. James followed. Snow hit them. Snow covered them quick. James raised Sinbad's piece to the side of Lee's head.

Here it is:

Showtime.

James said, 'Best lie is the lie that's the truth, Lee. Remember that, wherever the fuck you are about to go.'

He pulled the trigger. German gun – a Walther. *Niiiice.* A fire flare, Lee's brains, part of an ear splattered. They plugged snow.

Lee dropped to the snow; through snow that kept falling. He hit white-carpeted pavement. He made a soft thud. James fritzed at the sight. *Someone will wail for the death of Lee Palm.*

He raised the gun again. He crouched. Lee eyed him: James pointed the Walther carefully, pulled. Did Lee with a second bullet.

Lee went under. James knelt by him as snow fell on them. James unfurled a fist. Careful now. Lee's ichor was everywhere. Lee's ichor was vivid.

Crimson on white; blood confetti.

He haemorrhaged.

He kept on haemorrhaging.

He no longer eyed James.

He would be dead soon.

James placed the pistol in Lee's unfurled fist and stood up. He still wore his gloves. The snow near blinded. It masked CCTV. He walked across the street to the Rover, and tapped on the window.

Sinbad wound the window down.

'Can I have my phone back. *Please.*'

Frederick chorted. 'Of course – Dazzler.'

Dazzler handed it over. James said, 'See you.'

Frederick – still laughing – 'And I wouldn't want to be you.'

The Rover pulled away. James turned and walked towards the Griffin and made inside.

He laughed. It was the E, chisel. It was Frederick/Lee/the two muppets/*everything*-FUELLED.

He clocked Elvis at the bar, Dana dancing.

He made the bar.

James said, 'My shout. Bloody Marys all round. Three fat ones please.'

The drinks got fixed up. Elvis went to the jukey, and hit the best cheese he could find. A Swedish number named 'Strandbar' flooded the juicer.

Dana and Elvis – jigging.

James turned with the drinks, and joined them. A piano riff cut the place apart. A sense-tingler for this time in the a.m. James grabbed Dana and Elvis. They group-whooped. Bass hit the piano. Bass and piano pinballed off ceiling onto floor.

Elvis hit a disco track up next. It was titled 'Got My Heart Up'. It leapt into the pub. Elvis sang: 'Got my heart/you can too/*let's go.*'

Silliness.

Music.

More music.

Finally: they left the place. The snow fell. It piled high and dangerous. In drifts. The street scene was eerie. Changed: the Ditch was a foreign country, whited-out.

James looked for Lee. There was no Lee. Not any more. No crimson splatter. He was gone and buried, frozen, petrified.

Silent forever.

They said their goodbyes. They meant something. They walked away through the white streets.

Part Two

Beauty a Flower Unfolding

TWENTY-THREE

20 December, 10am

Frederick watched the feed.

He saw:

Camilla.

She examined the crack pipe. It was stained and crudely fashioned. It gave her chills – *blissful days, fried nights.*

Frederick read her look: if she had some she'd do some, right now. Cook it, toot it. *Do it.* It's been a long time, too long.

Too short.

She turned and saw pictures of Frederick.

She froze.

WHAT?

Three black and white photographs. Frederick head shots – actor glossies. They hung from the ceiling, above the crack paraphernalia. She gasped and sucked air.

She sat at the kitchen table.

What the fuck?

Whoever did it took care – string threaded through the corners of each shot so they hung down in place.

Frederick watched her mind-whirr:

Who did it?

Elvis? Because of her and Frederick? Her and Frederick were old news so it felt wrong.

Frederick? But why? He was *anti*-emotional, opposite of her. It wasn't his style.

Who then?

She clocked the rest of the kitchen now. The place turned over, ripped apart. Drawers thrown onto the floor. Plates and cups smashed in the sink. Pans all over the floor.

Crack paraphernalia by the cooker. Serving spoon, a sucked-out bottle of ammonia, ripped baggies and wraps, two porno mags – *Fiesta* and *Asian Babes*. Peg the vermin as a middle-aged square. Definitely not Frederick.

She walked into her bedroom. The feed picked her up. Frederick chorted: this fucking bird, James and his weird imagination: getting Lee to hang those pics.

Camilla scoped the bedroom. It was wrecked – bed tossed, ripped cushions, duvet and sheets in balls, clothes, shoes, underwear everywhere. The window wide open – air freezing. She closed it and walked out and entered the bathroom.

The feed picked her up.

The bathroom the same – in pieces.

She walked into Elvis's room. The feed picked her up. The same: wrecked. Elvis's bed was done over. His records and Technics decks smashed. His MacBook smashed.

Chills.

Frederick caught her look. Frederick knew her. More than Elvis knew. They talked, they connected. He knew the look she wore, her take on him.

It emoted this:

NOW it felt like Frederick, the break-in, the pics. *His capacity for cold rage.* Like when they were together and he was jealous of Elvis. Jealous of his own son. Jealous of him being her boyfriend. He cured that by having Camilla and wrecking Elvis. He cured it by taking everything he could. Numbing himself with pharmaceuticals and booze and boosting money and gear from the poor fucks he arrested.

She went back into the kitchen and sat down. Frederick watched and chorted.

The three glossies: hanging from the ceiling; James M was a crazy fuck. Frederick liked *that*.

Camilla mind-whirred: WHY???

She pulled her phone – before she dialled, Elvis walked through the door.

He said, 'Hi'. He saw the Frederick head shots, the kitchen wrecked, their place done over.

'What the fuck?'

Frederick watched. Wade did good – the porno fuck fixed the feed like a pro.

Frederick hunkered down for the show.

Elvis emoting:

Chills, sweats.

His mind raced.

Elvis sat down next to her. Camilla cried – he embraced her; hugged his ex. The girl he once loved like an idiot, some fever-sick kid. He *shushed, there there'd* her.

She broke from the embrace: 'Wow.'

'What?'

'You looked spangled.'

'I am.'

Try to compute.

Obvious: *about Frederick.*

Tangential: *but who…*

Camilla waited.

'I've been at Fabric, then out.'

'Where?'

'You wouldn't believe it. You would have loved it. Went to a wild party. I mean wild. You know Wade – at his place.'

'Chigwell?'

'His place here. I've mentioned it to you – near Old Street.'

'First time?'

He nodded and pointed at the damage. 'What the fuck happened?'

Starting to compute.

'That's what I'm trying to understand. You think it's – is it Frederick, your dad?'

React like it stuns, speak like it jars. 'Why would he do this? Why would he put up some mad photographs of himself? It's weird and he's no weirdo.'

'Who then?'

'That's the question. Fuck knows. Has to be for a reason, of course–'

More shivers, work angles: if not his dad but *about* his dad, then–

Camilla, an odd tone: 'Who were you with, when you were out?'

'Eh?' He played for time.

Camilla, catching it: '*Who* were you with?'

'Oh – Dana and James – James Maroon. You know James, he–'

'Dana?'

Elvis nodded, waited for her to explode.

Here it came. 'You and her now? YOU AND *HER?*'

'And James.' He was goosed – one long night. It maddened Camilla more. She had that look – feelings revived: why they didn't work. Why she practically begged Frederick into her bed, seduced the ageing fuckbag. What choice did his dad have: her harlot act went at him. When he was off his cake on coke, everything else.

'Who is James?'

'You know – James Maroon. You *do* know James. He certainly knows you. Or, of you.'

'Fuck him. What about you and Dana?'

'What?'

'Don't *what*. You told me enough times, when you used to fuck me that you thought of her.'

'That was when we were flying. You were on that pipe. Making me say it. Am I lying?'

'What's the difference? You're off your head or not – you start saying: "Dana, Dana, let me fuck you like I never fuck Camilla." *What do you think I'm going to think?*'

'I know what you were thinking because you told me. Told me to say it. And you said all the time, "I love it when you say that Elvino. *Love it.*"'

'I was off my head on rocks. You know what I'm saying *now.*'

'I suppose.'

He didn't care any more – she knew it.

He smiled, touched her hand – pulled James's Ray-Bans from his pocket and put them on her.

Smiling: 'Seductive.'

Camilla stared: like she'd explode again.

No – she howled, pointed at the Frederick glossies. 'What about those?' She pointed at the wrecked flat. 'What about this?'

Elvis looked round. 'Come on.'

He led her into his room and saw the wrecked MacBook and stopped.

'Okay.'

He *knew*. Cold chills now. He fritzed: a message to him; it's playing big time as Frederick.

Frederick chorted hard at what he watched. These two. His fucking son.

Camilla said, 'What?'

'The place has been done over in a bad way.'

'I know that. But what do you mean – you know something, don't you?'

Elvis shrugged. 'I know this is not a robbery – some druggie who needs a computer for a couple of hits. Otherwise my laptop wouldn't have been smashed to bits.'

Camilla nodded. 'The bastard did crack. I found it all, the pipe, ammonia, everything else – it's in the kitchen.'

She took off the Ray-Bans, put them on Elvis. He thumbs-upped and Rolodexed options.

He said: 'I'm shagged. The weekend is starting to catch up with me – what a weekend, ending with this weird shit. I need sleep.'

'You're going to sleep here after what's happened?'

Elvis shrugged. 'Is there any crack left?' It drew Frederick laughs, he pointed at the feed. 'That's more like it Elvino.'

Elvis aped piping a rock.

'Haha,' Camilla said. 'There *is* a but, however, from me. And it's this – what happened to the calorie-counting DJ Health Food act?'

'Haha.'

'Mr Clean and Serene.'

'He'll be back.'

'Yeah, right.'

Camilla laughed, Elvis too.

A vibe between them – good times, old times.

Very old. *Waaaayy* before she showed herself. *Waaaayy* before the Frederick shit. *Waaaayy* before HE cheated on her first.

She said, 'You're not worried about what's happened? Who did this? Which creep or fucking creeps?'

'Of course,' said Elvis. 'But it could be anyone, anyone with a grudge, say, against Frederick. Someone he's arrested, someone he's got sent down. A family member – wife, girlfriend, son, whatever. Anyway, I can't feel too fucking worried, can I? All the shit I've done, it's been a bender and a half. I'm emotion-free except the stupid feeling pills give you. I am ready for a long sleep.'

He cleared up his room the best he could, fashioned a bed on the floor. Once – he would tell her how horny he was; try to get her interested.

Not now.

He got down to his boxer shorts, ducked his head under the duvet. 'That is nice.'

Camilla giggled. 'You're still wearing those sunglasses.'

He popped his head out, pulled them off, gave her a wink, pointed at the wrecked room.

'To be continued. Goodnight, good morning, God bless.'

He winked again and shut his eyes.

Snow kept falling. Camilla closed the door behind her, Elvis snored and snoozed.

Frederick could not stop chorting.

Fucking Elvino.

TWENTY-FOUR

11.15am

Frederick was in the boozer. What a weekend. It required celebrating. It wasn't over yet. The Marie Davies press conference was squared away. Lee was dead. Shot in the street by one of his more serious threats. Both understood what occurred if anyone betrayed him. James Maroon further understood he was hocked to the hilt to the Fred.

Like he hadn't been already.

See how that played with his delusions of grandeur.

Darren and Sinbad were patsies for Marie. Though they didn't know it yet. Fall guys fingered by James, whose tab would keep rising until it wouldn't/couldn't rise any more.

Correct?

Correctamundo.

'I'll drink to that,' he said to the empty Setless Sun. The juicer ran deserted – it was old-style pub, reclaimed. It was just past eleven in the a.m. on a Sunday.

What a time to be in here. What a time to be alive.

Frederick raised his pint of pale to the pub and slurped. James was smart. He played it the way only he could. Show he knew Frederick knew all about Lee's raid on Elvis's pad. James now further knew Frederick chose James over Lee for all kinds of reasons. James might need time to work it out. The explanation was simple. Spell it out for the moron smarter than the usual moron but who remained in that class. James was more useful than deadbeat Lee who lost any moves he had a long time ago.

And when James worked *that* out–

One more thing James could/should/would calculate if he had half the brain he believed. *If James failed to go with the Fredster for the foreseeable he was next.* He needed to stop the coming-man-of-the-Ditch act.

165

Stick to coming on the tarts he pimped. If not, IT would not be long. The Ditch teemed candidates to fill a situation vacated by Maroon.

He *would* be next sometime in the future, of course. But this way the future was still the future rather than the present. The Lee thing blew up in his face. It was embarrassing. For James. As in a chort-fest every time you thought of it. And yet: there would be zilcho surprise if James came at him more than now. Like properly. Like he failed to learn a big lesson from the Lee farrago.

If so, fine.

If so, who would want it any other way?

He killed his beer. He made the same conclusion he made since a kid. It was natural-order stuff. If James got him fair is fair. Natural order is natural order. You have a run. You play it. You try and make it play more. And more. See where it takes you. Where it goes. You enjoy the ride. To the end. Or *the end*.

Frederick said, 'Clive – another.' The boozer filled up. Clive slid him a fresh pint of pale ale. He leaned on the bar and slurped. Lee was gone. God bless his soul. A new partner was required. Someone trustworthy. It might have been James if James wasn't James. At the station there was the young DC. Jefferson. He was near James's age. He'd been in line for a while. He did well with that goon Ricky and his see-through phone-mugging bull. He would be Frederick's new man on the job.

What he really needed, though, was a fresh lieutenant for the real stuff. Out here where goons dealt shit and had it taken off them for their own good. Where the jump and jive and jig occurred. Lee was down, Marie Davies was dead, James was back-footed – for the time being.

So a man of character was required. Someone who knew the moves and knew Frederick Street. Who knew never *ever* to try and pull the kind of stunt that did for Lee and nearly did for James.

Frederick looked at the clock over the bar. He pulled his phone and looked at the time on that.

He asked Clive, 'What time is it, Clive?'

Clive said, 'Twenty past eleven. There's a fucking clock above the bar in case you've never noticed, despite you basically residing here and owning the place.'

Frederick didn't hear it. Frederick turned to the boozer door, cocked a thumb and forefinger at it.

It swung open. A view of snow presented visible.

Frederick – hammy: 'Someone is required who is precisely like a Mr Wade Long Esquire. Porn entrepreneur, general mover and shaker around town. And, a loyal soldier.'

Wade entered the Setless.

It played corny – precisely how Frederick wanted.

Wade threw a beam. His smile lit the joint. He was accompanied by a young lady of a certain type. He looked like he was having the kind of weekend he was having.

'Howdy pardner,' Frederick said to Wade. Wade switched outfit. He was goosed from various narcotics. He wore cowboy hat, black silk shirt, tight denims and shit-kicker boots. He walked to the bar. He looked faintly ridiculous.

'Howdy,' said Wade. His squeeze was done to the nines. Uber-trashy. She ran crimson lipstick, bottle-blonde tresses. She was enhanced everywhere and wore it well. She was *young*.

'Frederick, this is Felicity. Felicity ChicFox.'

Frederick waved them to the seats by his. Wade placed his Stetson on the bar. Felicity extended a hand of false and manicured nails.

Frederick said, 'Very nice to meet you Felicity. Don't think I've had the pleasure–'

Felicity deep-throated a laugh. 'If you've seen *All The Pussies In The World And Mine* you have.' She paused. 'You *have* seen it?'

Frederick winked at her. At Wade. 'At some point, surely. Of course. Wade, good, no, *grand* to see you.'

Wade said. 'How was earlier?'

Frederick laughed. 'Like a dream. A hilarious post-show show too. That feed of yours – big thanks. Felicity, what's your poison, darling?'

This bird, chic. That name. *Being with Wade here: she's vibing Wade protégé.* Get the round in and hit the Gents. Refresh les passages de las nasal.

'Pina colada, please.' Felicity locked eyes with Frederick. That's good. That's a fine start.

She drew looks from a group further along the bar. Wade too. That hardly surprised – considering today's ridiculous fucking get-up.

Frederick shot the group a look that shut them up. *His* suit jarred. It vibed out of place – anti-hip Hoxton.

'Pina colada it is, sweetie. Wade?'

'The usual.'

Frederick ordered another ale, Wade's Black Russian, Felicity's drink, and headed for the Gents. He stood in the urinals at the mirror. He spooned showbiz up both nostrils. It felt like alpine air. It hit his system near instant. The place went Walt Disney. He Daffy-the-fuck-Ducked. Senses spasticked, colours optimumed. He felt it. He felt it all. He *cognated*. There was meaning in everything. Leaving the pisser felt like a victory. He grooved on the ridiculousness of it feeling like this.

IT FELT TREMENDOUS.

He made the bar. The place sparkled, he sparkled. Felicity FuckChick or whatever her name was sparkled. Even Wade sparkled in that stupendously ridiculous get-up.

Wade clocked him: 'You've got platinum? Thought it was done.'

'That stuff is never gone. You know that.'

'Come on then, saddle me up!'

Frederick pulled the bag and palmed it Wade and winked at Felicity.

'Thanks,' Wade said, and headed for the Gents. Frederick was ready to move on Felicity. He felt tremendous. His eyes were ridiculous. Out of control. He couldn't stop scoping those enhanced tits. That back end. Her dyed-blonde barnet.

Felicity said, 'You seem a platinum type of man.' It was corny. It was cheesy. He didn't give a fuck.

'Platinum-plated baby,' he said. That was cheese and the gang. Cheeseburgers R Us. He rode spritzes, fritzed. Arrests he made. Deals he ripped off. The patter, the chat, the bantz. His general fucking everyday modus operandi. It orgied self-love. Self-aggrandisement.

Self-well-being. It made him feel tickety-boo. Who the fuck said self-ishness was selfish?

The selfish fuck.

He was ready to move on Felicity ChickFuck. But: fucking Wade. Here he came. Too soon – bowling out of the Gents. That shit-head was knee-deep in porno clunge every day of his life. He should step the shit away from *this* portion.

Wade said, 'Fresh drinks it is.'

Wade fritzed coke-boost. His grin went manic, disfigured his features. 'That P is tremendous. Never fails to hit the spot.'

He ordered up and paid, handed Felicity her pina colada, Frederick his pint, slurped his Black Russian.

Frederick – riding irritation jags. They gripped/took over. 'You're welcome to your drink Wade. You know that. And you're welcome to do as much platinum as you can fit up your wide and elongated nostrils. You know that – we've certainly done some nights and tarts on that stuff – pardon me, won't you Felicity?'

She shrugged.

'But Jesus, Wade, you are *not* welcome to do that prime shite then rush back just as I am getting to know Felicity. I *know* you *know* what I *mean*.'

Wade grinned – it didn't help Frederick's mood. 'Don't mind me. Felicity's been dying to meet you. I've told her all about you. All about Frederick Street, high-flying Met detective. A man connected in high places.'

Frederick felt P jags – a dip in the constitution – in the way he felt about everything. He said, 'I hope you haven't told Felicity *everything*, Wade.'

Wade chuckled – he hit up on the P ride, Frederick chugged down. The dipshit attempted to rule the roost, in *his* boozer. It wasn't particularly clever. Not when this batch of sniff could go the other way. *Was* going the other way – performing a U-turn of seismic proportions. The P was the P. It meant superstar highs, plunges into irate territory. And a circumstance like this. Being roosted by some fucker who needed treading on – the gnawing needed a release. That chainsaw urge to do something to someone. It was powerful, potent. *It ruled.*

Alternative: stick a smile on, make the Gents, do more P. Return like the guns of Navarone. Sink more ale. And hope this ire over a porno tart would evaporate. An ire caused by Wade Long in his Mickey Mouse Stetson.

Go for it. 'Wade, the P please.' Wade palmed it – he was lost in oblivion. Frederick slurped more ale and caught another notion.

He said, 'Felicity, do you fancy some of the highest-grade blow you will ever have had in your youthful existence?'

Don't wait for the reply – walk to the Gents and hear her heels rattle across the Setless floor. Turn and thumbs-up Wade, who's guffawing at the bar.

That's Wade's strength. He never gets ruffled. Unlike Lee, who panicked goon-style.

Inside the Gents – Frederick threw an expression that told punters to get out. They scarpered quicksville, grabbed looks at Felicity as they did. The urinals were thirty years behind the rest of the pub – stuck in Woodbines/old-man age – sepiaville, Frederick approved *this*. The rest of the Setless Sun had that reclaimed faux chic shit going on – he approved *that*: move with the times.

'You know those people?' Felicity said – tipsy, already.

Frederick laughed. 'Not particularly. I'm here a lot, it's my local, they may know my face. You understand me?'

'Sure.'

He opened the bag of chisel and laid it on his hand. He pointed inside his jacket. Felicity giggled, pulled the spoon out. She dipped it in the bag and did her left nostril, then her right.

Frederick took the spoon. Felicity closed her eyes – ride that platinum-plated pleasure. Frederick did a generous portion and was back where he belonged: in coke-land, where the P ruled, a sense fantasia, no words required.

No words as he leaned forward.

As Felicity leaned forward.

As they kissed.

As bliss moved through them. Protons stringed. It held a second, maybe two. Then, Frederick pulled away. He kept his discipline. Kept Felicity ChicFox hot for it.

He took two more hits of P. She did the same. He allowed one more smooch, pointed at the door, departed for the bar.

He heard her heels: following like the faithful kitten she already was.

TWENTY-FIVE

12.14am

Wade ordered up more refreshments. Frederick, floating: 'We should chat business.'

Wade clocked Felicity hanging from Frederick. He said, 'Of course, that's why I'm here so early in the a.m. on a Sunday. After entertaining your boy.'

A wink.

Frederick: 'It's gone midday but the point is taken. Cheers.'

They drank, Wade went for a refuel. The afternoon DJ set up. Frederick approved him – Frederick revived house music in the Setless – that sound he grooved on for years. The DJ knew Sunday afternoon was packed out with battered punters out on the re-batter. They wanted soothers/warmers. Sweet Balearic vibes. Sounds to float away on – get oh so cosmic, oh so off it again to.

'Felicity – Wade and I have to talk business, so could you give us a few minutes please darling.'

It was an order – Felicity took her pina colada, headed for the soft seats.

Frederick watched her. 'Okay,' he adjusted Wade's brim. It fell over his eyes: scratch ridiculous, he dressed *ludicrous*. 'As I said, that thing went well – as good as you'd expect from the Fredster.' A wink, a laugh.

Wade – quiet. 'He dead?'

Frederick shrugged. 'What you think?'

'James, too?'

Frederick shrugged. 'May as well be. *Will* be. James Maroon is a moribund man limping.'

A Frederick laugh – the baby baritone. 'As soon as you call and tell me he's at your place partying I come and got him and he does Lee.'

'He left after we spoke.'

'Yeah, to the Griffin, down from you. With Elvis and Dana, the reporter tart.'

'No problems?'

'He knew it was him or Lee. Truth, though, is it was always Lee.'

'Maybe James knew *that*. You know he's not stupid – not *that* stupid.'

'True. Who cares? How was my lad?'

'Blitzed, having a good time. It was a surprise he was with James.'

'It was part of James's plan – get Lee to do his place when Elvis is with him. Elvis is misguided, and I'm understating the fucking size of the issue.'

'What you going to do about it?'

'That's the question.'

They drank, the Setless filled up. They were given space – the joint drew a mostly young crowd: the man in the suit vibed wrong, keep out of his way.

Wade said, 'What about James?'

'He'll take care of himself. He nearly did with this Lee bullshit. Elvis is the problem. He's at your studio yesterday. He spouts his plan to you. He is full of it. He's dense. He can't see I am going to find out, going to know. That you are playing him. It's not funny, it's a shame. How can he not know, how's he miss *that*?'

Wade nodded. 'He was with the tart – the journalist. Plotting away. Putting her in the picture. Thinking he was putting me in the picture.'

'Like she's making a difference.'

'When he talked the double-cross on you, the Ricky Me deal, I asked him what the endgame was, what he wanted out of it. I said to him, "You sure your dad's not playing you?" Double-bluffed him. You'd have liked it – and the girl came through. But, like she meant it. She said the same, about you already knowing maybe.'

Frederick said nothing – what's to say? Wade wiped drink from his tache. 'Why *are* you doing it? Going through with this?'

A Frederick laugh – loud – heads turned. 'You can't guess?'

The DJ started up. A first Yuletide Sunday tune. 'You *can* guess, of course. You *will* guess. Work it out. It's not hard.'

A melody filled the boozer – aural candy – a vibe-builder.

Wade – blank. The fucker would die in that mode.

Frederick, staring: 'Elvis is my son. That's what I'm telling you. He mention Camilla?'

'It came up.'

'Bet it did. He's let it go, he's not let it go. All he tells me when he sees me. The hack is an interesting piece of skirt. Dana whatever her name is. He banging her yet?'

'You know her?'

'She's a friend of Camilla's. I knew her name when we were messing about. James mentions her, you say her name before, it reminded me about her.'

He stopped. He listened: the DJ brought a fresh track in – a fat fiesta sound – feel the mood lifting.

Frederick said, 'Seeing her operate at the press conference I think I picked the wrong young bit. You can bet Elvis thought that too, a long time ago – knowing him, knowing Camilla. *She* is loco.'

Heads spin, lights dip – the booze and chisel taking hold – feels like jig time.

The feeling – long. Since the old days. Since London/Manchester/Blackburn. The first summer of smiley house lurve.

Frederick swayed in his seat. He moved a shoulder. Wade clocked it, heaved laughter. Revellers clocked it too. Frederick hardly moved. He cut serious shoulder dips. Wade howled and spat Black Russian on the bar. Felicity fixed on him.

Frederick gave zero fuckeroonies. Revellers rubbernecked – who *is* the old geezer? They caught a buzz, grooved on the suited/booted old-timer. It's Xmas, it's Yuletide, it's *that* time of the year.

The vibe spread – Frederick virus-ed the joint – the place going off. He remained on his seat, shoulder dips went pronounced, his eyes shone. In it: *his element*. Like old times. Coming up with the firm from south London, Camberwell. He jigged/shoulder-dipped.

It's a moment, fleeting.

He got bored, stopped – the boozer carried on.

Frederick whisper to Wade: 'James put a fucking cannon to Lee's head and pulled the trigger. POW!'

It drew Wade chorts, Frederick too. They went back years – *waaaay* back. Frederick Street. The Fredster. His rule: forget blow and tarts and grafting. *Stay on the Fred's right side.* For fuck's sake. A fraught existence – ran a who-knew-how-long life expectancy. Fuck it, the gig rocked while it lasted.

Wade, laughing hard: 'Where's Lee now?'

'Where do you think, Soho cowboy? Along from your place. By the Griffin. In the snow, I fucking suppose. Petrified. Han Solo in that *Star Wars* flick. Unless they've found him already, which is highly doubtful. Going to need a snow plough and Search and Rescue the way the white stuff's coming down.'

He slurped ale. Wade – a long imbibe; he half killed his Black Russian. 'How did it feel?'

Frederick, hooting: 'I will not even dignify that. Lee was Lee. I will say it was nice. How it went down. Beautiful – he fell right outside, they're *all* in the Griffin – James went back in there, Elvis, the hack tart. I took the chance, opportunity-fucking-banged. Spook them. Teach them a little something about how out of their depth they are.'

Frederick rapid-fired chorts. 'Wade, Wade, what can I say? It occurred gorgeous – like a Western in the snow. In your world, think high-end arthouse fucking porno.'

Wade blanked, raised his glass. Frederick: 'Which reminds me – what I've meant to ask you. You go hard-on for Yank-land so much, all the West Coast, beach-and-surf bullshit, why you never move there?'

Wade shrugged. 'A good fucking question Frederick. Here–' He leaned forward, palmed the bag of showbiz, pulled the spoon.

Frederick loaded up – Wade held the spoon to his right nostril – Frederick did it in one. Wade held the spoon to the other nostril – Frederick shoved more platinum in.

It was by the bar – anyone/everyone could see. Who cared: Detective Inspector Frederick Street gave zero flying Fs.

Frederick, with the spoon: 'One for joy, two for G-force lift-off – fucking Cape Canaveral here goes.'

He waved Felicity over, reloaded the spoon. 'I do have to enquire, Felicity ChickFuck–'

'It's ChicFox–'

He hooted. '*ChicFox*. What *is* your real name? C'mon – Chick-fucking-Fox *cannot* be it. And by the way Wade, if you dreamt up Felicity ChicFox as this lovely young damsel's stage moniker, think again. You can do far better than that. Or could, if you possessed any creativity, imagination.'

Wade goofed, Felicity flushed – platinum surged. 'I thought the name up – my real name's Felicity Baumgartner. Means tree gardener.'

'In German.'

'Yeah – I was bum, bottom, backside gardener all through school. I'm sure you can imagine.'

She laughed. Frederick said, 'I am indeed *not* surprised.'

'Can I garden your bum? Can I plant something in your arse? It never stopped for what felt like years.'

She laughed again – Frederick joined her.

Now – Felicity made a move. She swayed to the music. Fixed her eyes on Frederick. He read her easy.

Wade resumed business talk. 'What you going to do about Lee – who's going to be your new partner in filth?'

'That's all squared off – don't worry about it. A lovely young man will be assisting Detective Inspector Street in his various enquiries.'

'I'm sure he's up to it.' Wade laughed. 'He'd better be.'

Frederick grooved:

This is grand, operatic. It's cocaine-hyped, what a ride – why he did the stuff, came back for more and more. Showbiz and booze: what a chemical reaction *that* was. What else gives the same heebie-jeebies: solving a murder/ripping goons off.

It's related, HOLISTIC shit.

'Go on then,' said Wade. 'Spill the beans. Who is it? Your new partner in solving and doing crime.'

He laughed at his quip, Frederick ignored it. 'Like I said, a nice young man. Has a bright fucking future. A DC called Jefferson, Larry Jefferson. Green, but a soldier. Has a brain but doesn't realise it yet – I'm talking relatively, obviously. Which is where I come in – he reminds me of Elvino, but obviously lacks his fucking pretensions of grandeur. Larry loves the moolah and the fun involved obtaining it – you understand? He gets that it's *the life*. He gets it in a way Elvis never has.'

Wade got brave. 'How does *that* make you feel?'

'What?'

'Elvis – the way he is?'

Frederick threw Wade a filthy grin. 'We talked about this. Best word for him is, as I said, misguided. The reason I'm letting him set me up, not pulling the plug on it, is I am going to teach him the lesson he needs.'

Wade chewed on it. Wade said, 'More shit? I'll get the drinks.'

Wade ordered up. Frederick did more blow. He stuck more up Felicity's nose. He stuck more up Wade's.

The DJ changed sound. He spun a Frederick fave. It ran from his era. He laughed at the lyrics. The tune gave him shivers, chills: the good ones. He shitted around, mouthed words. He mugged like the Working Mens Club' crooners along Columbia Road.

He felt tremendous. Stupendous. Top of the world. He linked arms with Wade. He yelled: 'Felicity-fucking-ChickFuck get your gorgeous self here'.

Felicity took Frederick's free arm and they drove back and forward by the bar. The crowd parted – *everyone* sang the chorus. Frederick's crooner act – genuine. His pipes surprisingly honeyed. Punters caught it, raised glasses.

As the man and woman unisoned on the song: 'Take this time/see what you can do/sometimes only sometimes it may be only you.'

It was apt – made the kind of sense that made all sense cosmic.

The crowd ratcheted up. Yuletide hit pay dirt. Frederick grooved on himself: on self-well-being, self-ease, the absolute wonder of being *him*.

The tune played out. The DJ let it run down.

Fade to silence.

A pause.

It lasted *lonnnng*.

Then: Frederick, Wade, Felicity traded grins, had a moment. The Setless Sun had a moment.

The silence broke.

It *exploded*.

A joy cluster-fuck. Shouts, whoops, yells and cheers. As, *slowly*, the DJ brought the next tune. It's sweet agony. Seconds that last a lifetime.

The DJ raised the volume until the place lifted, expanded.

Frederick closed his eyes.

He flashed childhood; those late teen years:

The summer of love, warehouse parties, police chases, the firm. Ibiza, capers. Three decades of shit and giggles Rolodexed. He flashed it all.

And: the pub, now. The transient moment. How it felt. How it *should* be felt. His senses exploded. He surfed affirmation; a wave of *yes – YES*.

For the Fredster. The Big F. Lord Frederick of Street. For what Detective Inspector Frederick Street existed for.

THE WHY.

Always plot, anticipate. He noted the clock above the bar – it's gone 2pm.

He waved Wade over, ordered another round from Clive. 'This is what's going to happen. I'm going to tip off that journo bird, her TV station, whatever the fuck it is, she works for. Then mosey down to the Griffin. Acting on my own info, of course. See the action.'

Wade was near full blitzo. He still retained some sense. 'Why do that? There's no need to take a chance you don't need to. Come on.'

Frederick laughed. 'Too late for that shit. Just as importantly, Lee Palm's my fucking partner. *Was*. It'd look off, not Frederick Street's style, to not have some inkling my partner's been done in. You know what I'm saying? At the station, and on the street. Also, and this hardly fucking matters but you can have it anyway – I didn't pull the trigger did I? James did. Imagine how that shit-head feels.'

'What if he tries to turn it all on you?'

Frederick laughs: 'A ridiculous notion. Almost as ridiculous as him trying to do it. You know how much dirt is on him. There's the tart who died at his place, who double-dropped there *after* previously doing a pill at his night in Ziggy's. He *offed* Lee, like I just said, pulled the trigger. And he's joeyed for me for yonks. You want more? You know why Lee was at Elvis's? You were there with me before – setting the show up. You saw what James did. Come on, what you saying about it?'

Wade shook his head, vibed reluctant to have the convo. 'He had Lee there to get back the film Elvis shot of him on his phone. I know about the film because I told you this because Elvis fucking told me.'

'I mean the real reason – for James having Lee break in?'

Wade blanked. 'Spit it out.'

'His real move was actually to send me a message, you know what I mean? I couldn't quite work it out when we're in there before, you setting the cameras up. But I got to thinking about it properly on the way here. Having my son's pad done over means James is a threat, or he thinks he's a threat. Which is the same thing. It means he doesn't give a fuck about me. That's what I'm thinking.'

Wade double-taked, face-flushed. 'You're telling me this *now*? What took you so long?'

Frederick grinned. 'I didn't see it at first. I only worked it out before. On the way here. What James was really doing. He tried to make a statement. What a shit-head thicko. So now I've worked this out, he's in even deeper shit. If it comes down to him accusing me of anything – oh fucking dear. It will be carnage. He'll be decimated. Going up against me.'

Wade grinned. 'And Elvis – you still think he can be turned?'

Frederick shrugged. 'Anyone can any time.'

Wade's grin – wider. 'James goes down for Lee and the girl who died in his place. He *is* fucked.'

Frederick shrugged. 'Who knows? Point is he *could*.'

'I see it.'

'At the moment we're got two prime-os for Marie Davies. And guess what? They are actually the right people. The street goons who sold her the gear. Well, the pill at Ziggy's. The one that made her nearly snuff it. She recovered from that, poor bitch. Then takes another two at James's place. Thicko bitch. She's an epileptic so she lacked a few brain cells doing what she did.'

Wade shook his head. 'What a mess. James gave her the two that killed her?'

'Answer is almost definitely.'

'What about Lee? Because you know a killer of one of your boys is a far more fucked-up deal than a tart who it looks like – sounds like – basically killed herself.'

'Good question.' Frederick drank. 'James is, of course, an option. A fall back, at the moment. If he fucks up even more.'

'Who then?'

'There is one very tempting candidate.'

'Stop teasing.'

'A street shit-head you and I both know.'

'You mean Ricky? Really? It's not his style. Guns, killing someone, anyone – especially a cop. He's hardly even a mid-range operator.'

'No, though remember – he's the goon Elvis is using to try and get at me.'

Wade said, 'Motive? I don't see it. What's his reason?'

Frederick shrugged. 'Fucking hell – motive? *Motive*? It's a detail. The little shit sells smack as well as gak, who's going to miss him?'

'Can't argue.'

'No, you can't. However, you want backstory, the press will want backstory and his family certainly will. We've bust him in the past. Of course we have. How the fuck were you introduced to him? When he used to joey for you. And, I was round his place last week, not with Lee, with Jefferson, so there's a trail there. A path to Lee – the revenge shit.'

Wade blanked then brightened. 'Mistaken identity? He does Lee thinking he was you?'

'Whatever. Details. Dear Boy. I'm saying he's an option is all. There are others.'

'What about Lee breaking in to Elvis's place?'

'Plays perfect to the rogue-cop-out-of-control dark secrets/problems narrative. Wade, you need to chill the fuck out. It's the same as always this shit.'

Wade, brave: 'Tell me for once. One time. No dicking around. Why? Why do it – any of it? What's it for?'

'Really – that's your question? You should know far better. You *do* know far better. This is smoke-a-joint-and-look-at-the-stars teenage bull.'

'Fuck it.'

Frederick cracked a grin. Wade stayed brave. 'Come on. What's it for? You've had a great run. Why continue?'

'Continue what?'

'You know exactly what I am saying.'

Frederick shook his head. Being drawn into this shit.

'I know the answer. Don't worry about that. I want to hear *you* say it.'

Frederick's grin widened. 'Here's one for you: why don't *you* stop? You've had a good run.' He adopted a little-boy voice: 'What's it all for?'

'You don't get away with it like that. Not like *that*.'

It got Frederick laughs. 'Since it's you, fuck it. The answer's going to disappoint. To stop boredom. As simple as that. There's nothing worse than being bored. That is it.'

A blank Wade look. Frederick, grinning: 'I will drink to that. Cheers.' He raised his glass and slurped. Here came the next tune. It was a dirty bit of tackle. It got Frederick inspired. He did more P off the spoon. He re-gakked Wade. He half closed his eyes. He jigged, re-entered the kingdom of platinum heaven. He *tuned in* to the sounds bashing fuck out of the Setless Sun. The DJ slid in a bootlegged pop ditty. The sample was hacked off where the melody went syrupy. It filled Frederick's head. It filled the heads of everyone else in the joint. It was a headless hook. It came like it mutated every time. Every time they got down to boogie to it.

'*Fuck*,' said Frederick. He took in the mob around him. He sucked up excitement. His senses went wah-*WAH*! Those who never went out couldn't compute. Going out was anything anyone wanted it to be. There was no secret. This mystery ran simple. A bomb went off when the music started and the whole thing started *occurring*.

A voice boomed into the boozer, from the record the DJ fat-vinyled into the place. 'MOTHERFUCKERS HAVING A GOOD TIME?'

A sonorous timbre. It got inside Frederick. It got inside him. Made his heart a sound system about to smash his sense up.

A cheer emanated from the crowd. It raised hackles, sucked them all in. The Setless forgot/memory-wiped. It forgot this morning, last night, the day before. It had everyone on their feet.

It *had* everyone.

The cheer subsided. Another one replaced it. Realisation broke. There was a mob on the track to match the mob inside the Setless.

Here came that sonorous timbre. It posited: 'HOLD ON, HOLD ON, *HOLD ON: CAN YOU???*'

Like any doubt existed – ever. It ran over a beat that sent the Setless mob batshit.

The voice wouldn't stop. The voice was relentless. The voice said: 'HOLD ON, HOLD ON, *HOLD ON: CAN YOU???*'

Volume dialled up. The roar of the mob on the track got matched by the Setless mob.

'MOTHERFUCKERS YOU ARE MOTHERFUCKING MOTHERFUCKERS.'

A punter went rogue – fancied himself an iconoclast shit-head. 'THERE'S A LOT OF MOTHERFUCKING GOING ON, FUCK THAT AND GET ON WITH THE MUSIC'.

It didn't pop the vibe. The opposite: delirious whoops, applause.

As: 'MOTHERFUCKING MOTHERFUCKERS–' faded out.

The Setless went silent. The DJ controlled the place. He held it a second.

The second went *longggg*.

He broke it – dialled up sound. The track restarted. The voice informed the joint:

'I KNOW HOW MOTHERFUCKING MOTHERFUCK.'

The track revived. It zoomed into the room, hit senses, revellers went ballistic.

As the voice told them: 'YEAH THAT'S WHO'S MOTHER-FUCKING, MOTHERFUCKING, MOTHERFUCKING, MOTHERFUCKING, MOTHERFUCKING, *MOTHERFUCK-ING…*'

The beat ran riot. The beat terrorised. It *felt* wrong. Why wrong was *right*. Frederick revelled, buzzed on sensation overload. Like ripped-up skies hurtled through his eyes.

As that fucking voice said: 'I GOT TOLD NOT TO MOTHERFUCKING MOTHERFUCK BUT THAT AIN'T MOTHERFUCKING GOING TO OCCUR UNLESS I DECIDE IT AIN'T.'

Here it came.

A single note of piano. It dropped from the speakers into the boozer. It plink-plonked. It bounced across revellers' heads. It disappeared. It was replaced by another, another, *another*.

The place felt it. The place expanded. The place like the end of the world happened. That this was it, right now. And it made perfect sense.

The voice posited correct: nothing was going to occur unless everyone fucking wanted it to. They all ran their own personal film no one else would ever see.

Frederick raised two thumbs – climactic.

To Wade: 'I'll see you later. I'm stepping outside. Calling the hack tart.'

He waved a ta-ra to Felicity. She didn't see him, Wade thumbs-upped. Frederick made the door of the Setless, outside – onto the white-covered pavement.

Snow fall, no clouds, Night Time coming.

Let's see. Hotshot time.

TWENTY-SIX

1pm

He crossed Columbia Road and entered the Silent Assassin juicer. The place near deserted. A pool game in the saloon bar. Balls clacked, bull-shit bantz bounced. He ordered a pale ale, set his phone to anonymous and dialled Dana's number.

Senses jumped. Frederick fritzed – ride the buzz.

A few rings – her voice came on. Sounding tired. 'Yes, Dana Gabrielle.'

He rang off.

He supped ale, scoped the joint. Spoon-snouted more platinum. He pulled a pay-as-you-go blower from his suit jacket. He tapped a text into it. He chorted at his fried fingers shaking. Read Dana's number from his main phone, punched it into the pay-as-you-go, read the text through. 'Go to the Griffin, Leonard Street. Body in snow.'

He hit send, drained his pale ale in two bolts. He headed for the Gents and stopped instant. There – *surely not?* In the saloon bar, at the pool table, addressing a shot with that shit-eater hairdo.

It is. Richard 'Ricardo' 'Ricky Me' Cliff – how very fortunate.

Frederick mind-whirred quick, got this: let's stir the pot. Let him see the Fredster, see if he takes it back to James Maroon.

Frederick *half suspected* Ricky might be snitching to James on him. He looked them up – they're cousins – more pertinent – Ricky was a thicko goon who could be twisted any which way.

So, let's have some fun.

Frederick hit the saloon bar, kept his back to Ricky. He ordered a fresh pale ale. Spoke loud: 'A pint of Hootsville please.' Watched Ricky in the mirror above the bar.

Now, Ricky, clocking the old geezer at the bar. A double take – is that? – a look in the mirror – Frederick a split-second linger – let Ricky catch a half glimpse.

Frederick grabbed his pale ale and slow-walked out the saloon bar, away from Ricky.

He took his time, heard steps behind, kept walking, hit the Gents. He took a cubicle, closed the door – locked it – heard the Gents door open again and coughed loud:

I'm in here, Ricky.

Frederick pulled the pay-as-you-go apart and flushed the SIM card down the pan. Chucked the rest out the window. He pulled his actual phone and listened – yes, someone breathing, too quiet, *surely* listening.

He dialled Jefferson's number, started speaking – OVERLOUD: 'Yeah Larry, Frederick – yes, Frederick-fucking-Street, how many other dudes you know with a name like that. Shut up now, listen – get to Leonard Street, outside the Griffin boozer, as soon as possible. Move it – I've had a tip-off. It's showtime.'

Frederick hung up, killed a snigger. What a hoot – play Ricky, play James Moron, Elvis, play every shit-head goon-fuck who came to try and play him.

He paused, let go a long cough – a warning, get out now Ricky, don't be seen.

He heard feet on floor, the Gents door going – off went Ricky.

Frederick exited, went straight out into the snow – took a glimpse through the juicer window: BINGO, Ricky on the blower.

He had to be calling James.

TWENTY-SEVEN

3.14pm

James caught a full-frontal look from Home Bar, along from the Griffin. He spied from the third-floor window. It Cinemascoped the view. He knew the manager – the manager *knew* his girls. Ergo, Maroon Inc. was owed favours on an ongoing/non-negotiable basis.

James returned to the scene of the crime. HIS crime. FREDERICK'S crime. He liked how this played: *ADORED* IT. The goon shithead gets him to do Lee. Now *he* gets snooped on and snapped as he *pretends* to find Lee for the first time.

Ricky came through again – good work, cuz. Keep it up and you might have a future of some kind after all.

James watched as:

The snow stopped for what felt like only a moment. The sky still whited out.

Frederick pulled up next to another car across from the Griffin. He double-parked alongside.

Frederick – got out, waved someone inside the other car to get out.

Here he comes now – James settled in for the show.

TWENTY-SEVEN A

Frederick to Jefferson: 'This is grim.' He buzzed – a cocktail of cold air/what went down/near-overpowering narcotic system slosh.

The Leonard Street snowscape dazzled. He caught a Xmas good-will-to-all-men-women tingle.

Hotshot time. Let's see.

'Larry – let's go.'

Frederick crossed to snow drifts outside the Griffin. Jefferson followed.

Frederick started digging. It was cold. He was drug-numbed, insulated. He kept on digging, Jefferson the same. The backup from the station would arrive soon. The media when they got a sniff. Amusing if Dana missed the scoop of her life by arriving post-them.

The snow fell icy, swirly. The wind got up. It bit. Frederick ruminated. He chewed. Jesus: what a way to go, Lee. You might say a certain honour in it. Dignity. In the line of duty, that kind of bull. His family might not be too heartbroken. Once initial shock died. That was Lee and his family. That was Lee.

Would *he* go the same way? Fuck no/fuck yes. There's no different way to go.

'Shit.' Jefferson whispered.

'Him?'

Jefferson raised a clenched and frozen fist. A bloodied forearm. The fist clenched a pistol. The gun that killed him. The pistol put there by James, post-snuff.

'It better be him,' Jefferson said. 'I won't be happy getting frostbite for a Joe Public joey.' He laughed. Frederick poker-faced – in case they were watched. You couldn't be too careful.

He stood and went over to Jefferson, helped him dig. The snow was ice underneath. The two detectives used batons and handcuffs to chip at blood-grimed snow.

It took time.

Then: Lee's whole arm came free. It was his left. They tried to pry the rest of his body loose. Lee's head, still buried. Frederick felt for its shape in snow/ice.

He peered at the scene. At the whiteout and their unmarkeds near covered.

Frederick felt a body part come free – snow and ice fell away. It had to be Lee's head. He waved Jefferson on. They chopped and hammered. They battered away at ice with truncheons and fists now.

Something *was* loose.

Frederick waved Jefferson off and he continued. He saw Lee's hair stuck to his face. Frederick cradled his partner's head as it came away.

The expression on Lee's face: a petrified half grin. His eyes stared at Frederick as a flash-*FLASH* came through falling snow.

Frederick looked up to see Dana and a photographer. Dana saw the look on Lee's face. The hole in the side of his head. Caked and frozen blood around it. She turned away.

The snapper took more shots. Of Frederick and Lee. The flash popped and strobed through the snow. The gun in Lee's fist looked like it would never be released. A teddy bear, a cuddly toy – comfort for the grave.

There was the shot, the picture: right there.

TWENTY-EIGHT

3.33pm

Elvis heard his phone going. Again. Should have left it on silent. How to sleep the weekend away with that thing going off?

He rolled over but it went off. Again.

This better be good.

He picked up.

'Yes?'

'Elvis, Dana. You got Periscope?'

'What the – Dana?'

'Yeah. You listening?'

'You just woke me up.' He took a moment. 'I'm lying in my fucked-over bedroom in my fucked-over flat – when I said goodbye to you, I got back here and it's been done over. Been ransacked. Wait a minute, where are you?'

'Freezing outside the Griffin. Listen, Lee Palm – he's dead.'

Elvis sat up.

'What?'

'Killed. He's been found here with a gun in his hand like he did it to himself, but it stinks. Elvis, he's been murdered. I'm sure of it. It's where we were before. Right outside the Griffin. Fucking creepy.'

'Lee's my– that's my dad's partner.'

'I *know* that. Now get on Periscope and watch. I'm about to interview him live.'

'Who? Lee?'

'No. Fucking hell – your dad. Frederick.'

'On Periscope?'

'Yeah, I got a tip-off – sent to me before, which is also weird. Though once you start thinking about it, maybe not. I came down here straightaway, with a photographer. Your dad's willing to be interviewed live – he found the body, he found Lee. He was already

191

here. Before me. Weird again? Or a coincidence? I don't think so. I'm going to do it in his car, via Periscope – as long as my 4G holds up.'

Lee dead: outside the Griffin.

Dana right: weird, creepy. Plays eerie.

Make sense of it. Being at the Griffin with James. Drinking, dancing, gooning around. *Zoom:* James left. *Zoom:* James came back. There's a link. Has to be.

'Elvis?'

Tell her. 'Later, we work this out. Now, if my Wi-Fi isn't wrecked by the break-in I'm on Periscope to watch the fucking show.'

'Easiest way to do so is find the *Shoreditch Today* Twitter feed – the link's on there.'

'Okay.'

He hung up, rubbed his eyes. Saw the MacBook on the far side of the bedroom. It was smashed up. His iPhone wasn't. He opened Twitter and found the *Shoreditch Today* feed. The link embedded in the tweet. The tweet said, '@DanaG about to go live on Periscope with breaking news about the death of a Metropolitan Police detective on Leonard Street, Shoreditch.'

Elvis hit the link. It brought up a frozen screen.

Now, a frozen image of Frederick.

He emoted stunned.

Now the screen moved.

Now the screen had sound.

Frederick spoke:

'He was my partner for more than ten years. I have to be careful as, you saw for yourself, there was a gun in his hand. But I just don't believe he killed himself. Not Lee. So whoever did this, I want to be clear – I and my colleagues at Shoreditch Police Station and our colleagues in the wider Metropolitan Police Service will ensure we do everything that we can to bring Lee's murderer to justice. If, as I strongly believe, he was murdered.'

Dana, off-camera: 'I know this is particularly difficult for you, Detective Inspector Street, due to your closeness to Detective Constable Lee Palm and the shock of finding him here on Leonard Street, outside the Griffin pub. But when I arrived I found you just at the very moment when you found DC Palm. Discovered his body.

'You were actually holding him – his head, that is, as the rest of him was still buried under the snow, the snow that has been falling for the last few days solid, almost. And is still falling now.'

Elvis heard Dana grasp for words. The apt tone.

'Can you – can you confirm how he died? How your poor partner died? That it was murder as you seem to be indicating?'

Frederick paused and looked straight at the camera. Tears formed in his eyes. One popped, and ran down a cheek.

Elvis zoomed what Dana got at when they spoke. Frederick was behind Lee's death. He killed him, or had him killed.

Shit: see even more now.

Outside the Griffin.

A message? Sure.

To: who?

And: why?

The answer ran obvious. To him. From Frederick.

HIS DAD MUST KNOW WHAT HE PLANNED.

And: James. He left, he came back. Was he part of it? Did he play them all night at Fabric?

And: the break-in, the pictures of Frederick. Weird overload. Another message. To him, again?

SHIT.

On Periscope, Frederick spoke. His tone, like every word, stabbed. 'My colleague DC Jefferson and I, when we found Lee, noted what appears to be a gunshot wound in and around his left temple. I'm no doctor or pathologist so obviously this is one for our forensic department, but, yes, I would be surprised if what we have observed does not prove to be that of a gunshot wound that was not self-inflicted. As I said before, Lee was holding a gun but I cannot believe he has taken his own life.'

Dana said, 'May I ask, DI Street, what brought you here?'

Frederick nodded – emoted surprised down the camera lens. 'As I told you before – off-camera – a tip-off. I believe this is what brought you here, too?'

'Yes, that's right.'

'Because imagine my surprise when you appeared, not soon after our arrival. And before the arrival of the backup I called in – that is here now.'

He pointed off-camera. Dana swivelled her phone to show a full crime scene. Marked and unmarkeds. Uniforms and plain clothes. A taped-off area. A white tent over where Lee fell. Other TV crews and media positioned in the snow. A few passers-by glimpsed near the car window as the shot returned to Frederick.

Zoom: Elvis made Frederick the tip-off merchant for Dana. He caught a shiver. He caught a laugh.

His fucking dad.

Jesus.

Dana said, 'It's the work of a journalist, to get tip-offs.'

Frederick stared off-camera at her. Like *she* might be the one tipped *him* off. Like he accused her of knowing stuff.

Rank it as a back-footing play.

He said, 'Hmm–' And let it linger. Then, curt: 'Any more questions?'

'Sure. What's the motive here?'

'It is too early to say.'

'Is it linked at all to the death of Marie Davies? The young girl who died in the early hours of Friday morning in Whitechapel?'

Frederick shrugged. 'As I say, it's too early to know what the motive may be. But I would not rule anything in or out.'

'One more question. Could poor DC Palm have taken his own life? You seem sure he could not. Why is that?'

Frederick's expression changed: angry/righteous. 'You have no right to ask or even think that.'

He reached towards the camera – the feed went down.

Premeditated? One hundred per cent. Frederick's shtick. It all was – he's never *off*-camera.

Shivers. He just killed his partner. He didn't care. He's being *interviewed* having just killed his partner. He ran a thousand lies a minute.

He is one sick fuck.

He'll get it – what he deserved.

He *has* to.
When? More shivers. Elvis fritzed on the answer:
It could be a long time. Too long.
He'll wreck more people before then.
Have to move quick.
Before he brings more down.

TWENTY-NINE

21 December, 10.47am

The *Shoreditch Today* website splashed on its picture exclusive. It was picked up by the BBC, ITV, Sky News, the national press. Copious other media outlets.

It was syndication pay dirt for *ST* and award-winning fourth-estate nirvana for Dana. The picture *and* scoop of Lee's death/the interview with Frederick: bona fide hacksville career-defining stuff.

The picture showed 'DI Frederick Street cradling the head of his trusted colleague and friend, DC Lee Palm,' the caption read. Frederick's expression as snow fell on him. As he held Lee's dead and frozen head in his arms. A snapshot of dignified grief and defiance. The bleak snowscape of Leonard Street framing Frederick as London town's police hero. A protector of people. Moral arbiter. General good-guy paragon.

Why would it not?

Frederick and Jefferson in Shoreditch station on Shepherdess Walk. In the incident room. They looked, they stared. A bank of TV and computer screens mugged the image of Frederick and Lee on myriad media sites.

Frederick and Jefferson fixed on *Shoreditch Today*. 'Dana Gabrielle,' Frederick said. 'She's in it now – and I think she's smart enough to know, understand what it means.'

The incident room – open-plan. Uniforms and CID buzzed around. Detectives huddled and whispered – they wanted to catch the scum who did Lee. There would be no rest until they started a *lonnnng* sentence. A throw-away-the-key stretch.

Frederick and Jefferson sat over coffee and smoked-salmon bagels. They were deep into a powwow.

Frederick bit a bagel. He said, 'It's why I tipped her off, why she got the exclusive: confuse her, confuse Elvis. He's got her helping him – trying to pull me – *us* – down.'

He lowered his voice. 'It's why Lee had to go.' He laughed. 'One reason, anyway.'

Jefferson's eyes popped. It was news to him. Frederick put a hand on Jefferson's shoulder and squeezed. Stop him saying a single damn word as the chief walked by.

The chief waved them into his office. Frederick waited for this. He wanted the chance. He stood, motioned Jefferson to follow.

'I'll talk. Get it?'

Jefferson nodded, looked straight ahead.

THIRTY

Midday

They hit the office. Frederick sat in a chair by Detective Chief Super-intendent Eldrick Hover's desk.

Jefferson stood until the chief told him to sit. He took in the DCS's crib.

Eldrick was an Arsenal obsessive. He tricked the crib out with club scarves, black and white shots of Liam Brady, Bob Wilson and Dennis Bergkamp. Arsene Wenger – this in colour.

Frederick possessed zero interest in football. He thought again: the obsession showed the chief as small. *Small–time.*

'Okay,' Eldrick said. 'First up, Frederick, I'm sorry about Lee. A damn shame. I, personally, went back with him a long time.' A sigh. 'Moving swiftly on, like we have to when fucking this happens to one of our own – great work getting the tip-off to find him before some snowplough driver mashed Lee up trying to shift the avalanche out the way.'

The chief fixed on Frederick. 'Where did the info come from?'

'It was a tip-off, like it says in the report.' Frederick pointed to the document open on Eldrick's desk. 'It came from one of the street goons in the frame in the Marie Davies case – for supplying her fatal Ecstasy. Darren De La Salle. Known as Dazzler on the good streets of Hackney and around here and wherever else he struts his pathetic stuff. I told him, he knows anything he might be able to parlay a little. His eyes lit up. They love grassing each other up, these shit-heads.'

The chief grimaced. 'I can imagine. We now know it's not suicide for sure. The pathologist's report came back. So what your file doesn't say is motive. The motive to kill – kill Lee.'

The chief tapped Frederick's report. Like it was a newly discovered Pentagon Papers draft.

Eldrick looked at Frederick. 'Why was he gunned down on my

streets? Who the fuck kills a Met policeman? This is not Detroit. Shit, it's not Brixton. What kind of fuckwit does this?'

'It is Hackney sir,' Jefferson said. Eldrick stared at him.

Jefferson: 'Well, it's near. Quite near. Pretty near. I mean, Hackney Road's just up the road from Leonard Street, sir.'

'I know where Hackney is. And I know where Lee Palm was found dead on my streets, Detective Constable.'

Jefferson flushed. Eldrick pulled at his tie. He drank from the over-sized latte on his desk, tapped Frederick's report. 'Motive. Where's the motive? You telling me, Detective Inspector, it's not in here means you haven't come up with one yet. Or—'

Eldrick Hover palmed hands and waited.

'You got it chief—'

Eldrick breathed out, slurped latte. 'Go on.'

'According to De La Salle, Lee was up to his neck in street shit. Was on the take where he could. Ripping off dealers, scum he was arrest-ing, the whole thing. He'd done De La Salle many times, he claims, loads of other goons.'

Jefferson swooned at Frederick's patter. His front – catch the seam-less act with 110 per cent gold-plated bull.

'What – and you had no idea?' Eldrick – like he could laugh. Like he *wanted* to.

Frederick shrugged. 'I had a suspicion, but what was I going to do? Never saw anything, never had any real, actual proof.'

Eldrick killed an incredulous grin. 'You believe it? That Lee did *that*?'

Frederick shrugged again.

The chief grimaced. 'So – what? Lee gets a gun in his head from someone he's been ripping off?'

Frederick placed his palms in front of him, facing up. 'That's the theory,' he said.

'You never saw him do any of this Street?' Eldrick looked at Fred-erick. At Jefferson – he cut a quick headshake. *Too* quick. Frederick would have to tell him to relax – it's DCS Eldrick Hover, that's all.

The chief, returning to Frederick: 'You understand I have to ask? You have to answer?'

'Yes, sir.'

'The answer?'

'Like I said – no, of course not.' Frederick smiled. 'If I had he would have been stopped straightaway. You know that.'

Eldrick said, 'How long you work with him?'

'On and off, more than ten years.'

An Eldrick pause.

'What are you saying Jefferson? Again: you ever see Palm doing any of this shit?'

'No, sir.' The reply calmer this time.

'*No, sir.* Okay. Now this is to go no further. But I hear all kinds of shit. About all kinds of shit. You understand? All the police who come in and out of my station. Especially detectives. This is for you Jefferson – you being greener than the holy Emirates Stadium sward: being a Met detective is a special kind of thing, a special kind of privilege and it means rules can be massaged. But that's as far as it goes.'

Jefferson kept quiet. Eldrick nodded. 'You *do* understand?'

Jefferson: 'Yes, sir.'

'You won't hear that from me again.'

'Yes, sir.'

The chief sighed. 'Anyone in the frame for this Frederick? De La Salle fingering anyone?'

'Of course. The usual shit. A compadre of his – the other goon in the frame for Marie Davies, was with him peddling shit at Ziggy's the night she died. Sinbad Williams. A black boy as black as you, sir. Dazzler's a white dude. Williams was pulled in with De La Salle for the Davies thing.'

'Could he have done it?'

Frederick liked the question. He manoeuvred for it – played the chief like a fiddle. Ricky Me's a candidate, Sinbad's another. 'Is Williams stupid enough to kill one of ours? He may just be. Because that's what this is about, what you have to be – to do that to my partner. Do Lee like this. As you say, chief – anyone who does one of ours has never been in the same postcode as a brain cell.'

It squeezed a chuckle from Eldrick. 'Sinbad Williams know his compadre is fingering him for this?'

'Not yet.' Frederick shrugged. 'Then again, who knows with these shit-heads?'

'Witnesses?'

'Lee was killed outside the Griffin, a boozer on Leonard Street, just down from Great Eastern, corner of Ravey. It was open at the time. There were punters in there plus bar staff, as it says in the report. We'll interview them – see if they saw/heard anything. It was snowing heavily so who knows what visibility was like. Passers-by, too – we'll appeal for them. But, the same problem. As with surrounding buildings. Leonard Street is bar/hip boutique shitsville plus residential. Don't know for sure, but CCTV is probably fucked because of all the snow.'

The chief smiled. 'Right Street – leave the Palm dirt out of the report. But follow it up. This becomes: Lee was murdered because of a grudge, long-standing or otherwise, held by some shit-head due to a previous arrest – make it fit. As far as I'm concerned, only we have discussed what Lee may or may not have been doing on the side – that he may or may not have been dirty. It goes no further.'

Eldrick picked up a mini football tricked in Arsenal red and white. He lobbed it at Jefferson, who caught it. 'What do you say Detective Constable? We going to catch who killed our dear esteemed colleague?'

'Hope so, sir.'

'No hope about it. We will. You must.'

Jefferson placed the ball on Eldrick's desk. 'Yes, sir.'

The chief pointed behind him at the window. 'Out there they will want action yesterday. This is a shitstorm in a snowstorm though it looks like the snow might be finally stopping, thank fuck. Can't stand the stuff. This is a murder of a serving police officer and we know how that can go. The press will be crawling all over it, more than they are now, to see if we're going to come up with who did it. Street – time to call in favours with your friends in the media. I know you got the most.'

Eldrick smiled. 'Try and make this work for us. Sounds to me like De La Salle may be a player here. How do we know he isn't playing Sinbad Williams off on himself? We don't. So, keep an eye on him.'

'I hear you,' Frederick said. 'I'm seeing Leesa later about the press conference. And don't worry chief. We'll nail who killed Lee, whether it was Sinbad, De La Salle, both of them or whichever piece of scum did this. We've got the press conference later – the message will go out loud and clear then.'

He pointed out of the office. 'Jefferson – come on.'

Eldrick nodded, called after Jefferson, 'You're blond like Lee, which will comfort Frederick, but they are big shoes to fill Larry – being his new partner.'

The first time the chief used Larry. Jefferson flushed. 'Thanks, sir.'

THIRTY-ONE

12.13pm

They left Eldrick's office and made their desks. Jefferson stared at Frederick, dropped his voice.

'You – *you* did Lee?'

Frederick laughed. 'You heard Eldrick. Big shoes to fill.' He threw Jefferson an oversized wink.

The junior detective laughed. 'It doesn't bother me. What I'm wondering, if you don't mind the question, is *why* you did it?'

Frederick weighed Jefferson up – it sent wobbles through him. Jefferson said, 'I mean, I know it was necessary–' He lost his nerve. 'Fuck it – none of my business.'

Frederick gave him a break. He lowered his voice. 'Lee was a liability. A walking snitch waiting to happen. Had been for a while, a long while. Its long-winded, a bore – Lee's backstory is too involved, redundant to go into. Especially now. It is old news. *Histoire.* Enough to say, plenty of reasons for him to go, plenty of candidates lining up to do it.'

Frederick threw a grin. 'Put it this way – his family won't be heartbroken he's gone. And the chief – did Blondie sense DCS Eldrick Hover as being deeply bereft to have lost one of his finest?'

Jefferson – dumbstruck. He *hadn't* noticed. 'You mean–'

'I don't *mean* anything. It is what it is. What it always is. Come on Larry – you may be the Aryan dream blond bombshell the laydees all love. But: don't try that innocent/oblivious shit on me. It's weak and see-through. As redundant as Lee was. And look what happened to that poor fuck.'

Jefferson stunned, floundering. 'What do I do to make sure that what happened to Lee doesn't happen to me?'

Frederick's grin – wide. 'A good question. Work out your loyalties. You understand?'

'I think so.'

'It's not rocket science.'

Jefferson – a hollow laugh.

He should feel befuddled – the way this set up was Russian doll shit. Enigma-in-cocoon stuff. There *is* only the one way out, just like Lee.

Jefferson said, 'What next?'

Frederick shrugged, kept his voice low. 'Next is simple. We keep on keeping on. At it – starting with our friends in the media. Then we pull in Sinbad Williams again. We take a full statement from De La Salle. Make sure it says what it should.' A wink. 'With this, and Marie Davies, Sinbad's looking at a stretch. A long one. The beauty being he was there when Lee was smoked.'

'He was?'

'Sure.'

'I thought–'

'I do the thinking. So, listen – Sinbad *and* Dazzler were there when he was done. You see why that's good? Neat and very tidy? Both of them are already living in it up to here.' Frederick pointed to the ceiling. 'They've no clue if they're coming or going or both because they're all of it. The way I'm seeing it, Sinbad goes down for Lee *and* Marie Davies. That leaves Dazzler so grateful, so goddam relieved to have been spared twice. He and Sinbad know who really pulled the trigger on Lee. But they won't dare say much – as in *nothing* – about it. If they do, who will believe them? If they do, there's no need to guess what happens to them.'

Jefferson, wide-eyed. 'You mean you. Right? You *did* do Lee.'

A Frederick laugh. 'The chief was right – you are green. No, of course not. No heavy lifting for the Fredster.'

Jefferson dropped his voice. 'Who? That chav coked out his mind last week – what's his name? Ricky, Richard. Yeah – Richard Cliff?'

Frederick smiled. 'Not on this occasion. But I like the thinking – was mine at one point. He's useful at the moment. No, our trigger-happy pal on this occasion, The Man Who Shot Lee Palm, is James Maroon.'

Jefferson's eyes – into blink overdrive. He took time to process it. 'The dude whose place Marie Davies was found in?'

'Yeah.'

'So it *was* a revenge thing then? Maroon was into the same thing, selling shit, maybe doing it at his night, before Marie Davies died. If he's into the same shit as Lee was, it makes sense he'd want to do him.'

Frederick sniggered, kept it low. 'You see, even you believe it if I let you. You're warm Jeffo, but a little off.'

Jefferson nodded, waited.

Frederick said, 'It was a revenge thing – actually, more a payback thing, and there's a difference. But not for Lee stepping on Maroon's toes. No, for trying to step on mine. Maroon didn't want Lee dead. *I* did. And James did it for me for a very particular reason. I mean, he had no choice, obviously. But I mean *why* I wanted him to do it. Maroon put Lee up to breaking into my son's place. You've met Elvis, right?'

Jefferson nodded.

'Of course you have. Who hasn't, right? Lee Palm, my late weightlifting, gym and steroid-fuelled bunny, decided it would be a good idea to go ahead and take the instruction of James Maroon. Over me. Moron – that's Lee. *And* James. As in James *Moron.* I've no doubt James threatened to blackmail Lee if he didn't do it, if he wasn't already blackmailing him. So maybe he felt forced into doing over Elvis's place, that he had no choice.

'But what kind of reasoning is that? It was counterproductive and ultimately futile. Lee should have come to me. But *could have, should have*, could and should go with him to Allah.' Frederick howled. 'A plethora of gakked-up, gagging-for-it virgins await Lee, so it's not all bad for him.' More howls.

Jefferson said, 'Why did James get Lee to do your son's place?'

'Is the right question. This is where it gets complicated.' Frederick chuckled. 'Like it isn't already. Like it isn't complicated every new day.'

'You don't have to tell me.'

'I know that. But this is important, so concentrate on this. Ready? Take a deep breath. The street fly you just mentioned, Richard Cliff – Ricky Me: Elvis is going to use him as part of a plan to try and turn me over. You understand? As in expose me, get me arrested. Fuck me over.

'How? Like this – stand by for his master plan: Elvis came to me for help. *Pretending* that is. Said he needs to rip off a dealer he knows – Ricky Me. To get him out of some shit he's in, money he owes, etcetera. The detail's not important. The idea is, he sets up a deal with Ricky Me for a weight of coke. And I, as Her Majesty's police, bust Ricky. We boost the coke and Elvis gets a fat portion of it to sell and uses the proceeds to get himself out of the hole he's in. You following?'

Jefferson wide-eyed, nodding.

'Good. Really though, what my darling son is planning to do is, as I said, turn me over. Record and probably film it all, a film starring me as a corrupt and dirty Met pig, all as part of his wish to do me over.'

'Fucking hell,' Jefferson said. 'Why?'

Frederick sighed and nodded at a detective who passed the desk. 'It's a long story, it's a short one. The short version is he thinks his dad is some kind of moral bankrupt merchant.'

Jefferson blanked. Frederick hooted. He didn't keep it quiet – it drew stares from the room.

'You heard me correct. The lad is twenty-eight going on sixteen. His ideas are stuck in the sixth form. Just in case you're interested – morals don't exist, unless you want them to. They went out with the dinosaurs. The time I ever had any doubt, ever cared about this kind of bullshit, was a long time ago. You understand?'

Jefferson nodded. This he got.

Another Frederick laugh. More stares. He kept near whispering. 'Now, to be fair to him, there is some personal history there. Between us. Pretty personal. Father–son shit. But that's not your concern.'

Another Jefferson vacant nod.

'Do me a favour – get more coffee.'

Jefferson made the machine, brought black for Frederick, white for him.

'Thanks.' Frederick slurped java. 'Okay. James Moronic Maroon – he gets Lee doing my son's place. Now, what's the point if I don't find out about it? You see what I mean? He knows I'm finding out about it, one way or another – probably from Elvis. He tells me his place has been done over, that whoever did it hung these big black and white headshots of me from the ceiling and I click straightaway who–'

'Were there?' Jefferson – wide-eyed again.

'Sounds odd but it's kind of James's style. Go weird. But he wants the message to get through to me *after* Lee's been in and out of Elvis's.'

Frederick laughed. 'The clown didn't bargain for me finding out *during* the break-in.'

Jefferson, getting this: 'So you could get to him with no warning?'

Frederick nodded. 'I'm told about it happening as it's happening. When I hear about it, I know for sure now Maroon is trying to do me, is after me. But he doesn't know I know – *yet*. I call a few people, find out where Maroon is at that precise moment. I'm told he's out getting blitzed. With, guess who?'

Jefferson slurped coffee. 'Who?'

'Elvis. And – who else?' Frederick leaned back in his chair, and watched the room.

The place buzzed. Case electricity. This one a zinger and down to the Fredster: solve the murder. The cold-blooded, cowardly take down of an esteemed colleague, friend and family man.

It gave him chuckles. It gave him tingles. Being Met Police was underestimated – live it, feel it. A privilege some of Frederick's esteemed colleagues didn't comprehend/appreciate.

Simple to do: enjoy what you have and *know* it. If you don't, what's the point? It's what Lee never got. What Wade and the rest never will. Elvis *knows,* but has twisted it to suit that narrow view of the world.

'Jefferson – how long you need? I know you've got a brain, otherwise you wouldn't be a detective. Who else was James out with?'

'I don't know.'

'You know *something*. You're sitting in Shoreditch nick, as a detective, partnered with me. That means you know a hell of a lot more than most goons inside and outside of here.

'Come on – who else was Moron Maroon out with on Saturday night, as Lee was doing over Elvis's place? Think. This is all part of the case we're taking care of.'

Frederick's tone ordered Jefferson to guess. He said, 'Darren De La Salle?'

More Frederick chuckles. 'I like how you're thinking. But no – I'll tell you who else was out with Maroon and Elvis on Saturday night, the night before Lee got smoked by Maroon.'

Frederick paused, annoyed. The chief strode over, Jefferson stiffened, Frederick beamed.

Eldrick said, 'What time did you say the press thing is today?'

Frederick, irritated: 'I didn't chief. To the best of my recall.' He switched mood, changed up. 'Only jesting Eldrick. Can't remember what Leesa said.'

He looked at Jefferson. 'Did she email you about it?' He blanked – big surprise, the lad would have to lose this act.

'Wait a minute chief, I have it on my phone.' Frederick scrolled through emails, saw the message from Leesa Zapata.

He opened and read. 'She's saying 4pm and she wants to give me a briefing beforehand, it says here. Like I don't know what our idiot friends in the press are going to ask. *I* should be briefing Leesa-fucking-Zapata about being around six years old in the head and having near zero clue about how to do a job which is supposed to be about helping me and the rest of the detectives who do all the actual work around here. Who keep Leesa in a job. No police work, no press officers, no Leesa Zapata.'

Eldrick concurred. 'No murderers, thieving scum and goons: no police.'

'Exactamundo, chief.'

Hover about-turned, went back inside his office.

Frederick shrugged. 'Now, where was I before he so rudely interrupted us?'

Jefferson clocked Eldrick's door. 'Er – the chief came out and asked you when the press conference was and you were saying–'

'That's right. You were trying to guess and failing badly about who else was with Maroon and Elvis the night Lee did his place over. I'll tell you who – the reporter, the tart, this one. *Our* reporter.'

Frederick pointed to a screen showing *Shoreditch Today*. 'Dana Gabrielle. Like I said, how the fuck you think she got the exclusive?

You see, her being out with Moron that night is good, very good. As in, she is in on this fuckwit plan with Elvis. When I know all this, when I know James is out, I see a chance to teach them a lesson. Elvis primarily. I set up Lee's snuff. I bring De La Salle and Sinbad along. They were muscle, options.'

Jefferson – on autopilot, trying to take it in. Dana Gabrielle being fed the 'exclusive' by Frederick. 'Sure. You think Maroon's smart?'

'And?'

'How you know he doesn't have any dirt on you?'

'Like?'

'You know – evidence, the same kind he was chasing to get back from Elvis?'

Frederick ham-sighed. 'If you need any more help to see the picture, let me put it another way. What evidence can Maroon possibly have that's going to beat the fact he pulled the trigger on a respected police officer and detective who was my partner for ten years?'

Jefferson shrugged, took his time. 'I see that. I'm thinking – say he recorded you telling him to do it, then what about that?'

'*That's* what's concerning you? Maroon had his phone taken off him when he got in the car, of course. He was frisked, to make sure there weren't any surprises. There weren't. I would have been surprised if there were because I told you – he didn't know I knew about Lee doing Elvis's place. Remember?'

Jefferson nodded. 'You're right, stupid question. James is fucked for all the reasons you say – but we still have to watch him, right.'

Frederick nodded. 'Everyone has to be, always. He's no different. There's no end to this – remember that. It keeps going and going. Understand?'

Jefferson nodded. Frederick said, 'There was a time when I could not have imagined Lee going the way he did. Shows what I know. You may think the same now, but be careful. People change, don't realise and don't know why.'

Frederick eyed Jefferson. 'How long have we done jobs together?'

'Since when I started here. When Lee wasn't around – on leave or sick.'

'Two, three years?'

'Yeah.'

'When he was off sick, on holiday – you think that was chance? This place is crawling with detectives who'd want to partner up. I knew a bit about you and asked the chief for you. Understand what I'm saying?'

Jefferson nodded.

'Good,' said Frederick. He offered a hand – Jefferson dare not refuse, the time was gone. Jefferson stuck out his hand, Frederick cracked a smile.

He said, 'I'm off to see that schoolgirl Leesa Zapata. To be "briefed". Whatever the fuck that is.'

He left Jefferson at the desk. Frederick walked through the incident room and out the door. He brain-whirred – ran options and moves. It ran Leesa Zapata.

THIRTY-TWO

1.35pm

Frederick took stairs to the next floor. To Leesa's office. The head of media worked a small room – the door always half open.

Like now.

She sat at her desk. He knocked and entered and closed the door. Pulled a spoon, a fresh bag of platinum, leaned over and presented it to Leesa. She bent forward, he loaded up. She did the lot in one smooth, hungry snort.

Like she waited all day for it.

Frederick did the same. He clouted twice as much showbiz as Leesa. The air went light. The day shifted. Stuff whispered.

Leesa wore tan slacks, a cream-coloured blouse open at the neck. Her hair scraped back. Like she was about to administer a bollocking to a hack who misquoted her. Or did the firm over. Or both.

She pushed back her chair. 'You want to talk strategy?'

Frederick goofed. 'About?'

'The press conference.' Leesa's smile sassy. She was overqualified *and* perfect to run media ops for Shepherdess Walk.

'You know my attitude,' Frederick said.

Leesa shrugged, pursed her lips. It signalled concern. For him, for the trap the media might lay. 'Marie Davies, now Lee. They are bound to ask if the two are related.'

Frederick touched his nose. He caught two flakes of showbiz, tongue-dabbed them. He swigged water from a bottle on Leesa's desk.

He said, 'Fuck them. My partner's been fucking shot. They should show some respect.'

Leesa's expression said: *okay, then*. Frederick caught a vibe. The same one she usually gave off. She guessed what happened. She guessed Lee, she guessed Marie Davies. She never mentioned her

213

guesses. Like now – her references were oblique. The media *might* try and link Marie and Lee. Of course they would – it's brought up to signal she guessed what he did. *And*: that she understood him. Comprehended what he was about. Why he returned to her time after time.

That was it. They moved on. Leesa got on her heels. She walked her end of the desk to the other. She went on her knees, unzipped Frederick.

She started blowing him.

Sweet music. *Everything* was.

Fuck the chief, fuck no-brain Jefferson, fuck Lee, fuck James, Elvis, that tart reporter, everyone.

Fuck the rest of the world.

Leesa smiled and stood, dropped her slacks, knickers, leaned on the desk. Aimed her sweet derriere at Frederick. He took a moment. He savoured the moment.

The afternoon stood still. London was outside the room.

They were inside.

He clouted more platinum. He fed Leesa. She clouted more. They moved through platinum-fuelled moments until they finished. They laughed. They re-garbed.

She said, 'You're briefed now.' A laugh. Frederick caught it, kissed a finger and ran it over his lips.

She said: 'Be careful.'

'I will. Don't worry. See you.'

He left. Headed to another press conference. Another meet and greet with a bunch of dull-heads. The world was packed out with them. Dull was inexcusable. Dull was duller than dull.

THIRTY-THREE

2.30pm

Frederick flanked by the chief, Jefferson to his left, Leesa on his right.

He stared out at the town hall's main room – crammed and standing room only.

Just like for Marie Davies.

A scrum, a happening, a shitstorm. *Apparently.*

Frederick bored. On autopilot: get this waste-of-time ritual over. Quick.

He saw Dana Gabrielle on the front row talking to a black girl he didn't recognise.

She tried to catch his eye. It came off as transparent. Hi there, we have a special relationship. I have an IN because of finding you with your dead and murdered partner. And, yet. You don't know what I plan with your son. So, really? *I'm not with you.*

Comedienne.

Dana Gabrielle, ace reporter. Gloat over the Lee Palm scoop. Think about this: who gave you it? Who set you up? Do you know *who*? Even if you do, so what?

Play her. Play the dullard like the rest of the dullards in here. The dullards at the station. The dullards on the street. The dullards of Dullardsville, UK, The World.

Frederick caught her eye. He hooded one of *his* eyes with a hand. Like he went incognito, fifth columnist. He threw her a wink.

Dana caught it. She returned a smile. She winked. *She* tried to hide it. Keep her IN with DI Street a secret from her hack rivals.

Laughable.

Leesa tapped the microphone. Leesa coughed, said: 'Thank you to everybody for being here. First of all, a few words from Detective Chief Superintendent Eldrick Hover, whose jurisdiction is Hackney and who is based at Shoreditch Police Station on Shepherdess Walk.'

The chief waited a moment. He started speaking. 'This is a particularly sad and tragic day for the police force of Shoreditch, for the Metropolitan Police Service as a whole, for anyone who is right-thinking and, particularly and most importantly, for the family of Lee Palm. They have lost a father, a husband and a man who was the head of their household and who was loved and liked by everyone who came into contact with him.'

Frederick wondered how Eldrick didn't laugh. How *he* stopped from chorting.

Eldrick said, 'Our thoughts – all our thoughts – are with Lee's lovely wife, Priti, and their two sons, Peter and NickLaus. And they, like all of us, want what is right – to see justice done, justice served. Many, if not all of you, will have seen the image of Lee's colleague and friend, DI Frederick Street, who is sat here next to me, finding Lee murdered. Murdered in the snow on Leonard Street, a few hundred yards from here.'

Eldrick paused, played the sense of occasion. 'When Lee was found by DI Street he was clutching a gun. I can now confirm officially that while this was an attempt, a clumsy attempt, to make it appear as if Lee had taken his own life, this is not the case. The pathologist's report confirms the twin gunshots that killed Lee, which were administered to his head, came at an angle that would be close to impossible to achieve if done by himself. In other words, a second party, at least, was involved. A second party being the person who shot and murdered Lee.'

Eldrick held the room. Frederick caught a post-coke buzz, he tweaked for more. That shit was evil. That shit was the fucking shit.

The chief said, 'In cold blood – Lee Palm was shot in cold blood. This was a calculated and evil act. So be in no doubt, it is a crime we will solve, most definitely. And in doing so we will bring to justice whoever did it, whoever the second party was. The investigation will be led by DI Street together with DC Larry Jefferson, who is also sitting here with me today.'

Eldrick indicated Jefferson. He looked at Frederick. 'I'll pass you over now to DI Street, who will, after speaking, take questions. Thank you.'

Frederick jagged. The post-coke buzz faded. He was left parched. He jonesed for a pint and a fat gak re-up.

He licked dry lips. He said, 'Thank you, sir. As the chief says, I am more than happy to take questions after I have said a few words to you all. First off, I have to say that the murder of my dear friend and partner Lee – Lee Palm – is something we are all heartbroken about and, as the chief said, all of our thoughts are with Lee's wonderful wife, Priti, and his lovely two sons, NickLaus and Peter.'

A pause. It held the room. Frederick got it: this is a career highlight for some. Maybe the highlight of their whole life. Fucking hell. Get one: a *LIFE*.

He said, 'Now, as the chief also indicated, this is a murder enquiry. We are currently and actively pursuing lines of enquiries. But I would appeal to the public out there, watching this and reading about the murder of Lee, or learning of it via any other channel, whether that be social media or whatever, to get in touch if they think they may have something, anything, that could help bring to justice whoever killed him. This is a grave and serious matter and whoever did this is a danger to the public while they remain at large.'

Another pause. He held the room a beat longer. He fixed on this: leaving this place, kicking back, getting funky again. 'Okay then,' Frederick said. 'Questions please.'

Leesa said, 'If you could just state your organisation before asking your question that would be very helpful. There is a roving mike.'

Frederick smiled and winked at Leesa. He didn't try to hide it. The first poser came from a hack near the back.

He took the mike. He announced he was BBC. He said, 'Lenny Mann, BBC News. May I ask DI Street if any motive has been established yet?'

The question was good. It might have been a plant – the chance to lay out how this would roll.

Frederick paused. Like he had to think on it. 'Yes, as ever, when trying to solve any case, motive is of paramount importance,' he said. 'At the moment, we are viewing this as a street-level hit. There was nothing professional about how Lee was killed. He was shot dead in broad daylight, outside a pub, the Griffin, that, although it was early on Sunday morning, was open. There were people inside. There may have been people outside. In other words, potential witnesses. This is obviously one line of enquiry. Even if there ultimately prove to be none – witnesses, I mean – a professional would wish to minimise the chances of being seen. This leads us to believe that it is street-level.'

'And the motive?' Mann said.

Frederick shrugged. Play urbane, in *uber*-control. 'As I say, we are working on this, and one theory is that this was revenge, possibly, from someone, a criminal, Lee may have previously arrested. He was a fine detective and policeman and man and there are any number of criminals he helped bring to justice who could attest to that. And who would also hold a grudge. The kind that may – just may – move them to kill Lee to get some kind of sick revenge.'

The hack throng buzzed. They rode career nirvana excitement. Frederick's line on a possible motive meant a revenge cop-killer headline: HACK WET DREAM FRONT PAGE SPLASH PAY DIRT.

Leesa said, 'Next question please.'

The microphone went to Dana. 'Dana Gabrielle, *Shoreditch Today*/BuzzFeed,' she said. Frederick threw her a smile. She said, 'DI Street, is there any link between the murder of Detective Palm and the death of Marie Davies last week?'

Leesa looked at Frederick. Frederick thought on it, *pretended* to.

'Hello again Ms Gabrielle, and thanks for the question,' he said. 'As you know, Marie Davies died after taking two Ecstasy tablets – these so-called clogs – after having previously taken one of this same batch earlier that evening, last Thursday.'

Keep the picture blurry, as convoluted as possible.

'There may be a relationship, or something stronger, between the two. Lee was killed outside the Griffin pub on Leonard Street, just near here. Marie Davies died in an apartment on Boyd Street in Whitechapel, having earlier that night been at Ziggy's, which is on Hoxton Square. There is less than a mile and a half between all three. So there is certainly a similarity of locale. Beyond this, I wouldn't like to say anything more at the present moment. As the investigating force, we cannot afford to get into the realms of speculation. It is counterproductive and does nothing to help any investigation.'

Leesa pointed where the microphone should go to but Dana held onto it.

'One more question please. DI Street, I mention Marie Davies because you were questioning two men, Darren De La Salle and Sinbad Williams, about their potential involvement in her death. If you are saying this may have been a street-level murder, of Detective Lee Palm, are they also persons of interests for you – for his killing?'

Frederick leaned into Jefferson and placed a hand over his microphone and whispered. 'Just doing this for effect and affect. Muddying the picture for these shit-heads.'

Jefferson's ears burned.

Frederick paused, withdrew, returned to Jefferson's ear. 'That's her. The hack with the exclusive. The hotshot reporter. Thinking she's getting me thinking. Like none of this is choreographed. Like it is not all worked out before – it is boring how unimaginative she, this lot are.'

Frederick withdrew again, shaped a smile.

It was supposed to look pained: *caught on the hop.*

He sighed into the mike, sound audible around the room. 'I can say, Ms Gabrielle, that the two men you mention, who are persons of interest in the death of Marie Davies, are also of the same and similar status regarding Detective Lee Palm. However, there is no need for anybody, you, I, the public watching this, your colleagues in the media, to speculate about this. This is standard procedure.

'I just mentioned that, given the proximity of where Marie Davies and Detective Palm died, this may be a point of interest. Therefore, it is not a massive leap for Sinbad Williams and Darren De La Salle to also potentially be the same – if you follow this reasoning? But as I mentioned previously, there are many lines of enquiry for us to pursue, of which this is one.'

He finished with an understated smile. Threw in hints of bashful. As if embarrassed. *Ever so deferential.*

Dana said, 'Is there any progress in the Marie Davies case?'

Frederick caught it – she didn't buy his act. Clever tart. 'I don't mean to be unhelpful, Ms Gabrielle, but this is a press conference

regarding the murder of Detective Palm. It is not about the unfortunate death of Ms Davies.'

Frederick smiled. He made sure she heard his tone. 'I am *ever* so
sorry.'

Leesa waved the mike on again, got nowhere.

Dana resisted: 'I, of course, respect that,' she said. 'And it was on
that basis, the basis of today being about Detective Palm, I was asking.
But pardon me, my fault, I should have made myself clearer. Given
they may be persons of interest, Mr De La Salle and Mr Williams, is
there no concern, then, they won't try and abscond?'

Frederick laughed. It played like he was being patient. '"Abscond?"'
He looked at the chief, Jefferson and Leesa, came back to Dana.
'"Abscond"? What do you think this is, Ms Gabrielle? An episode of
Miss Marple? I'm sorry, but this is a little–' he fought to keep a straight
face. 'I am sorry, Ms Gabrielle. I understand you're doing your job but
there is no concern that will happen. The reason being that the police
cannot possibly keep constant, ongoing tabs on any person or persons of interest they come across during the many of hundreds, maybe
thousands, of investigations they do each year. I do hope you can see
that?'

It played as sound and correct because it was. It wiped the floor
with her. The room hubbubed – *move on, she's had her questions.*

Frederick cleared his throat, addressed the whole hall. 'Ms Gabrielle
does helpfully bring me on to the one other thing I wished to mention. And the reason I do so is it may help us catch the killer of Detective Palm, which is what we all want, and is directly related to his
discovery on Leonard Street on Sunday so requires clarifying.

'On Sunday afternoon I, personally, was given a tip-off that led me
to go to what proved the scene of the crime – where Lee was murdered. There is nothing particularly irregular in this but it is worth
pointing out that it does not occur all the time. Again, it is not always
normal practice to make this kind of information clear, publicly, as I
am doing now.'

He fixed on Dana. 'However, as Ms Gabrielle – along with her
photographer – found me there, outside the Griffin, just at the
moment I found poor Lee, it is only correct that this is clarified. The

picture of me finding Lee – *holding Lee* – that you have all seen in the media, was taken by the photographer, as I say, who was brought along by Ms Gabrielle. And the reason she was there at all, with a photographer, was because she also received a tip-off.

'Why is this important? Because it suggests whoever shot Lee dead wanted not only the police to find it out but also the media, to ensure maximum coverage. This is a pretty significant clue and so I say to the public, I appeal on behalf of Lee's family and the Metropolitan Police, be alert. If you know of anyone who has a fixation with the police and the media, shows a particular interest in this case, in what is the brutal killing of Lee, let us know. You can, always, speak anonymously. Always remember, please, that any little thing may help. Could be a vital clue.'

He paused, smiled out at the rows of gathered media. 'Now, any more questions?'

'Sure,' said Dana. 'I have one.'

Leesa – near furious. She glowered at Dana. Frederick humoured her, played the crowd.

'There is a surprise. You might want to think about not hogging the conference. This is not a one-on-one. I feel like I'm being interrogated. Remember who the good guy is here.'

Loud laughs from the room. A classic Fredster message to her/Elvis/James – this is taking the piss:

Remember who the good guy is here.

'My question is, DI Street, are you looking into who tipped you off?'

'Of course. That's what the police do, that's what any detective does.'

Frederick – faux cheesed off, feigning hurt pride, quasi-disbelief.

Dana – ready with her follow-up. 'In that case, why haven't you contacted me?'

He didn't skip a beat. DI Street was ready. And it *was* a good question, a slick move from her. He *admired* that.

He was ready, too. 'You Ms Gabrielle? You saying you tipped me off? Because if so, that is a serious matter.'

It played for time, back-footed her. 'That's not what I mean. And I think you know it,' Dana said.

Frederick smiled. He got the response he wanted. 'Well go on then, Ms Gabrielle. Since you seem to be full of ideas. Enlighten us all as to what you mean. Because I have to say, you've lost me.'

Dana flushed. The room guffawed. Frederick hushed the laughter, tapped the microphone. 'That's enough. Let Ms Gabrielle speak.'

Dana flushed more. Frederick showed her up – the throng didn't see it. She said, 'I mean, and I think you know this, why haven't you contacted *me* to ask *me* where *my* tip-off came from? I don't actually know, it was anonymous, as you say yours was. But I'm a little surprised you haven't contacted me.'

Frederick caught subtext: like she cooked it up with Elvis. This was the surprise at the Marie Davies press conference: that there were not more plays like this, dreamt up by them.

He said, 'I can maybe see why you've asked the question but I'm not sure it's appropriate for here and now. I will, however, answer it. And the answer is pretty simple. We will contact you, as a matter of course. I don't want to sound patronising but I hope you appreciate this is a fast-moving and complex investigation. Not everything can be done at once, straightaway or instantly. Again, and my apologies, there are all kinds of lines of enquiry we are following up.'

'Thank you.' Dana smiled, passed the microphone on. She fixed the smile on him: Frederick got the point. Frederick smiled back.

Game on.

More questions. Regulation stuff about DI Street. The hero cop found his colleague and friend murdered – *how did that feel?* There's a cop killer on the loose – *what are the police doing about it?* How common is revenge murder of a serving officer? Could it be terrorism? Probably not given circumstances but nothing ruled out at this stage. And back over ground Dana covered.

Frederick fielded most of the posers. The chief fielded a few. Jefferson got asked nothing.

Leesa called it to an end. Frederick, Jefferson and the chief left the top table, followed by Leesa.

Dana followed them with the black girl.

'DI Street, may I have a word?'

'You just had about ten thousand.'

Jefferson, Leesa, the chief corpsed. The laughter bounced off walls. Frederick kept walking, the black girl whipped out a mike, camera flashes flashed, TV cameras pointed, hacks closed in.

The black girl said, 'Shanique Mannan, *Shoreditch Today*.' Her cameraman appeared from the throng. He locked Shanique and Frederick in shot. Frederick kept walking. Shanique kept doorstepping him.

Shanique said, 'Can you confirm that while you have questioned Sinbad Williams and Darren De La Salle about Marie Davies you have not done so with James Maroon? Despite Marie Davies dying in James Maroon's flat.'

Frederick kept walking, started laughing. The cameraman caught it, the media pack too.

Flashes strobed – there's the shot.

Hold the front page: the Met's investigating detective laughs at reporter's question about his other investigation.

Jefferson and Eldrick followed. The media scrum followed. Frederick's laughs kept going long. He gaslighted Dana, the rest of the hack goons. Dana, Elvis: get used to it.

The fun starts here.

Leesa stopped Shanique and Dana – she couldn't get to the cameraman. 'You are being totally out of order. You had your chance to ask questions *and* this, as DI Street said, is a press conference about the murder of Detective Lee Palm, not Marie Davies.'

Shanique said, 'The conference is over, it is ended. We've moved on, you closed it down. Remember? So why not ask about Marie Davies and James Maroon? It's a free press.'

Leesa snorted. She shook her head and started walking, caught Frederick up.

'Shanique, leave this to me,' Dana said. 'Go and send the stuff back, we're headline news. Again! DI Street loses his shit with *Shoreditch Today*. Twice. Make sure you mention in your camera piece how Street laughed as he walked off, when you asked about Maroon. I'll be doing when I write it up. And get it over to BuzzFeed, too.'

She caught Leesa and Frederick at the door – Jefferson and the chief scooted off.

Frederick threw Dana a beam. She ignored him. Change-up: 'Leesa, can I have a word?'

'What?'

'Look, I'm sorry if you're upset, but can we go off-record?'

A Leesa snort. Frederick beamed more. 'Go on,' said Leesa.

'If DI Street won't say publicly, can you give me anything on James Maroon? Is he to be interviewed about Marie Davies? It seems a legitimate question. We're not the only ones wanting to know. Everyone does. I'm here for BuzzFeed too. And I know the BBC have been asking you, ITV, the national press, so why nothing on this?'

Leesa shrugged. 'I can say to you what I am saying to everyone else on- and off-rec. I cannot confirm, as in any ongoing case – investigation – who we have or have not interviewed. But I can assure you, anyone who is of interest will of course be interviewed.'

She looked at Frederick. He kept quiet – the beauty of silence, wind Dana up.

Leesa continued: 'If they have not already been interviewed. Obviously you know he – James Maroon – gave a statement at the time?'

Dana glowered. 'That's not what I'm talking about. I mean, on the same basis as Sinbad Williams and Darren De La Salle have been interviewed – questioned. You know what I mean.'

Leesa stifled a laugh. 'As I say, anyone who is of interest will of course be interviewed. Now, please excuse me.'

'Sure,' said Dana as Leesa opened the door for Frederick. 'I can excuse you. But can you excuse DI Street?'

Nothing from Leesa – she walked off. Frederick paused: 'No comment.' He double-thumbed her. He mouthed 'L-O-S-E-R.'

It was infantile, puerile. It made him laugh more.

Who gave a fuck who saw?

He left the town hall door swinging.

THIRTY-FOUR

5.30pm

FICTION! located two corners up from Hoxton Square. It was old-style pub rebranded as old-style pub. It had been called the Ring O'Bells. It featured a chic-distressed sign that showed the heads of Shakespeare, Hemingway and Dickens in triptych. Scribbling royalty, masters of the prose, kings of FICTION! Get it, understand, *comprende*? It located where Mundy and Hoxton Streets crossed. Ground-Zero real estate for the happening-hip. Its Googlemap flyer: *Cool, vibrant, on three floors with soft seating, roof terrace DJs, pizzas and burgers.*

Frederick and Jefferson took a wood-panelled booth. Frederick sipped pale ale, Jefferson a Kronen 1664. They looked out of place. Frederick couldn't give a hoot. He *always* jarred, non-sequitured. It was part of the fun.

Vanessa boosted through the stable mews-style door. Pussy fiend Jefferson went wide-eyed. The done-up piece of crumpet – who IS she?

Vanessa clocked and ignored them. She scooted straight to the bar.

'There she is. Looking as good as she did coked-up at Ricky's.'

'Yes Blondie. Keep your dick out of your hand if you can. No Viagra required, right? She's your kind of age, maybe *too* young. Maybe you wouldn't be up to it. Maybe one for the Fredster. You feel me, brother?'

A blank Jefferson look. 'That's your young cats' lingo, right? Your talk, chat, jive?'

'You would, I suppose – do her?'

'You don't even have to ask Larry. *Jeffy-O*. You have to admire a tart who goes straight for a slurp, not asking us, the Po-leese, the muscle, the *law*, what we might like. If we may be fucking thirsty, perchance?'

'Our drinks are nearly full.'

'Not the point Blondie. Now shut up because here Vanessa Compton comes.'

She took the seat next to Jefferson, across from Frederick. She raised her Bloody Mary. A celery stick stuck out. 'DI Street. I did not have you down as a Hoxton hipster kind of man.'

Jefferson spluttered a laugh into his '64. Frederick did the real thing, hooted. Vanessa smiled – it frosted Jefferson.

Frederick, smiling: 'You just don't know me do you Vanessa? Hip in all kinds of ways.' A wink. 'On which note, this is DC Larry Jefferson. You've met before, of course. My partner. Blondie, meet Vanessa – again.'

They shook hands. Jefferson's grip was tight. Vanessa said, 'Your *new* partner?'

Frederick studied her. 'You follow the news I see. Yes, tragically, sadly, my old one, Lee, is dead. A fine detective and finer man. But we move on. We *have* to move on. And on this note, what news do you have?'

She caught Jefferson staring at her. He blanched, Vanessa said: 'What's in it for me? You said last time I had no choice. I was thinking. I do and I don't. You know what I mean?'

She leaned back, threw Jefferson a wink. Frederick read it. 'I know what you think you mean, sure. The only way you win out of this is to know what is the best thing. The best thing for you to do. You understand me? I'm sure you do, you possess a brain. *I* know that.'

Vanessa laughed. Frederick said, 'Don't get me wrong. You want a kickback, no problem. A loyalty payment, it's fine, normal. It's business. I wouldn't have it any other way. It's part of the deal, the thing.'

'Okay.'

'Okay, then. So, what is that boyfriend of yours saying? Has he met Elvis yet? Had Elvis's plan outlined to him by the little shit?'

'I don't think so. He was going to meet him before, I think. A few weeks ago.' Vanessa sucked Bloody Mary. 'He might have talked by phone. Who knows?'

The answer was yes – from Ricky in the Audi, outside his pad, the day he got 'mugged'.

Frederick said, 'Yeah. This "plan" was supposed to happen before.

We put it together but – let's say it didn't feel right. So I cancelled. And I was proved right by this – what's actually behind it.'

'And now?' said Jefferson.

'We're here, aren't we?' Frederick eyed Vanessa. 'No contact then? What I want you to do is let me know as soon as there is. Make sure you find out. You have been keeping an eye on him?'

'Of course.'

He smiled. He watched FICTION! clientele. They got gradually blitzed. 'Make sure you keep doing so. I want details.' Frederick's eyes locked on her. 'The full breakdown of what's being planned. Elvis is going to tell me one thing, obviously, and plan another. I know he's been calling him. I want to know details. Be a good and clever Secret Squirrel. That is *your* job.'

Vanessa scowled. 'I have a question.'

'Shoot away.'

'If you know your son is trying to set you up, why are you going through with this at all?'

Frederick smiled at Jefferson, pointed at Vanessa. 'I know what it is now. Something different from when we've met before. You've had your hair done.'

'I may have added some highlights.'

'I like it,' Jefferson said. He near panted. 'They're kind of like – tresses. Golden.'

'Hark at the poet here. Move over Shakespeare, Hemingway and Dickens, there's a new man of the written stuff in town.'

Jefferson flushed. 'I didn't mean–'

'No,' Frederick said. 'Do not start apologising for your dexterous way with words. There is not enough individuality in this world. Never be scared about what you think and feel. You hear? And that goes for you, too, my dear. Now, your question. Jefferson, listen the fuck up to the poser young Vanessa has just put on the Fredster. It's the kind of question you or any self-respecting partner of mine should be asking. What the fuck is he doing this for? If he knows what his son, his own flesh and blood, is the fuck up to, what the fuck is *he* up to?

'Now I could say, what the fuck has this to do with you, Vanessa?

Ms Compton. Correct? It's between my son and I, end of. Or I could say, who gives a fuck why? Or close the subject, the question, down any other way. But no, I'm not going to do that. Why should I? Right? I'm not going to.'

He slurped ale, threw them a wink. 'Instead, I'm going to be clear and transparent. You never know, it may empower you to hear the reason. Which, by the way, is clear and simple. And, inspired by Jefferson, the bard here, I'll give you the explanation via an allegory which should offer some illumination.'

Another wink. 'Before though, how about refills? I'm parched.' Jefferson and Vanessa nodded. 'Off you go then Larry. I'll buy, but no way I'm approaching that bar.'

He handed Jefferson a fifty-pound note. 'Be quick now.'

Larry flushed and walked off. Frederick laughed at him, Vanessa rolled her eyes. 'I like your act but I'm wondering if it is an act.'

Frederick grinned. The girl was the latest in a long line of Frederick-studiers: Fredologists, Fredostines, Fredfans. It lightened the soul, made senses soar. Such interest and fascination.

He said, 'It's an act. It's not an act. Who gives a flying motherfuck? Correct?'

'If you want to be like that,' she said. 'Be like that.'

Frederick nodded, Jefferson returned with the drinks. 'Right on cue Larry. Ms Compton was opening up a Sigmund Freud routine.'

Jefferson, bleary-eyed. Like he bolted a sly shot or two at the bar. For courage. He said, 'She can do any routine on me any time.'

Frederick and Vanessa howled. Vanessa clocked Jefferson's height and Tarzan torso. He squeezed next to her, a look flashed across her features.

Frederick said, 'Now, if you're still interested, you asked why, if I know Elvis is trying to set me up, am I going through with it? Easy: I'm happy, content, sorted, as simple as that. I know what I want and I have it. Even better, though, even more important: I know what I am like, *who* I am, and like it.

'So, this thing with Elvis is part of that. First, do not write off the score I will be scoring from your wonderful boyfriend, Vanessa. A fat delivery of some half-decent product – I know where he sources it from.'

A wink. 'The Elvis element is thornier – I understand his, let's say, reservations, *issues* with the way his dad operates. But fuck that shit. You're a patsy, Blondie's a patsy, Elvino's a patsy and the Fredster's a patsy. Everybody's somebody's patsy in some way.'

Another wink. 'Elvis needs to understand. To *comprendo* the fuck out of it. I've tried every which other way. Now it's time to try some direct action, some direct recruitment. Let him see me working from the inside out. *On him.* Maybe he'll start seeing what's worth seeing. He lacks the smarts currently. To be *able* to see, he needs that window on the real world, on *himself,* shown to him by me. Sure, you're going to cod-analyse, you might be right, I *might* give you this: I wasn't around when he was a kid, fuck it, right, that's me. So here I am, now, being the dad to him he needs, going that extra yard he deserves, showing him I *do* love him and that I can see well beyond the shitty small horizons he's got now. I can see how he can really kick fuck out of life, of *existing*, by doing this, now. It's the hard option. Jesus, the easy, lazy choice is let him float along in his little immature, do-goody mindset.

'No way, no. Fuck *that*. I'm here to show him *what* waking each day is actually about, snap him out of the mind-numb mindset he's stuck in, realise what is actually out here–'

Vanessa, laughing: 'And if he doesn't – see it?'

Frederick, laughing: 'He *will* see it. Just a matter of time – timing. Like everything else. And if not, then–'

'*I* get it,' Jefferson said. '*I* see it.'

'Good. No need to wonder if the lady does. She gets it, correct?'

Vanessa shrugged. Frederick said, 'You've had your explanation, your one-on-one. Time to move on, get to the evening's real business. Listen very carefully now – to make this worth it, I mean really worth it, I want Ricky to up the amount of the shit. At the moment, Elvis is talking a quarter of a kilo. Let's raise that to a full one. Question is, has Ricky got a connection for that amount? My snitches say yes – but is he able to handle that amount, Vanessa?'

'That's a big increase from what's agreed,' Vanessa said. 'You sure?'

'Answer the question.'

'If he can get a quarter why not a full one?'

'You ever see him with that much?'

'Do I look like a set of scales?'

'That's a no then.'

'Who's saying no? My answer's the same. If he can get a quarter of a kilo then why would his man not trust him with the rest?'

Frederick smiled. 'Now we *are* in business. Which is where you come in. You have to persuade Ricky to do this. Up the weight. Do whatever it takes.'

'You don't think he'll go for it?'

'Do you?'

'You may be right. He lacks backbone.'

'I work on Elvis, this end. You work on Richard "Fuck Me Good Vanessa And I'll Do What You Want" Cliff.'

Jefferson giggled, Vanessa stared at Frederick. 'What's in it for me?'

Frederick snorted and caught a laugh. 'We back here? As I said – no need to repeat myself but I will. You will be rightly and justly rewarded for your help, diligence and persuasive powers. This is cooking up into a fine scheme and your pivotal role will be recognised.'

Vanessa said, 'I'd rather talk numbers. You pull this off, you're going to be considerably richer.'

Frederick leaned back. His voice went near quiet. 'May I ask you to shut the fuck up? For your own good. I'd say you had some front for a teenager but we already knew that by way you're packing a strap-on from behind up your boyfriend.'

Vanessa, demure. 'Now Frederick, what's the point in recruiting me if I can't do what you ask?'

'Meaning?'

'All I'm asking is a bit of precision on numbers, a kilo is worth a lot on the street. Worth even more to you I'm thinking.'

'How much?'

'Let's say its 40K for a kilo – a quarter of that.'

Frederick could not believe what she said. He looked at Jefferson.

He winked. This tart. 'Ten grand. For what, exactly, am I paying you this?'

'For what you're asking. Upping the deal by four hundred per cent. You just said it's supposed to be a quarter. You want it to be a kilo. I guarantee that for you, why not? Your suit's probably tailored. Shoes cost the best part of a thousand big ones. I guess, if you live round here, it will be in a skyline apartment in Wapping or Victoria Park – one of those mansions down there. You can afford it. So why not?'

Frederick hooted. '"Why not?" Did you not hear me suggest you shut up?'

'This sounds like a yes. Or – a let's negotiate, at least.'

'How does shut the fuck up sound like that?' Frederick hooted more – he couldn't help himself. Jefferson bolted booze – the Fredster was going to explode, the tart didn't know what she unleashed.

'Your tone of voice,' Vanessa said. 'Forget words, it's tone, how stuff is said.'

Frederick: 'A career as a psychoanalyst waits, this much is clear. Analyse this, Vanessa Cunty: you do what you're promising you can have five grand and be grateful, very grateful. Put it this way, what are you going to do if the deal is nothing to you but not being arrested and being done for all sorts of shit that will ruin your life before you hit twenty? Go to the police and complain?' He fat-winked them both, took his time. 'You understand me? I mean, you are seeing this with that perceptive fucking mind of yours?'

'Sure,' Vanessa said. 'Clear as daylight. That's a deal.'

'Alright then.'

The FICTION! DJ started up. A Frederick grin – hear those house music vibes – Vanessa and Jefferson returned it.

'More drinks,' Frederick said. 'Come on – let's have a few more. Fuck it. Think I know this tune, young Elvis, the little shit, plays it – one thing I can't fault, apart from him being my offspring of course, is his taste in music.'

THIRTY-FIVE

22 December, midday

They were downstairs at Shepherdess Walk, in Interview Room 2. Frederick and Jefferson eyeballed Sinbad Williams. They sat at a table. The three of them. There was regulation audio-recording gear. Two cameras for filming. A laptop closed on the table. Frederick was ready to start recording.

But, not yet.

He said, 'You're in the frame for Marie Davies. We all agree on that. Now, I have some shitty news for you. You're in the frame for Lee Palm, too. This is not your day Sinbad. It's very unlikely to be your next couple of decades.'

Sinbad in his normal rig – oversized strides, leather waistcoat, black pirate bandana, John Lennon shades. 'The frame for Lee Palm. Hoho. Merry Christmas. Who the fuck is he?'

Frederick grooved on this dipshit. He *loved* his redundant routine. 'It can be easy or hard, this. What do you want?'

Sinbad enjoyed his moment. 'I said, who the fuck is he?'

'You've met. Of that we can all be sure, too. Let me jog that memory of yours. My partner, my *former* partner. Last seen in the fucking East End snow. Two bullets in his head. Blood everywhere.'

Now he computed. 'The policeman? That dude who was in your car the other morning. *I'm* up for that. You must be fucking joking me. Was your friend did that. *Your* buddy.'

Frederick slammed the heels of his hands down hard on Sinbad's. This black b-boy, hip-hop nut, whatever he thought he shitting was: what a dickhead. Where did these dickheads come from?

'Let's get this clear,' said Frederick. 'You shut the fuck up in here. And listen. We talk. So, listen. We can put you at the scene. It's your prints on the weapon. If you remember? Was a hire car. You drove the wheels. Your prints are on the steering wheel, too. You were so out of your head you can't recall *any* of this?'

Jefferson repeated: 'We can put you at the scene. Because you *were* at the scene. There are prints, murder weapon, the whole show.'

Sinbad's jaw stuck. He tried to speak. Finally he said, 'At the scene?'

'Outside the pub where Lee was smoked.'

'Oh yeah.' He relaxed again. Leaned back in his chair. 'You got a group photo? A selfie? Me, you, the victim and the murderer? This will be good. You going to see that splashed all over Sky and the BBC and every other fucking news outlet like the heartbreaker of you and your dear, beloved partner you ordered shot through the head? Ho fucking ho.'

'Larry.'

Jefferson flipped open the laptop. He scoped the white-walled room. He took his time, à la Frederick. 'Sinbad, oh Sinbad. What would your mother say?' He winked at Frederick. 'Just give me a second here. Pardon me if the suspense is killing you. Here you go.'

Jefferson called up snapshots. The first picture showed Sinbad driving the sled. Snow fell. The Griffin lit up in the background. The second picture showed Sinbad with the gun James shot Lee with. *In his hand.* The angle like he brandished it. POINTED IT. At something or *someone* out of shot.

'Fuck me.'

Frederick chorted. 'That's correct Sinbad. Fuck you. Big time. You are *fucked.* You still have the gun don't you? I'm betting you haven't even thrown it away.'

Sinbad blurted. 'I haven't, no – was going to but not got to it yet.'

'Because you're too busy doing that pipe all the time.'

'If I do the pipe, so do you. So does fucking everyone. That's the way it goes – open your eyes.'

'Fuck me gaffer, it's the long-lost son of Aristotle.'

Sinbad shut up. He lasted around three seconds. 'Fuck me.' He repeated it. He saw them, the room, for the first time. What it was. Where he was. *Who* they were.

Frederick said, 'I'm going to start recording now. But I'm feeling generous. So a freebie. Some free fucking advice. Heed it or not, your

choice. Your big pal Dazzler grassed you up for this. We have a statement. It is a beauty of its kind. Verbose yet precise. Lucid yet complex. Most important: damning. Put it all together, the evidence we
have, the case is made. Even the Famous fucking Five could solve it.
What can you do? Sometimes it is just not your time. Jefferson, read
me Sinbad's record again, please. Refresh the memory a little.'

Jefferson smirked. 'Make yourself comfortable, boss, this may take
some time. A sheet longer than Hackney Road.'

'Not his record of peril. His record – his *bio*. CV.'

Sinbad laughed, Jefferson flushed. It drew Frederick laughs. *Funny,
hoot-fest*: not the Sinbad laughs, but Jefferson *not* laughing. *And flushing.*

'Jefferson, could you go any more beetroot? What the fuck is this?
Countryfile? How Red is my Beetroot? No wonder Sinbad Williams, cop
killer and ender of a young girl out-for-a-good-time lethal E supplier,
is chorting here in pen 2. You're the Blond Bombshell, the future of
the joint. And you're flushing in front of a suspect, *our* suspect. What
the fuck do you have to say for yourself?'

Frederick haw-hawwed. Sinbad full-out belly-laughed. Jefferson
flushed until colour drained.

Then – he perked.

He fixed on Frederick. He said, 'I tell you what I have to say for
myself boss – let it the fuck go. You know what I mean? Cut me some
slack for once.'

Jefferson stood up. He rated six feet and five inches. His Tarzan
torso strained at his button-down shirt. He packed meat-plate hands
and blond locks. He seethed – billboard beefcake closing in on rage.

Frederick liked it. He grooved on the Bombshell. Look at that! He
showed some stuff! 'Fuck me twice. I didn't think you had it in you.
Welcome to your future.'

Jefferson grinned and flushed. He saved face, received zero aggra-
vation from Frederick for raring up.

He sat down, across from Sinbad.

Frederick said, 'After this heartening development, let's have this
goon's life of heartache. Read the bio, Larry.'

Sinbad, laughing: 'You two? For real? Really? Who's Arthur, who's Martha? Fuck me.'

Jefferson brought a fist down on Sinbad's right hand. A cracking sound, Sinbad screamed.

Jefferson read from the sheet in front of him. 'Stephen Francis Williams, twenty-four, born Homerton Hospital, 10/3/91, attended Betty Layward Primary School, N16. Secondary school, The Urswick School, E9. Then, Hackney Community College, took music, dropped out after a year. Lived, still lives, with his mother, Desiree Josephine Williams.'

Frederick cracked a grin. 'Hold it there. Rewind to the college years. Or should I say, year.'

Frederick shrugged. 'What the fuck happened, Sinbad? What the fuck occurred? College, doing music. I'm having you down for a grime cat, steeped in his black music soul standards. Music shows creativity, a spark of *other*. A chance to break out, away from the dog-shit hovel and life that is growing up in Hackney in this cursed millennium. Of being *from there*. You feel me on this, don't you? You're the kind of cat that does. Loves that street jive. *Lives it.* And what the fuck happens? The pipe, the bitch, the STREET. Correctamundo? I think so. Larry, this is when Sinbad is how old?'

'Eighteen, gaffer. He left Hackney College sometime in 2009.'

Frederick fixed on the dipshit. He emoted nothing – Frederick grooved on *that*. 'The last year of the last decade. How poignant is that Larry? Sinbad, you would agree of course? You're eighteen, it is 2009 and you walk through and out the gates of that august institute known as Hackney Community College, alma mater of so many of our fine society's upstanding pillars. And: that is it. Your life as having a life ends. It is over. Finito. And: six years later it is here. We are here. Where we've always been. You are there, in the seat, the electric chair. And you are fucked. Just like you've always been. You following this? You following me?'

Sinbad nodded, the tough-guy stare returned.

Frederick nodded. 'This is where I come in. With the advice, another freebie. It's the kind of man I am. The *kind* kind of man DI Frederick Street exists as. Who knows what a cop killer gets these days, in these times? Exactly, *precisely* I mean. But you can guess. The fucking terrorists killing everyone everywhere – the last thing needed is someone smoking a police, a good policeman who is one of the very people on the front line. One of the brave few actually trying to fight the fuckers. Who is most in peril from Isis, the rest of that scum.'

Frederick fixed harder on Sinbad. 'Here's the thing. I'm going to hit the record button very soon – in a moment. I suggest you start thinking about what role Dazzler had in this. How he was the brains. The brains with maybe a grudge against Detective Constable Lee Palm. You understand me? How it is actually *his* weapon, *his* plot, *his* scheme. The same as goes with Marie Davies, God rest her soul. Muddy the waters. Make them as opaque as you fucking can.'

Sinbad said nothing. Frederick said, 'You understand me? I mean really comprehend this?'

Sinbad stuck in tough-guy mode. He waited. Frederick waited. Sinbad blanked.

Now, he nodded.

Now, he said: 'Yes'.

Frederick smiled. He hit the record button. He and Jefferson started taking the statement of Sinbad Williams, twenty-four, in the case of the shooting, the murder, of Detective Constable Lee Palm on Leonard Street on 20 December, 2015.

Frederick closed holes.

THIRTY-FIVE A

2.19pm

Time to close another. He walked out the station into light snow into a coming dark sky. He clutched a Styrofoam cup of java. He dialled Dipshit Central and Goon Residential.

The blower got answered. 'Ricky.'

'Fred– *Frederick?*'

'Don't sound so surprised. It gives the game away instant you're not being straight with me.'

Ricky drew a breath. And another. 'I – I am. Of course I–'

'Now you're fucking stuttering. No wonder you never move up from remedial lowlife street school and hit the Ivy League. Which is why I'm calling. I've just been working. Working damn hard, as per.'

Frederick faux stifled a chort. He over-loud slurped java. Get in this fuck's face. Give him the shits.

'Now listen, I've just had to put some dumb fuck right about the murder of that poor epileptic who couldn't handle her pills and bought the farm fucking wholesale. He's going down for a stretch, a long one, it looks like, the poor bastard.

'I'm thinking – I'm *knowing* it could be you if you don't remember who the fuck you're working for. You don't want that to be *your* future, trust me on this one, Richard.'

He guzzled more java, let it hang.

Ricky said, 'Sure, of course. There's nothing at the moment – more, I mean.'

'You sure? You don't *sound* so sure. And one thing you *can* be sure of is Uncle Fredericko will find out sooner than you can tell me if there's something Uncle Fredericko should the fuck know about.'

'I know. And I'm squaring with you. What more can I say? It's like being interrogated by the fucking filth, this.'

Frederick hooted hard. 'I *am* the filth, Ricky.'

Ricky paused/laughed. 'Good point – yeah.'
Frederick said, 'Ricky?'
Ricky said, 'Yeah?'
'As long as you can sleep with yourself.'
Frederick hung up.

THIRTY-FIVE B

2.22pm

Elvis called Ricky. He answered *too* quick. 'Yes.'

He sounded spooked. 'Ricky, Elvis.'

'I know who it is you student.'

Elvis sighed. 'In that case, why you sound so fucking surprised?'

'I don't like this – not after your old man turned up at my place.'

'We discussed this.'

'I know we did, whopper bollocks.'

Elvis laughed. 'Not *everything* has to be an insult Ricky.'

'I don't like it – your dad snooping around.'

Elvis made a decision – throw Ricky something to chill Mr Thicko out. 'Look, I said before it was probably a coincidence. Now, well, I've been thinking. I reckon it's far more likely, because it makes sense, that he was checking you out because of what's going down. What we've got planned – he and I, I mean. Not you and I. All that matters is that you and I are tight. You see that, don't you? He can't know you're in on this. He can't know you're snitching him to me. If he asks – laugh at him. Front it out. Say, fuck Frederick, I thought I was the dense one: as if *I'd* have the balls to try and do that to *you.*'

Ricky, loving it: 'That's brilliant. Proper student deep-thinking bollocks. I feel far better now.'

Elvis said, 'You should do. Let's meet later, to firm plans up, shall we say–'

Ricky hung up.

THIRTY-FIVE C

2.28pm

James took the call while back-ending a gyppo tart at his pad. She was a fresh piece of quiff. She ran dark eyes, a mane of hair. The Albanians offered her up – via the Tahiri shit-head: *do you need a new whore, my friend?* Business was good, biz boomed. The answer was: yes, why the hell not?

It was the usual agreement – a road test first, then: get her up and running in James's pop-up enterprise: Pieces-of-Quiff-R-Us.

He did her on the roof terrace, under a heater, watching snow fall. She made kitten noises, wore an old-time garter James dug. She slid off, pissed off, when he took the call.

He hung up and ordered her back on all fours or it would be a fat no to Tahiri and she could go back to her shithouse country as an illegal.

She did it – *reluctant*. It got James's dander: he packed a never-been-harder boner.

The phone went again. He took the call again. The tart's meows mutated to other sounds as she relaxed.

James laughed at who called: Ricky-fucking-Me.

He said, 'This better be good because I'm into something, listen–' He held the phone to the business end of the transaction. Sounds hit Ricky's ear, James put the blower back by his ear, *didn't* slide off this time.

Ricky said, 'What was *that*?'

'It doesn't matter. Shoot.'

Ricky sounded stressed, wired. The muppet ran a gargantuan gak habit. He was potential 24-7 paranoid. 'I've had both those Street dickheads on – they won't leave me fucking alone.'

James kept up a regular rhythm with Lady Gyppo. He didn't falter. 'They've called you?'

'Wish they fucking wouldn't.'

James cut him a break. James resisted telling him to shut up – this was the game they were in.

He said, 'Cousin, cousin, *cuz*: relax. Just tell me what they said. Let me do the brain work.'

Ricky paused. 'That's it – it was a load of hot air that has done my box in. First of all, the Street pig calls and gives me a shitting warning that I have to tell him everything or else I'm going to be done over big time by him.'

James stifled a small groan – the piece got *more* into it.

'What?' said Ricky. 'What you say?'

James sighed. 'That's regulation shit from Frederick. Just get on with it – what did Elvis say?'

'A load of gobbledegook, too. I did what you said. When I told you about his old man coming round, then coming back again, warning me in his car. Bullshitted Elvis his old man has got me frightened.'

'*Fuck*,' groaned James. The quiff turned a trick with her butt. To Ricky: 'Repeat that.'

Ricky did.

James stopped his stroke. He said, 'You haven't told either of them about me, have you?'

Ricky scoffed. 'No – I know that much.'

James believed him. James resumed his stroke. He took in the view – a thing of beauty and a total fucking joy forever.

He said, 'So you're saying you made out to Elvis that Frederick's spooked you, like I told you?'

'Yes.'

'And?'

'And what?'

'Fucking hell Ricky. How did it play? What did Elvis say? Does *he* think Frederick's onto him?'

Ricky could answer that, was *confident* of that. 'No way. He thinks his old man is just checking me out because I'm the one he and Elvis are planning to rip off.' He paused. 'To be honest, it's all a bit confusing.'

James finished, exhaled a loud grunt. Panting: 'Like I say Richard cousin, don't worry about it. Let me do the thinking. You just make sure you keep on spying and snitching for me. And make sure you keep keeping my name out of it.'

He hung up, told the tart: 'You're in but definitely don't defy me again.'

THIRTY-SIX

3.12pm

Elvis was in the Oak, across from Ricky's place. The thicko hung up before, refused to pick up subsequent calls. He tried his landline again, his girlfriend's number. Nothing, no response. It was why he was here. If Ricky refused to answer again and showed in his window, left his pad, he couldn't escape.

He *shouldn't* refuse. They were in cahoots. The thicko was on the payroll. He gave Elvis a headache he didn't need. He shouldn't shit himself about Frederick.

Fuck that.

Elvis redialled the landline and worked on his pint. The Oak's wide windows showed Ricky's two floors. Elvis eyed them as he heard the first ring. He waited for it to ring out.

But – no.

On the fifth ring, Ricky. 'That you Elvis, you student? Is it you who's been calling all the time – we only just talked.'

'Yeah and you hung up if you recall. And if you answered my calls they wouldn't be missed would they? We need to chat, remember. We have a plan to sort out. Why you think I'm calling again?'

Ricky laughed. 'Where are you?'

'Across from yours. In the Oak. Fancy a pint or three?'

'If you're paying.'

Ricky sounded wired – he *always* sounded wired. This time though: off the charts.

It might help, keep him from freaking out and shitting ten bricks at Frederick sniffing around. And, it might help getting him to spill his guts.

THE PLAN NOW: try and discover if Frederick had got to Ricky. If his dad played him from that end.

He should be here any moment–

Here he came. What a sight: he packed that questionable barnet, nth-degree follicularly challenged, every day a bad fucking hair experience. His Mohawk cut 'in' a long decade ago.

Ricky made the bar – he scoped the Oak: empty. 'Where's my pint?' Then: 'Fucking snow.' He brushed flakes off his knitted cardigan – the kind cats around here sported for ironic giggles.

'What you having?'

He said, 'Whatever you're having please Elvino.'

Elvino.

Elvis stiffened. He flushed and popped a sweaty chill.

Calling him *that*.

Frederick called him that. No one else did. Elvis brain-whirred, Rolodexed to this conclusion: his dad might have said Elvino when speaking to Ricky about him. *Plotting* with Ricky about him.

Ricky said, 'How do you like my new phone? It just arrived – before you called.' He showed an iPhone. 'Box-fresh sucker.'

'New?'

It drew a Ricky laugh. 'I mentioned it fuckhead – it's a long story, remember. I'll tell you one day. Let's just say it involved a nigger.'

Elvis recalled – that shit story Ricky told him about – got his dad round there, Frederick catching on to it instant. He said, 'Don't worry, you told me enough.'

Ricky finished laughing, slurped his pint. 'We still on? You still good for this "deal"? This con of your dad? After his performance at my place, I'm even more motivated to do him. It's going to make it a beautiful Chrimbo!'

Elvis stiffened – what happened to the shit-scared-of-Frederick act? He played for time. 'That's why I'm here.'

Ricky said, 'Still the same weight?'

'What we talked about. A quarter.'

Ricky drank his pint. His eyes darted. 'That's the thing – I've been meaning to mention.' His eyes – everywhere.

Elvis, stiffening more: 'Yeah?'

'My guy is moving up,' Ricky said. 'He's *moved* up. Will only do kilos now.'

Elvis's shit detector hit red. This had to be *why* his Frederick fright ended. It was less than an hour since they spoke. Ricky was in bits, then. Ricky was back to chipper-thicko Ricky, now: *zero* mention of *Frederick, his fright.*

In fact the opposite – *he wanted to up the deal?*

Unless.

Unless – a wrong read. He *did* sound content, reassured at the explanation Frederick checked him out *only* because of the deal.

Let's see.

Elvis said, 'Oh, I see. Your friend will only do kilos now, that right?'

Ricky grinned – he liked the way Elvis sounded. 'Sure is. Now – excuse me a moment. I've got to go to the khazi.'

He winked and headed for the Gents. Elvis watched him, chewed on it. Elvis saw Frederick – it *had* to be his move.

Run scenarios, compute: ask Ricky/don't ask him.

Concurrent: what did it matter?

Frederick – playing like this: he WANTS you to enquire.

He WANTS you to run anxious.

If Ricky IS snitching to Frederick he can report back his son is confused – his son doesn't know what the fuck to think/not think.

Ricky returned quick, eyes re-gleaming. He sniffled, grinned *larrrrge*.

Elvis said, 'That was hasty.'

Ricky winked. 'Fancy a bump?'

'Ricky, it is Tuesday afternoon. No, thanks. But let me ask you a question. When you came in here, you called me Elvino–'

'Did I?'

'The question is, why?'

'That's simple. Because your name is Elvis. Shit, I thought you were the brainbox student.'

Elvis shrugged. 'You ever call me it before? Because I don't remember you doing so.'

'Fuck knows. More importantly, who gives a shit?' His eye sockets bulged. He was goosed; showed zero concern at being quizzed.

Elvis made the decision – shrug it off. 'You may be right. Forget about it. I was curious, that's all. Not many people call me Elvino.'

Ricky grinned. 'I already have. Now, back to business. Can you do a kilo? Which means – do you have the money for it? It's a step up – big boys' time. Especially for a student – you lot are always skint.'

Elvis shrugged. He ignored the 'joke'. The real issue: IF Frederick was behind the up-weight, what's the endgame?

Beyond trying to scramble his head.

Elvis tried to see any other WHYs – how could it be a classic Frederick play? He couldn't see any.

First off: he now *knew* about it.

Second: because he knew, he would let Frederick know he knew about it by telling him: we need more dosh now.

It's a puzzle.

He decided: if a Frederick move, it's to confuse and nothing else. The reason was that: there is *no* reason. *That* is the reason. Confuse, make him think. Like he did now, right now.

Fuck it.

'What's the price?' Elvis said.

Ricky would never see the money. He had plans about the moolah – about the way the deal was going to occur. Plans Frederick wouldn't ever know. Plans Ricky wouldn't ever know. Ricky might be fed *errant* adjustments. If he snitched to Frederick it would throw the fuck off. If he snitched to Frederick the false info might boomerang back and Elvis would know for sure Ricky snitched.

Back to the biz in hand. And this:

A ZOOM.

Four times the amount of chang was four times evidence against Frederick when the sting came.

He liked that a lot. So if it's a Frederick play, it would rebound on him big style.

He liked that even more.

Wait until Dana hears this: the way it went, she headed for hack-of-the-century status for her exposé of a top-ranked Met dick caught ripping off a kilo of street coke.

And, of course: HE *was bringing the old soak down.* For the right reasons.

The Prime One: Frederick's betrayal with Camilla.

Admit it for the first time: this is about revenge. Revenge? *So what?* Revenge wasn't revenge. It was the wrong word. KARMA.

Call it now – that's what this is. Karma payback.

Ricky said, 'It'll be 40K. For the kilo. You have the coin for that? Or rather, does your dear old pa?'

Elvis nodded. 'Of course, or I wouldn't be here.'

'You were here for a quarter, remember?' Ricky played it slick if he rused with Frederick. 'It's a big hike – 10K to 40K. I have to be sure you can get it before I order. You have to be sure. Know what I mean?'

'We've done deals before.'

'We have. And you've backed out before.'

'Once.'

'The last time. Over a considerable fucking hike in amount then too.'

'True.'

Ricky grinned. He flew Gak Airlines. He fiddled with his iPhone, took a selfie. He moved alongside Elvis, papped them. Elvis clocked Ricky's cheeseball grin. Mugging for the camera.

He said, 'I'll send it you. Wait a moment.'

Elvis said. 'You're the one wants to up this from a quarter to a full kilo.'

A ping. The photo landed on Elvis's phone. Ricky said, 'I didn't want to do a deal at all. That's you. You've chased me. Remember? You've got me involved, which reminds me. My cut was going to be a grand. Well, four times the weight means four times on that which is 4K. Also, I've been thinking – a grand to help fuck over a big shithead pig is chickenfeed. Where's my danger money? So I want 5K for that too – that's 9K total.'

Elvis said, 'Fuck off.' It was a play, make it seem genuine. Ricky was right: a grand for what he asked shouldn't have cut it. 'I'll give you two grand for danger money and three for the weight-upping.'

Ricky thought about it – it didn't take long. 'That's my fucking student – deal. I knew you'd see sense.'

Elvis pointed at his phone display, the selfie. 'You have a freakoid smile going on. More than usual. It *must* be good blow you're shovelling down. Is ours the same batch?'

'The same man is what I know. All I need to. Which goes for you.'

Now Ricky turned tables. He reassured Elvis. 'I don't see why you're so worried about the weight anyway. We're mugging your dad off, right? We're setting him up, you're getting your dirt, I'm getting a nice kickback. There's 40K there. He's supplying that. From how we plan this – the coke goes back to my man and we boost the 40K. But I need to know it's there in case this goes tits up and the shit gets seized and I still owe my man. The filth having it is no excuse to these Albanian fucks.'

Elvis nodded, brain-clicked. Ricky showed something – Elvis sensed it. How much of his cockney-boy manner was an act?

Ricky said, 'The same question again – answer it this time: the money – can you guarantee it?'

'Like I said – of course I can. Frederick's got mountains stashed away.'

'We're in the wrong business.'

'No,' said Elvis. 'You are. I'm quite content thank you, and in this thing for a real reason.'

Ricky, blanking: 'Whatever.'

Elvis, bored. He wrapped it up. 'How do you want to play this? When is it coming?'

'Yesterday. As in it's already come.'

'Let's fix a time.'

'Any time.'

'Tomorrow?'

'Too soon – these things need arranging.'

'You said any time.'

'I didn't mean *any time.*'

The dopey fuckwit. 'That leaves Thursday, Christmas Eve. I take it the shop is closed then. The sooner we do this the more chance–'

'Open all hours. This is the twenty-first century.'

Elvis smiled. 'Where then? Your place?'

Ricky paused. 'You dicking around? You think an amount like this is going anywhere near my place? Some free advice: do the same.

Make sure it is nowhere near you. Where you eat, sleep, pull your pud. Understand?'

Elvis laughed. He said it to sow a seed. The plan was never for there. He said, 'It is really not like you to be so serious, Ricky.'

Ricky got on one – this is his field of expertise, let the thicko bull on. 'You take my point, keep the dope away from you,' he said and winked. 'Now, excuse me a moment, I need a piss. Another one.' Another wink.

He disappeared into the Gents to do more sniff. It took less than a minute.

'More drinks?'

'Thought I was paying.'

'Seal a deal like this and it's champagne time.' *Another* Ricky wink. 'Prosecco at least. Let's order a bottle.'

The fizz came, filled their flutes until bubbles popped over the sides. They drank the first flute fast, refilled, re-drank. Elvis got tipsy near instant. Senses went light, senses went happy. Frederick was knee-deep in shit. The brown stuff piled high, and stank the sting out nicely. The snow fell ceaseless, Christmas was whited-out 24-7. Frederick should enjoy it. He would be doing a long stretch for the next foreseeable Yuletides. Elvis was convinced. Elvis could *feel* it.

He hit a new curve – visioned options, saw a rosy future. No more cold and snow, *feel that* sun, beach life. The Music Man would hit Ibiza: would reside there, *Music Man* there. Live the long-held dream.

How would he do it? *Finance it?* That got sussed out recent. He didn't tell Dana, Wade.

Simple: finagle serious coin from the fat of the East End. Remove Frederick and opportunity banged in Shoreditch/Hackney. A Mediterranean of opportunity.

This caper with Frederick showed him – change-up, 180/360. He *still* wanted to end Frederick ripping off punters, ruining them. But fuck any moral crusade.

Now: take advantage of *him* long-term.

Be high on the future. Dreams of it. On himself.

To Ricky: 'Come on then Ricardo, where? Where the fuck do you think our deal of the century should be done?'

'Is the right question at last,' he said. 'I know a perfect place. Right by here. The old park out the back. It's sheltered, no fucker goes there unless they're a junkie because of those fucked-over towers.'

Elvis chewed on it.

Ricky said, 'It will probably still be snowing too. Extra cover. Not that we'll need it. This will go off easy. The way I see it. I'm sure you'll agree.'

'Go on.'

Ricky grinned. 'Tell your old man, 2.30 Thursday, come to the park. I'll be there. You won't see me at first. But I'll be there. About. When I see you, I'll keep watching, making sure everything's how it should be. And when it is–'

He trailed off.

'When it is?' Elvis wanted to hear it for himself. Make sure Ricky remembered.

'I'll ping you a message. I won't be there like we planned. I mean, I will be there but as soon as I send you the okay, I'll scarper. The shit will be where we said, you tell your dad, you go in together, and from there it's up to you, right? You do what you got to do. Just don't forget you're now going to owe me five K, whatever happens. But you do this right and we've done a deal like Leonardo DiCaprio in *The Wolf of Wall Street*, Al Pacino – my man, in *Scarface*.'

Ricky hooted – the sound of a thicko.

The way Elvis *actually* planned it; how it *would* go down – just wait and see, Ricardo.

Elvis nodded. 'Yes, all of that's how it should be. And don't worry the five-large is yours.'

Ricky goofed a smile. He was near bombed out of his mind. Good – ramp it up, make it look genuine. 'Thing is Ricky, how I know you won't try and rip me off?'

Ricky laughed. 'You won't, will you? Not until you're holding your kilo.'

Elvis thought about it – *pretended* to. 'Okay.' He fritzed, did heart leaps: this was on; the pieces fell in place.

It's a sensation tsunami.

He RODE:

Booze thrills/giddiness. Telling him – get on the bugle that's blitzing Ricky.

Fuck it: 'Can I have some of that tackle you're on?'

'A cheeky bump or three?'

'Yeah.'

Ricky pointed at the Gents, palmed him the gak. Elvis drained his drink, Ricky said: 'I'll get another.'

Elvis meandered towards the Gents, howled at a smooching couple – they broke their clinch. He howled more, hit inside, a cubicle – locked it.

Out came his keys, steady now – hands shaking/jonesing for showbiz, riding a big booze glow.

He grooved on it ALL making sense.

The dickhead Ricky walked half blind into it. DI Frederick Street was full-on blind. He would need Braille to decipher what happened to him *post*-when what happened to him happened. The Fredster? The Sheriff of Shoreditch? Ho, ho, *ho*. Santa Claus is on his way.

He keyed the coke, flew it into him: left nostril, *whoosh*! Right nostril, *whoosh*!

It's Christmas – repeat.

Whoooooooosh!

Ready and primed. Walk back out to the bar, see Ricky with a fresh bottle of Prosecco.

He poured, they chinked. Elvis got coke backwash. It riviera-ed down his throat, via nasal canals. The taste: sweetly sour.

He caught the Oak's vibe – seasonal reboot, contentment and warmth. Palmed the chizz back to Ricky.

Ricky said, 'Watch this.' He bent over the bar and dangled an arm into the open till. He dipped a hand in and snagged a fistful of cash, pocketed it quick time. He grinned. 'Merry Xmas.'

The barman turned and clocked nada. He ambled over, closed the till, carried on tending.

Ricky howled. Elvis's bugle buzz racheteted, his legs spasticked. He scoped the Oak – near empty. The canoodling couple faced the other way.

'What did you do that for?'

Ricky aped bewildered. The look suited him. 'What?' He sniggered. 'I thought you had a sense of humour, even though you're a student.'

Elvis said, 'You get caught doing that, with what we're planning, what happens?'

Ricky blanked. He said, 'Shit, yeah – I never thought of that.' Another snigger. 'But, you know, fuck it.'

The dude was thicker than thick. He dished out advice about where to stash the coke. Then pulled a stunt like this ahead of the deal. The criminal class lacked intelligence on an industrial scale. It was a regular Frederick observation. Elvis saw why: Ricky could mess up any moment and Frederick would walk.

'You need to start thinking a bit more. Use this.' He laughed and tapped his head.

Ricky, near blotto-ed. 'I did time in Brixton for this kind of shit.'

'Dealing?'

'Robbing.'

'Houses?'

'Bars and pubs, like this one.'

'You got sent down for stealing from tills?'

'You deaf?'

'Fucking hell.'

They refilled their flutes and slurped Prosecco.

Ricky said, 'The chisel.'

'I gave you it back. You put it in your pocket.' The bag came out, Ricky held it to the light. Elvis scoped the pub, Ricky put it away.

Elvis: 'Fucking hell.'

'Chill the fuck out. Just admiring a sweet eighth – clear crystals in the lump. *Nice.*' He winked and wobbled off. Elvis watched him meander to the Gents – a minute later, meander back.

He gave the bugle to Elvis. Elvis did the same, hit the Gents. Elvis handed it back, Ricky dawdled.

Elvis mock admonished him. 'Get on with it – let's get unclean and un-fucking-serene. Totally Betty Forded.'

Ricky fixed on Elvis – this student.

He handed the bugle to Elvis again.

He made the Gents, hit a cubicle, took a fat snort up both nostrils. He was bang back at it.

He relapsed.

And, now, here it came – a surge on *that* memory; *that* scene. A tidal wave of memory.

Back to *then*.

As clear as it was when it happened; when *this* happened: walking up the stairs to the flat and the sound. *That sound.* Feeling what it was before he knew what it was.

The sound of night time; *of the night.*

Sex sounds.

Agony, torment; opening the door and walking in quiet. The sound got louder, more intense.

He *had* suspected; now creeping forward in the flat, he *knew*.

In the hallway, outside the bedroom, *their bedroom*; the door open, seeing them, catching them:

AT IT:

Camilla and his dad in bed.

He couldn't help it – some instinct – he didn't interrupt – stood transfixed – his dad taking Camilla from behind. Wanting to cry and be sick and near fainting – bolts of terror – a boy again, *young, back to then, knowing something, about his dad, about HIMSELF.* Lifelong knowledge, *then.*

His dad moving, grunting loud, Camilla giggling. His dad fell off, out of her – his girl. His dad naked on the bed – their bed – Camilla turning, stroking his dad's chest.

More Camilla giggles – she started stroking him down there again–

FUCK, ENOUGH.

He tiptoed out. He got it – this was it, that moment – time to go for Frederick; bring the shit-head down.

They went at it at THEIR place. His ex and his dad.

Frederick then and now:

EX-DAD.

Forever.

He snapped back to now. Coke bolts sent him near crazed; he wanted to kill that fucking–

Revenge is wrong.

Revenge is self-defeating.

Revenge is sweet.

Revenge is the only game in town.

Act on it.

Elvis poked a finger in the bag and did more showbiz. *Aaaah, aaaah-aaah: FORGET FREDERICK AND GET ON THIS SHIT-HOT SHOWBIZ: STUPENDOUSLY STUPENDIENTE.* It's *the* burn. *The* instant uplift. *The* only way to fly. He brain-whirred on Frederick. Rolodexed the plan. Options: he *could* still leave it all alone; walk away. Rise above it. Let the fucker hang himself. He surely would.

Wouldn't he?

No.

Not now – not after living *that* again. Not having to live every day trying NOT to REMEMBER.

Frederick has it coming to him. Frederick IS about to have it ALL coming to him.

He bolted more showbiz, left the Gents and hit the bar.

He palmed the bag back to Ricky. 'Next time, just do it at the bar. No need to waste time racking up in the khazi.'

Elvis ignored him, scoped the Oak. A non-sequitur: 'This place went off didn't it? Back in crazy time?'

'When we first met.'

Elvis smiled. 'Remember it – there was a pool table where the restaurant begins now.' He pointed to the back of the boozer.

Ricky dropped into third person: 'Ricky pulled many a bird over there – "Here darling, fancy a line, I'll lay it on the side of the table. Here's a note, away you go darling."'

Elvis, riding a soft coke wave. 'The place is fucked now, corporate shit. Just about okay for a pint and chinwag.'

'For business.'

'Fuck business, give the magical miracle stuff back.'

They did more toots off keys and fingers. Timed them when the barman turned away, dared the Oak clientele to do something about it.

All day/night/week: toot and booze – what a way to exist.

'Clean and fucking serene,' Elvis said to no one. He felt his phone buzz and pulled it.

Frederick – calling.

Ignore it – keep the whopper guessing. To Ricky: 'Come to the jukey. Let's see the kind of crap that's on there. I'm betting it's the same that's found everywhere, you know what I'm saying?'

Ricky shrugged.

They made the side wall and a pimped-to-look-old Wurlitzer – polished wood, lemon tubing, chrome-finished.

Elvis flicked through songs. Ricky said, 'Go on then Mr DJ, what's on it?'

'As I said – usual shit. Can't even read this stuff out.'

'What we doing then? We're wasting valuable drinking time.'

'No time is wasted Ricky, remember it.'

Ricky blanked – Elvis wondered if he played dumb to cover his dumbness. 'Doesn't matter. This, however does.' He clocked some half-decent pop. 'You got any coins? A couple of nuggets.'

Ricky dug in his pockets, brought out a fistful of wraps, loose powder, broken Es, coins/notes.

Elvis took two pounds and dropped them in the Wurlitzer. The machine popped light, fairground bright. Numbers flashed, whizzed.

'Look at this.' Elvis saw Ricky in the jukey reflection. The dude ran vacant – out of it.

Elvis hit play on a Britney Spears number, 'Baby One More Time'. Cheeseball melody/words hit the Oak louder than expected. Elvis grooved on it. He foot-tapped, grinned, got a Ricky smile. The joey joined in. He danced a half-gone stumble.

Elvis belted out lyrics. The clientele had to hear him.

He sang: 'Give me a sign/Hit me RICARDO one more time, *PUR-LEEASE!*'

Elvis belly-laughed in his face. Ricky goofed and said, 'Jesus Elv, are you off your nut or what?'

'It's Christmas, Ricardo,' Elvis howled at him.

Ricky, slurring: 'Britney Spears? You like a bit of Britney in her school uniform, you fucking perv?'

'Who doesn't? And it's top cheese-pop. Has that *thing*.'

Ricky teetered. 'Thing?'

'Gets you here.' Elvis indicated his guts. 'Think we both know what I mean.'

'Whatever.'

Elvis's blower went again. The Oak swayed, snow hit windows. His phone showed Dana calling.

He hit answer: 'To what do I owe this rare pleasure?'

His tone – halfway blitzed.

Dana said, 'I wondered how it was going, that was all.'

Elvis winked at Ricky and pointed to the phone and stepped away.

'I'm still here, at the Oak. Going good. We've finalised the plan, so it's kick-back-and-relax time.'

'You sound drunk, out of it.'

'I will not deny I am having a few looseners. Rude not to after the powwow. And it is Christmas time, mistletoe and wine, remember?'

'And it is, oh, at least seventy-two hours since you were getting fucked up with me and James in Fabric. And *after* Fabric. Don't you think you should be keeping a clear head?'

Elvis giggled – couldn't help it – the Dana effect. 'Seventy-two hours: how precise of you – is it really that long, my dear? Have you heard from James?'

'James? No, should I?'

An impatient tone – old news he didn't trust James. 'Just thought you might.' Let it go, say: 'Why don't you come and join us?'

'Not sure 'Ricky Me' Cliff or whatever he's fucking called is going to be my tipple, to be honest.'

'Fuck *him*. What about The Music Man? Elvino, The Elv, *Elvis*? Elvis is here, for it is he!'

'You *are* out of your head.'

'It is Christmas time – mistletoe and wine.'

'You just said that. You on that evil shit again?'

Elvis howled. Loud: 'Really my dear – *sssssh*!' The Oak rubbernecked. He didn't give a shit. He had a nagging sense he should. 'Not on the phone. You do not know who could be listening. But if you must know, the answer is, YES! I HAVE BEEN SNORTING THE SHIT!'

The Oak re-rubbernecked.

'Elvis, pipe down.'

'Sorry, *sorry*. But I'm thinking, you know, being here, listening to Ricky, *observing* him. And my dad and James, for that matter. This lot are nothing. We – we can really do something. You know what I mean? They're all thickos. We clout them, take them down – pull that off, we can take over ourselves. Be whatever we want. I forgot to mention, the deal is now for a kilo. Think of what we can do with that if we boost it, do this properly.'

Dana sucked air. 'First of all, *you* shut up now about this over the phone – take your own advice. Secondly, I thought you were worried Frederick might get to Ricky – now you're writing him off as thick. Thirdly, we need to talk.'

'I only mentioned that about Frederick and Ricky to raise it, for us to be careful.'

'I'm on my way.'

'Exactly, that's what I said, that's why I invited you. I knew I could persuade you.'

'For all the wrong reasons,' Dana said. 'Now keep it shut if you possibly can until I get there. And if also possible – get rid of that idiot you're with.'

'You coming now?'

'How gone are you? That's what I said, wasn't it? Just don't go anywhere.'

'Why would I?'

'I don't know. But you're sounding like your dad.'

She hung up. Elvis looked at his phone, put it away. Ricky nudged him, held out a hand, opened it to show a wrap.

Elvis smiled. 'Don't mind if I fucking well do.' He faced away from the bar, wet a finger, stuck in the wrap and tooted a fat one.

He might have been seen. He might have given a fuck. Once: like pre-Fabric; pre-this whole thing.

He did a second toot, nudged Ricky. 'How's that bird of yours?'

'The Paki? Not seeing her any more. Had a new cunt for a while.'

'Richard – that language does not become you.'

Ricky cocked a drunken eye. 'She's coming over any time. You'll like her. She's white for a start.'

Elvis resisted telling Ricky that didn't bother him. The only thing to do was order more drinks. Feel afternoon slide into evening, the night wobble, go off somewhere.

Columbia Road street lights came on – they tangerine-glowed falling snow through the windows. Elvis said, 'I look forward to meeting your latest squeeze. What's her name?'

'Vanessa. Lovely, and I mean a lovely piece. Having that sat on your cock with a fuck-load of bugle wedged in your nose is boss, let me tell you.'

'How's her rack?'

'Rack?'

'Tits.'

'Is the right question. Lovely – she loves a bikini and her tits in one are firm as fuck, rock-hard, they're not plastic, they bring home the bacon. Got that jiggle on them – does me every time.'

Jesus – Elvis, non-compliant, grew a half boner. He said, 'Nice.' Tried to move proceedings on. 'Very lovely, I am sure.'

His phone went again, he pulled it. What did you know: Frederick. He can't stop himself.

Okay – this time.

'Give me a moment, Ricky.'

THIRTY-SEVEN

6.01pm

Elvis walked away from the bar and out the Oak. Moonlight – beams. The night clear, a few stars showing through London night haze. He crossed the street and answered his phone. Frederick rung off at the same time. He missed the call – could not care less.

He made back inside the Oak. Ricky was in the same spot by the bar. He talked to a girl. It had to be *his* girl.

It wasn't – Dana.

Dana turned, saw him. 'Hi. I introduced myself to Ricky. His hair *is* distinctive.'

Ricky said, 'You didn't say *your* girl was coming.'

Elvis near swooned. 'Dana is a friend. A good friend. Drinks?'

'Of course,' Ricky said. 'Get them in. I'll have a '64.'

'Dana?'

'G&T, please.'

He ordered. The Oak packed out – the clientele rich and square like the rich and square manor the manor had become. The drinks came, they slurped them. Ricky insisted on buying the next round. Elvis mimed faux surprise. They ploughed through these. Dana's round next. She insisted on paying. She waved Elvis off. Declared it time for chasers. She ordered three tequilas, the barman put a tray on the bar with salt pot and lime wedges next to the shots.

They did these.

The night woozed. Elvis fed the jukey more nuggets. He found some New Order, hit up 'Blue Monday'. He made the bar – asked if the volume could be dialled up. It was: loud – it sounded louder. 'Blue Monday' blared into the Oak. A Yuletide vibe built: the juicer warm and inclusive. Punters rocked in their seats, jigged on their feet. Bar-crowd hubbub went loud. It headed past 9/10/11pm. The Oak got blitzed.

Ricky's showbiz stash was endless. Snow piled up outside. A coke blizzard ran inside.

Vanessa arrived. She wore a knee-length faux fur coat. She wore it open. Revealed the tits Ricky dug in a low-cut dress. Elvis dug them, too. Who wouldn't?

Dana said, 'Wow, a girl with a chest better than mine.' Vanessa dug *this*.

She said, 'Vanessa, nice to meet you.'

'Dana.' They shook. Vanessa and Elvis too. Vanessa to Ricky: a fancy-seeing-you-here smirk.

'Drinks?' Elvis said.

'Yes please, I am parched,' Vanessa said. 'Bloody Mary, double.'

'Sure. Ricky and Dana – same again?' They nodded. 'Vanessa, we're onto slammers now. You in, or too early?'

'I'm in.'

Elvis ordered the drinks, he dished them out. Ricky dished coke out. Vanessa fingered a toot, another, one more. Then, a long one off a key Ricky held for her. She downed her drink, did her slammer, ordered the next round up.

Elvis caught a sense – she's different. Dana shared a laugh with Ricky – she forgot wanting him gone.

She was on her way to being gone.

She boosted over to Elvis, her eyes half closed. 'He's not so bad.'

Elvis laughed. 'You've changed the tune. I've heard it all now.'

'I can be stuck-up sometimes. You know what I mean? Once the drinks and drugs start working, we're all the same, aren't we – what's the difference?'

'I cannot argue with that.' He dropped his voice. 'I've got a good feeling about this. I think the whole thing is going to work like a dream. As far as I can tell, Frederick hasn't got to Ricky. Hasn't got him working for him to try and fuck us up.'

Dana – quizzical look.

Elvis said, 'I'll rephrase that. I don't *think* he has but so what if he has, this fucking thing is on.'

Dana threw a shrug. 'First of all, that talk on the phone before about taking over from Frederick – can that, okay? Can it big time.'

Elvis grinned. 'I like you when you're bossy.'

'I'm serious. Otherwise I'm out of the whole thing. And you won't see me again.'

'Sure, I get it.'

'Really? You promise?'

'Yes – *yes*.'

She sighed. 'Now, about Ricky being got to by Frederick – why? What makes you think he would? That would mean he knew what we planned.'

He couldn't get into this – it would mean telling her Ricky was co-opted. Not a smart move.

Play it straight: 'It's my dad is why. DI Frederick "Born and Will Die Bent" Street. We have to be careful. Do I have to spell it out? Think what happened to Lee. Think what Wade told us. Think about why James has enjoyed a free walk over Marie Davies. I'm just raising this, is all – that's it.'

Dana snorted. 'I am aware of all of this. I am still asking. You raised it, then said he hasn't got to Ricky – how can you be so sure?'

Elvis futzed with his glass. 'Like I said, I can't be sure. But does it matter? Ricky's told me everything else so far. He's told me enough. I've not even asked him if it's Frederick who's behind upping the weight to a kilo. You know what I mean? You see why? Let Ricky take *that* back to him if it is one of Frederick's fucking moves, trying to wind me up. It's on now, so who cares?'

It makes sense, say: 'Think about. And think about what upping to a kilo does. What is that about if it's not because he wants to make a killing on the scam – make it worth his while? It's just like him.'

Dana, quick: 'Or, if he's playing you – and his play is go along with it and spring something, then he could be thinking make it worth his while that way as he does so. You see what I mean? I don't trust him at all.'

Coke logic told Elvis she was wrong. Coke logic told him to say: 'Maybe. But fuck it. And fuck him. Let's waste time on him when we have to. Cheers.'

He stopped futzing with his glass, raised it, they chinked.

Elvis, howling. 'Looks like you have a fan. Ricky can't take his eyes off you. I'm sure you don't mind now you have seen the light and think he's cooler than cool.'

He watched her – felt stupid for doing so.

She laughed. 'You have to be joking. I was winding you up. Well – he's an okay guy, but Jesus, no way.'

Relieved jags hit Elvis. They built, and boosted him. He felt that soar. More drinks, toots. The jukey went from 'Blue Monday' and 'Bizarre Love Triangle' to Yuletide pop standards. No one cared. The Oak was rolling drunk – the joint swayed, tipped, the clientele surfed along on a Tuesday night Chrimbo high.

Elvis watched snow through a window. The booze/drug buzz made the view glisten.

More drinks. More toots. *More, more.*

Elvis hit the Gents, took his drink. The coke binge gave him the horn. As per usual. But – tonight: *fuck.*

He hit a cubicle, took a leak. He read john-wall graffiti that asserted: 'No fuck you'. An arrow pointed to a crossed-out message. It ran: 'Fuck all Muslims in the name of Allah.'

He laughed, finished, put the seat down and sat on it. He finagled a wrap of showbiz off Ricky. He got it out and laid it on a knee, started jacking off. He did a large bolt of chang, heard the door go – Ricky's voice; Elvis stiffened. He might want his chang back. He heard Vanessa's voice – she was with Ricky. He got it: they came to do their own toots. He continued jacking off, the next cubicle door opened. They entered and Vanessa giggled. He heard them bolt chang. The sound bounced off walls. Pub noise reverbed further back – it's an aural soundscape.

There was a silence. There was more snorting. The toilet flushed, Elvis used the noise as cover to bolt more gak. He half spilt the shit – gak spilt down his nose onto his chin. He licked it off his face and sniggered. He bolted his drink – enjoy that ice-cold G&T, double.

Now, noise. The door opened. They left, someone replaced them. There's two of them. There's giggles. Jacking off felt good. It felt great. Another bolt of chang and it felt better.

Sounds next door – he caught a sense. Chills: he brainwaved next door was going to do the wild thang.

Sounds – clothes fumbled, kissing, muffled laughs. The latest bolt of chang CPR-ed Elvis. He felt like fucking – *himself*. How gorgeous was *he*?

How eminently shaggable???

The JOLT was brill. He jacked to the sound of next door. The sound of copious sex sounds. Groans and grunts. He grooved on Vanessa. On those tits.

The noise ran louder. It came off as Vanessa. It sounded like her. It *was* her – she's doing Ricky; they returned for a quick go.

And, here *it* was. And, here *they* were. Here *he* was.

Elvis lost control.

Elvis nearly died of pleasure OD.

What a way to go.

NO.

Something was wrong. Something *sounded* wrong. The voice. *That voice.* It *wasn't* Vanessa's. He only just met her. He only heard her speak a few words.

It didn't matter.

He knew.

He knew because he half recognised the voice next door.

Ricky, laughing: 'That was amazing. Better than with Vanessa. She don't like it filthy, you know what I mean? She thinks she does but does she fuck.'

Elvis froze.

The girl caught her breath. She said, 'That *was* good.' Giggles, pants, sighs.

DANA.

It was *Dana* – Dana's fucking voice.

Elvis stood up, pulled his boxer shorts and jeans up.

He yelled: 'GREAT!'

He left the cubicle, slammed the door.

He exited the Gents and made the bar. He threw Vanessa a look she couldn't ignore. He leered at her.

Now: here came the happy couple. Dana let that scrotum sack do her.

She enjoyed it. He failed to comprehend it. He could not believe it.

Ricky staggered by. He threw a wink. He took Vanessa's hand, kissed it. A cheeseball move he saw in a movie. Dana staggered up. She stood by Elvis.

He knew she knew he knew.

He said, 'Fun?'

She was gone – a smile – she did not give a fuck.

Elvis: 'I'm waiting.'

She kept on with that fucking smile.

'What for?'

'An answer.'

'You want one – here it is. It was great, I loved it and it's none of your business. Okay?'

Elvis ate it up; *chewed* on it. He was half gone, not totally blitzo-ed. He could make a decision – the right one.

It was hard.

There – do it. Say: 'Fancy a drink?'

Dana smiled. 'Yes please.'

There – time to forget. Now – time to roar into the night.

His phone rang. The phone was always ringing. He pulled it from his pocket. It was Frederick. He ignored it. He ignored his dad. That felt good and brave. One thing: he had to admit, concede.

Frederick did it his way. *That* had to be admired.

'Okay,' he said. 'Same again?'

'Yes.' Dana ignored Ricky. He grooved on that. It felt *something*.

Elvis ordered more drinks, they arrived. The slammers went down. Music played, it's a tune riot. They tooted tackle. Drink/tunes/toot tackle. Shoreditch and Hackney repeated. London repeated.

Elvis adored it.

The night.

The night.

The sound of the night.

He popped thoughts and grooved on existential conclusions. Saw it all, saw nothing.

He howled.

The mind bullshitted. Thoughts coke-atrophied.

His phone buzzed.

It was Frederick.

Quelle surprise.

Nosh more bugle. Take the shit-head's call this time. Prime yourself. Be as ready as you can be given your state.

He walked from the bar. He made the door, went outside. Snow – falling lightly. Columbia Road glowed lamplit orange.

He stood in the doorway. Pulled his phone.

'Hi Dad. How are you?'

Thoughts jumped/synapses snapped. Did Frederick think that he thought that Frederick might think he knew?

The sting: labyrinth-constructed, spaghetti-plotted. Who knew what went on at any given moment?

Frederick said, 'There you are. At last. The Scarlet Pimpernel is a lot easier to locate. And I mean a lot. I should put a tag on you. Curfew you. Ankle-chip you.' Frederick grooved on his shtick; those duffer-than-duff jokes. He hooted long down the blower.

Elvis let it die. 'I'm related to you pops, after all.' He never used 'pops' before.

'You are indeed, my boy.'

'Been a busy few days.'

'True. I thought I might have heard from you before.'

'You thought wrong.' Soften it: 'You always tell me to leave your business alone – police business.'

'I meant our business.'

'True.'

A pause. Background noise from Frederick's end – party noises, girls, three maybe.

Frederick said, 'On that note, down to business. You fixed it all up?'

Elvis saw his chance. Back-foot the bastard.

'Yeah, of course. Why – you're not saying, you're not ringing me to say you're reverse-ferreting out? Again?' Elvis laughed now.

Frederick's tone remained even – cool as per usual. 'I certainly am not. And I will certainly be happy when you stop mentioning it, too.'

'Once this is done it is ancient history. Until then–'

'Go on then. Pray tell, the suspense is killing me due to your Pimpernel act. What's the form?'

'Thursday, half-past two.'

'Christmas Eve. How very fucking festive.'

Hit him with it. See how he sounds. 'One thing, the deal has changed – I'm with Ricky, he's saying the weight has gone up. We have no choice.'

Frederick missed zilcho beats. 'Really – by how much?'

'To a kilo.'

Frederick sucked air. He near gasped. 'By four times?' He answered instant – an act? Difficult to decipher.

Elvis said, 'As I said – up to a full kilo.'

Try this:

'What you think – deal-breaker?'

Frederick chorted. 'You must be off your head. Elvino, this is splendid news. Merry Yuletide. Goodwill to all men. Especially Ricardo Prime Fuck Up Me. Think of the score we have on our hands now. And that's 'we' because, don't you worry, you my son will be righteously rewarded, too.'

Elvis stiffened. The coke and booze buzz flatlined: Frederick called him Ricardo Me? *Ricky* Me, sure. But Ricardo Me, no.

He said, '*Ricardo* Me, dad? You have been engaged in extra homework.'

He watched snow flutter, shimmer in street lamps – he stuck a hand out, let flakes hit his fingers.

Frederick, still even-toned. 'Yes, Ricardo Me. I have now had the pleasure of meeting him on a face-to-face basis.'

Wait, see how he plays it.

'I was coming to that next,' said Frederick. The background noise ramped up. Someone put music on. 'The last time I saw you, at the church, our last meeting when they sang fucking hymns–'

'Carols.'

'Yeah – those. After I saw you, guess what happened the next day?'

'You reinvented the wheel?'

'Ho ho ho. There was a call to the station from Ricky. He called on this shit insurance job.' Here it comes – Frederick offering up disclosure on the Ricky visit: clever.

Frederick, continuing: 'Saying his phone had been stolen, he needed a report, all that bull. A pal at the station weighed me in. I told him to let me know if Ricky came up – any call comes with his name attached to it, I'd take it.'

Jesus – clever. It sounded plausible. Why? Because it was; because it was the exact same reason he gave Ricky – that Frederick checked up on the dealer Frederick believed they were going to shake down.

Frederick continued. 'So there it was. Opportunity knocked, Elvino. I took it. Went to Ricky's place on Columbia Road opposite the Oak. You'll know that, of course–'

Elvis opposite Ricky's place now. 'I'm standing outside as we speak, talking to you across from his pad.'

Frederick said, 'There you go. I go to his pad and check him out. I have to say, even for a dipshit street-fly, he has close to zero brains. Means he is ideal for our little plot. Means fucking well done to you.'

Elvis laughed. His booze/coke buzz returned. 'Aw shucks dad, thanks.' He watched revellers slide by in the snow. They hit the working men's joint. They hit the Silent Assassin. They hit the Setless Sun. 'Why were you there? What was the job?'

'I told you,' Frederick said. 'Homework – research the goon. The job was a saddo insurance stitch-up.'

'And?'

Frederick chorted. 'You're jumpy. If you can't handle the drugs, then–'

Like he had to know.

But: he's a near-impossible read *because* he's so transparent.

Think fast: 'Jumpy? No – cautious. This is a big deal, just got bigger. You think it's odd that I want to know what happened when you went round to Ricky's? I'm hearing about this for the first time.'

Frederick sighed. 'Okay – he's there with his tart and, well, he gave a good explanation – have to give him that. When I saw the piece of paper he wrote his bullshit 'mugging' yarn on I pointed it out to him. You know what the goon said? He said he wrote down the details so as "not to forget".'

Elvis howled. 'Then what?'

'The usual. I find his stash. Guess where – in the shitter. The lad has the imagination of a pigeon. And, well, I took it. For personal use.' Frederick sounded bored. 'He must keep the main stash elsewhere.'

Think – ask: 'If we're up to a kilo my cut has to be bigger.'

'How fucked up are you? I said that, didn't I?'

A pause, Elvis let it linger. Frederick said, 'You still with Ricky now?'

'Yeah. I'm with Ricky, Vanessa – his bird you just mentioned – and Dana – Dana Gabrielle. I think you *know* her.'

Frederick's tone shifted slightly. 'The reporter? I give her the exclusive at Lee's murder scene and she breaks my fucking balls at the press conference. She gives me a grilling every time I see her. She tried at the Marie Davies press conference, too.'

Frederick repeated it. 'I give her an exclusive when I find Lee and she still gives me a hard time. The jumped-up tart.'

'That's her job.'

Frederick chorted. 'You think so, do you? I'd say, no, her job is favours for favours. Her job is business. To be in the business of trading up for info. Exclusive shit. Which is what I furnished her with – that interview was a one-off, career gold dust thing and she tried to fuck me over as a thank you?'

Elvis allowed a pause. He said, 'Maybe *that* was the business. The business of keeping up appearances on a public basis while the real business happens on the quiet.'

'That's bullshit. I don't read her clever like that. You do – obviously.'

'She's smart. I believe that – know it.'

'Smart. Or unpredictable? That's what I'm seeing more. Believe me, we had a chat after the chat we had that went live on Lee's death. We came to an understanding,' said Frederick. His background noise revived. 'Or so I thought. We get to the Lee presser and she tries shitting on me in front of everyone.'

Frederick didn't *sound* touchy.

'In that case, why care about it?' Elvis said. Who gives a fuck, right?'

'I don't care about it. I didn't then and don't now. But we're talking, aren't we? You and I. You're with her now, it's a natural course of the conversation. *It came up.* So catch what I am about to say to you about her. Do not be telling her anything about us and our little shakedown on Thursday.'

Frederick paused – a ham act. 'You have kept your mouth shut?'

'Now you're insulting me. What do you think?'

'I think you're trying to bang her, you might tell her anything that could help get you into her knickers.'

Elvis howled but caught a thought. Dana told him nada about the post-interview chat. She never mentioned it. It might mean nothing.

It might mean – he flashed on an image of Dana and Ricky; Dana banging him in the Gents.

His coke buzz flattened. What if Dana turned him over for Frederick?

He ran calculations:

Should he ask Frederick?

Dana, could he trust her? He shoved it away. He didn't think straight, the amount of shit that juiced his system.

He said: 'We should meet before it goes off on Thursday – earlier that day. Talk it through. Properly. I'm busy at the moment, as you can tell – celebrating Yuletide, you know how it is.'

Go in on him. Ask: 'How's the investigation going? You got anywhere on Lee? Fucking big shame that.'

His dad sucked air, play-acted. 'You know I can't really say, but – sure, it's a shame. Looks like the same goon mixed up in the Marie Davies snuff killed Lee.'

Don't mention James. 'Yeah – who's that?'

'Two goons who were in Ziggy's selling pills and coke on the Thursday night she died, who we think sold her the pills – one has fingered the other for Lee.'

Elvis laughed – Frederick *had* to be behind it. 'That was good of him. Honourable. Loyal.'

It's all neat and tied up. Lee's murder had Frederick's fingerprints all over it. Whether he pulled the trigger or not.

Elvis said, 'What does someone get these days for being a cop killer, murdering the partner and close friend of DI Frederick Street?'

His dad laughed. 'A long stretch. His life is *over*. You know what I mean?'

Elvis said, 'Yeah, I know what you mean. The lad is fucked and he deserves it for killing Lee. That's what you get if you mess with you, right?'

'You know it.' Frederick sighed. 'Okay, then. How's the snow?'

'Still going, it hasn't stopped. Where are you?'

'Out.'

'On a job?'

'Always. Kind of. Always be on a fucking job. Correctamundo?'

'Correcta-fucking-mundo.'

Frederick chorted. 'Let's meet on Thursday, early on Xmas Eve, like you said. You want to come to the house?'

'Your place?' Think. 'Nah. Not very festive. How about the boozer.'

'The Setless?'

'Yeah.'

'Where are we meeting Ricky – to do the deal? I'll scope it out beforehand. Take a look.'

He lied. He said, 'It's near here. Behind the Oak. That wasteland near the end of Columbia – going towards Durant. You know it?'

'Sure,' said Frederick. 'You want to say midday then, Xmas Eve?'

'See you then. Bye.'

'Bye. And get some sleep.'

The phone went dead. Elvis looked across Columbia at Ricky's place. He'd done bugle and pills in there, recalled banging a bird in Ricky's khazi. That was a long time ago.

The kilo could be stashed in there now. Forget Ricky's patter about storing it elsewhere. That might be bull. The lad was an amateur. He operated a brain paucity. But, he *would* have muscle behind him; *would* be connected. Dealing in his amounts you had to be. It didn't mean he was *protected* though. He could be a goon, and nothing else.

It threw up a poser: what happened when word got out Ricky had been ripped off by a pig? At a deal involving the pig's son?

Because: word *would* get around.

Ricky would be laughed at. He'd be hunted. In the brown stuff big time. But, what happens to the son? What would happen to Elvis?

Fuck it.

The snow thinned. The sky showed. The moon still flowed. Stars still illuminated. Elvis was blitzed. The whole city the same – the metropolis got goosed on chemicals.

Take those away and what was left?

No Elvis. No Frederick.

No city. Nothing.

He stepped back inside the Oak.

Dana and Vanessa talked close. They whispered. They conferred on something. Ricky stood along the bar, fully, finally oblivious.

'Come on,' Elvis said. 'We're going to a place I know. The night is still young.'

He knew a venue that teemed punters and gear. He knew the promoter. He could take a guest spot when he wished.

DJ Elvino.

The Music Man on the decks throwing sounds. Making the people smile, the dancers dance.

Let's do it.

THIRTY-EIGHT

11.44pm

Snow, thicker again.

Columbia Road drunk scene. Revellers hit pub after pub. The Setless Sun, the Silent Assassin, the Stingray, the Oak. A start on a night of oblivion around the Shoreditch Triangle.

The gear ran endless, the booze fountained, emotions got wrecked.

A black cab took them further east on Elvis's instruction. Hackney Road became Temple Street became Old Bethnal Green Road. Became Clarkson, Ellsworth, Bethnal Green Road.

Then – Cambridge Heath Road.

Vanessa said, 'Where we going? Ricky doesn't like going too far – he's adventurous like that.'

Ricky resurfaced. 'No place like home, Elvis.' He slurred, pulled a wrap of bugle. He opened it. Offered a bump to Vanessa. She did a fat one. Powder spilled onto the seats. The driver took zero notice. Elvis and Dana followed. Ricky drooled. Ricky lucky-dipped his nose in the wrap. Powder went everywhere.

They re-upped. The night went coke *craaaazed* again. 'Ricky, should we take Elvis and Dana to a real party?' Vanessa said. She near panted. She gleamed *something*.

Ricky brightened. The obese toot of tackle worked. He presented half sober. He lucid-upped for a moment. 'Dong's?'

Vanessa laughed. Ricky laughed.

She said, 'You interested?'

'What is it?' Elvis said. 'The place I'm taking us to is a giggle.'

'Wait and see.'

He chewed on it – took a second. 'Okay.' He clocked Dana – clicked this is a set-up. They talked it through at the Oak. Her and Vanessa. The bar-confer. This was *always* the plan.

Vanessa leaned and talked to the driver through the window. He

277

nodded and veered right to take Whitechapel Road. He gunned the cab past poor-town shops, fried-chicken joints, late-night pubs. Beyond East London Mosque and Muslim Centre, Altab Ali Park, until they were near Elvis and Camilla's Princelet Street pad. South of it. North of Boyd Street – where Marie Davies died at James's joint.

The driver stopped by Osborn, on the bottom of Brick Lane. They jumped out. Elvis paid the driver and wondered why. It's their gig – they should pay: Vanessa, Ricky and Dana.

The cab gunned away through Whitechapel to Aldgate, scooting out of sight. The snow still clumped. It's a winter wonderland, London-by-the-Alps. It's *verrrry whiiiite.*

Elvis said, 'Now what?'

Vanessa pointed across the street and started walking. She crossed Whitechapel Road, they followed. 'We go the back way for Dong's.'

Ricky giggled. 'Don't call it that. Not when we're inside, anyway.'

Vanessa headed left, then hit Back Church Lane and went right along it, cut back through an alley behind warehouse buildings.

Elvis said, 'What *is* the place called then?'

Vanessa laughed. 'Cocks and Cunts.'

She rang the bell – crackly intercom sounds, a pause. 'Yes?'

'It's Vanessa Vag and Ricky Roger.'

'Guests?'

'One each. Boy, girl.'

The door cracked open. It went fully wide. They walked in. Vanessa pointed to the lift.

They took the elevator up three floors. Vanessa stepped out first. The place lit in dim-red Soho '70s chic. A Bangkok Soi Cowboy aesthetic. It was *soooo* unoriginal/ironic.

There – close-to near-naked beefcake everywhere. They garbed devil masks, they donned horns. The women were clothed *and* showed copious flesh. They wore cat and kitten masks. Bikinis, swimsuits, lingerie, high heels, bling and vamp make-up *de rigueur.*

The joint swam in beefcake and clunge. The clunge could not stop eyeing the beefcake.

The walking Adonises were steroid-issue muscle. They were

thonged-up and appeared Equus-hung. Schlongs hosepipe-esque. Serious portions of dick. They went white, Asian and black.

The clunge was white, black, Asian. It wore lascivious expressions and hungry eyes. *It* was being serviced, *not* the beefcake.

That was Rule One. The only rule.

Cheesecake ruled, okay?

Pants and moans, grunts and groans emitted in cacophony. Sound arrived off-stage left, right and centre. It pinballed around the joint. It went in and out of range.

A man garbed in old-London elegance approached. His accent toned cut glass. He handed them masks. They donned these. Vanessa and Dana's were Bond girls. Elvis and Ricky's regulation Mephistopheles.

The footman said, 'Ladies and gentlemen. What will it be? A drink? A service? A service while you drink.'

A gaggle of Eastern European-looking clunge roved by. They eyed Elvis and Ricky. Ricky collapsed on a velvet lounger. The clunge walked on. It giggled. Elvis wanted to follow.

'A drink first,' Vanessa said. She followed the footman. She waved Ricky to do the same in quick time.

The joint opened onto a bar that ran semi-circular and was on a mezzanine. It looked down onto a vast fuck-pad where vast copulation occurred.

'What *is* this place?'

'Elvis,' Vanessa said. 'What does it look like? It goes all day and night. Costs serious dollars while it lasts. You can see why. Ricky knows the people who run it. It's cost you nothing to be here, so enjoy.'

Ricky staggered up, made the bar. He ordered drinks.

Elvis cornered Dana. 'Why does this place not get shut down?'

Dana shrugged. 'It's a pop-up, done by that big porno guy who has places in Soho. This is old warehouse space. The answer is the same old answer. The police are paid off. Looks like the sort of place Frederick would be right at home at. And the local councillor and MP. You know what I mean?'

Elvis nodded. 'And Tarquin and Cassandra, Ricky, Vanessa whatever her fucking name is–'

'Compton.' Dana pointed. 'There – I rest my case. A local MP *and* deputy mayor, Margo Firmin.'

'Where?'

'With the tall white guy, green mask.'

Elvis blanked. He lost interest, returned to his thread. 'Hopefully this is an Elvis and Dana kind of place, too.'

Dana didn't bite – she blank-faced; like she didn't hear.

He said, 'How come you're not aware of the place until now? Wouldn't you know? *Shouldn't* you know, as part of your job?'

Dana cracked a smile. 'How do you know I don't?' Another smile. He couldn't read her – felt stupid pressing her more.

His coke and booze buzz sagged. Refuelling was required rapidly. Copious drinks. Shots, shots and more shots. Beyond the far end of the bar were half-doored cubicles. The view showed legs akimbo, heads bobbing.

It's a cunnilingus/BJ riot. A couple/trio fuck-fest.

'Come on,' Vanessa said. She pointed to the nearest door.

They carried their drinks. They followed. Stairs down to the main fuck room. They entered.

The vibe – amphitheatre.

Punters stood and watched. Punters stood and goosed their mojo. The view: a super-sized four-poster sans the posts. On it, three girls being pleasured by three beefcake.

Vanessa dug it, wasted no time. She kicked off her shoes, got on the bed. A tall portion of beefcake jumped on and joined her. She/he made it a quartet of couples. Elvis was transfixed. Ricky grinned and bumped bugle. Dana grinned and bumped Ricky's bugle. Ricky kept on grinning. Dana joined Vanessa on the bed. She got involved, it drew a fifth portion of beefcake.

The crowd clapped. The crowd whooped. Elvis did a generous bump of Ricky's bugle. He stood transfixed. What a show, what a night.

He pulled his phone, the clock showed post-2am. This day now, then the next was Xmas Eve.

What a day *that* was going to be.

THIRTY-NINE

23 December, 3.54am

The party spilled out of Cocks and Cunts into the snow. Elvis and Dana went arm in arm. Ricky and Vanessa kicked up a slanging match. Their voices sailed across Altab Ali Park. The subject was incongruous. The subject was forgotten. It wasn't the point. Ricky stopped. Out came a wrap. It ran inevitable. As the white stuff that wouldn't stop fucking falling.

James watched them. James rode coke bolts and mind-surges. He sipped a Peroni Gran Riserva. He dialled the heating in the Merc up. He dialled the house music on the stereo up.

Off they went now. On to Whitechapel Road. James bolted more chang. Sipped more Gran Riserva. Put the Merc into first and watched them a few more moments.

He pulled away. He drove the other way. To Boyd Street. To his place.

He didn't trust Ricky, cousin or not. He didn't trust anyone.

FORTY

23 December, 10am

Frederick tooled the unmarked from outside Shoreditch station on Shepherdess to City Road, Jefferson riding shotgun, that blond bombshell grin fixed on. City to Old Street roundabout became Hackney Road. Frederick made Cambridge Heath. He made left. He made Mare Street and gunned along.

He double-parked outside Hackney Empire and they jumped out. It was a cold day. Clear. The air froze.

But.

The snow: it stopped.

Finally.

It was that kind of morning.

It was that kind of fucking day.

They made Starbucks. Frederick ordered a black Americano and a large latte for The Bombshell. They snagged a window booth. The view showed across the square, past Hackney Town Hall, to the museum.

'We do this.' Frederick pointed in the direction of the museum. 'Then we go see Wade, word him up about sorting out Thursday with Ricky Me. After that we *do* Thursday. Sort Elvis, fuck up Dana-fucking-Gabrielle, sign up Ricky, palm off the score and Larry, you shit-head, it's a Xmas Eve to remember.'

'Then what, boss?'

Frederick's eyes gleamed. 'Then, we move on. Upwards. And onwards. Silly question.'

'Move on?'

'Yes, Jeffo. What else? Here she is.' Frederick slurped coffee – pointed towards the museum again. Jefferson wiped foam from his lips.

He looked out the window. 'Her?'

Frederick nodded.

Margo Firmin was Conservative MP for Hackney South and Shoreditch. She was the Deputy Mayor of London. She was a brilliant orator, fox-hole politician and ran a *wiiiild* coke/crack habit – call her The Freebase Queen.

Margo arrived, ordered, sat across from Frederick, next to Jefferson. She wore '80s-style shoulder pads, a pleated skirt.

She sipped her double espresso and indicated Jefferson. 'Who's this young man, Frederick? Lee's replacement?'

Frederick said, 'Yes. God rest Lee's soul. This is Detective Constable Larry Jefferson. Larry, meet Margo Firmin, Deputy Mayor of London.'

She offered a hand of manicured nails, and they shook. She winked at him, smiled. Jefferson coloured – for some reason. Frederick caught it and laughed. Jefferson crimsoned deeper.

Margo ignored it. 'Very nice to meet you. Frederick, stop laughing.' She sipped espresso. 'What's the deal then?'

Frederick lowered his voice. 'How much would you like?'

Margo smiled. 'As simple as that. How much can I have?'

'That's what I'm saying – whatever you want.'

Margo shrugged. 'Enough for a white Christmas and powder-perfect New Year?'

Frederick nodded – no problem. He switched subjects. 'How's the mayor doing? Still pushing this inclusive agenda bull?'

Margo shrugged. 'He has to. You know that. It's politics, stop taking it so seriously.'

'Sure he does. But he believes it, too – that's the problem.'

'You *could* be right.' Margo shrugged, dropped her voice. 'How is the Lee Palm thing going?'

Frederick mock grimaced. 'How the fuck do you think?'

'The mayor was asking.'

'Tell that Muslim fucker I ask the questions. Tell him too I ask the questions he has to answer. Tell him Lee is dead and the murder is about to be solved. It *is* solved. The media and the world just don't know it yet.'

Margo looked at Jefferson, gave Frederick a raised eyebrow.

Now, taking her time: 'Calm down.'

Frederick paused. Her act worked – he cracked a grin. 'It's a good thing that fucker is useful or–'

Margo shrugged and he winked at Jefferson. The young detective caught it right this time – she's being friendly, including him. Saying – Frederick really *should* know better.

Margo said, 'One day he won't be, remember that.' She smiled.

'You know it and then – so what you saying?'

Frederick – a pantomime left/right nostril snort.

'Now you are asking – a half ounce should make it a cool Yule. One to recall in my dotage. If I'm not being greedy.'

'Sure.'

'Price?'

'On the house.'

Margo smiled. 'Merry Christmas.'

'You know why.'

She nodded, killed her espresso. 'I have something for you, too. I know you adore your son, even though you show it in mysterious ways.' Margo smiled. 'In your own *particular way*. Saw him last night – at that pop-up brothel in Whitechapel.'

'Pollack's?'

She nodded.

Frederick said, 'The Hun showing zero class as per usual. Cocks and Cunts? What a fucking name. Yeah, Liebling, we get the joke. You're the anti–Paul Raymond, you're muscling in on his territory. But the attempted irony is flatter than some of the young men he's a predilection for.'

Margo shrugged. 'Is that so – I thought he went both ways.'

Frederick: 'You were saying about my son?'

'Elvis looked like he was having a good time is all.'

Frederick said, 'Good – it's Xmas, he's young. Don't tell me – he was with a short chav with a dodgy haircut and two girls.'

'I don't know who he was with, the place was very busy. It's closing after Boxing Day.'

Frederick cracked a grin – fucking Elvino.

A bright sun flooded the square. It was turning snow to ice. Frederick said, 'That's good to know Margo. Thanks.' They kissed. She kissed Jefferson.

'Right then – bye, have a good one.' She stood and left, walked across the square towards the museum, her surgery.

Jefferson said, 'An interesting lady.'

'Going places. A smart cookie. She toots but who the fuck doesn't? Correct Larry?' Frederick answered himself. 'Correcta-fucking-mundo. She's worth cultivating – keeping onside – until she's not.'

Jefferson nodded. 'The mayor sounds a fuckwit.'

'Straighter than straight. Which presents a challenge. You might call it a problem, Larry. You'd be mistaken. Mayor Patel's a challenge, nothing else. And the way I see it, he's going to be in all kinds of shit.'

'When?'

Frederick shrugged. 'Who knows? Sometime. It's a detail. Let's forget about him and talk Thursday. What's the chief fucking aim of this caper? What did I tell you?'

'A fat score, and show your lad the light.'

'That is correct. And the girl? Dana Gabrielle?'

'Whatever.'

'That is correct. Let's see how it goes down. And Ricky Chavs-R-Us Me?' Frederick mimed quotation marks: 'The dealer?'

'Done in such a way he has no clue about Elvis setting him up.'

'Un-correcta-fucking-mundo. Done in such a way that Elvis has no idea I know I'm setting him up – with Ricky Me's help. With Ricky Me as double agent. Elvis thinks Pricky Me's working for him. Un-correcta-fucking-mundo. He's double-agenting for moi.'

Jefferson grimaced, killed it fast. 'That sounds – how do you know he's not feeding you loads of shit? Doing you over?'

'An understandable but rather amateurish question. A quick lesson – listen, you'll hear this once, that's it.'

Jefferson nodded.

'Okay then – what do we know? We know Elvis plans to try and turn me over, using this dope deal with Ricky. We know Ricky's in on it – Elvis has promised him fucking chickenfeed to be so. One thousand pounds. Little enough chickenfeed for the thicko – even this thicko – to decide it isn't worth trying to help take down me. His plan was to rip Elvis off before Elvis and I got anywhere near doing this fucking thing. Boost the cash, some vague, plan-less, *brainless* idea like this. So, I intercede. With Ricky, tell him how it's going to be. I intercede with Vanessa, get her to up the weight to a cool kilo. Now, Vanessa is of particular interest in this particular plot. Elvis does not know about Vanessa and I. Ricky does not know about Vanessa and I. Vanessa and I go *waaaay* back in time. To like the original mention of this plot and plan to do it. Said plan was pulled out of by yours truly. For two reasons. As a ruse that would give Elvis something to moan about to me and thus blindside him. Second reason was more practical. I needed to check Ricky Me out. Who the fuck he was/is/might be. And I needed to get a suitable spy and mole–'

'Vanessa Compton.'

Frederick – surprised at Larry's powers of deduction. 'Exactamundo. I do both these things. I know the kind of dipshit Ricky is and I have Vanessa. I approach Elvis to reactivate his plan. You see, whatever he does, whoever he tries to fucking co-opt, get to snitch or turn against me, this thing is fucking happening because this is about me and him. Not about a kilo of showbiz. It's about him waking the fuck up. Like I keep saying. So, to get back to your original question: how do I know Ricky won't feed me shit despite him double-agenting for me on Elvis. Because of–'

'Vanessa Compton.'

'Correctamundo. Vanessa C is single/double/treble/quadruple agent and where I'm getting a load of the more pertinent info from. Example, she got access for Wade to fix up the feed so I could watch him. When we went round there on that fake mugging call, I knew all about what he was going to say, the amount of shit he'd put up his nose that morning and etcetera.'

Larry went white. 'You're kidding, I–'

Frederick ignored him: 'I know how Elvis took the upping to a kilo when Ricky raised it, how Elvis got a bit paranoid when Ricky called him Elvino during the same conversation because only I, his deeply loving father, call him that.'

Frederick paused. He said, 'You see, Larry, you might be astonished and say "you're fucking kidding" but you were there at the boozer when I met her, when I strong-armed her. Why did you think that was the first time? It was the tip of the iceberg.'

Jefferson nodded, took it in. Got a new look – like he understood more what Frederick was about.

'I get it,' he said.

'The latest plan Vanessa Cunty tells me is some half-arsed thing about how this is *supposed* to go down is that Ricky is not going to be there, that Elvis has to drop the money, then I come in. That's what Ricky's telling me and that's what Ricky's telling Cunty so I know it's right. You see, remember this Larry – Ricky cannot be even trying to turn me over or he will be arrested for the shit he's scoring and planning to sell to Elvis. You see that?'

'Yeah – what I don't see is why he doesn't pull out?'

Frederick grinned. 'Because he can't now. I won't let him shit all over how I am going to show Elvis what's right and wrong about me, about how it all should be. Try that and I'll fucking pop him for all kinds of shit. I already called him to remind him so after we did that shit-head Sinbad. And with Ricky's sheet he wouldn't be that far behind bad man Sin the cop killer for length of stretch.'

Jefferson took a breath – he tried to take it in. 'You not going to pinch Ricky then?'

Frederick, impatient: 'When *are* you going to learn? Of course not. He's an absolute muppet, true. But absolute muppetry makes him ideal – too useful to nab. He can snitch for us. He can fill a couple of vacancies now Sinbad and De La Salle are going down. Understand?'

Jefferson liked it. He cracked a smile. 'Loud and clear. Now what?'

'Finish your ladyboy latte and let's go. Time to meet Wade.'

'Where?'

'HQ.'

Jefferson went wide-eyed. 'HQ? Is that wise?'

Frederick caught it. 'At my house, you dopey goon. Not at the station.'

Frederick stood, Jefferson followed. They made outside of Starbucks and the Audi. It was double-parked – a warden walked up, saw Frederick and grinned. Frederick wound his window down, said: 'Merry Christmas.'

He started the Audi. He swung right, gunned along Mare Street, towards Victoria Park.

There were light skies and the sun. London dazzled. It was the day before Xmas Eve.

James sat in his Merc across the square and watched Frederick and his pig honcho drive away. He clocked the Starbucks scene. He recognised the piece they met. Not instantly. He googled her: Margo Firmin, Deputy Mayor of London and local MP.

Frederick had friends everywhere. Frederick was connected. Frederick ran a thousand-and-one snitches/shakedowns/schemes a day/night. Good, coolio. All the better when the old dipshit's taken down.

He put the Merc into gear and followed Frederick and his sidekick. He caught them up, stayed three cars back. He saw where they headed – Frederick's joint. He stopped trailing them, pulled the car up, pulled his phone.

He dialled Ricky. 'Yeah me, cuz. Frederick and his honcho are at his house. I–'

'What you call now for? You dickhead! I was just getting my cock sucked.'

'You're the cocksucker – *cocksucker*. Just listen, you got anything new, come on, spit it if you have.'

Ricky's tone brightened. 'Yeah, I have, dickhead. It's up to a kilo – the weight.'

James thought about it. The news: it brought a smile. 'Great.'

No need to ask why, whose idea it was. He didn't give a flying. He said, 'You know where it's happening at, then? How it's supposed to go, all that shit?'

Ricky said, 'Yeah, of course.' He started explaining, put his blow job on hold.

James listened – the amount of detail his pigshit cuz offered up made it obvious:

Ricky didn't leave a thing out.

The decision closing in – near the time to make it: make the move now or wait and see how this mutant father–son act went down.

FORTY-ONE

12.17pm

Frederick's place was an old-money London townhouse. They located in Belsize Park, Holland Park, Kensington, his stretch of Victoria Park Road. They went triple/quadruple storeys. They were ancient-cash and exclusive. Frederick was the gatecrasher in this polite society. He was feted for his high-ranking copper-ness. For making the toffs feel safe and secure – by being *non*-genteel, *non*-polite.

The Audi screamed to a halt outside in movie-opening-scene style. Frederick and Jefferson made the pavement and took steps to his double-fronted door.

Frederick stopped his partner and said, '*Ssssh*.' He said, 'Listen.'

He put his ear to the keyhole, Jefferson put his to the door.

A Frederick grin – rakish.

What was heard: sounds of enthusiastic copulation. Within those: some off notes. They registered too high. They registered dissonant. As if someone – *a tart* – laughed, *too much*.

Frederick, again: '*Ssssh*.' He put his key in the door, turned it slowly. 'Come on.'

They made the hallway, the sound went louder.

Frederick, whispering: 'Upstairs.'

Jefferson followed him to the first floor. The noise ratcheted up; it ran close to deafening. Man/woman fun and frolics, stopping and starting. Punctuated by desperation.

At last, the noise halted, ceased. *Part* of it did. The man went silent, the woman could still be heard.

She laughed – those discordant notes again. Here they come – she's *belly-aching* laughs.

Now, a voice. 'What the hell you laughing at?'

'Can you blame me?'

'I can't help it.'

'I can see that. Let me have another go–'

'That won't work. It's all that Chas and Dave I've stuck up my nose.'

Frederick corpsed. He nearly died of laughter, repeated the words through machine-gun laughter.

'"No-that-won't-fucking work. It's-all-that-Chas-and-Dave-I've-stuck-up-my-nose." HAHAHAHAHAHAHAHA!!!'

Frederick's voice boomed into the hallway; boomed through the door to the unhappy couple.

Frederick respooled and repeated. He *had* to. He *couldn't* help himself. He didn't *want* to be able to help himself:

'It's all that Chas and Dave I've stuck up my nose!' He fixed on Jefferson. It ruined him – Jefferson corpsed, exploded laughs. He held his sides, caught a large stitch that was tremendously painful. And, tremendously hilarious. This got Frederick going again. They did their nuts – howled; creased up big time at the gone-tits-up sex scene. They couldn't stop laughing because they couldn't stop laughing.

Then, nothing.

Silence.

In the corridor. In the room.

Then, the woman laughed again.

Then, the door opened and Wade appeared.

He was butt naked. Apart from his I am the Walrus moustache.

'Phew-ee,' said Jefferson at the length Wade packed.

'Fucking hell, that thing *is* bigger than Xmas,' said Frederick.

Wade scoped them both – addressed Frederick: 'Why don't you fuck off?' Now he laughed, had to – what else could Wade do? He pointed at his drooping length, followed up sotto voce: 'It *is* all that Chas and Dave I've been sticking up my nose. I swear to you Frederick. It's not even the P.'

Frederick grinned, threw him a bone. 'Or it could be the tart. Not doing it for you. Who is she?'

It drew a 'Haha!' from inside the room.

Wade dropped a grin and winked. 'That would be telling. No doubt you will recognise her when you meet. Let me just say for now that inside your well-furnished spare boudoir is one of the many bits of fandango who want to be in my movies. Who is ready for their close up with Mr De Long.'

Another 'Haha!' from the room. A 'Whatever, Wade-baby,' from Frederick.

Wade re-entered the room to retrieve his clothes. His voice dropped. Her voice dropped lower. They spoke – laughter between them. He re-emerged wearing boxer shorts, and carried the rest of his garb. He closed the door and joined Frederick and Jefferson.

Frederick said, 'Come on.'

FORTY-TWO

12.46pm

They made downstairs, entered a kitchen that was Grand Hyatt suite size. It was understated – showed Frederick had taste, an eye for the elegant, fancied himself an aesthete on the quiet.

He said, 'DC Larry Jefferson, meet Wade Long. My brother-in-arms – *my partner*. Wade – ignore the antic features, admire the torso, the muscle ripple.'

'Great to meet you,' said Jefferson.

'You too,' said Wade. 'Ignore him – you're handsome, as if you didn't know it.'

Wade got fully dressed – into classic costume. A flaming red shirt with a tropical-bird design, rhinestone boots, tight jeans.

He primped his tache, said: 'You with Frederick now? I mean *with* the Fredster?'

Jefferson looked at Frederick, who said, 'Wake up, shitwit. Why would I bring him here if he's not? Jeffo/The Blond Bombshell: he's my new partner, since Lee's sad and unfortunate demise. Come on, how stupid can you be?'

'Calm down Freddy boy.' Wade threw Jefferson a wink. 'If you're in Larry, great, welcome. Now, you can hear what I have to say – about Elvis, Frederick's boy. Frederick, brew some coffee, and hold on tight because you are not going to want to hear this.'

Frederick shrugged. 'Doubtful.'

He went for the coffee, loaded a Krups grinder and blitzed beans. The aroma hit Frederick's kitchen – made them feel alright. 'I probably know it all. And if I don't, I probably will.'

Wade smirked at Larry – OTT-ed cheek blows. 'So, you know Elvis is at the studio on Saturday morning, with the hack tart, that girl Dana, before your media thing about the piece who carped it at Maroon's night?'

'Marie Davies.'

'Marie Davies.'

'You told me all this.'

'Just refreshing your memory – humour me.'

Frederick finished the coffee and poured. He fluffed milk for Wade and Jefferson's lattes, poured them, handed them out. 'Go on – pray tell, the suspense is killing me.'

'We're there. We're listening. Elvis is laying out his plan. To her, to me. Like I told you, how the plan is to turn over Ricky, how that afternoon the journo squeeze is going to grill you at the press conference, try and set you up–'

Frederick laughed. 'That went well.'

'And Elvis is banging on about how he's going to record you at the Ricky thing, film you, get you shit-canned, shit-storm you.'

'You've refreshed me. The point?'

Wade shrugged. 'Point is what's coming next. What you might not want to hear. What I thought at the time and can't stop thinking about. Which is what happens if he pulls this off? If Elvis manages to do it?'

Frederick sipped coffee. It was strong and black. He took his time; he would always be taking his time – even when he was not.

Finally: 'That's it? That is the reason you're at my place to see me? The reason you are banging a wannabee porno piece in my guest room? The reason you can't bang her, maybe? Because you're getting all worried that Elvis – *my son* – is going to reverse what's being going on for years and turn *me* over?'

He laughed hard – the sound echoed around the kitchen.

Finally – he stopped and grinned; threw Wade a wink – the fucker should know better.

Frederick said, 'Jefferson, I do hope you're observing this and learning. This is how my business partner, *my business partner*, moves. If you can believe it. Credit it. This is why he is Wade Long and I am Frederick Street. I have a great fondness for Wade. A fondness founded in all that is right about being fond. His undoubted and unswerving loyalty. His ability to do tanker-loads of dope and booze and come up smiling for more. But Jesus Christ, Wade. Don't doubt.

You hear? You know why? Because there's no need. *Ever.* If I don't care, why the hell should you?'

'Because, I do – care.' Wade flushed, got a child-like look in the eye.

Frederick saw him and near raged. The same rage as always: grow up and grow a pair. Grow into being a *man.* Do what most men did not.

'Sure you do,' said Frederick. He got bored. He said, 'And it's noted – that you care. It's noted most weeks. That's why you're sitting there drinking my coffee and Lee is where the fuck he is. However – this is business. *Business.* You hear me? The long business. The short business. Making the green stuff. What's better than loads of moolah? *Making* loads of moolah. You know all about that – in your business.' He flicked a thumb at Jefferson. 'Larry has heard all about you – *your business.*'

Wade nodded – he tried to talk to Frederick, no more. It was case closed; as it always was.

Frederick said, 'Wade – you think Mr Teutonic could have a future in your flicks?'

Frederick and Wade shared laughs, Jefferson blushed. 'You don't even have to ask,' Wade said, and bolted latte. He pointed at Jefferson. 'Look out though – he's keen.'

A deeper Larry flush. Frederick smiled. 'Jefferson, don't. There are enough fuckers out there and enough chances for them to blackmail you in our line without one of Wade's screen tests, shall we say, "falling into the wrong hands".'

Frederick smirked and winked – he might jest/might not; Jefferson did not know what was true, was not.

'I could arrange a private screen test,' said Wade. 'I'm kind like that.'

Frederick, enjoying this: 'Kind *and* complicated. He'll offer to fit you up in front of you with the smile and the aw-shucks act.'

'Screen test sounds fun,' Jefferson said. 'Get to bang porn chicks and it won't go in any actual video.'

Frederick, laughing: 'You know you show here a naivety I admire for its untouched sweetness but really Jefferson do not. You know why? Because if you ignore the free advice and do it, Wade will keep your test in his library and don't think it won't be there, waiting.'

Another wink and smirk; another is-he-pulling-the-new-schmuck's pisser? 'The library is – what would you call it, Wade?'

'Sinecure, pension, insurance policy.'

Jefferson grinned. 'The way I see it then – what's the difference? Don't think I'm *that* green that you haven't already got a bulging Stasi file on me, if you did want to do me that way.'

Frederick and Wade howled at this – *look at the smarts on Larry*. He joined them, had hit the right note: deferential *and* balls out.

Frederick said, 'Wade's library – something to behold. Movies *and* stills. Audio *and* visual recordings. You want dirt on Mayor Patel? Wade's your man. You want shit on Deputy Firmin? Wade's your man. Stuff about DI Palm his post-death family could do without knowing? That's right. Chief Eldrick's predilection for Muscle Marys? Shit on the brief who finalised my divorce? The manager of Bethnal Green Waitrose who's a landlord of icky properties?'

Frederick smirked, twinkled. 'I need to continue, Larry? We may be fucking around, we may not. On various levels. Take note. Wade is a broad-church curator kind of guy. There is no stratum of our lovely filth-ridden society he hasn't penetrated.'

Jefferson's smile went shifty. He didn't know what to believe. 'I've got a question – that okay?'

'Fire away. I'm making fresh coffee.' He started doing so. He said, 'Go on.'

Larry said, 'We're here about Elvis, right? What's going down tomorrow?'

They nodded.

'I know he's your son,' Jefferson said. 'I know what you just said to Wade, but why not just pop him? I don't mean *pop* him, of course, he's your son for fuck's sake. I mean archive *him* – get him on film, bring it to him, say back the hell off, or else. You know what I'm say-ing?'

A Frederick snort. *Bored and the Gang*. 'Archive him? Do him up? I can do that all day. What can't I do – that I'm trying to do?'

Frederick stared hard at Jefferson; Wade stepped in – twinkling:

'He cares for Elvis. *Says he does* – that's his patter and he's sticking to it. That he's doing this for real love, meaning his loyalty to his son, his care for Elvis.'

Jefferson shrugged – what the??? 'This is what it's all about?' Like he didn't buy Wade's routine. 'Tomorrow – father/son love?'

Frederick poured fresh coffee, slurped the java, winked at Wade, then Jefferson. 'What else could it be, young lad? This is about getting Elvis to see he's loved. Get him to see and feel it for the first time. *See it.* See that *and* see what the world is, what it could be and should be for him. Not just as a citizen with potential, with heart in the right and only place – like you two dickheads – but as my son. That's the kind of love I'm dealing in and, trust me – the little runt will *feel it.*'

More winks – leave it ambiguous, let Larry decide whatever he wants to. 'See how his dad rolls is the only way to roll. Which means – take control. As much as you can. Fuck, phone hacking? *Phone hacking?* You think that's it – that kind of shit? Funniest thing about that was how well it played. It was a smarto fucking play. By all involved – Murdoch, the spooks, top brass, *us.* Elvis is trying to do me? And? *And?* So. The. Fuck. What?' He smiled, winked again. 'And that, Larry, is it. Father-and-son love, oh yes.'

Jefferson smiled – thin: what could he say? Frederick drained his coffee, held the cup up.

'More?'

Jefferson still tried to take it in – gave up. 'Sure, yes please I'll have another cup.'

'Me too,' Wade said. 'Larry-O, you want a game of pool?'

Jefferson nodded, followed Wade as he walked through the kitchen to the corridor.

It was wide – like the house was two houses knocked through, joined together.

Up they went.

FORTY-THREE

1.17pm

Wade took the back stairs with Jefferson, Frederick trailed them. They went three floors up, hit a room – Frederick's den. It ran spacious and plush. Tricked out as a gentleman's club. Chesterfields. A drinks cabinet with cut-glass accoutrements. Four super-wide 4D TVs. A treadmill. A pool table, dartboard and oche. One wall was a French window-fest. It opened onto a wraparound terrace. The terrace became an orangery when required. The terrace housed a corner place with hot tub. A bespoke brick grill. There's loungers, two more 4D TVs. The terrace showed a horizon that went east, west and south to the Thames.

'Let's start,' Wade said. He handed Jefferson a cue, racked up the balls, addressed the table.

Jefferson chalked his cue and eyed the TVs. They beamed in sports and news and miscellany. One piped in gulch from China. Another a re-run baseball game from the West Coast. One a subtitled flick. One a porno.

Wade pointed. 'For fuck's sake Frederick, where's the loyalty? Get some of the Long product on. Real smut.' Wade smirked at Jefferson. Frederick smirked at Wade.

Wade said, 'You seen *The Longer Goodbye?*'

'Think I have.' Jefferson ran enthusiastic. 'That actor from *Friends* in it? Elliott someone?'

'No, thicko. *The Longer Goodbye*. Starring, directed and produced by a certain Wade Long. Now *that* is a porno. This Dutch shit Frederick's got playing here? You need some fresh fandango on your cock or some sparkling showbiz up the nasal passage to get off on that shit. It's *soft porn.*'

Jefferson nodded. He looked and he learned. He said, 'I'll break.' Cued the white ball into the pack at speed.

Balls fizzed off cushions. Two or three dropped. Wade, eyebrows raised: 'A bandit if I ever saw one.' He eyed the eight-ball as it moved near a middle pocket.

Jefferson scoped the table. He said, 'Stripes.'

Felicity entered the room. She was done to the nines – a high porno aesthetic.

Frederick threw her a wink. She threw one back.

Felicity smiled. Felicity said to Wade: 'Oh, you're dressed now.'

Wade, grimacing: 'Oh, so are you.' Wade said, 'Detective Constable Larry Jefferson, this is Felicity – Felicity ChicFox.'

They shook hands. Her smile dazzled. Her plastic boosting had a direct effect on him.

She said, 'Nice to meet you.'

'Yes,' said Wade. 'I don't think you have met before.' He cracked a grin. 'Though you may be familiar with the *sound* of Felicity's voice. A fucking whiny sound.'

Jefferson brain-whirred. He grafted overtime, got there in the end. 'The bedroom – before.'

'Yes, indeed. *The bedroom before.*' Felicity winked at Jefferson; Wade winked at Jefferson.

He chuckled, addressed his next shot – there's five stripes remaining plus the eight-ball. He potted the first one, then the next, then the next – so on. He cleared the lot, chuckled louder: Wade got cleaned out, whitewashed.

Felicity tittered – Frederick finally got who Felicity was – she's the tart from the Setless Sun on Sunday – big deal.

He said, 'Fucking hell, Wade, dickless in the sack, ball-heavy on the table.'

A Frederick/Jefferson/Felicity howl. A non-Wade howl – he grimaced, raised two fingers and issued them, raised the bird next, invited them to *swivel*.

'Come on Wade,' Frederick said. 'Shake the lad's hand.'

Wade did it reluctant. Frederick said, 'Alright then – coffee anyone? Felicity sweetheart – we meet again. Coffee?'

'Anything stronger on offer?'

Frederick grinned. 'It is booze o'clock as far as I can see. What would you like?'

'Beer for me,' said Wade.

'Jefferson?'

'Beer sounds good.'

Felicity said, 'Do you have any bourbon? If so, with coke and ice please.'

Frederick gave her a beam, got the drinks together. Wade said, 'Jefferson, rack them up again. I'm after revenge. And since the sauce is coming I'll rack the lines up. Let's get this party started. You're not on duty are you?'

Jefferson – bold. 'I'm with the Fredster – who gives a fuck what I am?' He racked the balls up, Frederick smiled and distributed drinks, Wade laid out lines, Felicity watched.

They tooted tackle – a sniff quartet. They drank – a four-way knees-up. It's a mini pool tourney. It's a laugh a minute.

Frederick and Felicity rekindled their meeting in the Setless.

Frederick said, 'Ms Baumgartner, I believe.'

'The Sunday afternoon dancer, I do believe.'

'Haha.' Frederick blushed. It was a rarity – catch it while you can.

Felicity asked Frederick about his walkout. 'Where did you go? You left rather abruptly.'

'Where did I go?' He blanked, couldn't remember.

Felicity smiled. 'Come on – Sunday, the pub. You left before us – you've forgotten already?'

He memory-flashed, got it: the Silent Assassin, that's where he went. After exiting the Setless. He tipped off Dana – the dummy-phone trick, pay-as-you-go, untraceable. He flashed more: Lee dead in Leonard Street snow, outside the Griffin, shit-head gimp James Maroon doing him.

Frederick said 'I have a busy schedule. I remember your name, don't I?'

'True.'

The showbiz started to work. The four of them took off; the four of them *flew*. Wade gained revenge on Jefferson at pool. Wade beat Frederick. Wade beat Felicity. Wade *ruled*. Frederick hit up some tunes. It was a mix by Elvis, a Frederick fave: disco/Balearic stew. House stuff with hooks that crept up. Kept on creeping. The more you listened. They sidled up, they stalked you.

Frederick and Jefferson eyed Felicity. They kept tabs. They *surreptitiously* stalked her. Wade took a backseat. Following his non-performance.

Felicity presented a porno-fantasy dazzle. She's here, she wiggles her rear. When addressing the white ball. When moving. When merely and stupendously *existing*.

Jefferson coached her. Frederick noted it. Frederick wondered if he should make something of it. Pull rank.

Fuck it – The Bombshell could have his moment. He would learn soon enough.

More lines. More refills. More games. The tally ran copious. They lost count. They lost themselves. It's a blizzard. It's a booze binge. The bugle bolted. The showbiz slung shooting stars. Elvis's tunes took over. A sunshine-and-beach vibe.

Frederick flung the French windows open. He goosed the heating. There's Hackney darkening. Swivel to Bethnal Green. Swivel and see Stratford stretch into Essex. The day before Christmas Eve became night. A 100K-plus lights lit the Smoke.

Wade and Frederick watched Jefferson and Felicity rack another game up.

Wade said, 'Mañana?'

Frederick shrugged. 'What we said. You know the place – back of Columbia Road?'

Wade nodded.

'Bring yourself, park near. Set it up. Watch. Record.'

'Anyone else?'

'Told you. Yes, at least two. Don't tell them what's going on. Just tell them not to be fucking late. They go where I said. They film it. You direct.'

Wade nodded. He spooned bugle and offered it Frederick. He noshed a generous bump, Wade did the same. They refocused. 'Where's the shit going?'

Frederick wiped his nose. 'To that weirdo MP – the Deputy Mayor bird. Some of it.'

'The dyke from Mare Street?'

'She's no dyke. Though she munches muff.'

'Who doesn't?'

'True.'

'The chief?'

'Eldrick?' Frederick chorted. 'He doesn't do that shit no more, *bruv*. He says. And I believe him.'

'No way.'

'Not after his little incident. You must recall.'

'What the fuck?'

'You filmed it, shit for brains.'

'Did I?' Wade blanked. The dipshit's cells ran puddled.

'Don't worry about it. Boring story short – a time arrived, he was reminded of what occurred and he backed off.'

Wade beamed a big one. 'I remember. The state of him, the state of the film.'

'Exactamundo.'

The spoon re-emerged. They bumped bugle. The spoon re-vanished. Wade caught a coke-brave buzz. He opened up, bared his soul. 'Truth is, I didn't have any blueys.' He pointed at Felicity.

Frederick caught it, played nice. Get Wade to spill his guts *then* rip the thicko to bits about it. 'You should have said. If I knew you were bringing her over I would've told you where they are.'

'They're not in the usual place, that's for sure.'

Frederick chuckled. 'Took a good look did we? You cheeky man.'

'Had to.'

'The state of you, poor bastard. I don't get it. Porn's about performing? On cue? Demand? Correct?'

'Correctamundo Frederick.'

'Yet you go soft when it's *not* business? When there's *no* lights, camera, action? Weirdo shit.'

'Perfect sense if you think about it – you crap on about your big brain, never shut up about it, you can work it out.'

Frederick snorted. 'You're going to give the same excuse – you take blueys for your pornos.'

'No, actually not. Well, not *all* the time – sometimes I do, sometimes I don't – it's different, a different set of circumstances, on set, banging some cheesecake actress.'

Frederick laughed. 'Jesus, Wade, stop taking yourself so seriously. Has to be said though, if you can't get if up for Felicity ChicFuck, then–'

Wade grimaced. 'Thanks a bunch.' A pause, then he cracked and guffawed, raised his beer. They chinked and slurped. 'You going to bang her or what?'

Frederick said, 'If young Larry lets me, the cheeky fuck.'

'That a yes or no?'

'A clear yes and you know it.'

They watched Jefferson and Felicity. They were mashed; they pinged balls around the table and found it *rather hilarious.*

'I was right,' said Wade. 'He's a bandit.' Change-up: 'What happens to Elvis *after* tomorrow?'

Frederick shook his head. 'I keep on being asked this. I haven't a Scooby why I keep on being asked this.'

'He's your son is why.'

'Elvino is about to learn a lesson he should have done an age ago. How many times I have to tell you? Then, he'll be fine. Set up. Welcome to the rest of your life, as in the *start* of your life, Elvino.'

'You ever think about, you know, leaving him alone?'

Frederick winked. 'He won't leave *me* the fuck alone. I didn't ask to be set up, did I? By my own son.'

'True.'

Frederick winked again.

'What's his endgame?' said Wade. 'Does he actually want to bring you down?'

'That's what I can't quite work out. Either that or the same reason I'm doing it,' Frederick said. 'He's trying to turn *me.* Reform *me.* Beautiful isn't it? The Fredster's sixth sense says if he did pull off what he's plotting he might walk away from actually doing me – I don't think he has got *that* in him.'

Wade said, 'Call him. Speak to him. Or don't turn up. I've got a bad feeling about it. This is all I'm saying–'

Frederick double-winked and chorted. He poured more bourbon, pointed at Jefferson. The junior detective leaned over Felicity as she took her latest shot. He 'coached' her.

Wade said, 'If you're going to give me the how-long-have-I-known-you spiel – don't.'

'Usually works.'

'Just answer me this first.'

'What?'

'Why not call him? Give it a try.'

'I've tried it, I've tried everything. I haven't tried this yet. You understand? If it doesn't work, he gets the fright of his life, and won't be trying anything like this again. You know my guess? My guess is he knows that I know. What he's trying to pull. That means he's thinking, shit, dad's still going through with it. Means he's thought should *he* pull out? Means if he doesn't it's because he *can't* back out. He'll be kidding himself hubris has got me. But, hubris has got *him*. You understand?'

Wade nodded. Showbiz buzzed him. Arteries surged coke. 'You think it's a hundred per cent chance he goes through with it?'

'Who gives a fuck?'

A *lonnnng* wink – close this down. Leave Wade nowhere to go except the spoon welded to him. Gear was gear. A buzz, a hoot. But ruled by it? Ruled by class-As and booze? The lament of the mediocre masses.

Frederick bumped more showbiz from the spoon, left Wade drinking his bonded bourbon by the bar.

He boosted outside and stood in the orangery.

Alone.

The snow fell soft. The skyline skidded lights. There's a pale moon, stars – there's the ether.

Chew on it/ruminate: ride the coke carriage and Rolodex thoughts.

Elvis: you fool. You know it. This is a sick-funny way to teach you a lesson. It shouldn't be required.

Fuck it. And, on this one, *fuck him*. Thursday would go down.

Thursday would reverberate post-Thursday; aftershocks would be felt.

Then, one day: Elvis would laugh about it. Joke with him about it – *reminisce*.

Do you remember that time when…

Frederick wheeled from his sky-and-moon confer. He fancied taking up where he left with Felicity. She wanted to get into one of Wade's big productions. There was a bigger production to star in. Directed by DI Frederick Street. Featuring DI Frederick Street. Starring Felicity ChicFuck up close and personal.

He made back inside, hit the pool table. The baize was off-blue blue – Jefferson addressed a shot, chiz spotted his nostrils.

Frederick said, 'Good shot. Hey Ms ChicFox, fancy another dance?'

He pointed at the speakers around the table, above the bar, dotted around the den. 'Next tune coming on is a goody.'

He held a hand out to Felicity. 'Let's relive our stuff in the Setless.' It was cheesy. It made her laugh. She got it – *him*.

Jefferson got this, too. He palmed his drink and sank in a seat and watched.

Felicity took the Fredster's hand. The Elvis mix was monikered *The Elvino*. The sounds light and happy – the vibe childhood/celestial/the shit in-between.

They danced. They entered a Class-A bubble. The bubble enveloped. The bubble had its own sound system. The bubble had its own bar. The bar shook up cocktails. The bubble shook them up. It's mesmeric. It's magic. It's ChickFuck – she keeps moving. Keeps tantalising. Twirling and twirling.

Jefferson whooped. Jefferson yelled, '*Yeah!*' Wade made the chesterfield and sat next to him. Wade grinned. He thumbs-upped Jefferson and Frederick. Thumbs-upped Felicity as she glided by. She was plastic-boosted. She was a natural.

Frederick and Felicity clasped hands. Frederick spun – stars flashed by through the orangery. Wade and Jefferson flashed by laughing. The stars again; Wade/Jefferson again.

Elvis's mother never danced like this. No woman before ever

danced like *this*. It was the next one and the next one. The next woman *always* danced like this.

Jefferson whooped more. Frederick mind-whirred on the deal unfolding tomorrow. Its moves, the choreography. *See this in 3D. To the rhythm of the house music Elvino pumps in the mix.*

Was there anything missed? Wade and Jefferson were told what they were told. *He* had other plans. But, who knew every eventuality? He could do without it backfiring. The Yard heard about it – *bad shit*. They would get him out of it, then get him *out*. Make him a dead man limping. Wade's archives didn't run *that* far. Not yet: the library *was* extensive. The library *lacked* a wing.

So, run through it again. Had he missed anything? Felicity giggled as they twirled. What did he miss? There had to be something. There always was. A detail that might/might not be crucial.

There was something at the church. When he met Elvis. Last set eyes on the little fucker. Linked to James and Lee. The night at Ziggy's, the night Marie Davies snuffed it.

The gig wasn't ripping off goons. The gig was seeing it *all*.

He left Felicity twirling. Her hands trailed off his. Their fingers gently touched, released. Frederick stepped back, she continued. Jefferson rose.

Jefferson took his chance.

Frederick winked at Wade. They watched Jefferson. He tried the twirling routine. Felicity: give me a twirl. Wade winked back, joined the Fredster at the bar. They poured bourbon, mixed it up, did bumps. Wade weaved over to the dancing couple. He shovelled showbiz up their noses.

He weaved back.

Frederick, laughing: 'Look how this is going down.'

'I know.'

Jefferson had a hand on Felicity's rear. The music went deep house-ish. Frederick hit a dimmer by the bar. It threw light on Jefferson and Felicity. Jefferson's other hand was behind Felicity's neck. She smiled – Frederick and Wade caught a clear view.

The Elvis mix threw a chugger out. A slow melody. A sleazy

rhythm. The dancers caught it, moved with the tune, with each other – they danced nice; they danced sweet together.

Jefferson went to kiss Felicity. She pulled her head back. He tried again. He got the same. He tried a third time and found Frederick's hand at his throat. Jefferson was slammed against the pool table. Jefferson was pinned.

Jefferson, seeing the Fredster – his eyes saying: *Come on big man, do something.*

About it.

About *me.*

Wade reached them. He said, 'Calm down Jefferson. She said no twice.'

Frederick said, 'I'm saying it a third time. Understand?'

Jefferson's eyes bulged. He said, 'Yes boss, sure.'

Frederick released his throat. He machine-gunned laughs. 'You okay Ms Baumgartner?'

Jefferson flew at him – a bad move. Frederick took him down with one action, used the detective's height and heft, his momentum.

Jefferson lay on the floor – making a keening noise – flushed, his features softened.

'I'm okay,' said Felicity – like she could handle Jefferson – Frederick's alpha-male act was too much. Jefferson tried to kiss her: big deal. He got carried away: big deal.

She held out her hand. 'Come on Larry, get up. No hard feelings – at all.'

Larry took a moment to stand. He got up, looked sheepish. Felicity got a concerned expression.

Frederick didn't like it. 'Apologise Jefferson.' This fucker.

Jefferson, catching his breath: 'Of course, of course. I'm really sorry Felicity, I really am. And to you too boss, I'm really sorry.'

He turned to Wade. 'Sorry to you as well.'

'Fucking hell Larry, you don't have to apologise to this goon and his ridiculous moustache – what the fuck?' Frederick howled.

Jefferson tried a watery smile.

Felicity said, 'You didn't really need to apologise to me either. These things happen.'

Jefferson fixed on Frederick – like he knew the boss wouldn't like it. 'If you say so, I mean–'

The bitch – she played it *this* way, did she? 'Larry, you still came at me,' said Frederick.

He winked: 'Payback time.'

Frederick dropped his suit trousers, boxers, pointed.

He waved Jefferson over. 'On your knees.'

'What?'

'You heard. You're sorry, you do the biz.'

Wade held it a second. Then burst – he howled and corpsed.

Jefferson got it. Here's a chance, it might save him. Keep him *okay* with Frederick.

Jefferson dropped to his knees and started working. Felicity backed off. She didn't like it – Frederick's a bully, he's warped.

The music went acid-disco – a floor-burner. Frederick closed his eyes. Jefferson's head bobbed. The track's vocal screeching: '*Acieeeeeeeddd.*' Screeching: '*Hahahahahahahaha.*'

Wade backed off, chopped lines on the bar. He waved Felicity over, she did hers, Wade did his. They watched – they had to, the sight transfixed. Frederick grunted. He *fuck-yeahed.* Jefferson's head bobbed. Frederick emitted a guttural grunt. He finished.

Frederick sighed and looked round the den, dazed. Jefferson got to his feet, averted eyes, fixed a smile on. Frederick bowled to the bar and did his Wade-chopped line. He re-refuelled. He waved Jefferson over – here came junior.

Jefferson did his line: *get past this moment, take refuge in more drugs.*

Frederick grinned at Felicity and Jefferson. 'Larry, I have to say, you make amends. I have also to say, that I am fucking warning you – pull something like that again, a similar trick, and you will have no chance to make any kind of amends.'

Jefferson nodded, Felicity avoided eye contact – this bitch. She isn't over yet, not by a long way. He knew just the thing. Suck her in – co-opt her.

Jefferson and Felicity racked another game up. She split the balls. Two dropped down pockets. The music moved into disco territory. Frederick grooved on the tune – Elvis educated him. Elvis helped him reconnect to his time. The vibe now and the vibe then. His late '80s/ early '90s era. He ran wild – the scene was the Wild West, zero rules, frontier stuff. He got nearly pinched copious times. He ducked and dived – used his brain; pulled stunts; made money.

Then, realised who the real stunt-pullers were. He joined the force. He crossed *over*.

Frederick winked and pointed at his dick. 'That's better. Cleared the air. Like those golden days in Stokey.'

Wade smiled. 'The day I left there is the day Wade Long was born.'

Frederick said, 'You still hear from anyone?'

Wade shrugged. 'Have to say it's been a while.'

Jefferson won the pool game, Felicity made the bar. She handed Wade the cue, he boosted to the table. He racked the balls up – Jefferson broke the pack.

Felicity, next to Frederick – uncomfortable.

Frederick, clocking it – fuck her.

He said, 'How do you like your friendly neighbourhood police?' He cracked a shit-eater; threw a Fredster twinkle. She fixed on him – recognition in her eyes – she got it, this is an icebreaker, a sly entreaty: Frederick's not *so* bad. Frederick has a particular sense of *humour*.

She smiled. 'An eye-opener. I don't think–'

'Don't think. What's the point? I avoid the process as much as possible.'

Felicity flushed, Frederick offered her a drink – she was into double figures.

He poured bourbon, coke and ice, handed Felicity hers. She said, 'Thanks. I chose the wrong career – I should have been in the police.'

'Wise words,' Frederick said. 'Looking like you do – maybe not. It's not PC but, baby, it's impractical for a squeeze to be any kind of proper police. It's about us. The chaps. It's not an anti-woman thing. It's just the way it is. Met shit – police shit – is not what anyone thinks. We're the biggest firm in town. The only firm. Fuck gang families – the Bartons – gangsters, we're *The Gang*. We're out of control. We're *in* control. The only way to be.'

'You seem to be – both.'

Frederick chorted. 'I'm not sure – I am fucking sure of *this*.' He bolted bourbon and did a bump, loaded Felicity up. She snorted – down it went.

Frederick revived the thought: how to suck her into the gig. He said, 'You want to be in the police? I tell you what, that can be arranged. On a temporary basis.'

Felicity swayed. 'Is that so?' Her words slurred. 'When?'

Frederick clocked his watch. 'About this time tomorrow.'

'Really?'

'Really.'

'Alright.'

'Alright.' He bolted bourbon, did more bugle. He reloaded Felicity – she wolfed the bump. 'It's going to involve a lad named Elvis. He's a DJ. This is a mix of his you're listening to. And, he's my son – that's right, yeah. Also correct, he needs teaching a lesson. Now, being my lad, there's a way of teaching him a lesson he will not receive any-where else. Understand? I mean, jail time will not occur. I will go to jail before him. And *that* is never happening.

'I digress. The plan – the part of the plan you can help me with has a certain beauty to it. Tomorrow will be filmed. Like today. Smile – you're on camera.' He jested, spooked her up – she didn't catch it; Felicity was near blitzo.

'You know Wade of course. Has a penchant for a camera, *adores* a close-up. What you will be doing is clichéd yet essential. You will create a diversion. What you need to know, will be helpful to under-stand about what is really going down tomorrow, is that Elvis – my lad – is trying to turn *me* over.'

It half sobered Felicity. 'Why?'

'How long do you have? It's incidental and insidious and frankly, a tad tiring. It/he bores me, too. But if you have kids that's the deal, correct?'

He hooted, answered his own question: '*Correctamundo.*'

Felicity said, 'This is involved.' Her voice wobbled – was it regret? Does she want out?

Too late lady.

Frederick said, 'Wade.'

'Yeah.'

'Come here.'

Wade boosted over from the pool table. His moustache was freshly primped – gak flakes flecked it.

Frederick bleary-eyed Wade, fixed a stare. Unnerved the wannabe Malibu Beach dudester. Wade got the message – keep your mouth shut. Just play along.

Frederick pointed at Felicity. He said, 'Why is she not in one of your pornos? I mean, like the *better* ones. Not this shit.' He waved at a Wade flick playing on a screen. Wade gave his generous length to an ingénue porno squeeze. Down an alley in red-lightsville.

Frederick hit pause on the remote. It caught Wade's faux genuine oh-the-ecstasy-is-agony rictus/grimace.

Cue group laughs: Frederick, Felicity, Wade and Jefferson corpsed.

They recovered. Wade said, 'She's more than welcome. I'm near begging her. She knows that.'

Frederick looked at Felicity. Then at Wade. 'What's the problem? Can't see that I can see one.'

Felicity and Wade laughed. He said, 'Her act. Her desired routine. How she *views* porn. The fucking skin-flick biz.'

'"Views?"'

Wade shrugged. 'Felicity won't do straight porn. As you and I and all of coke-and-wank-to-oblivion Christendom know it. Oh no. Not any more. She's moving up. *Apparently*,' Wade said. 'Fact is, all she wants to do is jack off. Men/women. You know what I'm saying? A straight wank movie.'

Frederick – interested. 'Go on.'

'That's it. End of story,' Wade said. 'She won't fuck onscreen, like she won't fuck in real life. She'll only jack off. You, me, her, whoever. She wants to do a series of motherfucking wank flicks. I'm like, no, won't work. Won't sell. Passé. P-A-S-S-E.'

'This true?'

Felicity threw a beam, followed by a pantomime wink.

Frederick *got it.* 'She was trying the routine on you? When Larry and I got here?'

'Why do you think I couldn't get off?'

'Thought it was no Viagra and an embarrassing problem with your cock.'

'Played a part, too – sure, yes.'

Frederick laughed and set Felicity off. 'For fuck's sake Wade. You plastic rhinestone cowboy. You're knee-deep in wank-fests everyday of your life and you can't get off when this lovely girl is jacking you to kingdom cum?'

Felicity said, 'He called it my audition. My chance to convince him there was scope for my proposed contribution to porn.' Felicity giggled. 'And I giggled, at the wrong moment. I tried to hold off, but there was only so long–'

More laughs.

'For fuck's sake,' Frederick said. He took the pool cue from Wade and pointed it at him in mock inquisition style. 'This true?'

Wade was sheepish. 'Might be.'

'Ha ha ha ha and fucking hahahahahahahahaha.'

Jefferson joined the laugh, caught on to the conversation. 'You never know boss, it might be her technique.' A hammy pause. 'Or might not be all that.' A wink. 'You know what I mean?'

Frederick smiled. 'Nice Larry. I knew you had it in you to seize the fucking issue when it presents itself to you. And what you're saying, as well, I suppose, is we should make our own judgement. Maybe Wade had no choice but not to enjoy, not to get hard as fuck and vinegar-stroke like he was being electrocuted. Or, maybe, Felicity knows *precisely* how to do the job.'

Felicity laughed. She saw where this headed – threw Jefferson a look. 'I'd give *anything* for a second chance to impress, you know. To show Wade he should invest in me. That I'm worth it.' A flutter of eyelashes in mock Marilyn Monroe style.

Frederick and Jefferson grinned.

Wade said, 'Don't look at me. One, I already tried the routine out and failed. Two, I'm goosed.'

'Don't worry, we weren't looking at you. And neither was Ms Baumgartner. Correct me if I'm wrong?'

'You're not.'

'I think I, Larry and Ms Baumgartner are all agreed. Larry is the no-brainer go-to on this. He's a fine specimen of a young man and as he has a weak spot for this fine lady, it seems only apt he should be the one who should host her second "audition".'

Jefferson's eyes bulged. He *loved* the idea, the turn of events. He revelled in anticipation, got lost in fantasyland.

The absolute dream of Felicity ChicFox jacking him off.

Frederick had difficulty holding back laughs. 'Ms Baumgartner. If you don't mind.'

Wade sniggered, Jefferson gulped. Felicity said, 'Certainly not.'

She approached him, reached inside his trousers.

He closed his eyes. She took hold, let go.

She said, 'Drop your trousers.'

He did.

She took hold. Felicity began pulling. Clawed nails glistened in the den's lights.

'Close your eyes, stand straight. Don't move,' she said.

This – a ritual handjob. Slow, slow, slow. Each back and forth was painful. Was pleasurable. Jefferson moaned, Frederick grinned, Wade grinned. Jefferson went rigid. His features rictus-agonised. Felicity stopped. She diced with the vinegar stroke. She ordered Jefferson to shut the fuck up every time he moaned and *pleaded*.

The v-stroke went nth degree. Nth, *nth.* Then, at last. Jefferson was reduced to helpless. Jefferson begged; begged more. He got his wish. Jefferson tripped stars and moons, the light fantastic.

He flashed and burned.

He went *limp.*

Felicity said. 'It's not over. *You're* not over. Close your eyes.'

He whimpered, closed his eyes. He jammed them open. 'I can't – *again.*'

Felicity looked at Frederick. 'You got any Viagra?'

'Sure.' He found the blueys and told Jefferson to open his mouth. 'Two – enjoy.'

Jefferson popped them, glugged Frederick-fed bourbon. 'Thanks boss.' He whimpered again, jammed his mouth shut.

Felicity went at it once more. She worked Jefferson from limp to rock. The routine was the same. It took longer this time.

'*Aaahh!*' Jefferson near squealed. Now, a third time. Fuelled by more Viagra and Wade's bugle. The degradation of what he did.

'That's it! That's fucking it!' Jefferson's eyes jammed open. He ripped himself away. 'Any more and I'll die of cardiac arrest, I swear.'

He pulled his trousers up and collapsed on a chesterfield. He ran near out of breath. He flushed, sweat soaked his temples. His heart pounded.

'For fuck's sake Larry. I was close.' Frederick was stroking himself.

'Same here,' Wade said.

Felicity beamed wide – she fixed on Wade. 'At last.' He was hard – Wade laughed; Frederick and Jefferson joined in.

Felicity's eyes flashed. 'Do I pass the audition?'

Frederick nodded. He looked at Wade.

Wade said, 'I still maintain there are a thousand and one handjob flicks that no one buys because they're out of fashion. Went out with the Ark.'

'Come on,' said Frederick. 'You're being unreasonable and unrealistic.'

Wade shrugged and took his time. He came up with a grin – devilish.

'Tell you what Felicity, do Frederick and you have a deal.'

She smiled. 'That's it?'

Wade returned the smile. He said, 'Frederick won't agree to it. That's first off. No one controls Lord Fredster. Secondly, he agrees, he won't be some over-hormoned beefcake like Jefferson. You understand me?'

Frederick laughed. He appreciated how Wade played him – *tried* to – reverse psychology.

Wade said, 'You in?'

Frederick shrugged. 'It looks a hoot – a hoot and a half, eh Larry? As is blowing off your cod-psychoanalysis of the Fred, Wade. How the fuck could you not fucking die to be jacked off by this young lady?'

He winked, waved Felicity forward. 'Wade, chisel me up. Jefferson, pour me a fat one.'

They refuelled him. He bumped bugle, swigged a bellyful of bourbon.

He threw that Frederick twinkle. 'No blueys required, Wade, Larry. Put those away. High on today – rock-hard on anticipation.'

He closed his eyes, felt this London afternoon, a blissful sensation. It's Yuletime; it's the big Y of *Yesssssss*.

Here it was. Bring it on.

Frederick – harder than the lesson he taught Elvis.

Felicity went ritual again. She took *even* more time this time. It was drawn out. Wade and Jefferson were transfixed.

Felicity took him close. He loved it. She took him to the cliff, led him back again. He roared. He went, 'Fuck yeah! Do it! Felicity. Fucking agonise me! THAT IS AMAZING!'

Felicity had him teetering. It's a fall – a long way down, off the Grand Canyon. The fall won't ever quite come – this bitch; she *is magic*.

His eyes jammed open. She told him to shut them. He went, 'FUCK NO – WHO'S CONTROLLING WHO?'

Felicity let it go. She let it *all go*.

'FUCK AND FUCK AND FUCK – *YEAHHHH*!'

The sound of Frederick. Of the afternoon exploding.

Frederick jammed his eyes open. Felicity ordered him to shut them. He cracked a grin. A wide one.

'FOR FUCK'S SAKE OBLITERATE THE FUCK OUT OF THE FREDSTER!'

Then – a few pants.

Then – post-vinegar stroke bliss.

NOW – a smirk.

And pull those pants up.

Frederick, breathing hard: 'Jefferson you fruit – heart attack? *Heart–a–fucking attack?* Oh fuck off. You're not careful, that puff-cake Lee Palm will have a longer innings than you can ever hope for.'

He laughed, addressed Wade: 'Wade, give this girl a starring role how she wants. Fuck, I'm equal partner, aren't I? Look at her. You're telling me punters won't go wild for young Ms Baumgartner jacking her way through the menfolk of this land?

'Felicity, you have a future. In Wade's pornos and, more materially, tomorrow. Your role is to be essential and casual. To be the distraction you naturally are and provide Wade and his crew with some never-to-be-forgotten footage. This will be a classic of its kind.

'I'm meeting Elvis tomorrow in the pub. To seal the deal on how we're going to "rip off" Richard Cliff later. He's a dealer. He trades in mid-range street weights. The plan is simple and obvious. We'll meet in the pub where we met – the Setless – and get ourselves oiled. I know from previous experience that Elvis can be a little deviant. Some may say perverted but *I* would never say that about my son. I mean: a son of mine – deviant? That would beat the fucking band.'

He cracked a grin, started laughing. He clasped his hands on his knees and bent double.

He recovered. 'I want you to turn up at a particular time. This will be confirmed later. It will allow you to ghost in and inveigle yourself with Elvis. We all know what I mean. Your task is to take him to the limit, that is, seduce the little fucker and do your stuff in the Gents of the establishment – an establishment I basically own – and cause him to enjoy himself as violently as you've made us all do this afternoon *and*, more materially, to make him come close to missing this great big clumsy white elephant of a sting he believes is going to snare me, or something.'

A rakish smile. 'Comprende?'

She did.

They all did.

FORTY-FOUR

Xmas Eve, 9.54am

Sweet dreams; diazepam dreams. The hills of Ibiza. The *swoosh* of the surf of Sri Lanka. Running pills from London to Blackburn to Crete and back. Hazy *hazed* days.

I am Frederick Street.

I am–

Total blackout.

He woke to a pillowed morn.

Xmas Eve, early.

Sunlight lit windows.

The house Victorian; the fat day ahead.

Christmas card Christmas.

Why not?

And, YES:

Show time, the scheme. Later. This Elvis plot – a laugh a minute; everyone running around chasing their fucking tail.

Except the Fredster.

The main point, the *only* point:

A swag bag of coke. Richard 'Ricardo' 'Ricky Me' Cliff – the patsy. Elvis – the patsy. Everyone else: welcome to patsyville from DI Frederick Street, the President of P-ville.

The remnants of slumber – half-sleep reverie of Camilla – of girls – of women past – past schemes.

The past to *come*.

London shrunk to puppet size. The chief's a lame duck. Lee's gone. Jefferson: God help him. The boys at the Yard. The mob at West End Central and Tower Bridge; everywhere all in line.

Beauty: a flower unfolding. The scale of it all. Small and grand.

He never slept better. This house built on self-realisation. The power to will.

The big secret???
There is no secret.

He slipped his robe on, made the kitchen, ground fresh coffee. He loaded the French press. There's a butcher's bird in the cooler for Xmas roast. Pigs in blankets – look at all the trimmings already prepared; how very traditional, domestic. He adored a caramelised carrot. A Yorkshire pud with gravy. Home-done stuffing.

He clocked the time: that's four minutes. The coffee will be done. He took a cup and poured. He grooved: the money rolling in, dough salted away. Legit dough. The station packed out with goons and joeys. Everywhere was.

Frederick slurped his coffee and clocked the TV. Some overly made-up bit of snatch shit on and on about carols. This *special* time of year. It was special like every fucking day is special. Make it so.

He rung Wade. 'Mr Long, how you doing? Head like a basketball fucking a grape I'm guessing. I am speculating. That was shit and giggles for sure yesterday/last night, whenever the fuck it was. Yeah, you left, course you did. How you think you got back to the townhouse? You are in the townhouse? Good.'

Frederick put Wade on loudspeaker. He blitzed porridge in the microwave, sliced a banana into it. A dab of honey. Slurped more of that good-stuff coffee. Blacker than Sinbad Williams. The poor fuck – what is no chance?

Wade said, 'Same time you said for the meet?'

'Yeah. The Setless at eleven. See ya and God forbid I'd ever turn out to be ya.'

He ended the call. That tremendous portion of quiff on the television was reviving all the lovely powder and booze in the system. It was instant-boner time. The way her tits held so delightfully in her blouse. Too much lipstick was never enough. Her tantalisingly delicious youth.

He knocked a quick one off. He kept it businesslike. He kept pleasuring himself. Who said business and plez didn't mix? The thicko fuck.

Jesus!!!

He still teemed loads of vim and vigour; when that ran out, well–

He closed the TV down. The bird was decent young stuff, that couldn't be denied. But ageing quiff, in its thirties/forties/fifties, whatever. That went lumpy but still garbed a short skirt, a bit of tit, whatever. There's the action.

That's what the Fredster loved. *Adored.*

Who the fuck did not?

Time for a shower. A freshly laundered bespoke Savile Row whistle, throw it on, some of the expensive-shit cologne.

Hit this day.

FORTY-FIVE

10.33am

The disused park, a wasteland now, was perfect. Frederick scoped it. Like he chose it for the shakedown. Except he didn't. Elvis did. No, *Ricky Me did*. Making it all the sweeter.

He would bring two lads along. For appearances' sake. Go along with it as if nothing changed. To gee Jefferson the fuck up. *And* to have cover, collateral, options as potential pull if required later.

The towers that surrounded the place were abandoned. They were apt for this. You could pack whatever was needed into them and remote-control it.

It was the second time he checked it out. It felt better than the first.

He left. He turned to take a last look. One last time at where it would occur – apparently.

Then, satisfied. As satisfied as you could be: he walked around the corner. He headed for Columbia Road, the boozer.

It was before eleven. A Christmas Eve sun still burned. Frederick hammered on the Setless Sun door. Snow melted quickly – on the street, off roofs, fell from cars.

Seconds went and went.

Now, the double doors unlocked. Clive came through them. 'Okay, OKAY! I'm fucking here, it's only eleven now–' He clocked Frederick. 'You never heard of a mobile phone? Where's your key?'

Frederick walked past him. The joint was morning-empty. Perfect for a quick tipple, the powwow with Wade. Clive went behind the bar, flipped the tap, poured Frederick's pale ale.

'Merry Xmas.'

'To you, Clive. Have one.'

'It's too early.'

'It's Xmas Eve.'

'Consider my arm twisted.'

He poured a pint of ale. 'What's occurring?'

'What isn't occurring? Business and pleasure as always. Who says they don't mix? Fuck that, fuck them.'

Clive left it there. He was not completely stupid.

Wade arrived. Clive clocked him and started mixing his Black Russian. Wade in surfer-dude mode today. The look ran wild: Pacific Highway shades hiding yesterday's eyes. A *Swell is Up!* T-shirt. A North Face windcheater. Faded denim cut-offs that hung below the knee. Deck shoes worn sans socks.

'Warm out there, is it?' Frederick said. He threw a wink at Clive.

'Sun's out.' Wade was groggy. His head whirred with a late night/early morning fuzz.

'Been catching a wave?' Clive said. It drew a Frederick chort.

Wade peered at the landlord – who worked for *him*. 'Oh fuck off and hurry up with that drink.'

Clive finished up and slid it over. Wade slurped his Black Russian. Clive and Frederick swapped winks.

Frederick said, 'First of the day?'

'Kind of. Had one at the pad. But it got interrupted.'

'By?'

'Having to get rid of last night's tart.'

'You get it up?'

'I had your blueys didn't I?'

'This is true.' They laughed, Frederick nodded at Clive – fuck off down the other end of the bar.

He did.

Wade said. 'It's all ready?'

'Will be. Just came from it. You?' He kept the pretence up. This way Wade could/would play his part perfect.

Wade said, 'Same. My boys are setting up about now. Could do without the fucking hangover from hell.'

'The last time you *didn't* have one?'

Wade grimaced.

'Exactly.'

He tried the face again. Frederick shook his head, he ordered them a second drink.

Frederick: 'All you got to do is sit in your nice warm car and direct your picture. Think of it as second-unit stuff, experience for when you hit LA, get your big break, are ready to film your West Coast close-up.'

'You never get tired of the same lines?'

'It's the repetition that makes it funny. *Is* the joke.'

'I've heard *that* line too many fucking times too.'

'Not enough.'

'And that one.'

They drank.

'When's Elvis due?'

'I told him 12.30. Give me time to get him oiled. And let Felicity work her magic.'

'He'll go for it?'

'If he does he does. If he doesn't he doesn't.'

'The Gents?'

'As always.'

Wade finished his first drink. He slurped at the fresh one and made the Gents.

He was back in quick time. 'Done.'

'A livener too.'

'You know that.' Wade wiped his nose.

'Let's have a look.'

Wade unlocked his phone. He said, 'Clive, paper needed in the Gents.'

Clive shrugged. He palmed two rolls from under the bar, and made the Gents. He entered the urinals, appeared on Wade's phone. Crystal clear. He made the cubicles and did the same. There's Clive – in clear view. Frederick double thumbs-upped his partner. They guffawed. Clive grimaced – zero khazi paper needed. Wade played a joke – it *wasn't* funny.

They guffawed more. They watched Clive boost back through the urinals and fell into a *nothing–to–see–here* act.

Wade winked at Clive. Frederick studied the *Standard*'s back page. Clive gave Wade the bird.

He said, 'Loser.' He threw the rolls at Wade, who batted them over the bar. Clive went back around and carried on cleaning glasses.

Frederick's guffaws died. He said, 'The same over there, where it's going down. Cameras set up?'

'Sure.'

'What's up?'

A Wade headshake. Frederick said, 'What?'

'I get setting up there. Of course I do–'

'But not here?'

'What's the point?'

'Same reason as always. Security. Never leave home without it.'

Wade finished his drink, told Clive to do them a fresh one. 'The same old lines, all the same old time.'

'That's the way it goes.'

The new drinks arrived. Clive walked off. 'What's next? After this big lesson you're teaching Elvis?'

'How long have you got? London at Yuletide is a goldmine. You know that.'

The booze cleared Wade's hangover. He grinned. 'Correcta-fuck-ing-mundo.'

'Got a thing going on some junk our African-extraction friends are high-rising off Mare Street.'

'How much?'

'Two, three kilos. Whatever – it is coming the Fredster's way.'

Wade nodded. 'Good news. Makes a change. What else?'

'The usual shit.'

Wade nodded. It meant a coke-and-pill blizzard. The smut impresario threw a grin. 'I calculated once you could retire on your coke and E reserves alone.'

'When was that?'

Wade shrugged. 'Fuck knows.'

'Sweet. How about Mr Long?'

'I'm behind. We *both* know that. How is the nine to five?'

'The girl snuffed at Maroon's – nearly all done.'

'Lee?'

'The same – nearly signed, sealed and delivered.'

'This afternoon – you going to pinch Ricky?'

Frederick shook his head. 'He's more useful roaming the shitty streets grafting for yours truly.'

Wade pondered. 'Anyone else a candidate for a DI Frederick S collar?'

'There are options. I'm keeping them open. Who knows?'

Wade *that's-cooled* his features and finished his drink. He clocked the clock above the bar. 'Better go. Don't want Elvis to see me here chatting with his arch enemy *and* adoring pater. He'll never forgive me if he finds out I've been batting for your team all along.'

He winked, Frederick chuckled. Wade zipped his jacket, raised the hood. Went OTT mock incognito. He left Frederick grinning. He left the boozer, saying: 'See you on the other side.'

James parked up on Columbia, along from The Sun. He caught a clear view of Wade. The porno goon hit the bright sunshine. He crossed over Columbia. James cracked his window.

Wade spoke to himself. James heard it crystal, Wade saying: 'Frederick's right. This is the gig. Warm and snug in the sled, monitoring close circuit, watching that lunatic weave his dark-arts shit.'

Wade got in his Range Rover and pulled out. Boosted away from Columbia, James following. Wade parked a couple of streets away. A couple of streets from where Ricky Me was due to meet Elvis with a kilo of coke. The poor fuck. The *two* poor fucks.

James grinned. He knew what went down. Ricky called. Cuz was a muppet who stayed loyal. And for that he would be remembered and rewarded.

NOW: James debated THE option.

What it was all about. You're the coming man of Shoreditch: come *NOW*; come *LATER*???

Scupper their play/let their play play?

Scupper it.

No.

LET IT PLAY.

He learned a lesson from snuffing Lee. Frederick taught him well.

Know when to *back off*. Know when to *be patient*.

He tooled the Merc past Wade and parked in a side street. He brought his Canon DSLR. He brought his Canon 800-mm zoom lens. Fuck the iPhone – he wanted to get in close. Get the dirt. *Leverage the dirt.*

This was it, now.

He had a good feeling about this. He felt a vibe incoming.

The vibe vibed HUBRIS.

For Frederick, for Elvis. No need to intervene *now*. Do not be hasty. Keep on watching.

HE KNEW WHAT TO DO.

THIS IS A LAST-MAN-STANDING PLAY.

LET FATHER AND SON FIGHT. LET ONE CANCEL THE OTHER OUT.

THEN, THE VICTOR:

MOVE IN ON HIM.

TAKE THAT SHIT-HEAD DOWN.

THIS – TO BE CONTINUED: AT A LATER DATE. START THE NEW YEAR HOW THE NEW YEAR SHOULD BE STARTED.

FORTY-SIX

Elvis walked in the Setless Sun a half-hour later. He loaded a small backpack. It was 12.31, according to Frederick's watch. It was time to get this over with. Show Elvis the error of his ways.

They hugged. It was a long one. *Overlong* – Frederick feeling for a wire. He asked for Elvis's blower because 'it had a better camera' – and took a dad/son selfie.

It was REALLY to make sure *that* wasn't recording. It wasn't. It confirmed. Elvis had no snitch from Ricky that things changed. He *still* planned for it going off at the waste ground.

All of this played *obvious*. Frederick made it clear to Elvis what Frederick did.

Not a word spoken about it. There was no need – they both knew, were uber-aware of what occurred.

'Drink?' said Elvis.

Frederick said, 'You know the answer to that one Elvino. A drink each and every minute of the day if I had my way.'

'It was rhetorical.'

'As was the riposte.'

'Like it. You're on the ball and ready for this. Not like last time.' Elvis tried to backfoot the old man. Or played like he did: shadow-box the shadow boxer.

Frederick grinned. 'Will you move on *pur-lease* from the last time? Stop shitting on about that.'

Elvis caught Clive's eye. 'What *is* this shit you're playing?'

Clive knew the script. 'We just opened. Your dad was desperate, big surprise. Banging at the door like the hounds of hell chased him.'

'You know him so well.'

Frederick laughed. 'Where's the drink?'

Elvis nodded. 'Come on Clive. No drinks and fuck this shithouse music. What *is* going on around here?'

Clive fixed the drinks quick. He slid them to Elvis and Frederick.

Elvis said, 'You not playing any Music Man's mixes? Shame on you.'

Clive shrugged. Clive said, 'Sure.' Clive fixed his I'm-the-whipping-boy face on. He made the sound system and opened up The Music Man mix list.

Elvis said, 'I've got a new one – if you want to play it?'

Frederick said. 'Do it Clive. The young shaver's tunes are his only redeeming feature.'

Clive raised an eyebrow. 'That's it?'

Frederick sipped pale ale. 'His dad's dark and sultry looks may have been inherited. Past that, absolutely fucking zero.'

Clive laughed – forced it. He said, 'You got this new mix Elvis?'

'Certainly.'

He pulled a memory stick from the backpack, lobbed it Clive. The barman hooked it up to the Mac. Elvis said, 'You'll love this. So will the punters if they ever get here – hit up the Night Time Cool mix.'

Clive found it, pressed play. Frederick said, 'Night Time what? It's the middle of the day.'

'File under technicality. And fucking. As in fucking technicality.'

'It'd better pump out Yuletide spirit and copious goodwill to all men.'

'Wait and see.'

Elvis liked how it went. Frederick was loose and confident. As always. It would make this all the sweeter. Sweeter than sweet when what went down later went down.

It moved right. *He felt it.*

The first tune came on. 'Turn it the fuck up,' Frederick said. 'Loud. You have my permission to do so.'

Music flooded the Setless. It was spacecraft-taking-off stuff. The vista conjured was spectral deep space in a universe far away. Elvis stargazed a moment. He *dug* the moment. Elvis in the mix let the track linger a few moments. Then, the spell broke. The moment ended. The next moment arrived: regulation Yanksville house.

Clive dialled the volume down a notch. Elvis said, 'Another feature in terms of family lineage that is certainly not enjoyed by the old fella but is a boon for the young one is I am hung like a fucking python. DI Street, I'm afraid, most certainly isn't. And you can quote me Clive.'

Clive choked on laughter. 'How can you know? For sure?'

'I grew up in the same house. My mum told me. I've "heard".'

Frederick chorted. He grimaced. He mugged for them. 'Hey now Elvino, your mother's been dead a few years but there is no need to disrespect her.'

Elvis said, 'You're not denying the main thrust of my point, then?'

'I do not need to dignify that false and heinous accusation with a direct response. You know that.'

A Frederick/Elvis shared grin. They clinked glasses, Clive walked away. The boozer filled.

Elvis's phone went. Elvis pulled it.

It's Ricky: right on time. Here's the call. Elvis said, 'Excuse me' and crocodile-winked his dad.

He stepped away, made the Setless doorway. Stepped out and eyed the snowy vista.

He said, 'All set?'

'Yes Mr Student. All fucking set.'

Ricky sounded juiced. Just the *right* amount.

'Any developments?'

Ricky laughed. Good and even. 'If there were any I would have said. No is the answer. It's all to occur as discussed.'

Elvis paused. He took in his tone, *felt it*; liked what he felt. 'Great.'

He hung up, walked back in the Setless and rejoined Frederick.

He picked his glass off the bar, slurped double G&T. The liquor burned nicely. 'So.'

'So,' Frederick said.

'Everything is in place?'

'You tell me.'

'My end is sorted.'

'Money?'

'You're supplying that, remember?'

'I jest.' Frederick showed a roll of money from inside his suit jacket. 'That's 5K. I'm packing eight of those. He gets half before, half after it's handed over. That's the deal.'

'Sure.'

Frederick gave the 5K rolls to Elvis. He loaded them in the back-pack.

'Give him half, show him the rest if he asks.'

They ordered more drinks. The place filled up. Xmas Eve fell into full swing. Zero grumbles at the non-Yuletide music. The hipsters and older-clientele mishmash gave up moaning a long time ago.

Frederick cracked a grin. 'You nervous?'

Elvis scoffed. 'Why the fuck would I be? You, maybe. Me, no way.'

'Is that so?' Frederick said. 'And why would that be? This is the day-and-night job.'

'Was thinking about it on the way over. You've got the most to lose if it goes wrong.'

'Really?' Frederick chuckled. 'You *do* sound nervous.'

Elvis said, 'Maybe you're right. Maybe what I wanted to ask was why you're not? Ever nervous.'

'About what? This? *This*? You serious? I told you. This is meat and drink – bread and butter. Like drawing breath. Listen.'

He lowered his voice. Like he levelled, allowed a big IN on a matter of heavy-duty gravitas. 'You and me don't always see eye to eye. You know that, I know that, *we* know that. But Jesus, I would never do you wrong.'

'Let's not get into this. Again.'

'You know what I'm saying.'

'You always say that. But fuck it – not now.'

Frederick slurped ale, and drained the glass. Told Clive to build him a double G&T, and do the same for Elvis.

A pause until the new drinks arrived. They didn't say a word.

Then, Frederick: 'I was just saying, is all.'

'"Just saying".' Elvis bit. This fucker – why not? 'What about Camilla?'

A new pause. Frederick examined his glass. Like he played for time *and* acted. Hammed the whole thing up – knew Elvis would raise *her* and played up to it.

'This I have also said before. But here goes – she was into gear, as you know. Heavily. Fuck, it's why you went clean, right? Again, you two broke up over what that stuff, that life, did to you. She was into powder, getting jacked on it and I am – me. Big revelation. She was there. And, it happened. It was wrong, I know that. But it was mutual. She didn't force herself on me, any of that bullshit. But it happened. I apologise. Again.'

Elvis emoted cooler than cool. He didn't give a fuck.

'The point is, you say – you just said – you'd never do me wrong.'

'You'd basically split up from her.'

'So you say.'

'It was on the rocks.'

'So you say.'

'You weren't supposed to find out. You *wouldn't* have found out if she hadn't told you. I never have thanked her for that courtesy.'

'Point remains.'

'Okay, *okay*.' Frederick slurped G&T. Elvis watched him cackle at punters – at *their* double take. He stuck out to new clients, those not used to his incongruity to the supposed Setless vibe.

He said, 'In the spirit of this festive time of the year, let me ask you something?'

Elvis nodded.

Frederick sighed – this wasn't going to work; the stuff you tried to do.

He said, 'You ever *ever* do anything wrong? In your life? Like that you *really* regret?'

'Point is?'

'The point is you *know* what I mean.'

'Yeah I do.'

'So can we leave it, please? For now, at least.'

'That's what I said.'

They did; they left it. Felicity arrived – here she came through the door. She wore a cheap and demure get-up. She acted on Frederick's instructions. He knew how to stoke Elvis's kitchen – curves and tit bulged *all the more* for the attempt to look respectable, dowdy. Her lipstick was dull and thick. She wore secretary's glasses. The more her dweeb look was examined the more it ran geek next door *and* porno central casting. Hugely non-original; of course it was. The allure, the horn, the *fuck-yeah* was *all* about the cliché.

She threw a dazzler of a smile. She slid onto the stool next to Elvis as the fresh G&Ts came. She said, 'Elvis, I presume.' She stuck out a hand, casual.

It sent a charge through him.

He shook her hand and looked at Frederick. 'This is Felicity Chic-Fox. This is my son, Elvis.' He smiled. 'ChicFox is her stage name. Felicity is an actress.'

'So very polite, Dad.'

Frederick threw a sarcastic face. Elvis wanted to make her from pornos – from a Wade opus he soundtracked. But he could not be sure. He parked it. Got down to the delightful business of surreptitiously prowling her tits. Her backside. Those features.

He said, 'You know Wade – Wade Long?'

She laughed. 'Who doesn't?'

Elvis went brave – the G&Ts kicked in. 'You're an actress – have you been in any of his films?'

'Not yet. I'm working on it.'

Frederick winked at Felicity. 'A little early for bourbon I think. Babycham? Clive, we got Babycham?'

Clive nodded. Frederick said, 'Elvis – Wade introduced me to Ms Baumgartner, in this very pub. Would you believe?'

Mock *mock* big surprise.

'Where else would it be?' Elvis locked eyes on Felicity. Then unlocked them, and watched the floor.

Her drink arrived, Frederick said: 'I have to correct you about Wade's films, Ms Baumgartner. Technically, you are correct about not yet starring in a Wade Long production. But I assure you, you've been in a skin flick in the industry here in the last ten, fifteen years, you've been in a production Wade most likely had a slice of.'

'And you of course, Dad.'

Felicity threw a grin. 'Porn entrepreneur too?' she said. 'How intriguing.'

Frederick aw-shucked and drank. It got a Felicity laugh. Elvis said, 'You look like you might drink something stronger than Babycham.'

It got *another* Felicity laugh. 'I'm just warming up. But you should try Babycham.'

'Sure, if he will.' Elvis pointed at Frederick.

Frederick nodded. 'Get them Clive. If you have any more left over from the Ark.'

Felicity faux grimaced. Elvis eyed her chest. Frederick smirked. Clive caught it. 'I may have a few. For the old ladies who come in.' Hoots all round. He poured them, they drank. Elvis and Frederick drained theirs. They tried to out-macho each other. They played it knowing.

Frederick was the first to break ranks. He said, 'If you don't mind Ms Baumgartner, I'll return to the usual tipple, it's Xmas Eve and drinking time is wearing on. Elvis?'

He looked at Felicity. She nodded, smiled. He said, 'Think I'll stay on Babycham.'

'Hahaha,' said Felicity. She smiled. 'I'm with you, Frederick. Whatever you're having, *I'm* having.'

A pause – Elvis got it. She mugged him off. Before his old man. It got big Fredster laughs. The sight of his son's face got Felicity corpsing too.

Frederick said, 'Clive. Double G&Ts for the lady and I. And a second **BABYCHAM** for Elvino here. For the young 'un. For *junior*.' He played the audience.

Elvis grimaced. 'Fuck that. Clive – make it three G&Ts.'

'And keep the Babycham?' Felicity said.

'Do not keep the fucking Babycham.'

'You've changed your tune,' Felicity said.

Elvis thought: you could go off a tart. Even one who was a total shag.

The drinks arrived. Elvis raised his glass: 'Cheers.'

He clocked the TV above the bar. It piped in BBC News with the sound muted – Night Time Cool played on.

A picture of Lee Palm came onscreen. Time to front Frederick. Elvis, pointing: 'Real shame about Lee. You know who killed him yet?'

Frederick went reverential-quiet. 'We *know* who did it. He's bang to rights. But you know I can't go further than that.'

Elvis face-palmed *it's-a-shame.*

He said, 'I couldn't believe it when I saw he'd been killed. Saw you all over the news. Again. After that girl who died–'

'Marie Davies.'

'Marie Davies. Been quite a week. It's throw away the key time, right? For the fucker who did Lee. Make sure he'll never forget who he was.'

Frederick nodded.

The subject bored – his son bored: how the hell *were* they related?

'That friend of yours did okay didn't she? The reporter. Fucking hell – I'm there, I've just found my partner and dear friend murdered and she rocks up, starts filming it on her phone.'

See how this next move goes down. 'You gave her the interview, though,' Elvis said. 'That was a surprise – to me. Bound to win her an award. Scoop-of-the-year territory. Or so she thinks. An exclusive – on that? It's a massive deal, result for her.'

Frederick shrugged. 'Once she takes the picture she's got the story. Fucking hell, what else could I do? It's a live situation, she's got me holding my dead partner in my arms.'

Frederick tried a rueful smile. Like it's *clear* what is being got at.

'She's certainly not complaining.'

'Where is she today?'

'Dana? Working, I think.'

'Xmas Eve? What a trade.'

'News never stops.'

'Could be. Handsome girl that.'

'Handsome?'

'What I said.'

Felicity: 'You didn't tell me your partner had been killed. How awful.' It sounded hollow, false – like she guessed *something.*

'As Elvis said, it's been quite a few days, even for my dirt-filled business.'

'Poor you.' She stroked Frederick's head. It jolted Elvis: intimacy was usually off-limits for Frederick; caused an instant reaction.

Nothing – *that* was the reaction. Frederick smiled. He told her: 'Thanks. But it's nothing. You get used to it in my job. Funeral will be hard but that's life.'

Look at him. Pretending he is the kind of regular, deferential, straight-laced joey he cannot abide.

Elvis caught a sense: Felicity could be a stooge, in on Frederick's play. Whatever he planned – the way she acted, how Frederick acted with her.

Elvis chewed on it. He had to process it fast.

Felicity said, 'You brave boy'. It was more near patronising of Frederick. Again, zilcho irritation. His dad threw a benign smile. *Too* benign. Like he over-sugared it. To send Elvis a message that was not needed.

Frederick took the piss. Frederick's subtext: we know precisely what's occurring.

Felicity said, 'Just excuse me, I have to go to the Ladies.' She near simpered.

'Okay,' said Frederick. 'Powder your nose with this. Get into the festive spirit, sprinkle a little festive cheer.' Laughs as he palmed her the showbiz.

Felicity beamed and trotted off to the Ladies. Elvis watched her. 'She certainly has got *something*.'

'Wait until you hear what her *thing* is.'

Elvis smirked. He was a few drinks in, but business remained. 'I look forward to you telling me. While she's away, can we talk this through – what we're going to do?'

Frederick yawned, gave a big show of doing so. Teach this stiff of a son a lesson. *That's* what this is about. That's what *he's* about to do.

'I'm not sure what else there is to say. It is simple. You meet Ricky at the time agreed. As soon as the kilo of coke is handed over, my crew pounces. You do a runner – some of them chase you. I get very fucking grim with Ricky. Tell him I might be able to cut him a deal, of some sort. Make him a CI, maybe – an official Met Police informant. We process him, and that's it. Merry Christmas. It's a sweet score to keep us all warm and tinselled and engulfed in festive cheer. Correctamundo?'

Elvis managed a smile. He didn't try too hard. 'A merry time for all.'

'Exactly, champ. Now you *are* talking.'

'I have a question.'

He paused. This moment now, between them. The Elvis mix played a tune with a lyric: *I'm loving what is a remarkable day*. It repeated, drifted across the boozer. It vibed anti-carol.

Frederick tapped his fingers on the bar. He said, 'Only one?'

Elvis ignored him. 'Someone like Ricky – why don't you just take what he's got, from him? Once you know what he's doing?'

He called his bluff. 'That's the question? You look like you really want to know, so here's the answer. Look at the size of the score we've got here. And the size of the future ones. Ricky coughs up the kind of information I'll ask for him to remain un-pinched, to remain out and about – not looking at a stretch – he'll be the kind of super-snitch who should wear Y-fronts with SS for Super-Snitch on the outside of his too-tight jeans.'

Elvis chorted. He had to. Frederick said, 'Here comes Felicity – call her ChicFuck after what I'm going to do for you. Let's have a few more snifters then go do Richard Fuck Me Over Cliff.'

'You're sure everything's lined up, how it should be?'

'My end, of course. As long as you've lined Ricky up? That's all you had to do.'

'Yeah, don't worry about that. Was out with him the other night, he doesn't see past the money. He's a thicko.'

'Who isn't?'

Felicity returned from the Ladies. The secretary's glasses remained in place. Her eyes ran coke buzzed behind them. The coke gleam pulled at Elvis. The shape of her did; how she curved and burst from everywhere.

She read his mind and passed him the bugle. He clocked Frederick. His dad waved him on. Elvis made the Gents. He bumped a fat nasal fix. He made the bar again. He palmed the bugle to Frederick.

Frederick hit the Gents. It was coke-relay time, chased with booze. Elvis went wobbly. Frederick planned this. It was obvious, it was clumsy. Felicity's hand ran along his leg. Her crimson-painted nails moved lightly. He rode the buzz; the knowing he was being played.

And – *yet.*

He dizzied, he swooned.

He fucked it all up.

Frederick egged him on.

He became super-drunk, saw in double vision. There were two Fredericks. Jeez, two Felicitys. There's a pair of Clives serving up booze. Elvis was juiced – the alcohol rearranged sense; convinced him – ride that omnipotent glow.

The bugle came out permanently; they did it by the bar. Stuff, senses blurred.

What's this?

Felicity led him off, holding his hand – she led him into the Gents. 'What are you doing?' Elvis heard himself laugh – a far-off sound, odd, discordant. 'We don't need to be in here to do nosebag – we don't have to be careful. My dad basically owns the joint, and he's the police around here.'

Felicity smiled and kept quiet. The Gents ran packed-out and rau-cous. The crowd whoop-whooped when they clocked her. She fixed a smile on and took Elvis in the first cubicle. Shouts of 'coke-head'; 'lucky boy'; 'can I have a turn?!' followed.

The cubicle door was floor-to-ceiling flush. She locked it, they dabbed coke, they dabbed more. Their eyes locked. He *got* it – finally.

She unzipped his jeans and took hold. She said, 'Do not move, stand up straight.' Felicity giggled. 'And I mean *straight*.'

Elvis breathed hard. He said, 'Of course.' He'd do anything she wanted, no problemo at all.

She began. Slowly; *slow, slow,* expertly; the booze and coke didn't mess her up – she was smooth, in total control.

And, it felt good – the way she did it.

She paused, landed a slow kiss on him. She put two fingers to his lips. 'Shssh – *shsssh.*'

Elvis went quiet.

She had something in her *other* hand. She unclasped it, revealed a pill, an E. She kept smiling – the fingers that shushed worked his dick again. Slow, now: she put the pill in her teeth, it was brown-coloured, and bit it in two.

She dry-gulped one half, placed the other half in Elvis's mouth.

Flash – he caught the symbol on it. An embossed clog. Like the ones that killed Marie Davies. The ones that fucked up copious people. The ones he and Dana did at Fabric with James.

Too late. He necked it, it entered his system. Felicity worked him faster, the increase was incremental. She upped her speed in agonising fractions. It was pleasure and agony. The agony the pleasure. Torture that should not end. That he was desperate should not end.

Ever; please.

Now. Here. THE moment. Lights flashed in his head. They strobed. The walls crashed down. The ceiling rioted. Senses spasticked. Pleasure powder-kegged. It's an overload. It has to stop.

Pleeeease!!!

His breaths ran short. Gradually, they ran longer. Felicity said, 'You okay?'

He cracked a grin. 'Never better.'

Felicity giggled. 'The noise you made – I thought you might never come back.'

'Can you blame me?' He pointed outside the cubicle. 'Shit, did they hear?'

'Unless they're all as deaf as posts of course they fucking did.'

He tuned into the noise:

Whoops and cheers, banging on the cubicle door. She said, 'Don't worry about it. They're all as fucked themselves. It's Xmas Eve. You've been in your own little wonderland. I'm starting to feel it, too. That pill is coming up. That half feels strong.'

Fuck – the pill, a clog – what the fuck?

Frederick – he did this.

It's a set–up. It's too easy.

Elvis felt hazy, felt a first E tingle. That creeping sensation. That could not be ignored. Which would run stronger, more potent, would goose him.

'Come on, let's go and have a drink.' She gave him no time to think, led him out the cubicle, through the urinals. Through a *'fuck yeah!'* and *'go on son!'* cacophony.

They made the barroom and the bar. Frederick was wild-eyed, grinning; his eyes contentment, benevolence.

Elvis did not like it.

Frederick winked – goaded him to return it; Elvis winked back.

Wink and try to *think.*

Felicity sat across from Frederick. He grinned at his son: 'I told you.'

Elvis grabbed his drink and gulped and nodded. 'You did. And you were right.'

'What?' said Felicity. Like she didn't know. Wasn't in on it – big joke.

Frederick said, 'I told Elvino he'd be calling you ChicFuck.'

'Did you really?' She giggled. Her face joeyed – her half a clog gripped, her eyes fiendish. That body: those tits and lips and eyes were a cartoon.

Fuck: he felt it too. He goofed, the pub blurred.

Then: Frederick, Elvis saw, was on one too; glassy-eyed, a smile that looked disfigured. Elvis, cognated, sniggered: what a look: his dad like a clown – he seemed ridiculous, that smile was near ghoul-like.

Jee-ee-ee-sus.

He steadied himself – *tried* to steady himself. He said, 'I can see why these clogs killed that bird. They are rocket fuel.' His diction slurred. He leaned into Felicity. 'That was out of this world, what you did to me. I'm serious. I've been with loads of birds, you know what I'm saying?'

Bullshit tumbled.

REMEMBER WHY YOU'RE HERE.

What time is it? It's near 2pm. It's on for 2.30/3pm – which? Richard 'Ricardo' 'Ricky Me' Cliff packed a kilo of bugle smuggled in via Cornwall. The goon boasted about it being scarcely cut Peruvian flake. The bullshit merchant loved to bullshit.

He packed Frederick's 40K. He flashed taking it all – tax Frederick, see what the shit-head did.

The clog kicked in again. It punched senses, ratcheted consciousness. *Wait: it's subconscious what these things did.*

The sub-c ran above the consciousness. It kicked the fuck out of the c. Filters were shredded; the pub went big, the pub bounced.

Clive's head is expanding. It's a marshmallow. He's wobbling over the bar, as he brings drinks. More drinks, rivers and rivers of demon sauce. The glorious stuff we're diving into—

Frederick still grinned. He's a technicolour joker. Felicity moved, left trails – of sex and menace. These clogs were trippy. *This is what killed Marie Davies.* Felicity came on like a mystic. She's all women. All women flowed through her.

WHAAAAT???!!!

Time – shit: what time is it? Ricky Me.

The deal. The plot, the *takedown*.

Frederick snared him – he thought he did. Elvis saw, now; visioned what he had to do.

Night Time Cool banged in a track that brought the rest of the clog up. All the way.

Shudders – the track played tricks. The track was glorious, celestial, would never end.

It's a pink sunset over sea. A glorious orange vista. Nirvana nirvana—

Shit – this is head wobbles.

He said, 'Dad – it's getting… on.' It came out super-slurred, *sounded* to him drunk.

Slurrrred.

Everything is *blurred*.

His dad said, 'I'm buzzing here and you're mithering me like a bird. It's a deal, a rip-off, a nice touch. It's not a life-changer. Get with it Elvino. Get the fuck with it. Before it's too late.' He grinned, laughed a laugh that sounded like he cackled.

Elvis wanted to mention Camilla. Get back into that. See how that treated Frederick's pill. The softness. The eccy-fairness. But the *goodwill to all men* of this mad drug made it feel wrong. Wrong to do that to him.

Only good thoughts and words felt right.

Elvis said, 'Those Es.'

The words hung.

He *couldn't* say anything else.

Frederick said, 'We go when we are ready.' He placed a hand on Elvis's knee. Elvis ran a near-zero recall of affection – *touching* – when a kid from his dad.

Frederick said, 'I know what is going on. *Remember that.*'

Frederick confused/re-looped. That's his shtick, routine.

Elvis peered through the E haze, caught a giddiness surge. He rode an urge to hug the ageing conman.

Go then.

Do it.

He moved to Frederick. Felicity was draped over him, she kissed Frederick's cheek and saw him. She turned to kiss *his* cheek. Elvis accepted and looked at Frederick. Frederick saw him – a flash of surprise? The E worked its stuff on him? A glimmer of what was behind the front got shown?

The front behind the front – he was a Russian doll of fronts.

Then: Elvis hugged him. He felt it: soft, tender. He got it back, the feeling back – Elvis felt *sure* of it – Frederick rubbed his head.

Then – his dad went back behind his front. Elvis wouldn't let it go, he couldn't; he took Frederick's hand and kissed it.

Felicity saw him and smiled a big E smile. He felt his eyes shine, glitter; he broke the clinch and looked in Frederick's eyes.

He saw nothing: nothing but laughter. Frederick laughed, the shutters came down.

But *Elvis* knew.

And so does HE.

Frederick, through laughs: 'Son, this is worth a drink – I mean a *tipple*. Clive, bucket of ice, bottle of the best champagne.'

The pub wobbled. Frederick said, 'Here they are. Here they come. At last.'

He looked past Elvis towards the door. Two lads who looked like hipsters. The look was overdone – too much beard; too groomed.

Elvis made them as police. Here's Frederick's move – fuck it: he ran his own moves.

Frederick said, 'Robert Kone, Anthony Miller – meet my son, Elvis. This is Felicity. The drinks are on the Fredster.'

Handshakes all round. They were Frederick goons; his muscle for the job. They wore deferential smiles and took pints of Stella from their boss, hung back at the end of the bar like he told them.

The champagne arrived and Frederick poured. He palmed glasses of fizz to Elvis and Felicity and took one.

He said, 'Mazel tov.'

They drank. Elvis got smacked by E jolts; clog rushes that rubberised his legs and arms.

Frederick pointed to where Kone and Miller stood. 'They're good men – up and coming. Eager to please. And we like that don't we?' He winked. 'So was Lee. You know what I mean?' Another wink, devilish. 'You *do* know what I mean.'

He pointed to the clock above the bar. 'Half an hour, then we go.'

Half an hour?

Frederick goofed with Felicity.

Then – w*hat is he doing?*

That's what he is doing.

His hand was up her skirt. He looked over her shoulder at Elvis – that look: blitzed, *gone.* Felicity nuzzled him. Frederick waved Elvis over.

He wasn't *that* gone. He said, 'The beauty of this place? You want to know? Either way, I'm telling you. All of these–' He waved a finger around the boozer. 'They – *they* are all customers. Past, present and future. The ghosts of all my Yuletides come fucking truer than true. You know what I mean? Crawling with all kinds of wrongdoing, folk up to no good, not knowing what the fuck they're really doing. Criminals. Every shit-head's one. You know what I'm saying? I *know* you know what I'm saying. Why do you think I've got the joint?'

'I never thought about it.'

Frederick chorted hard. 'I'm telling you now. That's it. *This* is the beauty of the joint. The place is an absolute goldmine, a money machine.'

It felt like a play about something else. About what was about to go down; what they both did.

Wait – don't pre-empt. Play him at his own tricks – see what he does.

Wait – here it comes.

Frederick's eyes pulsed. He fixed on Elvis. He didn't say anything. It ran unnerving. What did he look at?

Then, it was over. The moment finished, Frederick cracked a grin. The clog was still strong – catch those *surges* – but nothing ruled Elvis, Elvino, The Music Man.

A spectral sound hit the Setless. The fancy shimmered – Night Time Cool took off. Elvis laughed and grooved to his tunes. The ones to come in the mix; that sound of himself knowing just what to play.

He closed his eyes and danced – got into the music.

He didn't see – missed it; who walked by him.

Ricky.

Ricky Me: what a sight; wide-eyed, blitzed on booze and gear, near full-gone.

Frederick clocked Elvis miss Ricky and grinned that grin.

Vanessa did it – Vanessa Compton – she did it right, how he wanted; Frederick knew he could trust her. She *wanted* in big time, beyond this low-level caper. She didn't snitch him to Ricky – she didn't snitch to Ricky what Frederick asked.

And it went off:

Now, beautiful; poetry in motion:

Ricky Me passing Frederick – *passing Elvis.* Ricky didn't see Elvis; Elvis didn't see Ricky.

That was the moment, right there:

Where it could have fallen down. It passed – came to nothing. Ricky moved towards the back of the pub, got lost in the crowd; back where Kone and Miller could watch him.

Frederick's blitzo bliss re-upped; he felt serene. SERENE AND CLEAN.

Elvis perked and opened his eyes. He kept foot-tapping – the new tune hit a nice groove; it was an Elvis fave, a Music Man classic: 'Last Night a DJ Saved My Life'.

A Frederick grin; he poured more champers. He waved Clive to bring another bottle over. He said, 'Elvino: MERRY XMAS DARLING SON!'

He shouted – it got lost in boozer noise – he raised the bottle.

That acted as a signal, a sign. Frederick's two goons materialised, his muscle was primed, ready to act.

Here they are – Kone and Miller, standing by Frederick. They didn't say a word, waited for Frederick to speak.

Elvis saw them, caught a chill. Frederick smiled. 'Bob, Ant, I appreciate your alertness and readiness. It's admirable. You can stand down.'

Frederick winked at Elvis – it was a warning – they nodded. Kone melted into the back of the boozer again. Miller leaned into his boss. Frederick smiled, nodded, pointed at Elvis. Miller turned and smiled. He was six foot four or more. He bloomed health. He was a rare black man who grafted for Frederick.

Miller leaned in and offered his hand. 'Good to meet you Elvis – I've heard quite a bit about you from your dad. The gaffer.' Miller, bashful. 'He told me to say to you who I just saw.'

'Who?' Elvis knew the answer – Frederick tried a wind-up; felt more chills.

Miller smiled. 'Richard "Ricardo" "Ricky Me" Cliff.'

Elvis smiled, tried to laugh it off. Frederick got heavy – Elvis caught a queer feeling.

Miller said, 'Nice to meet you.' He smiled – vacant, well-meaning. Frederick patted Miller's backside. Miller walked past him and rejoined Kone in the crowd at the boozer's rear.

They lurked there.

Frederick snapped into business mode. He said, 'What now? What's the plan? Your new plan?' He grinned and winked. He asked *Elvis* the questions, 'ceded control'. Of the shakedown, the situation.

It confused.

Elvis shrugged – he played for time.

Frederick pointed. To the back of the boozer – the crowd parted for a moment.

Shit – there IS RICKY.

WHAT THE–

Frederick smirked, Elvis's heart pounded. Frederick said, 'When I tell him, Ricky goes in the Gents, the first cubicle. Then, we make our move, the deal is done and we do him. You dish the goodies out, do your thing with him, and as you say so well, it's merry fucking Xmas for all.'

He gambled on Elvis buying it/having nowhere to go.

Elvis shrugged and cracked a smile. Frederick threw one back.

Chills.

It's all going down. Finally.

The clog sent bolts through him. Elvis fritzed; he fought to keep it down, maintain control.

Here he was. Here was Frederick.

Sensations spritzing; sensations cartwheeling. This fucker – time to finally get him back. For it all. For Camilla. For what he did to his mum. For what he did to everyone he ever fucked over in the name of Frederick Street. He's a Met Police detective. He's a city-wide crook. He's about to be finished.

Elvis grabbed his drink from the bar and sucked on it. He waited for Frederick's move.

His dad kissed Felicity. He waved her away, down the bar. She teetered off. He leaned in.

Frederick said, 'Let's get this straight, Ricky-fucking-Me's in here packing a kilo of Peruvian flake.' He howled, recovered. 'This guy is brilliant. He actually turned up. He's better than I thought. I told you about his so-called phone mugging? You see, it's goons like this that need policing. For the public and their own sake. This is what the public don't understand. They hear of corrupt police, a corrupt case, they think that's wrong. When the truth is there's corrupt and *corrupt*. Take your pick, you understand me? It's the only choice that matters. And it's easy/hard. You understand *that*?'

Elvis nodded – his subtext was clumsy. Give it to him straight. 'I've always understood you. Always. You understand *me*?'

Frederick cracked a grin. He said, 'Nice. The kind of stupid questions hacks ask – designed to wind the subject up, make them react.

You've been hanging around with that journo tart too much.' Frederick talked soft.

'Of course I understand you – I've always understood *you*. That is one reason, perhaps *the* reason, we are here now, right now, getting out of our minds in tremendous and magnificent fashion.'

Subtext overload. The message was overt, unignorable. It smacked the face; time to stop it – *stop him*.

Elvis smiled, he felt good now; finally, this is here. 'Come on Dad – Ricky isn't going to hang around forever. And he's pretty goosed. Who knows what the hell he might do? Let's get this done.'

He back-footed him. *Fuck him and his back–footing move.*

Frederick shrugged, played it cool. He said, 'Fuck him and fuck the rest of the world. Understand *that*. Ricky-fucking-Me? *Ricky–fucking-Me*? If he's in here with what he's loading– hahahahahaahahaha!

'Fucking hell, Elvino, he's not going anywhere, I don't care if he's blitzed or not. If he's thinking straight enough to be here, he's thinking straight enough to wait until he's told otherwise.'

Frederick paused. He held the stage, pointed at the sound coming out of the system, the tune taking over Night Time Cool.

'Now, if you'll excuse me a minute or five, I'm going to dance. It's Chrimbo Eve and it's time to dance. *Party*. You graft like I do all year, you got to have time to celebrate.'

The tune was a banger. Surprise, *surprise* – Frederick got *that* right. It ran a low bassline. A clapping beat. The melody spritzed emotions like there was no yesterday/tomorrow.

Frederick got to his feet. He swayed and pointed his forefingers. First, the left hand. Now, the right. Back and forth. He looked ridiculous. He looked alright. He was in the moment. Like he always was. He *loved* it.

The near-bar mob of punters caught it; caught the moment. There's the old man, he's goosed, he's having a brillo time – why not? They went wild, grooved on Frederick. He was tremendous; he was slightly scary.

Frederick hopped on a leg and smiled beatifically. He threw out a vibe – the right one. The tune approached climax. The near-bar vibe spread. The place hit the roof. Frederick and that grin. Felicity joined him. Elvis joined in. It was impossible not to. That tune. It wailed, it reprised, it was a choral hymn. A kaleidoscopic, sensate burst of everything right now.

Sensations ran overloaded.

His dad looked ridiculous *and* brillo. On top. He just *got* it. He took the joint with him. Ensuring *they* just got it. The tune ripped the place apart. Frederick ripped the place apart. Elvis was ripped apart. His dad *owned* the place.

Elvis looked for Ricky. He couldn't see him. He would still be here, somewhere. Frederick was right. As per usual. The record faded. The next one came in. He braced himself. If the last one was a barn burner, this muthafucker would cause a bliss heart attack.

The lyric came in. It roared. It informed the pub, 'DANCE ALL NIGHT TIL MORN, DANCE ALL NIGHT TIL MORN.'

It jumped and snapped and VIBED. Frederick led the Xmas Eve charge at stopping this moment ever finishing.

'DANCE ALL NIGHT TIL MORN.'

Elvis moved. He boosted towards Frederick. The E peaked – his fingers trailed. The place popped. His dad's eyes shone. Elvis's bulged. The place was charged. It fixed on the father/son combo. They linked arms. They freaked. They did not give a single flying one. They stepped forward, they stepped back.

'DANCE ALL NIGHT TIL MORN.'

They rocked and rolled. The place followed. Elvis aped a chicken hopping. Frederick stacked shelves, threw big-fish-little-fish shit. He was in his natural element. He tore the Setless Sun up. He was back in '88/'89/'90: the summers of love. The whole thing blurred.

'DANCE ALL NIGHT TIL MORN.'

They were out. They were about to turn over Richard 'Ricardo' 'Ricky Me' Cliff. They were about to try and turn each other over.

It mattered. It felt like it wouldn't matter. Not in the end. Not, ever.

Elvis wavered. He diced with fucking it all off. Fuck off Dana. Fuck off clean and serene full-time. For ever. Fuck off taking his dad down. And just accept it all. Accept the whole deal as it was.

No.

The dance continued.

'DANCE ALL NIGHT TIL MORN.'

Disco and house to break your heart. Mend the fucker better than it was before the fucker broke.

Disco and house: nostalgia for the future.

The tune wound down.

One last time – here it came:

'DANCE ALL NIGHT TIL MORN.'

It was over. It ended.

They raised flutes of champers. They clinked and drained them, put them back on the bar.

The place whooped. Elvis blew Frederick a kiss. Frederick returned it.

Now; right now.

IT BEGINS.

He threw a grin at Frederick. His dad tried to catch breath. He sat down on his barstool. Felicity ordered more drinks.

Frederick pulled his phone. He pinged Ricky a message. It said, 'Cubicle 1 now.'

Frederick waited for the reply. He waited more: now – here it came.

From Ricky: 'Ready.'

Frederick nodded at Elvis. He pointed towards the Gents. He said, 'Go in the Gents. I'm there in five.'

Frederick put his phone away. Elvis eyed him and grinned – Elvis came alive, styled it out; fronted it like Frederick would.

He waltzed through the back of the boozer. The Setless was Xmas Eve, gone. The streets caroused, London wobbled; the town revelried, ran blitzo-ed.

Elvis pulled his phone quick. He hit record on the voice app and positioned it in his jacket top pocket – quick.

Ready.

Take the fucker down. The E glow encased. This made perfect sense. This was sweetly sweet. He ran an emotion gamut. He rode feelings. This is *the time*.

Elvis hit the Gents. The urinals were crammed. Barroom josh mashed with legless bantz.

He scoped the place for Ricky: nothing.

Cubicle 2 was empty, the door open. Cubicle 1, the door was closed. He pushed it. Ricky sat on the pan – the seat was down, his eyes near closed. He palmed a spoon. A knuckle of bugle positioned on it. He did a big bump.

Ricky didn't blink. He said, 'Here.'

Elvis took the spoon. He did one. The shit hit his nostrils. The shit burned. The shit was the shit. He did another. The same result. Sensate buzz. The bumps cut through the booze, they clarified the clog.

He said, 'Fuck.'

Ricky said, 'More?'

Elvis nodded. They did more spoons. They went blitzo-ed nth *nth* degree.

He said, 'Fuck, *fuck.*'

Ricky grinned. It was a show, a grand smile.

Ricky said, 'Money?'

Elvis said, 'Product?'

Cartwheels, big dipper, light spangling. Fuck-oed.

Ricky pulled the kilo. A tablet of the good stuff sealed up.

He said it again. 'Money.'

Elvis pulled the wedge from the backpack. He gave it to Ricky. They exchanged – the kilo for forty grand.

Where was Frederick?

Where the fuck–

What's this?

Frederick rushed in. He badged Ricky, yelled: 'POLICE.'

Then: 'No! Stop!'

What the fuck is he saying?

WHAT THE FUCK IS HE DOING?

Frederick pulled his gun. He pointed it at *Ricky.*

He pulled the trigger. The sound came. The sound grooved – it's an intro – *sounds like that tune…*

NO.

He – HE shot Ricky Me in the head.

Blood spattered; coke spurted everywhere.

It's a bugle blizzard.

Flakes swirling.

Frederick turned the gun to *his* head. He pointed it at his temple. His eyes gleamed. A finger went to his lips.

He said, '*Sssshhh.*'

He cocked the trigger.

He waited. He went to do it.

Elvis felt the trigger squeeze.

Then.

Then – Frederick:

He un-cocked the gun, and dropped it to the floor.

He leaned forward and kissed Elvis.

The plan was blown apart. Ricky Me was dead. He got caked in coke – it went everywhere. There's a blizzard in cubicle 1.

Silence.

Frederick grinned. Frederick picked the gun up, removed the silencer, wiped it, put it in Ricky's hand and let it drop to the floor.

He gave his son the double thumbs up.

Frederick waited; a *lonnnng* pause.

Miller and Kone banged on the cubicle door.

Frederick reached into Elvis's pocket and pulled his phone. He hit stop on the voice app and pocketed the phone.

He grinned. He winked.

Frederick Street grinned; Frederick Street told Elvis Street: 'No one *does* coke any more.'

Acknowledgements

Special thanks to Matthew Brook, Scott Fletcher, Simon Hardaker and Ben Irvine: keep on Night Time Cooling XXX

To anyone who has ever smiled at Kid Paradise: XXX

Patrons

John Allen
Adam Altogether
Paul Ansorge
Mike Arrowsmith
Asim Ashraf
Victoria Atherton
Dave Aughton
Simon Bajkowski
Jason Ballinger
Chris Balmer
Tony Banks
Bhu Basilisco-Gurung
Jonathan Booker
Anna Bordewijk
John Brewin
Steve Broderick
Eleanor Brook
Simon Brown
Rochelle Byron
Lee Carter
Mark Chilvers
Tracy Clarkson
GMark Cole
John Colquhoun
Nicky Coonan
Jeremy Cross
Sean Crossey
Sam Cunningham
Gillian Dalgleish
Ian Danter
Rob Dawson
Melissa Dick

Wayne Dixon
Mark Dobson
Amanda Docherty
Andy Duckmanton
Luke Edwards
Cindy Ferguson
Kevin Garside
Jack Gaughan
Owen Gibson
Steven Gill
David H
Sandie Halpin
Paul Hayward
Simon Heggie
Ian Herbert
Roger Higton
Dips Hilderly
Paul Hirst
Dan Holloway
Tom Huelin
Rob Huntington
Jon In
Sonny and Martha Jackson
Stuart James
Jennifer JC
Paul Johnson
Richard Jolly
Mike Keegan
Ursula Kenny
Tara Kielthy
Gareth Kitchen
ian ladyman
Sam Lee
Don Logan
Samuel Luckhurst
Mike MacDonald

Alistair Magowan
Joe Mathews
Stuart Mathieson
Paul McCrudden
David McDonnell
Mike McGrath
Stuart McGuire
Jim Mitchell
sachin nakrani
Carlo Navato
Mark Ogden
Pete Oliver
Brian Oliver
Russell Openshaw
Anthony Paley
Phil Passey
Simon Peach
Jack Pitt-Brooke
Robert Pollard
Rob Price
Rachel Roberts
Katie Roberts
James Robson
Barney Ronay
Richard Saunders
Ok Shin
Sita Simons
Leon Sketchley
Michael Smith
Sammy Smith
Gabriel Stewart
Simon Stone
Stel Stylianou
Steph Toman
Liz Tray
VP

Louise Wain
Robin Wallace
Beth Whittaker
Ian Whittell
Andrew Whittle
Matt Williams
Paul Wilson
Jonathan Wilson